DARK AGE DEMONS

Book 1 of The Lost Hunt series

Neil Kay

CONTENTS

Title Page	
Prologue	
Chapter 1	1
Chapter 2	7
Chapter 3	11
Chapter 4	18
Chapter 5	24
Chapter 6	29
Chapter 7	35
Chapter 8	43
Chapter 9	48
Chapter 10	53
Chapter 11	61
Chapter 12	66
Chapter 13	72
Chapter 14	77
Chapter 15	83
Chapter 16	90
Chapter 17	98
Chapter 18	103
Chapter 19	111

Chapter 20	118
Chapter 21	122
Chapter 22	127
Chapter 23	133
Chapter 24	141
Chapter 25	147
Chapter 26	151
Chapter 27	158
Chapter 28	169
Chapter 29	178
Chapter 30	185
Chapter 31	192
Chapter 32	200
Chapter 33	211
Chapter 34	220
Chapter 35	232
Chapter 36	242
Chapter 37	252
Chapter 38	256
Chapter 39	263
Chapter 40	268
Chapter 41	276
Chapter 42	282
Chapter 43	290
Chapter 44	297
Chapter 45	304
Chapter 46	310
Chapter 47	314

Chapter 48	320
Chapter 49	326
Chapter 50	333
Epilogue	341
Afterword	355
About The Author	357

PROLOGUE

175 AD – The northern edge of the empire

Spurius stood at the back of the cone-shaped wooden and straw hut that functioned as the village tavern, and seethed as he watched the dice game. "You no wanna get your sestirius back from me?" Kai yelled to him from the circle of men sitting on the floor. Or at least that's what Spurius could make out; he was guessing a fair bit but the bald German idiot's Latin was intermixed with grunting sounds that Spurius took to be a language from whatever shithole Kai came from.

Kai had chipped away at the corners of the stone dice and rolled them enough times to be pretty certain which numbers would come up. Spurius was only along to 'lose' the first game, seeing a Roman soldier lose his coin would convince the pig-shit-for-brains farmers to gamble all that they had against the big German in the hopes of possessing one of the silver coins with the face of the man who some of the Britons were starting to name the wall after, the long dead emperor.

Sure enough, shouts and complaints soon started as Kai began to win game after game, and Spurius was forced to stop with the pretend sulking face and step forward to reveal that he was one of only two people in the tavern armed with a pugio, the only thing small enough to smuggle out of the fort but enough to terrify the farmers.

Soon Kai, who despite having shitty-accented Latin, had managed to pick up a lot of the local Brittonic dialect, was negotiating and calling in the debts for them both. Of course, the farmers would have no coin only worthless tokens the villagers used among themselves but the two soldiers would return to the fort with a sack of ale, a chicken for the pot or even a lamb for the spit, the farmers' wives and daughters would fix the men's boots and maybe even five minutes against the hut walls with a wife or daughter would be offered. Kai would certainly enquire about this, although Spurius, from the province of Phoenice thousands of leuca from here, was finding the companionship of the locals just as appealing as the weather.

"Is it worth it?" asked Spurius on the half-mile walk back to Housesteads. "It'll be at least two nundinae before we can go back there and be sure they won't remember us." Soldiers passed through the village daily, and it was soon clear that the villagers didn't really have much skill at recognizing the different faces of the much larger mainlanders.

Certainly the passing of two whole market days, eight days apart would be enough time for the villagers to forget the towering lean man who spoke Brittonic with a gritty German accent and his shorter, handsome, olive skinned companion who seldom spoke. Kai's left eye began to blink rapidly, a tic that indicated the big man was thinking about a reply.

"Got us lamb don't I!" he eventually offered in his best Latin, waving the dead animal tied up above his head like Otho waving Galba's head in triumph. Spurius started to speak choosing his words carefully.

"It's just there's not much more down south other than a bit of extra meat for us. If you really want to relieve the boredom of the wall then why not a raid north, find out what the Caledonians keep from us."

"Brass would crucify us if caught in the Picts land out of patrol," Kai said, his voice had become quieter and his Latin more intelligible – a sign he wanted to change the subject.

Once they were inside the fort their mood relaxed. They returned just before dusk, a good thing as the passwords changed every few hours and Spurius was in no hurry to be stuck outside until a centurion that recognized them could be found. That could take all night and one of many things Spurius disliked about this cold island so far from home was the wolves. So many and the size of the bastards! Twice as big as the ones back home in Phoenice. The ones in Caledonia were said to be larger and the incessant howling from the forests north of the wall certainly was a lot louder.

After listening to Kai and the villagers sound like a donkey in terminal pain while speaking. Spurius enjoyed the sounds and noises of the fort. Latin and Greek, of course his own native Aramaic, Coptic, and even a word or two of Punic that he understood escaped from the brick houses and barracks he walked past. Kai went back to the room the two of them shared with six other soldiers, Spurious said he'd join him in a moment. They both needed a couple of hours' sleep before their night patrols.

First, Spurius decided to visit the temple in the middle of the fort. A small rectangle with an open altar for sacrifices and ceremonies, the building was closed as usual, and around the altar were small statues of bronze and clay of the gods left by soldiers in return for luck.

Spurius looked around: he wanted to be seen. His last two

attempts to become centurion had failed he thought because he had refused to offer a sacrifice. "Men will not follow anyone not favored by the gods," his superiors had bellowed at him enough times. With soldiers at Housesteads from every part of the empire, it was not just the Roman gods that were worshipped here. Some of the small, crudely made statues were of what the Romans described as the mystery religions. He recognized Attis and Isis among the statues and one better designed than the rest – a beautiful naked woman with a snake around her shoulders, her eyes made of amber sparkled and seemed to be watching him as he knelt before the altar.

"Cursed thing must be worth a fortune." The only thing stopping him from stealing it was the thought that the owner was probably watching. Left it as bait to exhort blackmail from fools who couldn't think more than a few seconds into the future. That and that the statue disturbed him in ways he couldn't describe. A statue of his god would be unwelcome, he knew, so he prayed in Aramaic and drew the fish-like ichthys symbol in the dust hoping that any observers would assume this was a godly soldier praying to Jupiter, Juno, Mars, and the rest.

Patrol would start in a few hours. Getting the bare minimum of rest at the barracks should suffice. They'd barely seen any Picts over the past few nundinae. Usually, around this time of year, there was a slow trickle of them. If it looked like they wanted to trade rather than fight, and if they could survive the ditches and pits filled with sharpened branches and logs that were scatted all over the steep hill leading up to the wall, and their trinkets impressed the centurion on duty, then they usually were allowed to spend the winter laboring in the villages or hunting and fishing in the forests. With few field slaves surviving the long journey and harsh conditions, the Romans tolerated the extra hands that ensured the forts were fed.

This year, so far, next to none. Kai speculated that their harvest was so bad they'd resorted to cannibalism while the brass upped the number of patrols and training drills, fearing that the different tribes and villages had come together for a full-scale raid on the wall.

Spurius smelt it first; a tangy iron smell that he recognized right away and what followed it. After the smell of that much blood, the smell of shit was never far behind. He kicked open the door of his barracks and found Kai sitting on the floor his back against the far wall trying to speak but his throat had been slashed and he was choking on his own blood making inhuman sounds. His legs had been twisted into a grotesque shape with his knees twisted inward so they faced backwards, resting against the floor. His feet had also been turned backwards and flopped uselessly at an impossible angle. His left eye gave a final round of fluttering before closing forever.

'Picts!' Or the villagers? Surely none were capable and how would they get in? A fellow soldier jealous of the lamb or someone Kai had pissed off? It would mean death by stoning for whomever for sure, but as in every army, there were a few disturbed troops. Suddenly the door to the storeroom where the eight men kept their kit burst open and out fell Marcus. Spurious would recognize the Egyptian's body anywhere. You know a man's torso by sight when you live with him and that was a good thing for identification purposes as Marcus was missing his arms, legs, and head. A tumbling of body parts followed the torso and sure enough, a head soon rolled out, but it was that of Fronto the Spaniard who sometimes played the panpipes during their drinking sessions.

Spurius got on his hands and knees and made his way to the pile of body parts to see if anyone was still alive, his hand skidded across the already slippery stone floor. The front of his tunic was soon drenched in blood before he had identified Marcus, Fronto, Felix, Magnus, Rufus, and Philo all in various bits and pieces piled together in random order. Only Kai, the last to arrive had been left in one piece for all the good it had done him.

Wait, Kai was the second last to arrive. The last was… He pulled out his pugio and panting backed away from the gruesome pile until he had a wall to his back and slowly pulled himself up. It would take a whole gang of Picts or a pack of wolves to do this much damage. How would they get in unnoticed? And as for the fort? Eight hundred men in an area the size of one square leuca! No one heard the screams? No one noticed a hoard of blood-stained barbarians or beasts just strolling around? Even if whatever killed them wasn't waiting outside for him then he had to explain the unexplainable covered in his friends' blood but still alive. From the northern forest, the howling of wolves started.

Spurius tumbled out of the barracks. Shockingly the sky was black with only a full moon giving lighting up the sky. He'd only been inside for what? Ten minutes? How had it gotten so dark so quickly? He slipped and bumped on his arse a few times while descending the wooden stairs before he was greeted with the sight of hell itself.

Stacked on top of each other limbs twisted similar to Kai were bodies but also here the bodies had been bent or snapped into physically impossible positions. One's spine had been curved so much the victim's head rested inches from his arse. Another man had his neck stretched to the length of one of Spurius' forearms his nose now buried into his lap. Several had been flayed. Many were missing eyes, noses, and tongues. From the way the corpses' mouths were trapped in a permanent scream it was clear this had been done to them while they were still alive.

Spurius moved to another alley to be confronted with another pile of corpses in the same horrific condition. Some faces more familiar than others, but all looked otherworldly he'd never seen such screams or agonized expressions even in camp after a battle when the wounded were being treated. Eight hundred men, eight hundred soldiers plus however many slaves, villagers, and traders who were in the fort today, all gone in the cruelest fashion.

No army could have done this so quickly, killing so many at the same time giving no chance of resistance and certainly this was beyond a toothless gang of villagers upset that Kai had snagged some extra turnips to go with the lamb. Picts? They lack the numbers, discipline, and sheer strength to do this. It then struck him, the men's wounds, they had all been inflicted by hand. No one had the strength to do this. Wolves! The howls were getting louder but it took a massive pack to do this. At least fifty, probably more, and how would they enter and escape so deftly and quickly, and why just kill men and not eat them? And since when did wolves know how to bend spines?

"You know the answers to these questions deep in your heart," came the voice from behind him, "but you don't know why you were the one I spared."

Three things struck Spurius about the voice. First, it was female. Not unheard of to see a woman on the wall; some of the centurions had wives and daughters with them. Damn it! He thought there were the corpses of women and children somewhere in the fort. Merchants had wives too; they often camped from fort to fort. But these weren't the sort of women the Spurius would engage in conversation much less be addressed by in conversation himself.

Secondarily, the voice was speaking in fluent Aramaic. His

native tongue, not that unusual to hear it on the wall but everyone addressed each other in Latin. Did the owner of this voice know him?

Third, it was the most beautiful, commanding, enticing, magnetic voice he'd heard in his entire life. He turned around and by this stage was unsurprised to see a beautiful auburn-haired naked woman with a snake wrapped around her shoulders. The moonlight seemed to be drawn to her perfect face. Fair skin, full lips, an upturned nose, and striking amber eyes.

"The statue didn't have any goat horns." Spurius eventually said, looking up to the two curled and jagged spikes protruding from the top of her head.

"They know I have them, it's just a pain in the arse for stone carvers so over the years they've gradually dropped out of the stories about me."

That led to the obvious question from Spurius of "Who are you?"

"I have a lot of names," she said. "A lot of forms too, sometimes I'm male, sometimes female. Sometimes I'm young and beautiful, sometimes old and haggard. Sometimes human, sometimes beast. The form I've appeared to you as is one that you identify with at some level. Had I spared Kai I may have taken the form of a beautiful blonde man called Loki. Had I spared Marcus I'd be a green-skinned man called Osiris. But you are who I spared so this is me now. Call me Lilith."

"Why was I spared? Why did you do this?" Spurius said.

"I did it because I could. The inhabitants of this land, be it the wretched fools who've been here for centuries or you arrogant bastards in your armor who've barely gotten off your ships, all need regular reminders that they are only flesh to the likes of me, that means they are no more to us than beasts in the field to live or die at our amusement."

She closed her eyes and stroked the snake's head. It seemed to calm her.

"I saw you, drawing the fish sign in the dirt. You like the preacher that the Romans nailed up. Quite the speaker back then I saw him several times and the personality cult that exploded around him I've never seen anything like it. Virgin birth! Pah! I know that isn't true: still, credit where it's due. A society where a third of the people are slaves and he comes up with a religion that guarantees paradise after death for those that suffer in life. Genius! I give it two centuries before people tire of it!"

"That still doesn't explain why I was spared!"

"I have to leave this island for a while. I'm needed in my ancestral lands as well as other places. But I want to leave a replacement. Someone who will make the islanders new or old to these lands cower in fear. In short, you are the reason I came out of the woods, you are the reason all this happened."

She spread her hand to display the corpse piles.

"Corruption is one of the most alluring powers to hold, and who better to corrupt than a humble soldier one who thinks a mad man, who could have overthrown kings but chose to live in poverty and persecution cleansing lepers and loving whores, is a righteous man worthy of worship?" Her smile grew wider as her rant continued.

"I shall corrupt you, and you shall corrupt others, and we shall have no need of heaven of priests of prayers, we shall never feel hunger or pain or sadness again. Why do we have these powers? Why do these powers give us the urge to…"

She waved her hand at the corpse piles again. "Who cares? To keep them in line or to cull them or help us learn…" Here, she stopped and gathered herself. "It doesn't matter. We will be the mother and father to a race that will make this island one of the most bloodcurdling places in the world."

She took a step back. "I won't force you, just shake your head and you can join your comrades on the way to the next world."

Spurius was sure she hadn't told him everything, and that was a small part of what made him stand still, but her magnetic voice meant that when she was promising a life without pain or want, she was simply stating facts to him.

"I wonder where that snake went?" was his last human thought as Lilith's bones began to crack as her mouth opened to an impossible degree, her head nearly splitting in two as the snake uncoiled from the back of her throat and flung itself at Spurius' neck.

CHAPTER 1

365 years later – 540 AD, Subseaxe

Alfwen sighed as the rain pissed down. Bad enough to be stuck inside the hall all day, but she was stuck sharing it with her lackwit sister and nagging mother. Oh, and the village ox that had to be brought inside because it panicked during storms.

"Hel's tits!" she yelled when the ox did a giant shit on the hall floor.

"Do not curse the gods when they are pissing on us you stupid girl!" admonished her mother. Ignoring her, Alfwen leaned out of the door and screamed at the servant's wooden hut, where they were making a futile attempt to stay dry.

"Iga, get in here quick and get this ox shit off our floor!"

The door of the hut creaked open, and after a second's hesitation, Iga, the slave girl, made a forty foot dash through the torrential rain. She ran towards the larger wooden hall which had wooden beams supporting the straw. The servant's hut Iga was leaving had straw just stacked on, and sticks propped it up. It was looking like it would collapse at any moment.

Arse for brains slave owes me one or at least the ox one for getting her out of that thought Alfwen.

She ushered the girl into the house, and set her to work, noticing, as usual, the girl's left eye opened and shut rapidly when she saw the size of the mess she'd have to gather in her arms and dump a good way from the hall. The slave was about twenty she thought, but with her tatty, thin hair and sunken eyes, she could pass for twice that age. Alfwen thought about kicking Iga up the arse to encourage her but her mother called her away to help gather up the rushes.

~

The Nix stepped out of the forest he'd retreated into when the girl left the hut. He loved the rain. It allowed him to divert from the rivers and lakes, and this downfall now three days strong had allowed him to get further south than he'd ever got before. He still needed to stick close to the rivers, but that was where people lived so good for him. The rain just made it more comfortable and allowed him to keep a human form with more ease.

Usually keeping the human form was painful after a few minutes. Almost like holding your breath, or at least how The Nix remembered what it was like to hold his breath. It had been what 150 or was it 160 years since he'd been a Pict fisherman whose boat had sailed into a cave by the shore that was already occupied, and after that…sometimes the memories were clear. Usually, when he rested at the bottom of a lake the images were vivid. Sometimes he could even remember his old name. But not now, not outside. The respite the rain brought had its limits. For now, all he remembered was a fire in the cave, a walk through stone tunnels. His first meeting with an olive-skinned man with rams' horns, a snake's tongue, and eyes like gloom.

He focused on the present. He'd worked out the men were absent, the women unarmed, the two guards huddled inside their hut on the far side of the village. Everyone assumed this rain would put off bandits, and they were probably right. For the walk back to the lake to collect his knuckles The Nix decided to conserve energy by switching back to his real form. He made a wheezing, rattling sound, and the grubby looking peasant began to shake and grimace as his bones bent, and his insides curdled while they changed. Soon, the runty little man was a 6-foot tall figure with the head of a frog, a long green beard, webbed hands with claws, and covered in fish scales from the neck down. His bulging black and yellow eyes gave one last look at the village hall before he disappeared into the forest.

~

After disposing of the ox's offering, Iga had been sent outside to do all the jobs the chief's wife and daughters didn't want to do; the ones that would result in getting pissed on. Feeding the chickens, collecting the eggs, emptying the latrine pit behind the hut, trying to find firewood that hadn't been drenched. Just to be beaten by Aluhburg the chief's wife when she came back with only damp twigs. Aluhburg had encouraged her two daughters to join the beating. The youngest Aebbe looked shamed to do it, but the same couldn't be said for Alfwen. Her blonde hair bouncing, and her smile showed off her pretty dimples as she slapped Iga across the face twice.

Aluhburg spat, "You better not have been praying to Thunor for this rain thrall, we need you out in the field to…"

Iga then heard a muffled scream. She'd been half-listening as she sat on the floor scrapping a stone trying to remove mud from clothes. The two daughters were sitting on stools tying the rushes together, and Aluhburg was taking turns at poking the fire, and staring out of the tiny window slit to inspect and comment on the weather.

A microsecond after the muffled scream two louder ones started from the two girls, and Iga looked up to add her own scream.

Something was on Aluhburg's face. It was gray, it had no hair or fur, just a wet sticky slug-like skin. Aluhburg couldn't scream, but was in sheer agony convulsing, and soon the smell of shit and piss filled the room as she emptied her bowels and bladder.

It was then the grey thing slid off her face and rested on the floor. Slug or worm or leech Iga couldn't tell, but she'd never seen one the size of a hound before. Nor one with hundreds of tiny sharp-looking picks for teeth. Then a sight that would haunt her for the rest of her life, before her body crashed to the ground Aluhburg faced them. She had no eyes, she had no nose, she had no face. A socket less skull gave them a brief accusatory glare before she fell to the ground.

Alfwen slumped to the floor unconscious at the sight of her mother's skull, and Iga screamed for help. That left it to Aebbe to decide how best to save their lives, just seconds after the most traumatic event of her life so far. The grey dog sized worm thankfully was shuffling towards the open door at a faster pace than she'd expect from something its size.

~

The Nix sat hunched in the outskirts of the wood that faced the village. While not as sensitive to sunlight as some of the other creations, he still needed heavy rain clouds and plenty of shade to avoid bursting into flames. He was always sure to remain close to water, always close to water. He gave a wide horrible grin as he saw the grey legless worm dog leave the hall, and move towards the wood.

"Here, knuckles," he hissed. "Come here, my lovelies."

When the worm arrived at his feet, he hoisted it high in the air over his head and opened his mouth wide as he squeezed it. Blood and flesh poured from the worm's mouth into his mouth.

"Couple o'eyeballs, good knuckles," he burped between gulps.

When he finished, he reached into his leather sack and pulled out two more knuckles. He looked at the hall and heard the screams, but then rival screams came from the smaller hut. The soggy roof of the smaller hut had finally caved in after the girl escaped to the bigger hut. The Nix considered for a second before throwing the knuckles in the direction of the smaller hut. He then heard men shouting; the guards must have heard the screams. He retreated further into the bushes to make his move, and wait for the knuckles to bring him back some more treats.

~

Aebbe watched in horror from the window slit, as the beasts made their way to the slave quarters. They only had a few minutes.

"We must get father," she said to Iga while trying to prop Alfwen up. "Help me for Frigg's sake," she yelled at her. Iga helped lift Alfwen's other arm and clenched her face tight. She restarted screaming when she began to recognize the screams of her fellow slaves.

"It'll be us next if we don't get to father, help me and my sister live today and you'll gain your freedom I promise you thrall!" She dared to edge towards the door. "We can sneak around the walls…oh thank Woden those fucking guards have decided to wake up, my father will geld them when I tell him…" A spear flew out of the woods impaling a guard's throat. It then retracted back into the forest as quickly as it had come. It was also pink, fleshy, and twenty feet long.

"Let's go out the back way," said Aebbe.

"But that would mean dragging your sister through the latrine pit!"

"She won't mind… I think."

Five minutes later, the pair had dragged the unconscious girl through the pit, and took a second to gather their bearings. Behind the chief's hall was the edge of the village borders. Another huge forest was to the rear of the village, as well as the front of it. The other villagers' huts were a bit further out in clearings cut into the forest facing the hall, most of those huts would be full today because of the rain. Aebbe gave a quick prayer to the gods before she heard thuds coming from the hall. One of the monsters began to launch itself from wall to wall in search of a face to attach itself to. The ox gave the most horrible bellow before stopping abruptly.

"Let's go," Aebbe said.

Iga had never paid much attention to the younger daughter before. With drab clothes, a brown rat's nest of a hairstyle, and a projecting canine tooth, she looked so different to her siblings and parents that you could almost mistake her for a normal village girl. So quiet too. Iga had barely noticed her whenever she was called to the house. Usually, she just lived in terror of the other two's tyranny. One of her tyrants was still out cold, putting a lot of pressure on Iga's shoulders, and the other lay on the rushes without a face. It was the meek little sister that had taken charge, and talked rapidly in her ear, while they moved as fast as they could. Showing an assertive side, that had been well hidden until now.

"Father and the others will be at the stone building, it's a mile or two from here. We are heading in the right direction, thank Woden! They were hunting when the downpour started, so will have sheltered there, half the roof still remains and the roof is made of clay like our pots, a whole roof!"

"You mean the buildings what the giants built long ago?" Iga had heard of such things, but had never been more than a mile from the village since she was a child.

"The same. The walls are massive as high as three people, and outside there's a yard, where the floor is covered with little stones that make a picture. It shows a woman with snakes for hair, mother always said it gave the evil eye and we shouldn't go there…" She stopped talking. What had happened finally sank in. Aebbe dropped her sister to the ground and hunched over hyperventilating and sobbing.

"What creature of Loki and Hel was that thing that killed mother? And something killed one of the guards, something foul," she finally managed to get out through sobs.

CHAPTER 2

Digoth roasted the fish over the open fire. While the rain is like this the deer will look for cover, and finding them will be tough. But the good news is that once the rain stops, there will be scores of deer clustered together, ready for their spears. In the meantime, they used nets and traps in the forest streams to at least eat something that wasn't bloody parsnips or rock-hard bread for a change.

Fish were easy to catch too; something had thrown them into a panic. They were practically aiming for the nets at high speed.

He took a bite and stared up at the crumbling walls. The sight always made him feel awed. The giants must have lifted the stones to the top by hand, and how did they make the stones that perfect long cube shape that they were in? Digoth had seen wooden boxes and chests of a similar shape, but never another stone like the ones that had built this place.

"Digoth!"

He recognized the voice instantly. Aebbe! Sure enough, his little sister came crashing down the earth embankment that surrounded the stone building. Edging after her, more carefully was a tall woman with hollow eyes. Digoth recognized her as one of the village slaves, and on her back, a smaller blonde girl.

"Alfwen?" he said after getting them all undercover.

~

Thank Woden they made it to the building, thought Aebbe, landing on her arse. Iga had run straight into her. She watched her brother look disapprovingly when a panting Iga unceremoniously dumped Alfwen on the ground as Alfwen began to stir. The tussle of orange hair on his head suited the pinkness in his cheeks whenever he scowled, which was often. "What in Woven's name do you think you are doing, thrall?" he said, pushing his boot against Iga's face.

~

Iga had often wondered what had made one of the chief's children blonde, one brown and one orange. The chief himself was blonde, at least around the edges where he still had hair. Aluhburg had been grey for as long as Iga could remember.

Iga remembered another slave from when she was a girl. She couldn't remember the girl's name now, she'd died that winter. She had told her, "these that rule the land now ain't the same as us. They come from far away. My grandmother would tell about ships coming being bad news. Raiders you see, but these raiders stayed. We who lived with the giants either killed, or chased away, or slaves now." Maybe that was why the three siblings all looked so different.

Iga was waiting for Aebbe to defend her, and explain what had happened, but she appeared to be tongue-tied around her brother. She was still shaken by the events today and her breakdown in the woods. Iga's left eyelid was going haywire, as she realized in horror that the news about his mother coming from a slave would be taken as an insult, and in his grief, he might beat her to…

"My dress smells like shit," came from behind them. Alfwen was awake.

Iga breathed a sigh of relief that Digoth was beginning to turn his attention to her unlikely savior. Alfwen's eyes widened in horror, as she saw what was causing the smell.

~

"My favorite dress! It's covered in… what did you do? Drag me through the latrine pit?" Alfwen's voice shook with rage.

"Well, actually…" started Aebbe.

"You dog-faced turd! What the fuck did you do this for? I'm going to feed your eyes to the crows!"

"Shut up! Just shut up! You fainted straight away when that thing killed mother. More killed the rest of the slaves and the other villagers too probably. If Iga hadn't helped me carry you, they would have eaten you alive!"Aebbe screamed.

Alfwen's face grew ashen at the recollection of the last thing she saw before fainting. Soon she was mute, clutching Aebbe's arm. Her sister and Iga tried their best to tell Digoth what had happened.

~

Digoth needed to sit, and rested on a pile of collapsed masonry. Hounds with no hair jumping through the window slit, eating people's faces alive, mother's face? The girls must be mistaken. But all three women told the same story. They vehemently rejected any suggestions that it may have been some odd shaped wolf, boar, or bear, or indeed anything they'd seen or heard of. He began to grow weary. A wave of sorrow and anxiety overcame him making him try to hold back tears in front of the women. It was clear they weren't mistaken or making it up.

"Got the bastard!" bellowed a familiar-sounding voice, echoing in from the large holes in the building's walls and roof. His father, Ribald, the chief, entered the room, his spear bloody. A male slave was holding his wooden shield over the chief's head as an umbrella, even though he was wearing his helmet for no other reason than he was insecure about his bald dome.

He took his helmet off when he saw his son's expression. He sat, while some guards carried in a massive deer. They had missed the heart with the spears. Its head had been bashed in by rocks.

"Digoth, what's happened? Why are the girls here?" asked Ribald.

~

Later, Ribald's two exhausted daughters slept under the leaky roof in front of the fire, as the sun went down. Once he'd heard of these beasts Ribald insisted on both his guards patrolling all night, rather than taking shifts. He would grieve for Aluhburg in his own time. He also was considering who in the village and neighboring ones would be suitable for his next wife. But first revenge. Protect the family and revenge.

~

"Tomorrow at first light you and I return to the village together," he told his son.

"Ecgheard and Ecgbald will remain here to guard the girls until we kill whatever Loki and Hel have sent us. Ado we will keep taking care of the girls while we're away. If what we hear is correct we will need him to rebuild, but the female thrall we sacrifice in the morning to please the gods."

"Very well, father. She did help save the girls, according to Aebbe."

"I'll stick her in the neck from behind. She won't know it's coming."

"Merciful father, thank you."

In the section of the building missing the roof, the rain had reduced to a drizzle. Ado snored, while Iga lay awake in terror having heard every word of the two men's conversation.

CHAPTER 3

An hour later, Iga found it easy to creep out of the other side of the building unnoticed. Slaves were good at not being heard, and the two guards whose names she always forgot or mixed up, were loudly muttering to each other over some cuts of deer meat and a flagon of mead.

It was where to go afterward that was the problem. Despite being a slave, Iga had barely ever been chained or restrained. Only at the beginning, when she was small, and transported from the market to the village. Any slave who ran, would starve or freeze, or be raped and killed by bandits. Even if they made it to a town or village, with no one to vouch for them, they would quickly be returned to their village or re-enslaved. No need for chains with the prospects of freedom so bleak.

Her best option, she'd learned from many a 'what if' late night discussion about escape in the slave hut was to find water. Hit a stream, and go down river, was the standard advice. No one really knew what they were talking about but it was a mantra handed down in slave pens and quarters across the land. If you ran downstream, you'd reach a village or town, you shouldn't linger but food could be stolen from them, and eventually, the coast awaited. After that? Iga didn't have a clue, but it was preferable to ending up a sacrifice to the gods. Once over the embankment, she had no idea where to go so turned left on an impulse and began to run.

~

"You mean they are sleeping out in the open, and there're only two guards? Not the usual four?"

"Right, been stalking them two days now. They left two guards at the village for the chief's womenfolk, but something's gone amiss, no sign of the chief's wife or those two guards at the hall. They've brought the two younger women to the villa, and left themselves like sitting ducks."

The three men in the cave considered this, as outlaws they'd need to move quickly. They'd talked about squatting in the Saxon chief's hall after killing him and eating his harvest but had decided against it. The villages were close here. It was likely he had kin who would root them out and hang them but a quick smash and grab would be worth it. Saxon steel, Saxon grain and now they'd found out Saxon women were there to be taken.

~

Hearing conversations she wasn't supposed to was becoming a habit for Iga, as this was the second time tonight. She'd decided to risk approaching the fire coming from the back of the cave, confident she wouldn't be noticed with so many crevices in the walls to conceal her. Now having heard, she poked her head out to see who they were. Three figures, but only two lit up by the fire. Two were similar looking, pockmarked, bald, toothless men, around forty years old. One was missing a hand; he'd been caught thieving in the past. The one with his back to her looked bigger and younger, but it was hard to tell. Even not knowing much about fighting, Iga didn't fancy their chances. The two bald men looked weak from hard living and hunger, and she doubted they had quality weapons. Digoth and the two guards should make short work of them.

She heard noises. Of course they're getting ready now. A surprise attack is their only chance, especially if one of Ecgheard and Ecgbald are asleep. What if both of them are asleep? That would really shift the odds of the fight in the bandits' favor.

She should go and warn them. It's the right thing to do she thought, before being overridden with anger that those foreign bastards want to kill me for their gods. If it wasn't for the girls she would have let the outlaws have them, but the girls were sleeping while the men made their plans. They didn't deserve what the outlaws had planned for them. No one did. It was what made her turn back to the giant's building.

~

Aebbe groaned, as her neck was shaken. She was jolted awake by her head bouncing on a nearby rock.

"What is it? Alfwen, stop it or… oh thrall, I mean Iga, get back to sleep. I promise I'll talk with father tomorrow about giving you your freedom. Tomorrow morning they're going to…"

"There'll be no tomorrow if you don't rouse those two useless rat cocked flea sacks," she hissed, referring to Ecgheard and Ecgbald who were snoring away. "They won't listen to a slave, but will to you or your kin. Bad folk are coming tonight."

Aebbe's face turned white. "The things that killed mother?"

"No, these are from this world, but no less foul." Iga spat on the floor. "I'll wake Ado, you make for the rest."

~

Ado was up and lit a torch. Ribald was looking stern shaking Digoth. Aebbe frantically whispered into his ear when the first pockmarked man ran in screaming and buried his axe into Ecgbald's skull and left it there, unsheathing a second axe from his belt. Digoth raised his shield just in time to avoid a death blow from the man. Ribald slid his dagger into the back of the man's thigh. The man squealed in pain and fell to the ground. Ribald grabbed his spear and made sure to twist it as he pushed it into the man's belly.

"There's two more," warned Iga. "Another same type as him, and one I didn't get a look at."

Ecgheard, now awake, wrenched the axe out of his comrade's head. "Light," he said. "Just need one hand to hold it. The Britons up north have a few of these."

"Those sheep fucking savages seem to find decent weapons

just lying around for them to find. I swear Tiw is testing us by arming our foes." Ribald said clutching his fists. "What the fuck are the Brits doing so far south?"

"Hunger? Boredom? Maybe they want to try preaching their gods at us again?" said Digoth in reply.

"God, the savages only have one god. Got himself nailed to a cross he did. You wouldn't catch Thunor in such a state, Loki maybe although you can never be sure what…"

Digoth and Aebbe rolled their eyes as they began to hear this rant ranking the gods for the umpteenth time. Iga and Ado looked at the floor, not having the slightest idea or interest in what the angry man was yelling about.

Alfwen, having slept through most of the drama, stirred. "Stop snoring, Aebbe! Bad enough you have the face of a pig's arse, no need to sound like one." She patted the cheek of the snoring figure next to her and gave herself a self satisfied chuckle. The cheek belonged to the pockmarked man rather than Aebbe. His 'snores' were his death throes. Alfwen's shriek of fear and disgust when she opened her eyes and saw whose cheek she was patting did remind a sleepy Digoth to take the man's other axe off him just before he died.

"Two more you say, thrall?" Digoth checked. Iga nodded.

"Shit! They'll have the high ground due to the embankment, but they've lost the element of surprise, and we outnumber them so stalemate."

He shouted at the night. "Leave now and we won't pursue you, attack and you will die slower than your friend, and he died slowly."

~

Iga thought Digoth sounded ridiculous talking to no one but kept her head bowed. She'd deprived the outlaws of the element of surprise and that should give the girls a fighting chance of remaining free and chaste. Now she needed to slip away herself before they got the sacrifice idea again. Ado would want to join her to avoid becoming a sacrifice himself, and certainly if those terrible worms still awaited them at the village.

Ado was tall for a slave. A man on the road would make certain sorts leave her alone. If she had to give something back in return then Ado wasn't bright or handsome. He had never shown much kindness to anyone. He was pretty lazy when you thought about it. He always disappeared for an hour or two when it was time to work in the field. It certainly wasn't to go to the stream to bathe, as he stank. He was tall, though. Iga, who wasn't afforded the largest dating pool in the world, would be content with that.

Or at least she would have been, if an arrow hadn't torn through his throat a few seconds later.

~

Screaming and yelling filled the building as another arrow came down missing Alfwen by an inch.

Before long all of them were forced into a corner of the building. Concealed by a pillar and half of a crumbled wall. No longer visible or in reach of whoever was at the top of the embankment sending the arrows.

~

Digoth knew they were in trouble. The arrows they used for hunts were made for short bows to fire straight across a range of a few meters to hunt deer and boar. They did not have anything that could fire arrows so far and so accurately, nor anyone who could wield such a thing. Their one act of good fortune had been the archer probably saw Ado's height and mistook him for a warrior, if that arrow had been aimed at Digoth, Ribald or Ecgheard then they would be one warrior down. The girls had been trained to fight at close quarters. He made sure they shared the axe from the dead man.

~

Ribald was the first member of his family to be born on this island. His father had been a young man when he and his grandfather came first to raid and then to settle. By the time he was born the Britons had long since been forced out of these lands, which they soon called Subseaxe meaning the south Saxons. But in much of the area to the north and west, they still faced Briton resistance. It was futile, even though the savages had surprisingly advanced weaponry, (the giants must have left depositories of them up north Ribald assumed) the Saxons were winning.

Everyday more and more ships arrived, more farms and villages were established in these fertile lands. More and more Saxon babies survived to adulthood. With each growing generation, the sheer force of numbers was going to drive the already sparsely populated Briton tribes into exile, death, or slavery. Brief raids; futile attempts to regain lost farmland, and reduce the Saxon population happened from time to time. But they seldom came this far south or east.

Indeed since consolidating around a mysterious king called Arthur, and winning a battle that none of Ribald's drinking friends seemed to be able to agree on the location of, nor did any of them know a Saxon that fought there, the Britons had been content to stay on their part of the island. Rumors abounded that Arthur had not survived the battle, forcing the Britons into chaos despite their victory. So while likely Britons these attackers were more common bandits than warriors despite their weaponry.

This thought emboldened Ribald, and after noting the growing lengths of time between arrows, he figured whoever was up there was running low. He sent Ecgheard to the courtyard with his shield as cover to see if the path was wide enough for the five of them, well six, he'd take the thrall if he could, to evacuate together with enough shield cover and axe range for protection against anyone still out there.

~

Ecgheard moved out of the group's sight, and when no arrows fell he fell back. Ribald urged him to go further ahead. He then disappeared once more. He didn't reappear for five minutes, then ten minutes, then fifteen minutes.

"Where the fuck is he?" scowled Alfwen, who at least now had her own axe; Ecgheard having given her the spare he had wrenched out of Ecgbald's skull. "We don't need him anyway, I can fight as well as him."

Ribald ignored her and told Digoth to investigate further. "Take the slave with you," he said, mystifying Iga.

CHAPTER 4

Dawn had given them enough vision to see, as the two-edged out into the courtyard. Iga gasped when she saw the mosaic of the snake haired woman for the first time.

"That's what the woman giants looked like, I wonder how they kept the snakes calm when they…y'know," Digoth said.

Then they saw at the far end of the courtyard another pockmarked man with a missing hand, and a huge mountain of a man was waiting for them. At two meters tall he was the tallest man Iga had ever seen before. His chest stuck out like a pigeon, although his stomach and waist was lean through hunger she guessed.

"He didn't look so tall in the cave," she whispered.

At their feet was Ecgheard. His neck had been snapped, and his head lay on the floor at a weird diagonal angle. His axe was in his hand, and the tall man had a gash on his cheek so he'd gotten one shot in.

"Well met, friends," began Digoth. "I am Ado, one of chief Ribald's slaves, and this is his eldest daughter Alfwen."

Iga's head snapped around so fast she feared she'd do herself an Ecgheard style injury. Digoth quickly wrapped his hand around her jaw.

"The chief and his son long fled at your fearsome onslaught of arrows to get reinforcements. I was forced to stay and protect the daughters. Aebbe succumbed to the arrows, but here is Alfwen, a beauty I'm sure you'll agree and one the chief will pay a fine ransom for her safe return. So take her to your hideout from me as a sign of good faith, and if you leave us be I will be able to deliver the chief's offer to you once he returns."

He leaned forward and hissed in Iga's ear. "Just go along with it, we just need to get rid of them, if they think you're Alfwen they'll treat you well. We'll rescue you when we track down their hideout." It was a plan that Ribald had come up with while the arrows were falling, whispering it rapidly into Digoth's ear. Digoth thought he understood most of it.

"A chief's daughter!" piped the one-handed man in a high pitched voice. "A handsome ransom at least three deer I'd wager, and a warm bed for me in the meantime. Told you it was worth tracking these Saig."

The big man nodded, and began to speak: under a mop of brown hair, his face was pinched like he was perpetually in pain.

His voice was surprisingly light with a sibilant accent. "Maybe, maybe but why is the slave wearing a shield and axe, and the chief's daughter in slave rags? Did they trade clothes overnight?"

Digoth frowned: the Britons were speaking their savage tongue. When he made his offer he made sure to shout the important nouns such as 'daughter', 'ransom' and 'good faith.' Even shouted in Saxon the Britons would be familiar enough with the words after living alongside the Saxons for a century give or take. Also, every Saxon knew enough Briton nouns to communicate.

Digoth expected the same courtesy of the important Brittonic words being shouted with gestures to help the conversation go smoothly. He didn't expect the man's almost snake like dialect to confuse him so much.

"I say, could you please repeat that one more time," he shouted. His hand opened and closed in a speaking gesture while holding up one figure with the other hand.

Iga, who had grown up with various Briton and Saxon dialects being spoken around her in slave pens and huts, had a better but not perfect handle on what the huge man was saying.

"I think they want us to change into each other's clothes," she said hesitantly.

~

"What the fuck are they doing?" asked Saig as the two odd figures from the stone building began to undress. "Do these foreign barbarians offer themselves to their captors at once?"

"It looks like they are switching clothes," said the one handed man. "Nice tits on Alfwen."

"Her face is too long, she looks like a badger. You can have her. I will take the red-haired slave girl as mine."

"You have to look very, very hard I grant you, but I'm pretty sure from this angle Ado is a man."

"I am bigger than her, so she will be who I tell her to be." Saig was getting irritated.

~

Digoth had resisted Iga's suggestion, of course.

She persisted; "I didn't catch it all either but 'dilhad' means clothes and 'eskemm' means to exchange goods. What else could they mean? I guess they want me to be wearing clothes that have value once I'm handed over."

The slave was proving to be earning her worth by saving the girls and warning them of the ambush, somehow the gods have favored her. Digoth slowly nodded.

After changing clothes there was a five-second period that began when Digoth realized he was no longer in possession of his axe or shield, both attached to the belt that was now around the tunic Iga was now snugly wearing and ending when one of the many insects that lived in Iga's soiled dress of rags bit him on the arse, which convinced him he'd made a huge mistake.

~

This feeling intensified when the short pockmarked man approached them, and said, "Welcome Lady Alfwen you will be our honored guest during your time with me and Saig, as well as the weirdo you'll meet later. If you'd give me your axe and shield for safekeeping." She hesitated and was saved by the pockmarked man noticing Digoth begin to back away.

"You're not going anywhere Ado. The last woman we stole from the slave pens died of a chill last full moon. We need a new one to forage berries and firewood for us, gut the squirrels we catch, boil the water, mend our clothes and empty the stink pits. You're going to be a busy lass for us! Saig has a few other tasks in mind for you as well."

Digoth's face by now was a shocking shade of red. He wondered if he could snatch the axe off Iga and bury it in the man's skull. It would mean certain death from the larger man, but surely better than the alternative fate in store. He just hoped that despite the plan failing his father and the girls had used the time to climb the other side of the embankment and find a path home.

So why weren't his feet moving? Iga's blinking left eyelid flashed at him asking him the same question.

Digoth finally summoned up the nerve to move, he'd delayed for too long so despite being younger, faster, and having a hands advantage on the other man. It was going to be a 50/50 tussle for control of Iga's belt. Digoth got there first but the man pulled out his axe, and would have hacked at Digoth's wrist if he hadn't been impaled in the chest by a giant stone penis falling from above.

~

"Satan!" yelled Saig in horror.

"Who?" replied Iga and Digoth at the same time. They were all taking in the sight of a stone figure that had fallen on top of the short man. It had the body and face of a man, but the legs, tail, ears and horns of a goat. As well as a cock the length of an arm sticking out, that had crushed the short man's ribcage and had him trapped.

Ribald charged out ready for battle, and the balance was of power was now with Iga. She could aid Saig who with his size advantage may win with just a little help, or she could arm Digoth. Two on one would surely be too much for even a big man like Saig.

She heard a shout and looked up to see the two sisters hanging on to the edge of a piece of wall higher than the rest. They had climbed up a mostly decayed stone staircase, barely visible to the eye. Somehow they had balanced and heaved the statue up this narrow and fragile structure, and dropped it on the pockmarked man at exactly the right time.

"Great idea to change clothes Iga. It confused them and bought us more time," shouted Aebbe and even Alfwen nodded. Iga handed the weapons to Digoth.

Saig weighed up his options. He did not enjoy his chances of either two on one combat with warriors, or the fate in store should he surrender or be taken alive. He threw his axe at Digoth, the flat hitting him in the face, and knocking him out, before turning tail and running away.

"Go to Hel!" Ribald yelled, throwing his hunting spear which landed harmlessly several feet behind Saig. The big man disappeared into the forest.

~

"I'll carry him back, got practice now," said Iga, hoisting Digoth's unconscious body over her broad shoulders.

She stopped and nodded at the squirming, panting, moaning, dying pockmarked man. "Can he be your sacrifice?" Ribald nodded and got out his blunt-looking dagger, still soiled with the blood of the first pockmarked man.

~

Ribald explained the statue on the walk home. "Some of them are more daring than that, like they're some sort of women with their tits out, but their arms cut off. The giants must have had strange tastes. Of course the first time I showed the building to your mother she threw a fit, and demanded all these raunchy stones be destroyed. I did for most of them but buried a few in the grounds outside for…historical research, you see. Anyway, when Aebbe asked if there was anything that could be used as a weapon then the goat man with the large… he just sprung to mind."

"Neither of them was the archer," Iga said. "The runt was missing a hand, and a man same size as the other is trained in shield and spear, not arrows." Ribald nodded at this.

She continued "Must have been another one I missed in the cave. They said something to Digoth and me just before it went downhill for them about a weirdo I think was their words."

"I've never heard that word before," said Alfwen. "Is it a Briton word?"

"Think so. Never heard it from anyone else. It means madness but can also mean someone dangerous," Iga said.

CHAPTER 5

Milian leaped from branch to branch, like a squirrel somehow keeping his balance despite having his thin bow made of wood, horn, and sinew under his arm, and a quiver of bows on his back. Rog and Moe dead and Saig unarmed. He fancied his chances now to dump the bandit's life, and get back on the trail of The Nix.

He had a clear shot of the two girls when they were heaving something or other up to the top of the building. He let them live as he was curious as to what it was. When he saw Rog literally get fucked in the ribcage, he collapsed into a laughing fit, and by the time he'd pulled himself together Saig had fled and the Saxons were leaving.

Milian descended to the ground and sighed. He'd have to finish off Saig he thought. Can't have him running around and getting in the way of the mission. Merlin had been clear he was not to return until his mission was completed. He remembered his last talk with the great man.

~

"So, it's crossed into Saxon lands, it's not our problem anymore. Besides reducing the Saxon numbers doesn't exactly make me weep."

"Our king is a Christian now! Love one's fellow man and all that boar shit! Besides there are practical reasons to help. Eventually, we are going to have to share the secrets of this island with the Saxon bastards, even have them join the lost hunt."

"What you mean, tell them about the massacre at the wall and what happened after?"

"Eventually, for now, find a group of raiders or bandits to fall in with. Someone with your skills should be able to track The Nix, and lead them towards him as bait."

~

It hadn't quite worked out that way, but the movements of the fish in the streams, the lack of people on the paths, and a higher than usual number of empty villages and hermit shacks to squat in as they moved south convinced him The Nix was nearby. Now without being burdened with his idiot companions he needed to make his move. First, he had to head to the hideout to retrieve the rest of his weapons, he would wait for Saig and give him a fair fight. He looked forward to that at least.

~

The five survivors arrived back at the village. Ribald went straight to the hall. Digoth, now awake, followed him in. Iga comforted the sisters outside as they looked sullenly at the building while howls came from inside.

~

Iga left the family to their grief. She went to the grub-hut where the slaves lived. Blood was splattered over the walls and the thin rushes. Three skeletons lay intact. The monsters hadn't torn them apart but sucked away their flesh, blood and organs stripped right to the bone. Just half a day ago or so these skeletons had been living, breathing, laughing, moaning, crying, smiling, men and women.

~

In the hall, Aebbe had wordlessly wrapped her mother's

skeleton in linen. Alfwen gathered up the ox's bones. "We could use these to make soup?" she offered. Aebbe rolled her eyes, and Ribald shook his head. Digoth was resting under sheep hides, recovering from his injury. He had allowed Iga to keep his tunic and woolen trousers, but he had thrown her dress into the fire as soon as he could. He could have sworn he heard the cries of thousands of insects as it burnt.

~

Later sat at the table Ribald announced his plans.

"We go to Chichester and inform the king, well the reeve, and he will tell the king. We will all go together. We'll take the thrall and any surviving villagers we will need to be convincing. I'll make some deals with the traders, and we'll get some new slaves to rebuild. We'll allow Iga to rent a hide from us that should get her a husband, and new villagers will come. More and more boats from the old country are coming all the time. While we're in Chichester we may as well ride down to the harbor, and see if there are any strong hands."

~

Milian heard cursing and shouting from inside the cave a good 20 meters from its entrance. This gave him time to draw his bow and whistle.

Saig came charging out and stopped, suddenly nearly keeling over when he saw the bow and the raven haired smiling man wielding it. The purple birthmark that circled his right eye made him seem otherworldly.

"Hello, Saig," he said. "Don't worry, you'll get a fair fight if you want it the bow is just to stop you from coming right at me."

"Where the fuck were you?"

"Laughing myself breathless, did you see what that statue looked like it was--"

"It was that Satan the monks have been telling us about!"

"It was a fucking statue from Roman times! You halfwit."

"Well, I've lost two men and most of my weapons. What am I supposed to do now?"

"I was thinking we could fight. I would kill you. I'll go on my merry way, and you can see if the monks were right about them letting anyone into that heaven of yours if they're pious enough. Good luck with that mate! Why did you become a bandit when you used to be one of Arthur's men? I heard at Badon Hill a man your size broke during the battle. Killed as many of us as he did Saxons! Rumors were that he was spotted roasting his victims on a spit, and howling at the moon that night, before disappearing into the forest for good. But you wouldn't know much about that I reckon?"

Saig's face had turned the color of a plum, and he charged at Milian, but by now he was ready and dropped the bow. *They always go for the eye with the birthmark, makes it easy,* he thought as he ducked his head left. When Saig realized he was going to miss the punch he tried to turn his body in mid-flight, which left him a sitting duck for three quick kicks one to the chest, balls, and chin that ended the contest.

"There is no man on this island who can beat me Saig." He said to the wheezing sack of bones. He tilted Saig's head back so the big man wouldn't choke on the several loose teeth in his mouth. "I was put on this earth to fight things other than men. That's why it's time for me to give up the bandit's life. I say, while scouting the Saxons did you see any lakes…no never mind." He pulled out a Roman pugio making Saig's eyes bulge and held it up. "You helped get me this far Saig, a good clean death it is."

"Worms," or something sounding like it escaped from Saig's throat.

"What did you say?"

"Worms, the whimpering guard...right before his neck snapped. He begged for his life."

"Like you are doing now. I hope he said something more impressive than 'worms' for your sake."

"Claimed the old man had lost his wits, the girls had some story about a massive worm eating the wife, obviously the girls and the slave had done for the old girl, but old man believed their story. Guard offered to join us and take the village but I didn't like his face."

"Unlucky for him, are you quite sure that was what said?"

"Rog said it true; he had more Saxon than me."

"There are things I've seen in the woods north of the wall with jawbones rotted away centuries ago that have more Saxon than you, but you got a better look at this family than me so that's earned you a slight delay in meeting your nailed-to-a-stick god."

"Huh?"

"We are going to find that family together and that means finding a town, asking questions, as well as recognizing the family, your size will discourage any awkward questions been asked of us."

CHAPTER 6

Iga arrived at the hall with -talking news; two children a boy of six and a girl of eight were with her. Ribald recognized them as the children of Osric, a farmer, and woodsman who rented a few hides.

"They were all that was left in the village," she said. "Elsewhere, nothing but bones and blood. Some might have made it into the woods but none back yet."

And would they want to come back? She silently thought. She was still half thinking of running herself. Ribald had said she was free, but he seemed to be expecting her to stay and do the same jobs as before. She was hoping the trip to Chichester may give her some ideas about the future. She was a little excited truth be told, a city! What would it be like?

Ribald bent down and, asked the children their names. The younger blonde boy had lost the power of speech. His older sister managed to tell him their names were Winfred and Wiglac. Winfred explained their hut caught fire in the panic due to someone using a torch to fight the worms off. Among the blood-curdling screams, the two had been rooted to the spot in fear.

The worms had ignored them, "can't move, knuckles can't see," said Winfred.

"What's a knuckles?" asked Ribald.

Winfred continued, "Can't move, knuckles can't see, only frog-man can see, frog-man gets angry screams at the knuckles to eat us 'soft meat come collect knuckles,' he says. Knuckles can't see us, frogman opens his mouth. He has a million teeth, like needles they are. Then rain stops, and frog-man screams. Smoke comes from frog-man. He runs into woods along with knuckles. Only us and the bones left."

~

"Children say all manner of things," Digoth argued the next morning, as the now seven strong group started to make the long hike to the capital of Subseaxe. They dared not leave the girls or children in case the terror returned.

"They saw what they saw as did we," Aebbe snapped at him. None of the party looked particularly enthused as they climbed onto the wagon. Apart from Iga who was full of excitement to find out what the world beyond the village looked like.

~

An hour later, Saig and Milian arrived at the village, and the latter quickly found what he was looking for.

"See those tracks? Something with no arms or legs, the size of a boar made those at high speed. The bloodstains are still fresh. He must have fed on over ten of the poor souls. He'll be resting for while, shit. I need to get this area mapped, so I can work out potential hidey holes."

"Reckon they'll be back?" Saig said. Even though Milian shared a language with the big man he only heard, "rewpon dare d bak?" Saig's strong dialect had not been rendered more understandable with the loss of several teeth, quite the opposite it appeared. Still, if you listened hard, you could get it.

"Not a lot for them to come back to with their slaves and villagers dead, they've probably gone to find more which gives us a bit of leverage."

"What?" Saig was confused.

"No one is going to want to live and work here if they know what I know. It would be in those Saxon twats best interest to keep me happy. Still, won't approach until I know what I'm dealing with. I don't want them to give me a nasty surprise, like what happened to you and those two pockmarked bastards. We track them through the woods, so we aren't seen until we reach the city."

~

The larger party made their way to the edges of the city by dusk. Ribald decided to stay at a cheap thatched hut acting as an inn, about half a mile from the cities crumbling stone walls and ditch. He and his two daughters would take the floor space on offer. Digoth, Iga, and the two children would take shifts watching the wagon and sleeping.

"Keep a good eye on those two," he'd said to his son, regarding the children. "No parents, anyone could take them. Let's just say that they might be vital in replacing what we've lost." Digoth shrugged and set off for one of the shacks near the city walls that served eye-watering homemade mead and ale.

~

"You can't sell them as slaves!" cried Aebbe, after her father explained his plan. "They are just children!"

"Grow up, beaver face," said her sister. "It's just the way things are. How old was Iga when mother brought her to the village? Probably younger than those two brats. The boy can't even speak so training him to be a warrior is a waste of time. Do you want a bodyguard who stares at you mutely as someone from behind bashes your brains in?"

"The gods took his voice in exchange for his life," said Aebbe.

"And he's going to live isn't he?" Alfwen shot back. "Just not inherit his father's hides or anything else for that matter…"

"Shut up, the pair of you!" Ribald shouted. "Alfwen is right; the boy's use is limited as he can't communicate. Best get him working hard now, so he's as strong as an ox by the time he's grown and has value. I'm doing him a favor."

"A favor!" Aebbe cried. "You're selling him into slavery, and what about his sister? You know what happens to girls that get…"

"I'm sure that won't happen to her, she'll get a good family, those types you are worried about will be put off by her delusions. Much like the gods took the boy's voice, they took her wits in exchange for her life. Maybe the priests might be interested they say the mad are closest to the gods and…"

Ribald was cut off by Aebbe. "What if it wasn't delusions? What if she saw what we saw?" She gave Alfwen a stare, and she had the grace to look down at least.

Ribald pushed his chest out to speak. "We have only been on this island for two generations. It is possible there are foul things that lurk in the Britons' forests that we haven't seen yet, and that is what got your dear mother and the others. A man with a frog's head though? Sheer madness, neither of you saw one did you?"

They both looked at the ground.

"Now get to sleep," he said, climbing onto the main straw mattress. The two girls shared a much smaller one. "We need to present them to the reeve tomorrow anyway."

~

Digoth leaned against the wooden shack and took a swig from the pouch. A Frankish ship had run aground last week. Some of the wine barrels had made it from village to village to be sold and cut with watery ale, herbs, and salt, which made it taste vile but also created a warm, buzzy feeling. The taste made stocks last. Most of those who frequented the shacks had never had wine beforehand didn't notice the difference.

Soon, he was making soft snoring noises. A skinny little hand peeled open the folds of his tunic and darted around looking for the fold in his clothing that contained the purse of goods Digoth was trading for wine. The crunching sound and whimpering as the hand's owner's wrist was crushed, and jaw pushed upright was quickly muffled. Milian looked down on the sleeping man as Saig choked the would be thief.

"Looks like him, although I didn't get a great look at him from the tree."

"It's him, he looks different now he isn't in slave girl rags, but it's him. Ginger prick," said Saig.

"Some men have stranger hobbies than others, we should not judge Saig. Now watch over him while I look out for the woman and children this pot of piss on legs left to their own devices."

~

The Nix gurgled with delight when he saw it. He had had such a fun time when he was on his way down. Both wide and long as he liked. He'd had a fair few adventures here. He'd even thought about making it his new home but him, him, him… Spurius.

Spurius had come to him while he was having a long rest at the bottom of the river. He'd dragged down the odd fisherman and traveler on the banks himself and then he'd come across a small collection of huts. Some sort of settlement for the fishermen and even a local small farm. He'd decided to see how they'd react to the knuckles. It was that night Spurius spoke to him, while he was resting, with a full belly at the bottom of the river. Spurius could talk to him at any time and any place by speaking into his brain.

"Too exposed Nix! South, I say! South! To the woods! Let these German swine know what their new home holds."

After having fun – oh so much fun – in the Saxon villages. He was looking forward to trying out a larger settlement, when Spurius came to him again at the bottom of a lake, while he was sleeping
"Come, I wish to speak with you. Get yourself to the abandoned city as soon as you can." The voice hissed into his mind.

You couldn't say no to Spurius. He was more powerful than any other creation. He was their father. The Nix took his sack of knuckles, and sped up all the streams he could find, bounding across dry land in the dead of night when he had to. Now he was here. So much more fun than the lochs back home. They never flowed like this! He dived headfirst into what the Britons called The Tamesas.

CHAPTER 7

Chichester was one long dirt path surrounded by houses and huts, essentially a very large village. Main differences Iga could tell was the stone wall that surrounded the city. It must have taken years to build. Its height wasn't what it was, but the width! As wide as a man! It would be easy to hack an invader with spear and axe while he was trying to climb over.

The other difference was the alleys. In a village they'd be a few paces long, with nothing but a chicken coop or a stink pit. Here the alleys went on forever from her point of view, and had more huts and shacks on each side. Some huts were even on top of the other, pushing others further into the mud.

The houses that lined up on the main dirt path were stone made which surprised her. Further down the path, the fronts had huge open windows, with the wooden shutters flung open. This allowed view inside of the house, where they were selling their wares. There were a fishmonger, a blacksmith, a tanner, and more.

She looked the other way when they got to the next house: inside was full of men arguing and pointing at stacks of paper, piles of grain, slabs of meat, and whatever else could be used to barter. She knew at the back of that house was a pen full of naked, starving, diseased men and women who'd be dead within a week without a buyer to feed them the bare minimum.

She was also bothered by the noise and the smell, never having been in a large group of people before. She guessed at least a hundred people lived here as it was the highest number she could think of. Alfwen had laughed when she told her that. She said that her head was full of, "the brown water that comes out of your arse after eating Aebbe's porridge." But what was troubling Iga the most was the feeling that they were being watched.

~

The two Britons had a knack of slipping from alleyway to alleyway, not quite being seen, never taking their eyes off their prey. Saig proved his worth when they were noticed passing through a shack calling itself an alehouse. A sharp eyed Saxon warrior spotted them, despite being in his cups, and stood up to confront the strangers. Only to shit himself and look for an exit as soon as he saw Saig's face look down on him, and launch into a fierce hissing sound.

"I was only asking him what he wanted for the ale," complained Saig as they watched the Saxon party approach the great hall at the end of the street.

Milian laughed. "You sound like a hedgehog with a hair lip when you speak Brittonic. You don't want to know what your attempt at Saxon sounds like! Poor fucker probably thought you were going to eat him. Now we wait. I want to see how their king reacts to his people falling foul of Spurius' dogs. If he knew the half of it he'd have his people back in their ships sailing to whatever shit-hole they come from. Might not be a bad idea."

~

Iga and Digoth, Iga technically still a slave so not to be trusted with her account, and Digoth who hadn't witnessed the attack on the village waited outside. Ribald, his daughters, and the children went in to the two floor, stone hall to find the Reeve's quarters.

"How did they ever find so much stone the right shapes?" asked Aebbe while they went up the rickety stairs.

"Right around the time your grandfather arrived, they found one of the giant's palaces just west of here, a place called Fiscburna. Bit fire damaged, but otherwise in good shape. Stripped it to the bone the first settlers did and rebuilt this crumbling wreck of a city the Briton savages had neglected. Most houses in the city have blocks of Fiscburna propping them up," her father answered.

"Why didn't grandfather and the other settlers just move into the palace? I'd rather live in a palace than that cramped hall. In a palace, I could go to the other wing to get some sleep when Aebbe is snoring like a pig or Digoth is choking his--"

"That's enough, Alfwen," Ribald cut her off. "The palace was like the place in the woods, a strange place. Good enough to provide shelter, but it was not built for men. It would anger the gods for us to live in such dwellings and they might be tempted to…"

"Send flesh-eating monsters after us? Maybe the gods never intended the giant's dwellings to be used as shelter while hunting either!" Aebbe quickly said. Before Ribald could raise his hands against her, they found themselves face to face with the open door of the room where the reeve sat at his desk scribbling.

"What is that sodding noise outside? By the gods, Ribald, you've brought your whole family. Are those children new? No Aluhburg? Must be why my ears aren't bleeding, eyes too," he muttered the last two words under his breath.

~

Digoth and Iga sat in the shack acting as an alehouse staring daggers at each other in silence. While they'd initially agreed to drink together, Iga relieved at no longer having to babysit the children, and Digoth happy at any break from his windbag father and squabbling sisters, it became clear they had little in common so they decided to see who could get drunk the fastest. So far, Iga was winning, or losing depending, whichever way you looked at it. Used only to leftover dregs, which she sneaked sometimes when cleaning the dishes from a feast Digoth, who was often passed out at these feasts, had a head start on her in terms of drinking experience.

"Why are you so nervous?" he asked.

"What are you talking about?"

"Your left eye is twitching. We always took it as a sign you were up to no good and trying to hide something. Mother used to tell us to beat you harder if you ever started twitching when things went missing around the hall, or chores went undone. Alfwen said that it was probably because your mother was a horse."

Digoth wasn't as drunk, but speaking more freely than usual.

Iga decided to share her burden. "We're being watched. I got a look of them leaving here as we came in. I've had the feeling since we entered the city gates." She pulled Digoth's tunic towards her to get his attention. "And he was under a cloak, but one of them was a mountain of a man. I've only ever seen one that size before, as have you, I'd wager."

"Saig! Here? We need to let the city guards know."

"They know," grumbled the scabby man pooling the ale out from a barrel in exchange for whatever travelers had to offer, in Digoth's case kiln dried firewood and a small bag of wheat.

"Savage barbarian showed up in here, and sent one of my best customers running! Fella guards the walls always has quality scrap to use for tools, fuck knows when I'll see him again. Silly idiot panicking, and shaming himself in front of all his mates. Still, you did mention the unusual size and big he was. I thought the Britons were all tiny little bastards. Maybe he's a Jute, either way, bastard must have climbed over the wall ain't no way they let anyone like that one through the gates. He's being looked for by the warriors of this city that I tell you."

Iga and Digoth paused to wipe the spittle off their faces and wordlessly left to find the rest of the party.

~

The reeve was a portly man with a floppy quiff of blonde hair that fell over his face. "Worms, you say? Do you think this is worth bothering King Cissa over? Can't you just train your hounds better? Maybe keep the ale barrels away from the guards while they are on duty? This is very basic stuff…"

"The knuckles were just carrying the blood and bits of dead people for the frog-man. It was him who was hungry."

Ribald cursed, he had just intended the orphan children to look sad for extra gravity. Alfwen had been entrusted with keeping her hands over Winfred's mouth. Instead, she was staring mesmerized by her reflection in a glass bowl on the reeve's desk.

"Beautiful isn't it?" The reeve noticed Alfwen's fascination. "Found it buried out Fiscburna way several years ago. Still good stuff to be found there if you're willing to dig for long enough, and may I say your reflection looks radiant in it. Perhaps this summer you might accompany me out there for a dig or the next event at the amphitheatre."

The reeve noticed Alfwen's confused frown at the last word. "Oh, it's a type of fort the Britons must have used. Very impractical for marching your men with tight entrances, probably why we beat them so easily, but the view from the high seats is majestic. We use it for bear fights and public executions. It's a favorite of King Cissa. I would be delighted to invite you, my dear."

At least his waffling had made him forget about the girl's mad tales thought Ribald, and he suddenly had an idea.

"How about we begin to discuss how I'm to rebuild the village? We brought some rabbits for the pot, and a beaver pelt for your wife, if you'd be willing to have dinner with us tonight."

"My Hunburg sadly didn't survive trying to bring my last son into the world. She and the child are returned to the ground, but I will take that rabbit and pelt from you. In exchange how about a cup of Frankish wine, just shipped in. I feel we can have a fruitful discussion about how to fix your misfortunes."

~

The sisters and the children had been sent down to the first floor while Ribald and the reeve were having their chat, with strict instructions not to go outside. For once, Aebbe was pleased to hear her sister say, "Fuck this, no one is keeping me inside. I'm going to explore this shit-stained city."

She guided the two children past a couple of disinterested guards in her sister's trail.

They got about twenty paces from the hall when a man blocked their path. "Let's go back and find some guards," gasped Aebbe before she yelped as the man's size engulfed the whole group.

"Don't we know you from somewhere?" asked Alfwen, unfazed by Saig's size. Saig didn't recognize the sisters at all, not that he understood a word of what Alfwen had said.

"I think it's an idiot," she whispered to her group. "One of those that got kicked in the head by a donkey as a child. If we back away slowly it'll forget why it stopped us in the first place."

Before they could back out of his shadow, a second man appeared. Raven haired and with sharp almond-shaped green eyes, the purple splashes seemed to dance around his right eye. He was the most beautiful man Alfwen had ever seen in her life.

"She's wondering if they know you," Milian said to Saig in Brittonic. "They have seen you before albeit at a distance, these two are the ones that did for Rog with the Roman statue."

Then switching to accented, but intelligible Saxon, Milian said, "So how did your king take the news? How many men is he raising to put that frog-faced fucker down? He'll need good archers too to catch the knuckles, you can be sure for everyone you saw the beast has ten more. Never fought alongside Saxons before but if your warriors can give me cover I'll sneak in. I know how to kill The Nix you see, you can take me to see your king now he's aware of the danger."

"Ah, shame," said Alfwen. "They were both kicked in the head by donkeys. The handsome man more so it seems, well back to the hall."

"Knuckles?" said Aebbe. "Winfred dear, what did you say the bad man called the worms, and what did his face look like?"

The girl's face was white, she was shaking, and tears began to spill from her big eyes.

Her brother Wiglac spoke for the first time since their rescue. "EAT THE FACE KNUCKLES. G'ON MY LOVELIES YOU KNOW NIX HERE LIKES HIS LIPS AND TONGUE. GOOBLE THE FACE AND INSIDE BITS FOR YOUR MATE NIX. SKIN IS ALL YOURS, NIX DOES WITHOUT SKIN Y'KNOW GIVES HIM WIND. BLOOD AND GUTS FOR NIXY HERE AND LIPS OF COURSE…"

~

Aebbe and Alfwen finally managed to wedge his jaw shut. Not

only was he shouting at the top of his voice, but it was coming out in not the voice of a child but some inhuman croaky groan. Everyone on the street was staring at them, and when the sisters were sure his jaws had stopped squirming they let go, and he was back to the same old dead-eyed mute Wiglac.

The silence was broken by a shout.

"It's them, the two foreign bastards! They are the one that done for Yric."

Then a familiar voice Digoth's. "Bandits, these men are bandits! They tried to kill us and are now stalking us to finish the job."

"Did we kill a Yric?" said Milian.

"Dunno, probably," replied Saig.

By now the hue and cry had long since been summoned. Bystanders were surrounding the two men. Some were armed with axes or work tools. The guards were getting closer.

"Time for me to go Saig. See you in the next life maybe." Milian said. He turned to the women, and something told him that Aebbe was the one to address.

He leaned in next to her to speak. "You know what the children saw, you know I can help. Search for Milian. I'll try to stay local as much as I can."

With that, he jumped onto Saig's shoulders, and with a push landed on the roof of the nearest building. He leaped across from roof to roof until he was out of sight. Guards pushed them out of the way. They soon had their swords at Saig's throat. Saig let out a high-pitched howl, before holding his hands up in surrender.

CHAPTER 8

"I ought to have you whipped the pair of you!" screamed Ribald at the sisters in a corner room of the hall. The seven of them were all back together. Saig now held in the town quarry used as a prison to await execution. Yric turned out to be an unloved thief, discovered outside the city walls with a broken neck that morning. "Thank Woden Digoth found you in time."

"He didn't do anything as usual," Alfwen complained. "We were talking to the big man and his friend and maybe the children aren't quite as crazed as we believe."

"Because of the words of Briton bandits? Have you gone quite mad, girl?"

"Father, Alfwen is telling the truth." The words stumbled slowly out of Aebbe's mouth; she'd never used the word truth in the same sentence as her sister's name. "There was another man there that's true. He wasn't at the giants' place in the woods, but he knew the same sights that Winfred told us about."

"It was the archer," Iga offered. "Must have been, he were the only one unaccounted for."

"That explains it!" said Ribald. "He and that soon to be dead brute have stalked us. He must have overheard the girl's delusions, and needed to distract you to save his savage hide."

Aebbe frowned: that seemed unlikely but kind of plausible.

"Anyway my talks with the reeve were fruitful. He will bring our plight to King Cissa and has worked out how to restore our fortunes in the short term. Of course, some sacrifices will need to be made."

"Why are you looking at me, father?" Alfwen said.

~

The Nix came to the shores of the river. The sun was still going down, so he kept his head submerged for safety's sake. Not that he had to worry about being spotted. Spurius and his boss, who The Nix had heard whispers of but had never seen had done some tricks here a while ago. Once sixty thousand souls lived here, now no one but the creations roamed the streets.

The Saxon and Jute tribes now preferred to sail their ships along the coast. Too many disappeared while trying to cross the island using The Tamesas. The Britons knew this side of the island wasn't for them anymore, which the ones who were aware of what lurked in the abandoned city might even be grateful for.

The Nix had pulled himself up on the southern side of the shore, onto the marshy bank on which was the endpoint of the decaying bridge that spanned the river. He wanted to skip across the parts of the bridge where gaping holes were, or parts where the support beams were rotting and could collapse at the slightest touch.

He liked to play a game with himself about how many times he'd get dumped into the water, and have to climb back onto the bridge. He could leap so far he didn't need the help of the ropes that had been left under the bridge to help friends of Londinium in their crossings. Once he finished, he swam back to the southern bank and started again, attempting to beat his score.

When he had finally gotten to the northern shore, where most of the crumbling remains of Londinium lay, it was pitch black.

The Nix heard scuttling sounds coming from storehouses long since gutted by fire. The city wouldn't come alive until the darkness fell.

~

He wriggled through a hole in the wall surrounding the city. Waiting for him on the other side was a dwarf. Coming up to The Nix's waist he was just as wide as he was tall, making him look both comical and threatening. Nothing ambiguous about the dwarf's face, sheer malevolence, and violent intent was permanently plastered on his face. His skin was twisted at every curve, a spherical mound of flesh served as his nose, two pointy rags of skin were his ears. Only his hair still looked human, long black braids that went down his back to the end of the blood red tunic he was wearing. He smiled, showing scores of long pointy needle-like teeth not unlike The Nix's own.

"Bonum vesperam," said The Nix.

The Nix couldn't read, so was relying on decades-old memories since the last time he'd spoken Latin. The creations shared numerous native languages among them; it was a rule to use Latin when communicating. The Nix thought his memory and pronunciation had held up well considering, so felt a surge of anger when the dwarf replied with, *"patheticus,"* and then, "follow, he is waiting."

"Right you are Heslop." growled The Nix.

~

"No father you can't!" said Aebbe.

"Are you out of your fucking mind?" Alfwen screamed.

"Not that I disagree but isn't this a little hasty?" said Digoth.

Iga covered the children's ears and thought about what this

meant for her.

Ribald had announced the deal he'd made with the reeve. A new ox, the pick of newly arrived Saxons from the old country to work the land and repair the devastated village, four new slaves from the pens to replace Iga and her unfortunate contemporaries, four warriors to guard the land, a set of new weapons for them, as well as Ribald and Digoth, and enough crops to get them through next winter. This year's harvest would be severely reduced due to the destruction of the village.

All of this, and an audience with King Cissa in the amphitheater at the next public executions.

~

Ribald had come out of the reeve's room his chest swelling with pride. Aebbe had asked what he had to give in exchange, while her two siblings were congratulating their father.

"Well..." he started, his dome suddenly turning bright red. "The main thing is that after the harvest is back to normal levels, our tribute to the king and city is to increase from one-tenth of our crops to two tenths. Oh, the two orphans will be given to the priests for sacrifice, and Alfwen will marry the reeve."

An explosion of noise followed. Ribald cursed, stress always made his left foot tap impatiently on the floor. The sound of the tapping was beginning to rival Alfwen's howls and Aebbe's tears.

"He's nearly as old as you and he looks like a fucking rooster!"

"You can't do this! They're only children! The gods would want them to live! Even as slaves, they'd be better off!"

"I just think four warriors are too many to feed, especially with us losing so much of the harvest to the king."

Ribald's foot was sore by the time he'd swatted away his ungrateful children's complaints.

CHAPTER 9

The Nix followed Heslop through streets with rotting and charred wooden boards, and faded tiles on the floor. Past more and more buildings.

What were they once, houses? Barracks? Shops? It was difficult to tell, age and decay gave them the same shambling appearance.

One building still had two stone pillars left so probably a temple. Another was three floors so a grain storehouse to feed sixty thousand souls, or a palace to house the family of a governor.

~

The Nix didn't know or care enough about the steel men who had built this city. They had stopped bothering The Picts by the time The Nix was born. Born in that pink fleshy form before he was The Nix. After he became The Nix he had approached the fearsome wall. He was raised on tales about how his ancestors had charged it time and time again forcing the tall foreigners with their massive shields to retreat again, and again, before building the wall higher and higher, until it blocked the sun.

By the time he got to the wall it was deserted and not that tall: it only took him one run and jump to get over. He had been a little disappointed, to be honest. He was looking forward to seeing the knuckles' fangs go against the steel strips the sweaty foreigners were said to wear around their chests. Luckily, he'd met a gaggle of shepherds by the entrance to the nearest big river and his belly was full as he headed south.

~

Heslop seemed to know his way around alright, so The Nix asked him how long he'd been here. Their only prior meeting had been way up north not far from the wall about a hundred years ago. Spurius liked to hold what he called a forum every century or so to introduce new creations, and make vague proclamations about how "our time to reign as kings of this island is at hand."

The Nix and the other Nixes were directed to the underground pools by the dwarves who appeared to live in the caves that were hosting the forum. Heslop, foul looking thing, was the dwarves' leader back then. *Oh my!* The Nix thought, he hoped this meeting wasn't another forum.

"First set foot in this city about 250 years ago. I was one of Constantius' men sent across the sea to wipe out the last of those Frankish bastards the usurper Allectus was occupying the city with. Me and the lads made sure the streets of Londinium ran red that day," Heslop told him.

This all meant nothing to The Nix, but he guessed from the names ending in -us.

"You're a Roman?"

"Right. Constantinople born and bred, course it were called Byzantium back in my day. Bad luck changing a city's name, can't say I agree but it's the capital now greater than Rome itself, and...why do you ask you bug eyed overgrown fish? You think I was born in the caves? No more than you were born in a swamp! I had a life before same as you."

The Nix went quiet at that. It appeared Heslop had better memories than him of what it was like before. He wondered if spending time in the city helped Heslop remember what he once was, and if the dwarf saw that as a blessing or not.

"So you weren't always little then?" The Nix asked.

"The Britons eat frogs, claim they taste like chicken, call me little again, and I'll put these fangs to good use to see if the hairy bastards have the truth of it."

By now they'd turned a few corners. The scuttling noises behind the walls were louder. The sight of fierce fire-like eyes in a variety of colors were visible from the cracks. Under orders not to interfere The Nix assumed. They started to descend a stone staircase in relatively good condition that led underground.

~

In an open courtyard at the foot of the staircase, one large bath remained. Three other baths each attached to the corner of the courtyard were in ruins, pillars had collapsed into them, the tubs filled with stones. Plants and insects were in every crevice. However, the large bath in the center looked as new as the day it was built centuries ago. Marble tiles on the stone, steam rising from the water. The mosaic on the bath floor was still clear to anyone who approached. It displayed a pile of skulls that made the approaching person feel like you were looking up from underneath their jaws.

"Memento Mori," said the horned man shivering in the hot water. "Less of a message for us, Nix, but some who might stumble upon us will learn it soon enough heh?"

Spurius wasn't physically speaking. The Nix wasn't sure he could due to the large snake that he had instead of a tongue, but he didn't need to. His thoughts hit The Nix's' brain just as they did when he was at the bottom of the river. Although back then the message was just for him, this time from the slimy grin on Heslop's face he was sure that both creatures were hearing every word.

"So how did those Germans taste, Nix? Knew a German once, tall man, short of wits, came to a very bad end. That was a long time ago... shouldn't have given my Nix trouble. Short time back, some Saxon pirates decided to come up the river, must have ignored their comrade's warnings about how the river is off-limits. Anyway, I sent King Herla, yes the old windbag still insists on being called that, and his host galloping over the river to take some souls. It was pathetic! Just axes and clubs they use, and the bows have no range at all, and as for those that jumped into the water! Well, the sirens proved their worth. We ate well that night, several are still alive under the city in the cages I think, you never know when a new creation will come in handy..."

The snake then started to hiss. Spurius' way of showing he was amused but then he scowled.

"The greatest civilization known to man, replaced across the land by little more than feral beasts. It's surely a sign that our ascension is near."

The Nix nodded. He wasn't sure what this ascension would involve. Spurius enjoyed using words that left even the best Latin speakers among the creations puzzled. From listening to various rants over the years, he reasoned it was turning the whole island, maybe the whole world into Londinium; a dark, cursed place where they could all roam openly. The Nix just wanted somewhere wet to live and lots of lips and tongue to gobble.

As if reading his mind; which he almost certainly was. Spurius addressed this. "Food has been a problem over the past few centuries, these plagues and wars are out of my hands, and the population suffered further when the Romans left and took their slaves with them. You'd think those pig-fucking Britons would have learnt to farm themselves out of famine, but anything that doesn't involve sticking a spear into an animal or a dick into each other…or an animal now that I think of it appears to be beyond the useless pieces of camel shit."

After wondering what a camel was, The Nix certainly agreed with him that there weren't as many people as he'd like. After a feast, Spurius warned them all in their thoughts that they had to either lie low or find a new hunting ground far away. The Nix often chose the latter, which is how he'd found himself so far from home in the first place.

"You know the reasons why we still have to pick and choose our prey. Our numbers are still too few and there are those out there who know our weaknesses. We played our hand too soon once, and still have that infernal group of Britons playing their games with their 'hunt.' They are getting too organized under that new king. We lost a tribe of hobgoblins out near Salinae way just last spring to them. That's why I urge caution, Nix, always caution!" Spurius continued.

His snake-tongue spotted a rat as large as a puppy in the corner of the room. It shot out going under The Nix's legs to wrap its fangs around the unfortunate rat's neck before shooting back to Spurius' mouth.

"See, even I restrain myself…to a degree, but a man cannot live on rats. Excursions up north to where the Angles have settled are necessary. Farmers in the main so easy pickings, but rationing them is even more important. Tough land they've chosen to settle on, nearly as tough as what you Picts have to farm only they aren't as fierce as that. Anyway, it's the Saxons I wanted to talk about. They could be both an opening and a threat for us."

CHAPTER 10

"They don't look very strong," complained Digoth.

"Maybe back in your grandfather's day, it was warrior farmers that came off the ships," said the ship captain a bald man whose skin was raw red. "But not anymore, the rains back home never seem to stop. The Elbe burst her banks again last month, killed hundreds, destroyed scores of farms. What you see is anyone who had the reach to grab a branch or those who managed to skip the overseer's eye, and spend the day larking around on higher ground."

"They'd all be for the slave pens. I usually trade them for cattle and horseflesh but your reeve has told me you are to have your pick, and my trip home will have a heavier load, so do as you wish but no more than six, and don't take your time. I want to be in the city soon."

Digoth looked at the sorry group of twenty. It shouldn't be that difficult just pick the six that are most likely to still be alive this time next week he thought. He pointed to two tall men, and then a stout fellow, one of those barrel-shaped men who never seem to lose weight, no matter how sparse supplies get. That might come in handy he reasoned.

Now, he should pick some women to keep the men fed and cleaned and ensure there's a new generation of villagers. He decided to confer with the men he'd picked to see if there was anyone they knew from the old country, or from the journey over that they might favor. The tall men picked two blonde women huddled together, sisters he gathered who had worked together to survive the journey. The stout man didn't seem to care so Digoth picked someone with a flat nose and ginger curls reasoning her strong-looking shoulders might be useful. The man named Allyn seemed content with that.

~

Back in the city, Ribald inspected the slave pens, or rather Iga went inside as she'd know better than others what to look for with regards to the slave's longevity.

She checked the first man chained in the corner, banging his head against the post. Gods have taken his mind, maybe for the best from his point of view. Next one was a woman who blinked quickly and looked over Iga's head. Eyes are gone or going, no good.

She found four ones that would do. Not a word of Saxon among them. She used her sparse slave pen Brittonic jargon to convey to the Briton slaves where they should stand and walk if they wanted to eat tonight. It occurred to Iga again that she was almost certainly a Briton herself, but taken as a child before she could speak.

The handful of Saxon slaves, refugees that had stowed away or sold their freedom for passage on the ships were all in better shape, and spoke the language but the reeve's generosity had stopped there. Saxon slaves fetched a good price from city merchants. For the men to work as guards and clerks, and the women to work as cooks and bed-warmers they weren't to be given away to toil in the fields.

She arranged them behind the new ox, which was carrying the new supplies of weapons and farming tools. As she, the four new guards, Aebbe, Ribald, and the two soon to be sacrifices waited for Digoth to return from the harbor. Aebbe shot her a look that seemed to say 'how could you?' regarding her assisting Ribald.

Iga wasn't going to give away her plans to any of the family, but she was disgusted with Ribald's plan. Half of it, Alfwen spending every night for the rest of her life under the reeve's flabby belly did make her smile. She had a week to get the children away from him before they returned to the city for the wedding, an audience with the king, and the handover of the children to the priests. She would have to inform Aebbe, and maybe even Digoth. Their assistance could be vital in escaping with the children but she'd have to wait until they got back to the village.

~

Alfwen kicked the wooden posts that supported the room she was in, achieving little else but injuring her foot. She howled more in frustration than pain and sunk to her knees screaming.

"Shut the fuck up!" yelled one of the guards. "You might be some little princess out in your shithole in the woods but here you're just another useless mouth."

~

After her father had announced his ludicrous plan, he'd taken her aside. "I don't mean for you to go through with it, my dear. It's one of daddy's little ruses look, come with me into this room, and I'll explain it to you. After all, you're the smart one not like the other two."

Nodding at his recognition of her talents, Alfwen proudly strode into the small room in the corner of the hall's ground floor. When she turned expecting to face her father she instead saw the door slam in her face, and then a bang as from the other side the latch dropped down trapping her.

~

Three hours of banging and demands to speak to her father later, the guards finally told her that her family had left the city. She refused to believe them and threw the dinner they'd brought her against the walls. Soon hungry, she tried to rub dirt off the chicken leg and hard piece of cheese. It was better quality than what she was used to back at the village.

After more hours to herself and a further snack of bread and beer, she was feeling much calmer. She had a week to plan an escape. You can do this, you're the brains of the family, she told herself as she paced up and down the room. Then the door creaked open and the reeve stood there. By his side was a plump boy of around twelve and a pointy-nosed girl a couple of years younger. Both children had the trademark blonde quiff that drooped over their forehead or cheek.

"Greetings, my dearest. Children I'd like you to meet your new mother." The boy strolled forward and kicked Alfwen in the shin.

"Better make my turnips and beer same way mother did!"

The reeve gave a sickly smile. "I own a lot of land outside the city walls, so I can't spare any slaves for household duties, your father told me you were an expert cook and housekeeper so nothing to worry about. Stay here tonight, and I'll take you to your new home tomorrow. I just wanted to introduce you as soon as possible. Speak again tomorrow my dear."

Alfwen was shaking with rage when the door closed, and the candles went out with the breeze, leaving her in darkness.

~

They arrived back at the village at dusk. None of the missing villagers had returned yet. It was looking unlikely they'd see them again. Anyone who escaped will have either kept running, or will have fallen afoul of wolves, bears, or bandits.

The slaves were hurried to the villager's huts, and given wooden spades before being pointed towards the big pile of bones. Digoth was eager to see them all buried by the time the new villagers who his father was feasting in the hall retired to their new huts. The slaves shrieked when they saw the bones.

"Should have done this in advance," said Iga while trying to calm the slaves in broken Brittonic.

"We didn't have time besides…does she want to lay with me?" Digoth said, referring to a slave woman who was making a gesture of putting a clenched fist to her lips and pulling it back and forth. "I can't say it appeals, her warts have warts."

"No, I think she's making a snake gesture, listen for the hissing. Like a snake coming out of the mouth."

"What by Thunor can she mean by that?"

"I have no idea. Come on let's get them in line we can find out how useless these new guards are."

~

Ribald explained the history of the village to his guests over the deer meat they'd caught on their last hunt.

"Lands been in the family for forty years, now you have to travel through a bit of woodland to get to the better hides, but we've cleared paths most of the way and beasts won't bother you. There was a hermit who is best left alone but I think last winter must have done him in as we haven't heard his howling for…" he droned on.

~

Aebbe was confident that her father was drunk enough, and enjoying the sound of his own voice enough, not to notice her sneaking out. Especially as she had been put to work with the three new women settlers at the end of the hall, fetching beer, and boiling vegetables over the fire.

She met with the two children who were sleeping with the ox in its pen that night. She roused them awake. "You have to be calm nothing is going to happen to you but you have to trust me and listen to me, and do everything I say," she told them.

Wiglac looked at her as if he hadn't heard a thing. Winfred asked, "What do they mean by sacrifice? Father used to offer a goat to Freyr before each harvest, and two when mother had Wiglac in her belly. When they say we are sacrifices they are going to use goats instead of us right?"

Aebbe ignored the question saying instead, "We will probably have to leave this place soon."

"Of course, the frog-man is coming back. I can feel him on his way," Winfred said.

Despite it being the end of summer, Aebbe felt a chill up her spine.

~

They had calmed down the slaves by telling them the pile of bones was due to a plague outbreak.
However, while the Britons seemed to be unfazed by disease, the guards had cried out about it and refused to go near the bones. They even demanded to return to the city until Iga had come up with the compromise of burning the bodies.

Of course, with no flesh left on the bones a bit of peat and firewood was needed to get the blaze going. Then secure in the knowledge that neither evil spirits or disease lingered in the bones or the air, slaves, and guards alike crushed the burnt fragments into ash with their feet and sticks.

Digoth was beginning to overcome his arrogance towards Iga's status as an ex-slave and a woman. He was beginning to realize how useful she was always coming up with problem solving solutions. He said to her, "do something about the smell will you," and headed back to the hall.

Iga rolled her eyes and waited for the slaves and guards to return to their relevant huts and for the new villagers to return from the hall. She guided them to their new residences, making sure to keep them away from the hut furthest away which she had claimed as her own. She wondered if she'd get to spend more than a single night there, as she explained there had been a lightning storm that had struck the village the night before to complaints about the charred smoky smell.

"Never saw any storm from the ship," the strong looking red haired woman called Cwenhild said. "Was calm as a millpond."

"Ran blessed you with calm seas to welcome you to your new home the storm was inland." Iga's patience was running thin. She just had one more thing to do before getting some rest.

~

Aebbe didn't want to return to the hut so tried to calm the children into sleeping by telling a story she'd been told by her late grandmother, who came from the old country. It was a story about giant etins buried in the ground who one day woke up and gobbled up entire villages as if the people were peas before a great hero called…

"They are asleep." Aebbe turned her head around at these words and found Iga there. "We will work out a way to keep the priest's blade from them. First, tell me about the man who was stalking us. Not the brute, the one with the eye, the archer."

~

That night, Iga took the children and Aebbe to her new hut so the four of them could warm themselves together. There was plenty of space in all the lodgings with so many taken.

~

Digoth and Ribald snored off their ale in the hall.

~

Milian somehow managed to balance himself on a tree branch for the sole hour per night he allowed himself to sleep.

~

Alfwen sobbed herself to sleep in her cell.

~

Saig, chained by the neck to a post in the quarry, gagged to prevent his howls, was trying to remember what the monks had told him about eternal life and how to ensure it.

~

And in Londinium, The Nix was enjoying his farewell party.

CHAPTER 11

The amphitheater was one of the city's better preserved buildings. It was where The Nix had been instructed to demonstrate the skills of the knuckles for the amusement of the other creations. He strode out to mocking cheers and howls.

Looking around he saw the usual collection of animal hybrids; humanoid dogs, owls, bears, snakes. Spurius must have had quite the mood for them when he was making The Nix. Dwarves and Elves, Shades and Ogres, Goblins, and the pale skinned, yellow-eyed ones who looked human; The Nix's least favorite type sat on the benches waiting to see some gore.

One of the Saxon pirates was dragged out first. He slumped to his knees at the sight of the crowd. The Nix got a look at his eyes and gathered no one was home. This one had been tortured into insanity quite some time ago. He wasn't here for his fighting prowess though. He'd been dressed in Roman armor. Iron hoops fixed to leather straps that encased his torso and shoulders. His head was protected by a bowl shaped helmet with ridges that protected the cheeks and forehead.

Tempting as it was to throw the knuckles at the madman's naked legs or privates parts the whole point of his party trick was to show off their fangs power, besides the man's legs were covered with months' worth of dried shit and he didn't want the knuckles to get food poisoning. He gave a fearsome croak as he threw a knuckle with each hand, and one landed on the man's helmet, and the other hit his chest plate.

The one that hit the helmet gave a ghastly shriek when its fangs bit the metal, rather than try again it head-butted the metal again and again until a massive dent appeared in it. Blood began to pour from a gash somewhere on the man's head. Some of the blood ended up on the man's exposed face, at which point the knuckle caught the scent, and crawled down to lick up the blood.

The Nix was outraged at such a tiny amount of blood, and not a hint of flesh. Sure the knuckle would quickly tear the pirate's face off but that's only possible as the man's wits have fled, and he can't defend himself. A skilled warrior could have killed the knuckle by now. The Nix didn't have an infinite knuckle supply. Making new ones was possible, but it meant mixing a lot of fish guts, a lot of tedious chanting and it still failed most of the times he tried it.

He strode forward eyes blinking with rage to the jeers of the spectators. He tore the knuckle off the man's face before it could eat or drink anymore, and flung it to the ground. The Nix then, to more jeers, picked it up and squeezed the paltry amount of blood from the knuckle into his mouth. He then turned to the knuckle on the chest plate and bellowed a commanding croak.

The knuckle threw its head back, made its croak which sounded comical to the crowd who were beginning to get bored. In a blink, it thrashed its head downwards before hitting the floor under its own momentum.

Before The Nix could howl in despair, the man's chest armor suddenly split in two like a log hit well with an axe. The man's chest and belly were now completely exposed, and The Nix decided the knuckles had done enough for one day. He knelt, giving the man's belly a lick with his long tongue. Content that the flesh was succulent enough, his teeth tore the man's belly open and pulled out the stringy, ropey intestines to get to the liver a preferred piece for him.

He picked up the two knuckles and stuffed them in the hole he'd made in the man tasking them to consume enough blood and flesh to transfer to him later. He wasn't quite sure at what point the signs of life left the man's eyes but he gurgled happily to himself that it was quite late on. Adrenaline is good for keeping them going until the end.

~

In the section of the amphitheater which in days gone by had served as a VIP box for the governor and his family sat Spurius surrounded by his favorites.

Heslop was there as well as a pale skinned woman with yellow eyes and a bearded man who stood out as he looked...normal, just a regular sack of meat.

The Nix was beckoned over to sit and watch the next event.

Another nearly catatonic pirate again dressed in Roman armor was pitted against what would have been an otherwise pretty young woman, if not for the fact that her skin was green, and she had no eyes, not even holes, just skin where they should be.

She was chanting at the man in a language that The Nix had never heard before. Indeed, he wasn't sure it was of this world. She finished her chant and a burst of flame appeared over the man's head for a split second.

"Spells, Nix, spells, very much a work in progress but wouldn't you like to uncover the dark secrets? Imagine a spell that allows us to live under daylight, or if you could turn fish guts into knuckles with a mere flick of your fingers! We must keep developing and learning because our enemies will...now look at Alecto – I knew from the first time I saw her she had the gift, course she weren't Alecto then, but I had to have her now watch!" Spurius' words bounced around inside The Nix's skull.

The woman's chanting had left her exhausted. She was on her knees looking at the unfortunate pirate with hope. Nothing happened for half a minute. Then the man started to scream. The Nix strained to see what was causing it and his eyes would have grown wider if that was possible.

The man's helmet was melting, steam rising. "Yes," Spurius murmured. But then it stopped, the man was still screaming from his burns. The metal had hardened and turned cold as fast as it had begun to melt.

Alecto was now unconscious. Spurius snapped his fingers and had both wounded and prone figures were carried out of the area. "It's progress, progress is all I ask for, Nix. Progress! She'll get the spell perfect next time."

"Progress is what I expect from you now. You will leave Londinium tomorrow and return to The Saxons. You remember what I said? They are a gift from the dark gods. They breed like fucking rabbits! A permanent solution to our food crisis so I need you down there to fix a problem that has arisen."

"What problem boss?"

"Those fucking Britons, and their hunt. One of them is in touch with The Saxons my spies tell me. I thought they'd be at each other's throats long enough for us to exterminate The Britons, and welcome The Saxons across the island as our new sheep. I don't want that put at risk by them joining forces. I'll be frank with you Nix. Briton magic scares me. Back when I was…that person they were just inbred farmers not even worth killing, but we awoke something in them Lilith should have warned me, and…"

Spurius' face was contorted with concern. The Nix had never heard of him showing any vulnerability before even Heslop looked perturbed. "Kill them, Nix, kill The Briton in Saxon lands interfering in our business. Kill everyone he's spoken to."

CHAPTER 12

Iga's first week of freedom had been exhilarating. She hadn't expected much to change, after all, she was still tied to the village, and if Digoth or Ribald had asked her to resume her old tasks she would have had no choice but to obey. Alfwen and Aluhburg would have had her running around just for the power trip element, but both were now in very different places. She felt guilty for thinking that with a smile. Both men seemed happy with letting the new slaves handle running the household, and working the family hides.

That left Iga to her own hide which was far, far too big for her to do anything on her own with it. She still made the most of it. The plans for a husband and slaves of her own to do the work probably weren't going to happen. She always knew deep down that was for the best.

She spent her evenings getting to know the new villagers and hosting Aebbe and the children for supper where they discussed their next move over beer and gruel.

"He said that he knew how to kill it, and he'd need help because of the..." Aebbe mouthed the word 'knuckles'. Not even with making a sound and with her back to him, Wiglac still shook his head and began to hoot then laughed to himself. "That's what he called the things we saw, anyway. He called himself Millet or something, and said he'd be local that we were to look for him."

"Shit, we are going to need your brother's help. He knows the woods better than us and everyone else is new to the area," Iga said.

"He would never go against father's orders."

"Spineless ginger prick."

"Winfred! Stop copying the things I say when I get cross," Aebbe snapped.

"I guess it's up to me to come up with an idea," Iga said. Wiglac giggled and pulled out some raspberries impaled on a branch and started roasting them over the fire. "That's a rare treat."

"The bald man gives us lots of treats he says we should be looking healthy for the wedding coming soon," said Winfred.

~

"This porridge is too lumpy, you stupid sow!" The young boy yelled in a petulant squeak.

"What?" Alfwen turned her head to the monstrous boy and saw the bowl just before it struck her on the face. She hated the baggy dress that used to belong to the reeves' fat wife that she was now wearing, but still didn't want it to be soiled with the porridge she'd spent an hour making.

She took a deep breath and internally raged clenching her eyes shut while the plump boy sneered.

She remembered Hieu, the pointy nosed girl, claiming that her father would "beat you black and blue" if she retaliated to their bad behavior. She'd also made a big deal out of knowing the location of her late mother's collection of gems and the glass and metal treasures from the giant's palace she had been given over the years.

"They will all be mine now! If father finds any in your skirts he'll cut your hands off!" she'd shouted with a smirk.

Smirk and Sneer were how Alfwen was now identifying Hieu and Torold in her head. She trembled with anger as she returned to the pot to try to make the porridge looser.

"Sm…I mean Hieu could you please change the rushes while I remake your brother's porridge?"

"I'm busy!" She was bouncing a leather ball against the wall.

"When I was your age, I used to spend my mornings learning how to weave and helping my mother around the house."

"Well I'm the daughter of the reeve other people will give me their cloth and you are not my mother just some farm girl my father wants to rut!"

This waking nightmare for Alfwen had the sole consolation that the reeve returned her to her cell in the hall in the evenings but after the wedding… She sighed and went back to making Sneer's porridge.

~

Milian wrapped himself around the tree branch so tightly with his brown cloak hugging him that the two guards sitting under the tree had no idea he was just a few feet above them, no idea that he could just let go of the branch, and thirty seconds later walk away with two corpses lying at the foot of the tree.

He wracked his brains for an answer to The Saxons sloth. Three days now since they returned from the city and nothing. He'd made regular runs along the perilous forest path that would take him to the edge of the city without being seen several times now. He knew enough about their military to know that representatives from Chichester should be leaving all the time for the villages to form a fyrd but so far nothing!

It was maddening. Even the family had returned to the village, burnt the bones, and carried on as if nothing had happened.

The new faces around the village and the absence of the proud if haughty looking blonde girl had not gone unnoticed.

Something foul had happened when they talked to their king. Did these Saxon fools think that this problem would just go away with a new ox and new guards?

His cold ran cold. Could their king be in cahoots with Spurius? It wouldn't be the first time a mortal has had treacherous ambitions. He listened carefully.

~

"Plus side is there's fuck all to do and their ale supplies are decent," said the first guard. "Also these woods have been barely touched, meat is going to be plentiful."

"Aye, true enough," said the second. "But the problem is too much land for the men they've got. I heard that ginger prick means us to start helping out on there from next week."

"He can fuck right off. I didn't spend my time running between the shield walls dodging Briton arrows and Jute javelins to plant cabbages. I was assured that if I lived then I'd have women and slaves to do that for me. Speaking of which we have to sneak back to the city as soon as we can to get some whores and…"

"Not happy with the village women?"

"There's only a handful, the daughter is off limits, and the two blondes are already settled in with those lanky twats. That leaves the slaves, the redhead with the squashed face, and that tall one with the twitchy eye."

"Thought the redhead was with Allyn?"

"I think Allyn has his eyes on another redhead."

"You mean…"

"Yeah, fat fool is in love with Digoth."

"An ungodly type of feeling."

"Which god said that?"

"Now that you mention it I'm not sure."

~

Milian usually enjoyed his birthmark. It put fear into enemies and made sure that be it a creation he'd sent crawling back to Londinium with its tail between its legs, or a maid whose bed he'd just left that he would never be forgotten.

Here it was a hindrance. His first plan would be to get a drop on the guards and stroll back into the village wearing one of their tunics and helmets, but the eye would mean the first villager he encountered would raise the hue and cry and send him fleeing. So it was tedious spying sessions on the guards and villagers until he worked out a way to talk to the girl with the snaggletooth or the boy with The Nix's voice.

~

"No, I'm not going into the woods to guide my sister into the arms of a Briton outlaw so they can plot to ruin my father's deal with the reeve, thus dooming us to poverty and starvation, Iga. Why do you ask?" Digoth rubbed his temples in annoyance.

"According to Aebbe, before we caught up with them, he knew about what killed your mother! Aren't you at least curious?"

"All I need to know is they are gone, and won't come back!"

"How can you be sure?"

They'd been going back and forth all day. Iga thought she was making progress. She'd at least managed to get a promise that he wouldn't go running to his father telling tales. A worthless promise but a start. She decided to try shaming him.

"Saig is probably dead by now or at least in chains. The outlaw is all alone out there and you've got all your weapons, your guards, and you know the land better than him. Go and protect your family!"

"Why doesn't he just come down and break bread with us if his information is so important?"

"Your people have spent a hundred years maybe more kicking them out of their ancestral lands, killing, raping, and enslaving as you go! Don't you think there's going to be some mistrust there?"

"I'll think about it." Digoth rubbed his temples so hard he half expected to feel bone.

CHAPTER 13

The next morning Iga, Digoth, one guard called Aart, and Allyn left to track down the outlaw. One of the conditions was Aebbe and the children would remain in the village.

Digoth laid out his plan as they entered the woods. "Tracking him will probably take most of the day. Now Iga thinks the outlaw wishes to merely confer with us, but this show of force will make him keep his distance. The best case is he shouts what he needs to us, then disappears back to the damp hilly lands he comes from. There's no need to kill him and risk a feud with his kin as long as he fucks off so what I propose is…"

A small splat sound rang out and everyone froze. Aart fell to the ground unconscious, blood trickling from the side of his head. "Bastards got a sling," said Allyn, leaping in front of a surprised Digoth.

"I don't know why you bother giving them helmets if they're going to take them off every time they have to walk more than ten feet in the sun," Iga complained.

After a few minutes, a voice came from the woods. "Sorry about that, he should be okay. You didn't need him to do anything particularly taxing brain-wise did you? Like count how many sheep you have? Because counting beyond ten may be beyond him from now on…"

"Come out and we will talk," offered Digoth. Then the same voice came from a different direction.

"No, I haven't moved. Not even I'm that fast and quiet, just a trick of mine so you don't know where I am. Throw your axes down and I'll come out to talk. Refuse and I have enough stones to send you all to sleep, and I'll just walk down to the village and take your sister and the children under my arms to where I need them. This way is simpler don't you think?"

Digoth raised his arm and three axes clattered on the forest floor.

~

The three pushed Aart against a tree to make him more comfortable. They then looked around for an intruder's approach. They were unsurprised to see the cloaked man arrive in front of them from a bush without making a sound.

"Well met Digoth and Iga I believe. We haven't really had the pleasure of an introduction yet but I saw you parley with Saig at the Roman villa, and we briefly met at Chichester before I was forced to leave. It's no worry, if you hadn't raised the hue and cry then someone else would have. Next time I will choose a more discrete travelling companion."

He noticed Allyn. "This fellow is new, quicker than he looks. Digoth, I noticed he is very loyal. You are a lucky man."

He looked as if he was about to say something else but thought better of it. "We should sit and exchange knowledge. The Nix hasn't gone away you know. This time we have together could be vital. Do you have a pot? I caught these." He pulled away his cloak to reveal six dead squirrels on his belt.

"Never had squirrel before Allyn?" Asked Milian as he roasted one more of the furry things on a stick over the fire.

"Usually fish where I come from. Rivers so wide can feed us all you see. Once caught a heron, not so bad but tough to pin down, these squirrels aren't so bad."

"Pretty much most of what you find in the woods here is eatable, however, I do not recommend mole!"

"Shall we begin with your story Milian?" said Digoth. "I would certainly like to know what killed my mother, and how much if any of the children's ravings are the truth."

"The thing that came to your village is called a Nix." Milian began.

"They're a race of creatures found a way up north, further north than any Saxon has been I'd wager. They have giant lakes the Picts call lochs that they sleep at the bottom of for months after a feast of flesh. This one appears different. Greedier and stronger. They can take human form for a short time but usually revert to their frog form after a few minutes. Their weaknesses are sunlight and dryness, they need to keep their skin damp. What kills then and the other creations are up for debate. Where I come from the monks have taken to blessing the yew trees we make our arrows from. While I've got little time for this god on a stick, too soft for my liking, but whatever they did I don't deny it had an effect."

He paused for breath. "Certainly saw off those hobgoblins. They won't be stealing the little ones of Salinae from their mother's arms anymore."

Everyone was silent at that. "And do you happen to have any of these magic arrows with you now?" Allyn asked eventually.

"Not as many as I'd like, the hunt sent me south once they got reports that a Nix was moving faster and further than they'd ever noticed before, but I only left Avalon with one quiver we never expected this Nix to be so much trouble."

"And the worms?" Iga said.

"The Knuckles? Regular arrows should be enough or a spear, I wouldn't want to come at them with those axes, little fuckers are faster than they look." He caught Iga nodding. "So you've seen them? You know how fast they can rip flesh from bone."

Allyn shot Digoth a look of bewilderment and worry. "I'll explain later," he hissed back before asking, "if it does come back as you think it will for some reason, then what else kills it?"

"Again, it's debated but most believe the Romans had some success battling the creations at first, and certainly passed on some knowledge to our ancestors but at some point, the bastards got clever and turned the tide. More and more fled this island and then Londinium was lost. Whatever the Romans had if anything that worked against the vermin is long since buried who knows where."

"Romans? I don't understand," Digoth said.

"The ones you call 'giants' mortal men like you and me, they used to control this island but that's a story for another time. Basically, if you are without blessed arrows or magic artifacts from across the sea which is probably quite likely, your best bet against a creation is to stab, hack, spear, pierce, club, tear, punch, kick it as much, and as hard as you can. Then when the sun comes up it can't run for cover or water in The Nix's case."

~

They made their way back to the village with Milian saying he needed to talk to Aebbe and Wiglac in particular. Iga sighed: it was going to be her job to carry Aart back down through the woods but she was surprised Milan could hoist the much larger man up over his shoulders with ease. "One time, Saig drank from a well that had a dead hound in it, was carrying the fat bastard for days. My back has never been the same but once you get used to it…"

An hour later, they arrived at the edge of the village. Milian's appearance caused some chatter among the villagers but Iga and Digoth's presence calmed them. Allyn was quickly joking away about how the birthmark meant he ate a lot of salmon; "The freshest fish!" Milian had a knack for making people feel familiar around him even after a few minutes.

Iga led him to her hut where Aebbe and the children were waiting. Even the other guards found Aart's misadventure amusing, "if he gets to ten then it'll be an improvement," said one when Milian warned of his potential long-term injury troubles.

~

"Greetings Aebbe, I understand I have you to thank for the hunting party your brother arranged. Clever idea, probably the best way to avoid Saxon blood being spilt."

He saw the children. "Well met little ones, you saw The Nix and lived to tell the tale that makes you both very special." He turned to Wiglac, "And you, my lad, can you still do it? Speak with the monster's voice?"

"He hasn't spoken since last time we think he's been struck dumb with fear," said Aebbe.

"No," said Milian. "It's an illness…will be lifted once The Nix is dead."

"Nix?"

Milian then told Aebbe and the children a rushed version of the tale he'd told in the woods. "And you think he's planning on returning?" Aebbe said with a worried look on her face.

"Now that I'm here he'll be under orders from that snake tongued sack of shit, and the lad here means we've kind of given the game away."

CHAPTER 14

Later that night, The Nix appeared at the top of the river he'd been sleeping and swimming in. After checking his surroundings, he came ashore.

He stamped on the riverbank twice, and a large eel appeared at the top of the water. At The Nix's signal, the eel opened its mouth hissed, and the world seemed to shake. Everything in The Nix's vision shimmered and when it all refocused the eel was a man. The bearded man from Spurius' box in the amphitheater. "Good journey Nix, what was that thing that came up behind me back there a few hours ago?"

"Otter," said The Nix. "Had to give it a whack to get it to piss off. Next time turn yourself into something with legs if you don't want to end up in the belly of a bear, otter, or heron."

"If a beast attacked me I'd simply change form and ruin its day. A bear would be a challenge but I reckon a wolf could take it down. The boss man once told me that back in his day The Romans used these beasts for war in the desert and mountains. Like a cow but as tall as a tree, and with a long nose like a giant cock, tried to turn into one but the description doesn't do it, got to have seen the beast I reckon…"

"He was probably pulling your leg," The Nix said once they were both on the riverbank. "She should be awake soon, let's find her and cover some land tonight."

The two of them found the forest she'd been resting in, and after The Nix released his horrible croak waking nesting birds and making a pack of wolves in the distance howl but no animal would dare approach.

"The sun sets and she appears," the man said, pretentiously The Nix thought, as out of a hollow tree trunk the black haired, pale skinned, beautiful yellow eyed woman slithered.

The woman called herself Psyche, after a Greek from one of the stories Spurius was fond of, while the shapeshifter called himself Vitium, thinking it made him sound fearsome. Their real names were some garbled mess The Nix forgot the second he heard them.

They were both East Angles. "A swamp kingdom when this is over we can go there for a swim together Nixy fill our bellies feasting on the swamp villages," Vitium had promised. The Nix didn't like the pair. Far too familiar and inexperienced, they'd been stinking humans just twenty-five years ago, they wouldn't know as much as The Nix about how to get this job done.

~

The Nix had stamped his webbed feet at the Lud Gate by the Londinium wall as Heslop escorted him out of the city the next morning before sunrise after the amphitheater games. "There's an underground river next to the gate, you'll want to hop it there quickly and get underwater by the time suns up. Vitium is already down there waiting, not sure what as. Psyche will leave tonight, she can cover more ground so will catch up with you somewhere halfway. The boss will message to saying where soon…"

"Why do I have to play nursemaid to these porwigles?"

"The boss has tired of creations like us because we can't move among men easily. Look at how the new creations are more human like, can barely tell them apart from the stinking, decaying tasty ones. Truth is, you are only going because you have the boy's sight so can point them in the right direction. That's going to be the way from now on I reckon. Us and the ogres and shades, and whatever the hell you are, getting fat behind Londinium's walls while these shifters and yellow eyed freaks farm the land for us so train the pups well!"

The Nix concentrated on his reward: he'd asked for one thing in return for solving Spurius' quandary.

~

"Wait," he told his two companions and folded over his eyelids.

He seldom closed his eyes but he had to in order to see what the boy was seeing. The boy's eyes flashed open: he was awake, or had been awakened at least. He scanned his head around and took note of his sister sleeping next to him. Why were they were moving in the middle of the night? Voices at the front of the wagon, he saw a young woman with messy brown hair who told him to go back to sleep. One of the men at the front turned his head his way. Under the man's hood, no one else would notice, but he would: Spurius had told him what to look out for, under the hood the marked eye glistened and shined.

The Nix's eyes flashed open. "They are moving, headed towards the city. We could catch them tonight! Move!"

Psyche smiled as she began to hover in the air and the air shimmered as Vitium seemed to melt before remerging as a horse.

Psyche was now twenty feet in the sky and began to glide south.

The Nix whined at the horse. "Told you to become a mare, stallions are too difficult for me to guide. I won't tell anyone." Vitium just gave that a fierce snort, and grumbling The Nix climbed on.

~

"Explain about the illness," Aebbe had asked earlier.

"I don't know everything but the monster was about to kill him when the rain stopped and sent him scrambling that's right girl?" Milian said.

"Frog-man opened his mouth and showed his teeth, hundreds of them there were his tongue was long and headed for Wiglac's eye" said Winfred. "Then rain stops and frog-man can't move just starts smoking. Not sure after that just remember him being gone all of a sudden…"

"The Nix's have some form of venom on their skin. It's why we always fight them at a distance. If you get some in your mouth or eyes you become a thrall for The Nix that cursed you. Never see victims much after that. The thralls just walk into the lochs to be dinner but this Nix is different, stronger. He's able to use his curse to speak through the boy and see through him too. That's why we need to leave now. The bastard is probably watching us right now! I can use the boy to lure him out but I need more open ground and more men. We should head to the city," Milian explained.

~

So that's why Aebbe, Milian, Iga, Allyn, and two of the guards found themselves on the wagon in the dead of night going south to Chichester. Leaving just a day earlier than planned for Alfwen's wedding.

Digoth and two guards were to follow the next morning once he had told his father of the why and how of a large section of the village, including the children promised to the priests disappearing overnight.

The travelling party's hope was that the reeve would open the city gates to them, and they could rally the city guard before getting the king to raise a fyrd.

"How do you know he isn't lying?" Digoth had made a final plea to his sister.

"The children's stories and his tales match, you're just going to have to convince father! You know he won't listen to me!"

"And convincing the reeve? King Cissa?"

"We'll cross that bridge when we come to it."

Allyn, who Digoth had chosen as he felt he'd obey whatever was asked of him, was told, "If it turns out the Briton is deceiving us as one of their tricks then we've seen he's good enough to overpower the guards so get behind him and stick him in the back of the foot with this." Digoth had handed him a dagger.

~

Walking besides the wagon, Allyn made sure the boy was back to sleep before whispering, "if he's going to the priests anyway why not make it tougher for the monster to find us by you know…"

"We are not killing a child!" Aebbe hissed.

"I didn't say that, did I? I was thinking we could put his eyes out?"

"Thinking isn't your strong suit, Allyn, he's got our scent. I doubt he needs the boy anymore. Only needed him to identify who he's to kill," replied Milian.

"Who's that?" Allyn said frowning.

"Me and every Saxon I've spoken to. I have only given you a hint of what I know, and if the beast is returning he will want to silence us all. I can do without a blind child bumping in the way."

"Why are you so sure it will return?"

"I wasn't until I looked into the boy's eyes for the first time and saw the wretch staring right back at me."

"Maybe we should have waited till sunrise to travel," said Aebbe. "Didn't you say sunlight is dangerous for the monster?"

"Yes, but this one mimics animals of the swamp and pond. It could find ways to burrow or swim as it tracks us during the day. It's best to make haste and get behind city walls early. Also, it's a creature not known for its speed. It'll take a while to catch us if it's travelling alone."

"And if it isn't travelling alone?"

"It's very unusual for them to team up due to how conspicuous they are, but if he has friends we're pretty fucked, given how limited we are with weapons and manpower."

CHAPTER 15

Psyche approached the village. Once she had worked out from the skies that it was a small party heading towards the city, she had rendezvoused with the other two. It was agreed she would fly back to the village and finish off those who remained, while Nix and Vitium went into the forest to cut across the wagon before it reached the city.

She listened for heartbeats. Around thirteen, she thought, a lot to cut down in one night. She had a couple of hours at best before the sun came up, and although she made it look effortless, the flying tired her more than she could say. She looked around; lots of places to sleep during the day. She knew The Nix wouldn't approve but she didn't care. She planned to find someone else to do the killing, sleep all day, and awaken to a feast.

~

The Nix dismounted the horse and got his bearings. They were well ahead of the wagon now but were deep, deep into the woods to avoid being seen or heard.

"Good ride," he begrudgingly said to Vitium.

The shapeshifter had done very well only colliding with trees two or three times. He had tripped up throwing The Nix to the floor once. Blood was trickling from between the horse's eyes. The Nix wondered how that would affect him once back in human form. He wouldn't know yet because the horse gave a furious grunt before shimmering and turning into a wolf.

The pair edged closer to the mud track that the wagons and carts used.

The travelers had stopped for some reason, repairs or rest, either way, it was their rotten luck that they were sitting ducks for the pair. They were about twenty feet from revealing themselves when The Nix heard a thudding sound and an arrow hit the tree behind him.

The Nix expelled a snort. Fucking wolf growling must have woken a guard…wait he remembered something he'd heard in Londinium about how Saxons were poor archers, preferring spear and javelin to fight with. It must be the Briton he thought.

"I'll shove this right up his rump," muttered The Nix as he went to pull the arrow from the tree.

The instant the webbed hands wrapped around the wooden shaft pain tore through his body. It was like being on fire but on the inside. He let go of the arrow and writhed in agony on the ground. Another arrow missed Vitium by an inch. The bastard was getting closer. Soon, he'd have a clear view.

The Nix felt sheer terror for the first time in over a hundred years. If touching an arrow floored him what would one in the belly or neck feel like? The pain still tore through him, but he had to move. He waved his hands to the wolf who growled and started hysterically barking when he saw The Nix's palms, on each a slashed cut right to the bone surrounded by charred black flesh.

The third arrow would have hit Vitium between the eyes if he hadn't turned into a dormouse a split second before. He turned tail and scampered into the darkness of the forest.

"Bastard!" hissed The Nix, now on his belly trying to flee as well.

~

Milian lowered his bow when the wolves barking suddenly stopped. "I think it's scared off, must be without a pack. Strange for a wolf to be alone and so close to the city. Do you get many packs around here?"

Aebbe shook her head.

"Saxons and wolves don't mix," Iga said. "Both like deer meat and The Saxons have been outnumbering them heavily these days."

"Yes," Aebbe confirmed, "Father always said the wolves are a northern problem…well a Briton problem, sorry."

"No need, he's right. They usually travel in packs and even alone it takes more than three arrows to scare one off. This one must have been a weakling. The arrows were from the blessed yew. I'm going to be needing them later with luck. One of you come with a torch so I can find them."

~

Iga came with him as he picked up two arrows close to each other on the ground. She pointed to a third arrow with green goo on the shaft.

"Don't touch that!" Milian yelled. He looked around sharply and found a patch of goo on the ground, and a trail leading into the forest. "Shit, he was here!"

"Milian," said Iga in a shaking voice her eye blinking like a star as she guided the flame to beyond the green goo on the ground, to a leather sack which was squirming and hissing in a way that was all too familiar to Iga.

Milian and Iga returned to the path with the former clutching the bag tightly.

Now having worked out something was wrong, the bags were squirming harder. One was throwing a ferocious tantrum and Milian was struggling to keep the sack closed. Allyn and a guard came to assist him.

"Are they...?" asked Aebbe.

"Yes, three of the bastards. Not his full set but a significant dent. Quick! Iga my spear!"

She found it in the collection of weapons in the wagon and threw it to him. He made two quick thrusts and rattling screams came from the sack with the remaining knuckle having the sense to stop moving and whimper.

He opened the sack and pinned out the survivor with the spear while picking up the two dead knuckles and throwing them to the floor. "Will burn up in the sun but we should wait to check, means I'll lose any chance to track the vermin but I think he hurt himself so we shouldn't be troubled."

"And that thing?" Allyn pointed, not happy at it still moving.

"It's something to show the reeve king."

"I've told you they're different people, the reeve is the king's assistant, and he answers to the ealdorman who answers to the king," Aebbe said, frustrated.

"Well, whoever is in charge can see first-hand how destructive just one of them can be. In the meantime get some rest we're stuck here till the sun comes up and takes these two to the otherworld."

~

Aart grumbled, with two guards having scurried away in the middle of the night, along with that birth marked bastard before he could get his hands on the bleeder, he'd woken up to find out he'd be doing the graveyard shift solo.

He wasn't worried about his mates mocking him about losing his smarts. He'd had his helmet rattled before as part of the fyrd, last time it had been West Saxons, Jutes the time before that. Of course, Britons had clanged his head before and he'd always rewarded them with an axe between the eyes just as he planned to do when the bandit returned.

He had heard of visions after a head wound. Seeing things that weren't there. It hadn't happened to him but a mate once claimed to have heard his long dead mother after a blow to the head. Another made mention of coming face to face with a tall woman with red hair down to her waist, holding a spear with a dress made of the most bizarre colors who disappeared as quickly as she appeared.

It was a woman Aart was seeing now, no spear, and no fancy dress just a plain black gown but the woman wearing it -- a pretty, round faced, youth with chubby cheeks, long black hair, and yellow eyes --was not from this village. Aart wasn't sure if she was from this world.

The first time he saw her she was far in the distance at the top of a small hill at the back of the village. Just a speck really, she disappeared seconds later. Then a minute later he inspected the storehouse at the foot of the hill and saw a shape flash past him.

It took him twenty minutes to track back and cover the village. He thought he saw her sitting on the roof of one of the huts again she disappeared so fast he chalked it up to his injury. He did a circle of the hall where Digoth and Ribald were sleeping, when he saw her again. This time barely 10 feet away. He hissed as so not to wake those inside the hut, "who are you?" only for her to vanish again.

He sprinted now he wanted to get back to the guards hut and wake his mates. He needed someone else to see her. What if this was Hel herself come up from the underworld?

He stopped in his tracks as he saw her in the distance as he approached the villager's huts, and nearly emptied his bowels when he heard from behind him, "Godne morgen," good morning, in a dialect of Saxon he didn't hear very often. It was how the bogmen spoke, perfectly understandable but someone not from around here.

~

Psyche was just happy to speak her native language again. The shared part of the journey had been tedious although she was sure The Nix's stories would be just as boring in any other language, but his Latin vocabulary was so limited he kept muttering the same phases again and again, "aqua vitae."

"We get it, you like water!" she had complained. The Nix even gave petulant croaks when she and Vitium spoke to each other in Saxon what did he expect? Vitium was born just six villages over from her!

She had to act fast the land was unfamiliar to all three of them. She hadn't covered as much ground as she wished, and with recon taking a bit of time the sun was coming up in an hour. Still, just one little trick and a feast awaits her when she wakes.

She faced the man, handsome enough but the enhanced sense of smell she'd gotten when she'd become who she now was made her find all humans repulsive. "Good morning" the man replied. "Who are you, and what are you doing here?"

Psyche with lightning-fast reflexes scratched his cheek drawing blood. "Fucking bitch!" screamed the guard, reaching for his dagger but as he drew it, he looked into Psyche's eyes and forgot why he'd drawn it in the first place.

"You'll need your axe and dagger," Psyche told him, "Start in the hut where your friend is sleeping and kill him. Then I want you to go from hut to hut and to the hall killing all of them. Do so as quickly and quietly as possible. When they are all dead you will smash the axe into your forehead. A bit of brain might leak, but it ensures your insides will be nice and chewy when I wake up and find you."

Aart looked horrified but turned and started to shuffle slowly towards the guards' hut.

Psyche floated into the air and watched Aart enter.

A few seconds later there was an angry grunt. She smiled as Aart staggered out of the hut with tears flowing down his face.

When she first learnt how to make people her thralls, their mind was wiped, and they became unthinking beasts, she had asked Spurius for help, and together with Alecto, she'd worked out a potion to mix with her blood. She secreted it under her long black fingernails. It left her pets 100% aware of what they were doing but unable to stop. The look on a mother's face as she drowned her babies against her will brought joy to Psyche like nothing else.

She glided into the guards' hut. It was huge and was that a barrel of ale in the corner? She poured herself a cup and lay on a straw mattress. *Perfect* she thought as she took a long sip from the cup, and an even longer one from the vein of the dead guard's arm she'd wrenched off. She drifted off to sleep soothed by the screaming from outside.

CHAPTER 16

Alfwen paced around her cell. The guards hadn't slipped up yet, and the wedding was tomorrow. During the day Smirk and Sneer would terrorize her keeping her busy. The reeve's house was in the middle of town, too far from the city walls if she made a run for it. That's not to mention how she'd get back to the village without being hunted down by the guards, raped and killed by bandits, or have her furious father return her to the reeve in shackles.

"Think harder you mutton brained fool of a girl!" she whispered to herself. Then the door opened, and to her surprise, it was one of the main hall guards not the head guard of the reeve's house.

"You are wanted upstairs," he told her.

Alfwen was ushered into the reeve's room. She noticed there were more glass artifacts in here now. She supposed these were his late wives' trinkets that Smirk had decided she didn't want. Bowls and goblets mainly. The reeve himself was standing by the window looking out, trying to see something on the far side of the city.

"Ah, my love we have a bit of a problem."

For a minute, her heart leaped the deal has collapsed! She would be back home soon!

"It's your sister."

"Aebbe? You prefer her? Are you blind? I'm much…I mean sure, okay you can have her! We can still do the wedding tomorrow but with her instead. I'll return to the village and…what?" The reeve was looking at her like she was speaking Brittonic.

"What on earth are you talking about? Your sister is at the city gates with a Briton. The same outlaw that escaped the city guard. Reports are confusing some say he has her hostage; others say he's in the company of armed Saxon men. They're asking for you, both of us, in fact. We're to meet with the whole company in the town square."

~

Cwenhild was changing the rushes of the small hut she shared with Allyn, and getting ready for a full day's work alone out in the fields they were now responsible for.

She liked Allyn well enough, but he was awfully frosty when she tried to get him to lay with her. The other two girls had already noticed the glances he gave Digoth even if the men remained oblivious.

She was at a quandary eventually Allyn is going to have to put aside his distaste if only to make a child, but if he were clearly unhappy, perhaps Ribald could help her, and…she heard the first scream but didn't think much of it. Arguments between the other two couples had a habit of getting heated recently.

Then she heard a male voice, Alcred, she thought scream, "You bastard, why? Why? You fucking…" and a grunt followed by nothing.

This sounded like it was getting out of hand. Alcred and Emma wouldn't thank her for getting involved and it appeared to have stopped now.

"NOOOO!" For Frigg's sake! Now screams from Oswine and Wigswith's hut.

"Wigswith escape now! Get to the hall. Tell them the guards

are uuuhhhaah!" A frightened scream followed by some thuds, crashing, and banging. It ended with heavy footsteps and male panting.

By now Cwenhild was getting concerned and decided to see what was going on outside.

She screamed as she was greeted by the sight of Wigswith lying face down on the grass. Half her body was still inside the hut she was trying to escape, and an axe protruded from the back of her head.

Out of their hut stepped Aart, one of the guards, his tunic and leggings drenched in blood as he gave the corpse a vacant glare before turning to face Cwenhild. His eyes were red raw from crying as he simply said, "sorry," and pulled the axe out of Wigswith's head and looked down.

The wound on the right side of his head from the sling's hit earlier was gushing blood. Someone must have gotten a shot in, but with no weapons, it wasn't enough.

Cwenhild knew instantly there was no reasoning with him. She threw the rushes into his face before turning and beginning to run for her life.

~

"You should have left the wagon here at least. We are going to have to leave this afternoon to get to the city gates in time. I'm not spending another night in that inn, it was as drafty as the slave hut, and nothing had better happen to those children before the priests get their hands on them. Honestly, Digoth, you allow your sisters to wrap you around their little fingers. Whatever took your mother I will find out, but a talking frog it…"

Suddenly, the sound of fists furiously banging on the wooden door cut Ribald off.

"Who is it?" Digoth shouted.

"He's killing everyone! He's killing everyone!"

"Cwenhild?"

~

The guarded escort they got from the city gates to the town square really didn't know what to make of them. Hostile to the marked Briton they had their spears on, but wary of the two Saxon guards and one farmer who appeared to be protective of him.

At the front of the procession, Aebbe led with her arms around the two children.

A cluster of guards parted to reveal Alfwen, the reeve, and two children who, from their appearance, were clearly the reeve's children.

"What is going on here?" bellowed the reeve.

"Aebbe why are you here? And Iga, and the children, and the lunatic, where's father and Digoth? And who are these people? Why is that one rounder than the ox?" Alfwen had noticed Allyn.

Milian stepped forward and gave a mock bow. "Well met, reeve king."

"He's not the…" Aebbe then decided not to bother, it wasn't getting through.

"And to your lady wife."

"I'm not his wife!" Alfwen yelled getting strange looks from both the reeve and his children.

"I understand you dismissed the report you received about the deaths of Aluhburg, the wife of one of your village chiefs, and her villagers and slaves including the parents of these two little ones well…Aebbe, cover the children's eyes would you? Well, here I bring proof of the destruction that was brought about upon that day!" He opened the leather sack gingerly. "Oh, it's sleeping." He gave the sack a slight kick.

"Why does he talk like he's singing?" said Smirk.

"Because he's a foreign outlaw bastard," said Sneer. "Father told me they lay with sheep, and eat human flesh!"

"How ghastly!" his sister replied.

Then out of the bag shuffled the knuckle with Milian keeping his spear trained on it, lest it make any sudden movements.

He lifted the spear which allowed the knuckle to bear its pointy fangs drawing a gasp from the crowd. Smoke began to sizzle from its back as sunlight seeped through to the square despite heavy clouds. It began to squeal in pain so Milian covered it with the sack.

"It could be a shaved hound or boar even a baby bear just with its legs and arms removed and long fangs and hundreds of sharp little teeth added," said the reeve not sounding like he was doing a good job of convincing himself.

"Find me some shade, and an animal you can do without, and I'll show you what it's capable of," Milian told him.

Ten minutes later, they'd found a rusty old cage that could fit a piglet, and the knuckle and dragged it into the hall. By now the crowd of bystanders was so large that everyone had to jostle for space, but the reeves children barged their way to the front cursing and threatening anyone who got near their space with their father's wrath.

"Do you really think the children should see this?" Alfwen said.

She meant the reeve's children. Aebbe was taking care of

Wiglac and Winfred outside.

"Shut your useless hole," said Sneer, who then launched into a screaming fit as the piglet's intestine was spat out by the knuckle.

It was full of pig shit they discovered when it exploded upon striking Sneer in the face.

The piglet had the worst of it, there was a curved arch where its stomach and chest had been only 10 seconds before. The knuckle realizing there was no rush now used its fangs to peel the skin off the parts of the piglet that remained.

The reeve was trying to calm his hysterical children when Milian approached him. "King reeve, we've captured one and killed two of these foul beasts, but the creature that uses them as its cat's paw has several more at hand. It's currently in your lands. I wounded it last night but could do with your assistance in raising the Fyrd to shoot down these knuckles, while I fill The Nix full of blessed arrows that should do for him."

Eventually, the reeve noticed him. "I'm not the king you simple savage. King Cissa will arrive tomorrow for the wedding!"

"Well then, looks as though we're waiting here until tomorrow. Where do I sleep, and do you have any wine? Figured so near the coast you might have some of the Frankish stuff."

The reeve pushed back his flop of hair and pushed his sobbing children towards Alfwen.

~

This was a dilemma; he'd struggle to arrest the outlaw without spilling blood, not only was the Briton good and fast, the farmer, and the two guards even the woman with the twitchy eye could cause problems, and one dead city guard would be a massive headache for him. A screeching widow at his door demanding compensation.

He reluctantly shrugged, "stay here but the floor is the best you'll get. The lady Alfwen will doubtless enjoy the company of her sister in her cell tonight." Alfwen had the grace to only roll her eyes. "Rest of you, take the floor or the stables."

~

Vitium was not enjoying the day trapped in a narrow riverbank cave with a groaning Nix, and seven knuckles, who he hoped hadn't understood him call them "as ugly as a bear's arsehole" the previous evening.

Due to the cave being unable to support both of them, he'd turned himself into a newt, and was nervous about the previously small knuckles now towering over him like one of those long nosed cows he'd heard about.

"Why? Why? Why?" The Nix moaned and sobbed, holding up his ruined palms. Vitium didn't answer mainly because he didn't have vocal cords just a small sac that emitted a faint 'tic, tic, tic' sound, but also because he had no idea what had made those arrows so foul to The Nix's touch. He shuddered when he thought of what sort of pain would have been in had he not turned into a dormouse. It couldn't kill them, could it? The boss said that was just sunlight that they had to watch out for.

"The Romans had spells that me and Lilith didn't like, and put an end to a few early creations but they were experiments, weak ones not like you Vit. Besides, The Romans are long gone." He remembered the boss man's speech well. What the fuck was up with those arrows? Had the Britons learnt the Roman spells?

They managed to get some sleep and as dusk fell The Nix told Vitium his plan. 'Tic, tic, tic' was all he could say to the first half of it but it then got just dark enough, he pushed his small newt body into the river flinching in terror as a knuckle made a playful snap at him.

Once clear of the cave and sure that it was dark enough, the newt dived deep into the river to give himself a bit of space so he could return to human form while leaping from the water.

He swam back to the cave, now content to float outside, and clutched his bleeding nose. He was still suffering the effects of breaking it as a horse. After giving the offending knuckle a swat to the face he said, "go on Nixy I think this plan has legs."

CHAPTER 17

Digoth massaged his temples. "What do you mean Aart has killed everyone else?"

"What do you think I mean? He's made them all porridge! The other four are already dead, the other guard too. Godfrid didn't see him either he's in on it or dead…oh my, the slave hut! They have no weapons, most don't know how to fight we must tell them to run!"

Digoth saw something in Cwenhild's eyes that shook him out of his usual selfish, sloth like nature.

He ran to a chest by the wall and withdrew the sword he seldom took out. Preferring to hunt with spear and axe, the sword was made of several small pieces of iron which had been beaten together to forge a single blade. It was heavy and awkward to wield so no good in the enclosed woods but in battle, as his father said, "Hit a man with that and he stays hit."

Aart a veteran of the fyrd would be able to repeal spear, axe, and dagger thrusts despite whatever has addled his brain. Screams started to come from the cursed slave hut, only just rebuilt since the knuckles destroyed it, and slaughtered its inhabitants.

"Grab a weapon from the chest in case I don't come back," he told Cwenhild and a surprised Ribald.

~

Panic struck him halfway through his run to the slave hut.

While he liked to style himself a warrior, he'd felled many a deer, and boar, and even run his spear through the occasional bandit looking to rob him he had never taken on a professional like Aart. Even Saig's crew which was just one immensely talented archer and a freak of nature had given him trouble.

What if he couldn't do it? His father had last been in the fyrd ten years ago, and Cwenhild's fighting ability was unknown. A blood crazed Aart could break into the hall, and kill them both should he fall, and then what? Aebbe and Iga returning home to a destroyed village again?

Iga? Why had she sprung to mind as the last thing he thought of? He entered the hut and nearly vomited at the sight.

Two male slaves lay dead on the dirt floor, their throats slashed. Aart at the far end of the hut grunted and slashed his dagger at a female slave trying to get away from him. He ripped her cheek open, and instantly Digoth knew she had no chance. No one can survive that amount of blood loss.

Aart couldn't step forward to hit the killing blow as the only unhurt slave had jumped onto his back, another woman, she was biting at his neck and had managed to make some cuts despite weak and missing teeth. Aart's head wound, surely the cause of his madness was flowing. The woman had made enough scratches on his forehead to cause blood to run down his face making him look like he was weeping blood.

Aart was trying the shake the woman off his back, and when that failed he resorted to smashing the flat of the axe on her dome until she lost consciousness and slipped off. He looked across the hut at Digoth and screamed at him before sticking his dagger in the unconscious woman's eye. "You have to finish this, I can't stop!"

Digoth screamed, raised his sword, and charged. If Aart was surprised by this he gave no sign; he simply stepped aside to dodge Digoth who skidded and slid too far due to his own momentum and blood everywhere.

Seeing that he had bought himself some time, Aart left the slave hut and ran back to the guard hut. Digoth followed him just in time to see Aart emerge from the hut with a sword of his own as well as a round wooden shield and an iron spear on a wooden shaft. Suddenly disadvantaged Digoth ran back to the hall to regroup and hopefully tire Aart who was showing a display of stamina that was beyond normal.

Back in the hall Digoth told them, "we've got two minutes until he gets here."

Ribald with his axe and shield said, "I'll take the back you two hold the main door!" Cwenhild had a dagger in each hand. And they waited.

"Don't be afraid," said Digoth to Cwenhild. "It's three on one we have the advantage." And they waited. After around ten minutes Digoth called his father back from patrolling the hall's backyard and the three of them inched the door open.

Aart was sitting cross-legged on the floor and although his eyes were raw red from tears he was smiling.

He closed his eyes and they had changed from brown to yellow when he reopened them. He then started to speak. A jolt of fear went up the backs of all three of them at the sound coming out of Aart's mouth.

It was husky in a creepy way, it was in a different Saxon dialect, and it was unmistakably feminine.

"You've disturbed my rest by challenging my cat's paw sadly for you I don't need much rest. I can't come out to play yet so I will give the cat's paw some of my abilities. Not all of them, even a tiny fraction would reduce a human body to mush, but enough to deal with three stinking blood bags."

Aart's body shook, he closed his eyes, and when he opened them again they were back to brown.

"Kill me!" he screamed in his normal voice as he walked towards them.

Digoth stood at the front and raised his sword, and swung it downward, as Aart for some reason had thrown down his shield, and was slow to get to his sword. Perhaps cause by the trauma of what he'd gone through

Digoth smashed him right on his widow's peak with the hilt a blow that should have knocked him out, but it simply made him stagger backwards. Aart then wildly swung a fist at the sword hilt, snapping it in two. Digoth and Ribald watched in horrified awe at the iron broken by the guard's punch.

Cwenhild crept up behind him and slipped one of the daggers into Aart's back. Aart yelped in pain turned around and punched Cwenhild, sending her flying forty feet until she crashed into the slave hut. He then pulled the dagger out and looked at it before throwing it on the ground. Digoth and Ribald used this time to get back in the hall.

"What do we do now? How do we kill him?" screamed Ribald.

"There must be a way," replied Digoth who was frantically searching through the chest. Then the door was ripped out of the doorway by Aart's bare hands. He then ran towards Ribald, and with his sword and took his head clean off with a single swing.

~

Digoth's world stood still. His father's body seemed to remain upright forever and crashed to the floor in slow motion.

His father's head hit the floor and bounced a few times before stopping face down. It probably only took a few seconds but felt like hours to Digoth.

Too racked by panic and terror to stand he crawled. Aart just watched him, trying to conserve energy, he weighed up whether to kill Digoth or go outside and finish off the woman. Digoth was crawling to the part of the hall where the food was prepared, looking for a knife or something to use to defend himself Aart thought and decided to stalk after him.

He was not prepared for Digoth to put his arms into the fire and throw a flaming log at him.

Digoth looked back wincing in agony from the burns on his hands expecting to see the last thing he ever would, but instead of Aart charging towards him, he was convulsing with pain from the flames on his tunic, albeit he was somehow remaining upright.

So the bastard or bitch, depending on whoever was in charge, doesn't like fire, Digoth thought. He found it in himself to reach into the fire and throw another log, this one striking Aart in the face making him howl unnaturally.

Digoth didn't have the strength to throw anymore so he put his feet into the fireplace and kicked, forcing, at great pain to himself, another few logs to roll onto the dry rushes which quickly ignited.

The last thing he remembered seeing was the flames rising as Aart's figure flailed in the middle of them, and the heat getting unbearable as flames encroached further and further towards him.

CHAPTER 18

Alfwen and Aebbe sat in her cell talking. The children were sleeping and the guards outside either taking naps or playing dice.

Milian, Allyn, and Iga had found it remarkably easy to slip past the city guard who controlled the main entrance, and were probably in some ale shack right now. Aebbe voiced concerns about Iga a woman being out at night. Alfwen said she'd be okay with the two men although she didn't sound concerned, quickly changing the conversation back to her favorite topic; herself.

"It's a nightmare living here! You saw how those two brats talk to me and that fat old rooster will expect me to lay with him after the wedding. What was father thinking? How can I get out of this? Think!"

"You can't," replied Aebbe matter of factly.

"What! I thought you'd have some sort of idea, turning up early with new guards, the Briton, the thrall, surely part of this was to get me out of his shitty city."

"No, just needed to show the knuckles to the authorities so they'd help us. You're stuck with the reeve and your two little children." she paused. "It's just the way things are."

~

Noviomagus Reginorum was what Spurius had told The Nix the town was called.

"It has a new Saxon name now, but that's not important. It has a bathhouse just like in Londinium but this one hasn't been used for over a hundred years. Saxon fools ignore it all, latrines? They shit in the street! Amphitheater? Used for executions and drunken festivals! Bathhouse? They knocked it down and use it as a stone quarry! They inherited the greatest civilization ever to reign in the west, and behave like animals in the pen! Anyway, it won't be easy but a sewer tunnel into the city might still be there if you look hard enough, will probably come out near the bathhouse…" That had been the message whispered to him as The Nix lay whimpering in the cave.

Now he and Vitium were scouting for the tunnel's entrance by a quay slightly to the west of the city. The one they found was too small for The Nix but Vitium told him, "I'll go in and find out what's what. I'll relay the message to the boss in Londinium and he can give you the information you need." He closed his eyes and made the world around him blur for a second before turning into a grass snake.

~

One of Milian's steel axes and a spare pugio he had was enough to purchase them a couple of barrels of Frankish wine. Which they shared with anyone who passed by, and expressed an interest in chatting to the trio, who had unsurprisingly quickly become the most popular people in the city.

As Milian was fond of saying, "The most popular people become the most knowledgeable people."

They discovered the wedding was to take place in the amphitheater that lay outside the city walls. King Cissa himself was to attend making a rare trip from the great hall he'd built on the coast.

After the wedding there was to be a great feast, the execution of some vile criminals, and the priests would then sacrifice the two children as a blessing.

~

"Before that happens, we offer the knuckle as a substitute for the little ones. I'll have presented it to this Cissa by then and Aebbe can tell them it was made by…Low key?"

"Loki, the trickster god. He created these things. The Nix too, probably," Allyn informed him.

"His sense of humor is shit," Milian said.

"What if the priests refuse?" asked Iga.

"Won't come to that. The king will give me a fyrd, and I need the boy's eyes to lure the beast out, but if it all goes wrong, make sure the little ones are in my vicinity when the priests are ready to butcher and be ready to run. Either way, they leave this city alive."

He then stopped whispering and decided to get another conversation going with whichever town folk were in the ale shack.

"One more wine? How about it? What did you say your name was, mate?"

"Randolph," said the man sitting in the corner. "And yes thanks, one more and then I have an errand."

Milian frowned. "Not from round here are you, mate?"

"His accent is Angles," said Iga. "What's a bogman doing this far south?"

"I'm a shipbuilder by trade, more work out here."

Milian laughed. "The ships are bringing them in, you tool. They get made and fixed up back in their Saxon home ports! You want to go out west, some of my people have quit trying to fight you bastards and are going over the sea to a place called

Armorica. If you can understand their brand of Brittonic then plenty of work for a ship builder."

"Thanks," said Vitium, already disliking the man with the marked eye.

~

Vitium left the ale shack frustrated. Cities were full of food but too many armed men for him to turn into a wolf or bear, and devour his dinner without ending up stuck full of spears and left unconscious to burn up in the morning.

Close quarters made it difficult for him to quickly change form he needed a bit of space for that. So he murmured Latin words that Spurius in Londinium, eighty miles from here would hear as clear as day.
"They'll be beyond city walls so Nixy can come and play, but its open air during the day. What's our best plan, boss?"

He decided rat for tonight's supper and slipping behind some barrels changed into a black cat giving the night a meow as he disappeared into an alley.

~

Psyche felt ill, the boost she'd gotten from eating the guard was gone as she'd sweated out most of his blood when she'd been forced awake. Her skin felt like thousands of ants were crawling over it.

Even with her advanced pain threshold, she had felt her cat's paw being burnt alive. It was finally dark enough for her to venture outside.

The villager's huts yielded four dead bodies, all in decent condition so she tucked in although she couldn't enjoy it as much as usual due to a nauseous feeling in the pit of her stomach.

At the slave hut, she screamed and cursed. One slave, a woman, had bled out, she'd taste all sticky now. That's when she noticed the hall was a blazing inferno.

She did the math in her head thirteen heartbeats, four dead slaves, four dead villagers, one dead guard and her cat's paw burned alive. Some were missing. Doubtless, they're all charred bones in the hall she thought. The fire was too strong for her to approach it so she returned to the better-preserved bodies in the huts to eat.

~

A mile away in the woods their heartbeats just out of Psyche's hearing range Cwenhild collapsed. Digoth couldn't walk with the burns on his feet, but she had thumping head pains and probably broken bones from being thrown into the slave hut from forty feet away.

"I can't walk any further," she groaned as she lay Digoth down.

"Am I dead?" murmured Digoth.

"Not yet, the halls destroyed and the village is just blood and bodies, we had to get out of there. Aart is dead but something evil remains, that voice he spoke with I don't think that's dead. I will never return to that village." she promised herself.

"How did I get out?" said Digoth.

"I pulled you out. I saw... I saw your father. I saw what had happened to him. I'm sorry."

Digoth nodded. "I should have listened to Aebbe when she said the children were speaking the truth. What happened to Aart and what they saw must be linked. We must go to the city."

"How? You can't walk and I can't carry you far. We should rest here tonight."

~

Morning came and Aebbe comforted her sister who awoke and greeted the sunlight and dawn of her wedding day with a wild roar before dissolving into a tantrum.

Both girls had grown up with the knowledge that their father would force them to marry whoever could provide the most handsome handgeld.

Aebbe had expected a farmer with good hides that her father would incorporate into his land to be her fate, and just hoped he would be kind.

Alfwen the prettier and more spoilt of the two had dreams that one of the merchants might take her for a wife. A more comfortable life, a bigger house, even trips across the sea, and he would of course be handsome, kind, and do everything she said.

The reality of a boring old man with two monsters who was rich but known to be miserly was sinking in fast. A servant brought in a wooden barrel, and began to heat buckets of water over a brazier.

"Look Alfwen you're going to take a bath. What a nice treat!" Aebbe tried to cheer her sister up.

~

The owner of the ale shack woke up his three guests by banging his new steel ax on a rock that he used as a stool for customers. "Come on you lot, being an inn wasn't part of the deal, suns coming up soon and I need space for guards finishing a night shift."

"I feel like the ox walked all over me, rammed its head into my belly, and then pissed in my mouth," Iga complained.

"Getting used to the booze I see. So what happens now?" said

Milian.

Iga stood up and groaned. "We need to find Digoth and Ribald. They should have arrived last night or early this morning, they will escort Alfwen to the amphitheater and to give whatever goods they have as Alfwen's byrdgifu."A token gift that would remain untouched but would provide Alfwen with some short term security in the event of the reeve's death.

~

"What do you mean father hasn't arrived?" said Aebbe, when the trio arrived back at the hall with no knowledge of Ribald or Digoth's whereabouts.

"He has to be here to take her to the wedding grounds! And give her the new sword she's supposed to give to her husband! We don't have much time she's having her bath right now!"

"Lucky her," said Allyn. To explain the odd looks he said, "I like bathing, done it three times this year, hoping for a fourth before winter draws in."

Then the doors to the cell opened, and escorted by some hall servants acting as attendants, Alfwen appeared in a white linen gown, tied at the waist with a belt decorated with glass brooches and a crown of flowers on her head. Aebbe beamed. Allyn said, "You look wonderful, my lady."

Iga found it in herself to smile and offer congratulations.

"I don't want congratulations! I want someone to take my place," Alfwen hissed.

"That belt shows off your bum, it's as thick as a bowl of porridge," Milian said in Brittonic, and then explained, "A standard good luck phrase we use at weddings in my homeland. It doesn't translate to Saxon well."

~

"You look as sick as a dead rat," Iga said after following Milian out of the hall. He had told the others he would watch the city gate for arrivals.

"I didn't want the girls or Allyn to see my worry," he said. "There was a wolf with The Nix, right? I heard him just before I found the knuckles. That means The Nix has a beast with him or more likely a shifter…"

"Shifter?"

"A monster that can change from man to beast. Fuck, if he has a companion then I'm not liking Digoth and his father's absence, not liking it one bit."

CHAPTER 19

The candle clock in the hall showed that the reeve would be waiting at the amphitheater about now.

Allyn offered to be Alfwen's escort and a kind guard called Tilmund dug out his iron sword for Alfwen to present to the reeve.

"But if father and Digoth are delayed then the wedding can be postponed?" Alfwen said hopefully.

"Someone should check the road, all the way back to the village if need be," suggested Aebbe.

"I'll go," said Allyn, looking frantic.

"It'll have to be you, Allyn. I need to speak to the king and keep an eye on the little ones, let's hope the reeve doesn't mind a Briton escort for his beloved," said Milian.

"I'll come too," said Iga. "I've got nothing to do here, and you might need help on the road."

The two groups split up. One heading towards the amphitheater, and Iga and Allyn headed towards the city gates.

~

The directions and instructions from the boss were accurate. After jumping over the city walls in his cat form. Vitium met The Nix outside the amphitheater just a few hours before sunrise.

They started to work fast. They'd been told what to look for by Spurius. *"There'll be a chamber somewhere the place hasn't been used for its proper purpose for 200 years. Thieves have probably plundered the place countless times. It could be anywhere, so rush!"*

Vitium turned into a hawk to improve his eyesight, and a bat to pick up extra sounds. The Nix stamped on stones where the spectators would have stood and sat and cheered centuries ago.

Eventually, the bat transformation did the trick. Vitium made high-pitched clicks at the sound of one stamping.

The Nix lifted the stone to find, more stones, a lot more stones, but these were in a pile of rubble. Grumbling as usual The Nix scooped them up into a rope net. He tied the net to the horn of the ox that Vitium now was who made a grunting low as he pulled the rubble out of the hole.

Then there it was; the entrance. Vitium turned back into a human, and they both dropped down into the darkness.

~

As Alfwen, Aebbe, Milian, and the two children approached the amphitheater, the crowds grew and jostled.

They needed the city guard to escort them across the wooden bridge that covered the small river by the city walls. From then on it was a short walk across a few open fields where families were picnicking, although not everyone was allowed to enter the amphitheater it appeared that the whole town was taking the day off.

The guards guided them to the amphitheater gates, which were doorless, long since rotted away. Guards stood by the entrance keeping out the peasants.

Inside a festival appeared to be taking place.

Musicians played horns which people danced to, two men were wrestling in the ground with a crowd of onlookers betting their possessions, a gray robed priest was reading from a book of riddles, and long tables were full of people filling trenchers and ale cups.

A warty old man was leading around two bears, he would have them fight later, the bears malnourished, had their teeth and claws removed for them so they could fight again. The grey robed and grey haired as well as grey bearded priest noticed their arrival. "The lady Alfwen has appeared so we can begin and get back to drinking," he said to cheers, putting down the riddle book. "And you've bought us our two presents for Frey." He winked at Wiglac and Winfred drawing a disgusted glare from Aebbe.

The reeve was in a canopy style tent at the end of the amphitheater grounds next to it stood a much larger tent that housed King Cissa. "Remember keep the children within a few feet of me at all times," warned Milian, as he held the lead-lined wooden box that contained the knuckle.

~

"What do you mean your father isn't here? It's unprecedented for a bride to be presented to her betrothed by someone who isn't a kinsman, and doesn't even know the gods!" The reeve was annoyed by the unexpected issue.

"I'll permit it if there is no alternative." The priest clearly wanted to return to his ale and his riddle contest.

"Very well get everyone to gather around," yelled the reeve, and he emerged from the tent; King Cissa.

Milian gave a surprised look; after Merlin, this was the second oldest person he'd ever seen in his life, certainly the oldest Saxon. Although, given that when he came face to face with a Saxon what usually followed was Milian's axe hitting their skull, he shouldn't be surprised he hadn't met too many old ones.

Most of those in attendance in the amphitheater paid little attention to the wedding as a crowd of about twenty gathered around the priest and the couple. King Cissa was the only one sitting.

The reeve snapped his fingers and a servant brought something, something so amazing it almost stopped Alfwen's tears. A wooden chest that once opened glittered with its treasures. Silver and gold coins, silver spoons, gold bracelets, a silver figure of a fierce-looking giant cat with a shaggy mane with gemstones for its eyes, bowls made of green glass, a pearl ring, a golden cross encrusted with gems. The more Alfwen pawed through it with eyes like saucers, the more outlandish and wonderful discoveries she made; a gold body chain with amethyst at the center, a statue of a goat with impossibly long horns, a silver crane, more rings.

The writing on the coins and some of the bracelets she'd never seen before the characters were curvier and shorter than the runes the priests and merchants could read and write. "Your morgengifu, my dear, I'm supposed to give it to you tomorrow, I just wanted you to see it first." the reeve said.

"It's beautiful," Alfwen said with awe, perhaps speechless for the first time in her life.

"Your Fiscburna chest! It's bigger than I remember. Why I remember it was a hot day much like today…today…yes… today I'm going to a wedding, I remember my wedding. It was in winterfylleth, a cold time of year, her name was…is that your Fiscburna chest?" King Cissa went on before losing his train of thought.

"Fuck," Milian muttered under his breath he hadn't counted on the king being feeble-minded.

"I give you this handgeld as I am oathed to do," said the reeve to Milian presenting him with a smaller chest.

"Me?"

"You are father's stand in," whispered Aebbe. "It's for him."

"I'll be sure to keep it nice and safe for him," Milian said with a wink.

The priest then asked Milian, "Do you have the byrdgifu?"

Milian shrugged.

"It's the gift father was supposed to give to Alfwen!" Aebbe told him.

He shrugged again and handed over one of his arrows. "On the way here last night this certainly gave me a piece of luck."

Alfwen took it while rolling her eyes. "The byrdgifu is for security if, y'know, he dies," she said waving her thumb at the reeve.

"If father dies, you go back to your village," said Smirk, "and everything in the chest is ours!"

The reeve began to frown and the priest said, "Now the exchange of swords."

The reeve handed Alfwen a heavy iron sword. "I give you this sword for you to keep safe, and one day for our sons to use."

Sneer piped up, "That sword is mine!"

Alfwen took Tilmund's sword and gave it to the reeve. "With this blade, you must keep our home safe," she said.

"I now pronounce you married!" the priest said to a cheer.

~

Alfwen and her new family took a position at the head of the table as musicians played, the reeve clapped instructions and the feast started.

"Come with me," Milian said to Aebbe. "I look more trustworthy when I'm in the company of women, plus we need to keep the little ones close."

"We can't have the children in the tent if they see that…" She pointed at the chest with the knuckle locked inside.

"Fair enough, we'll have them wait outside, Tilmund watch them like a hawk!" The reeve sent some guards to escort them inside the tent.

Aebbe knelt and addressed King Cissa with, "My lord." Good to have someone with knowledge of local customs, Milian thought as he put the chest down and did the same.

"Who are you?" wheezed the king.

"Aebbe, the lady Alfwen's sister, and a Briton outlaw who claims to have information about a strange new beast that killed many villagers, including the lady's mother," said a young aide standing next to the king who licked his lips a lot.

The king closed his eyes for a while and just when they feared he had dozed off opened them. He said "I was sixteen years old when I set foot on this island for the first time. We raided Jute settlements forcing them back. I killed many a man but when forced into the forests it was Briton arrows that were our bane, when we caught a Briton archer rather than kill him we took his fingers from him and sent him back to his fellows a useless mouth."

He bowed his head. "We were cruel back then, I can see it now."

Milian shrugged. "A Saxon who falls into our hands loses more than his fingers. Besides, there are crueler things than men, hard as that may be to believe. Here my lord look." He walked towards the chest and got his dagger ready to be trained on the knuckle, he picked the chest up and opened it gingerly. The horrible hissing sound came from the chest and the king frowned at the sight.

"Such an ugly thing – is this what they said ripped the piglet to shreds?" His aide nodded. "Yes, I can see how such a thing could be trouble…put it away."

As soon as the chest closed the king blinked and asked them, "Who are you?" The aide looked uncomfortable as he began, "I was 16 years old when I…"

And Milian realized this was going to take longer than he anticipated.

CHAPTER 20

Allyn and Iga had made it halfway back to the village when people they were asking on the road began to tell troubling tales of fire. Then second and third-hand rumors from people who claimed to have spoken to people who had been to the village, to inspect and put out the fire. They spoke of blackened bones in the ruins and mostly eaten corpses.

"Must have been a huge pack," said one.

"Old Cissa needs to call The Fyrd if wolf packs of this size are coming south!" said another.

"Briton raiders I reckon, wolves can't light fires!" his mate claimed.

"Nah, since the Brit bastards were sent running, it's the West Saxons who are coming through the forest. Cynric can tell old Cissa is weak," an old woman warned.

"I spoke to someone who went up there right into the village, he fought in The Fyrd half a hundred times and he said the village smells like after a battlefield when both sides retrieve their dead for burning," the last man they came across said.

"Cwenhild and Digoth," moaned Allyn eyes welling up with tears.

"I don't think the village is safe, we need to return to Chichester," said Iga.

"We need to keep looking! Maybe some of them escaped, we can go into the forest and search." Allyn protested.

"It would be like looking for a cock on a cow! We need numbers and advice, and we get both back at the city!" Iga said.

~

Digoth and Cwenhild had barely slept. After resting as much as they could, they tried their best to put as much distance between the village and themselves but at a snail's like pace as they had to rest every ten minutes or so because of the pain of Digoth's burns and Cwenhild's broken bones.

Ten minutes on, ten minutes off, was the pace they agreed. Neither knew if it would get them to the city walls before nightfall. As soon as they could, they got within sight of the mud path but decided against taking it.

If bandits saw two invalids on the main path they would likely slit Digoth's throat, and sell Cwenhild to slavers after raping her. So it was working through immense pain that they gave up their rest to keep up with Allyn and Iga once they had spotted them, at least they thought it was them.

Iga was first in their line of vision and one dirty woman traveler looked much like the rest, although her companion was of a certain build that gave them hope. It was when Allyn turned so they could see his frame horizontally that they were sure they had the right people. Yelling out their names, they rolled down the embankment to the path.

~

"Thank Woden!" cried Allyn as Iga checked their injuries.

"Neither can walk, his feet need herbs and she needs rest to heal. We can carry them but it'd slow us we might be outside the city walls exposed at night," Iga said after inspecting them.

"What happened?" asked Allyn.

"The children and the Briton were right there is darkness unlike anything a man can imagine in these lands," Digoth said solemnly.

"Your sisters and I tried to tell you, too!" Iga moaned.

"Let's get a move on we can argue later," said Allyn propping up Digoth, leaving Cwenhild to Iga. "We can hail a wagon, trade some tools for a ride."

"If one turns up in time. Whole kingdom is either at the wedding or running back to their halls once they hear of the village," said Iga.

~

On the third showing of the knuckle, the king kept his wits for long enough to agree to raise The Fyrd. They got the aide to write the promise in shaky runes before King Cissa used his ring and hot wax to mark his seal before he drifted off again. "I was 16 years old when I…"

Milian turned to leave but Aebbe clutched his arm furiously. "Where you come from, do you leave a king in mid-sentence?"

"Where I come from, kings don't drone on with the same thing again and again! They fight!"

"So did he… once." They stayed for a while longer, until finally the heat and the wine made him doze off. Snores drifted from him.

Once outside the tent, a cold breeze started. Aebbe looked for her sister and saw her; still at the head of the feast table dressed warmly in furs over her dress. Another gift, it's not all bad for her, she thought, and then something was missing?

"Where are the children?" She panicked. "Wiglac! Winfred!" she screamed and, "Tilmund!" once she'd remembered the guard's name.

Aebbe surveyed the scene. In front of the long table where the feast was taking place, two bears were lumbering towards each other. The warty old man and his younger assistant had hounds on leashes barking rapidly at the confused and maimed bears forcing them together.

Behind the bears, carpenters were working on the stage the executions would take place on soon. She looked up as the sun was going down the amphitheater seats were beginning to fill up, families and couples had rationed enough from the feast, and were retiring to relax away from all the speeches, and the gruesomeness of the executions.

She frowned when she saw the guards had smuggled some whores in, knowing what women who spend all week on gruel would do for a chicken leg! That's where Tilmund has buggered off to, she thought crossly. He had better not expose the children to such…then she caught sight of the children and excitedly waved, but her joy turned to horror when she saw they were standing behind the stage with the priest and their hands were bound. She gestured for Milian who was walking behind her.

"What's wrong?" he said. "Oh, shit!"

CHAPTER 21

The armless man gurgled. If he could speak he would beg for death. He didn't know how he hadn't passed out yet the pain was so great but now...yes...yes...the pain is fading, thank Woden, and soon the darkness maybe, just maybe Hild his love, gone too soon in childbirth would be waiting for him.

Then the hound that was gnawing away at his stump looked up sniffed and gave an angry bark. The world seemed to flash was this it. I'm leaving this world finally, he thought but then a green eyed man with a shaggy beard peered over him.

Him? He was there at the start. He was actually with the monster before disappearing.

~

It was when he went up to the amphitheater seats with a cask of wine he'd snagged while the wedding ceremony was going on. He'd glugged half of it down and wobbled a bit not noticing a stone missing and he took a tumble into the darkness. He assumed that the bearded man who helped him up was another wedding guest who had fallen too.

Then the man grinned and said, *"Nixy! Ecce quid hicest!"* Complete gibberish! But a flashing sensation happened and the man disappeared. Out of the shadows stepped the monster.

~

Now the man spoke again, this time in Saxon but the dialect of the bogmen.

"Alright mate? Sorry to interrupt, looks like you were about to pass out on us, can't be having that, can we? We want you wide awake for all of this. Gives the blood and flesh a bit of a tang. Problem is your body is shutting down because the blood isn't getting where it should matey, but I can fix you so the party can go on!" Vitium stared into the poor man's eyes, took a few crushed leaves out of his purse, and sprinkled them into the man's mouth.

The man's eyes went wide with agony as the pain returned. "So, he'll be alive and conscious up till the end?" asked The Nix.

"Right, Alecto taught me what herbs to pick, and what to chant when drying them, pretty simple but he'll be awake right until the end. No dead dull meat for us. You want to have a chat with Alecto next time you're in Londinium, been teaching me and Psyche all sorts of tricks."

Switching back to Saxon he told the man, "Going to be here for the whole party feeling everything aren't you mate?"

In Latin, The Nix said, "I forgot you know their bastard foreign language. If I'd remembered I wouldn't have eaten his tongue straight away, we could have got information about how many out there now."

Vitium shrugged. "Don't matter, dark soon. We will see for ourselves." He turned back into his hound form and began lapping at the terrified man's stumps.

~

It was dark enough that Psyche was able to step out of the guards' hut she'd spent the day in, and just finding the twilight just a little itchy she sprinted through the forest. She decided not to bring attention to herself by flying; not with an archer around and not with the tools he had.

She'd been informed by messages sent from Londinium which

bounced around her head as she slept off her feast. The meat was dull and listless, that fool of a guard had slashed away at the victims, not caring for precision meaning too much blood had drained away.

However, she did get some fresh meat. Her hearing alerted her to groups of people coming to check on the fire. Still resting in the guards' hut, she hid under the straw mattress when her enhanced hearing reported a large number of heartbeats. It was shameful to retreat from toothless farmers and peasants but the sunlight was too much of a leveler.

Once when she was sure there weren't any other heartbeats around other than just a couple, she beckoned the two unarmed nosy passer-bys towards the guards' hut from its door. They hadn't hesitated.

Keeping her human form of an attractive young human woman had its hardships but a few benefits she thought. Her teeth ripped one man's throat out while her hand had made a hole in the other one's stomach, and was greedily hunting for the kidneys her favorite part. After all, she reasoned, the two men would have hardly been so eager to enter the hut had she looked like Heslop or old scratch forbid The Nix!

~

Alfwen was drunk, she proposed to herself she would remain this way for the next say thirty or forty years, and then she might just get through the marriage. Thankfully Sneer was fascinated with the torture of the bears and was leaving her alone. Smirk was pawing through the treasure chest that Alfwen had been given.

"Find anything interesting?" she asked and got a grunt in return. Deciding to put in a bit more of an effort, she passed over the arrow that Milian had given her as her byrdgifu.

"Here have a touch of this, the wood feels so smooth, I don't think we have trees like this down here. Of course, their arrow makers would be much more skilled, us Saxons prefer fighting at close quarters. Axe making is more important for us."

She looked beyond the stage where the first of the executions was happening. Some things struck at her as a little off; maybe the wine was messing with her head but it was so cold that even clutching the furs closer didn't alleviate as much as she needed.

Smir…no, she should start thinking of them as Hieu and Torold…Hieu was saying something to her but while she was listening, her head turned to give herself a pan view of the entirety of the amphitheater in her vision. The sun was going down and her view was lit by torches on the table and spread around the arena.

She saw the jugglers by the entrance, musicians with horns and pipes, a few couples dancing. King Cissa in his chair, reading to the three condemned men. She was startled to see the last man in chains was the huge man from the forest who was arrested in town.

The hounds biting the heels of the hapless bears delighting Torold and some other youths. Mini campfires now being set up with people bringing in their own meat and vegetables, the guards less picky about who enters mainly due to them being blind drunk. More whores, having gained entry with some guests, fucking openly on the seating area. Sprawled on the floor all over the amphitheater grounds and seats were drunken men and women either passed out or not too far away from it.

She looked for her sister and Milian: she wondered if he knew his former companion was here and due to die in a few minutes. She found them together with the two children but they were arguing with the priest and is that rope around the children's wrists?

When would Digoth and her father get here? she thought as that's when the racing between the two families that would signal an end to the party would begin. That brought her back to the start of her daydream as that's what Hieu had been asking her about.

"Well, if they don't come we will drop you and Torold off at your aunt's house, then your father and I will return home and..."

At the thought of the conclusion of today, Alfwen grabbed another cask of wine and started taking large gulps. Hieu then started screaming at the top of her voice in terror. *Has she just read my mind?* was the last thing Alfwen thought before she joined in with the screaming.

CHAPTER 22

Drefan looked at the old man as he started his speech again. He didn't recognize some of the words 'condemned', 'malicious arson' he just liked making fires. They calmed him after a beating from old dad, lying in front of the fire for hours made the pain go away. Soon he wanted more; starting fires while working meant beatings by the overseer which led to him running into the forest to start one to stare at.

His mother had pleaded with him to stop. He promised, and upheld it for a while. Rather, he kept away from the village, spending the nights out in the fields, and the wheat twinkled so prettily with the tiny flame. He didn't know that wind could spread fire so quickly, so was a bit confused as to why the next morning everyone was screaming at him, and his mother was crying. That's the last thing he remembered before the village headman rained blows on him.

He woke up tied to a post outside the hall. What bothered him most about the days that followed was the lack of fire rather than cold or hunger. His hands still bound as he was put on a wagon and then it was all a blur until waking up in the quarry.

Chained in the quarry with the bald man who had to be chained round the neck at an angle to stop himself from bashing his head against the rocks, and the giant man who made funny noises. He asked the giant if he liked fire but the bald man in a rare moment of lucidity snapped.

"He's a savage, you lackwit! Their tongue is different, can't make our words, they have to use odd sounds."

Nothing of note happened for a few days other than the foreign giant going into a screaming rant and making a cross-like sign with his bound fists at the sight of a grass snake one evening.

He asked the other two and the bored drunk guards when he'd be let back to the village because he missed his fires, the one the guards made at night was okay to stare at but a little small. The guards laughed and told him to shut up.

One morning, they had buckets of water poured over them, a bit of stale bread stuffed in their mouths, and were marched out of the city dodging the rotten fruit and pebbles passers-by were throwing at them.

Now after waiting by the gates in the sun all day. The sun was going down and the three were standing on the stage. The giant was chanting in his odd voice, the bald man spitting curses. He could see some people from his village in the crowd of onlookers, and his mother being held by the arms and made to watch.

The old man was sitting down reading from a scroll in a loud voice. Drefan had stopped listening he couldn't concentrate that long but then the old man gestured towards him.

Two guards grabbed him so tightly he made a yelp of pain but that soon turned to a gasp of delight when he saw the long stake erected on the stage had loads of kindling around it and big chunks of firewood at the base. He was going to see a massive fire!

~

"The children were what were agreed by the lady Alfwen's father, not some worm," the priest said.

"Trust me, the gods would favor the worm, these things are

not of our world," Milian explained.

Aebbe was squirming trying to keep the priest's attention and hopefully distract him. She had already taken Milian's dagger and was pinning the knuckle in the chest back with it.

She was hoping that without the burden of holding the chest Milian would sneak in and sprint the children to safety but he had turned his back to her and the priest.

He was looking at the execution stage where the chanting in a familiar voice was coming from.

"*Domine Deus omnipotens, Pater Domini nostri Jesu Christi...*" droned the voice she remembered from both the Roman villa and the streets of Chichester.

Milian found the chanting amusing. "I know those words. It's what the monks taught him. Ha! He doesn't have a clue what they mean. Fancy keeping the big dumb beast alive for this and…"

He caught Aebbe's look. She managed to look both disgusted and pleading at the same time. A useful talent, Milian thought.

He took back the dagger and chest. "Right, the children, look priest one way or another we are going to stop you from killing these little ones so you may as well make the easy choice and pick the knuckle here."

The priest puffed out his chest and spread his arms. "If I don't slit these children's throats in honor of Frey then may the gods strike me down right here and now!"

It was then the knuckle came out of nowhere and struck him square in the face.

Aebbe was hit by the most terrible flashback to her mother's death: the priest was convulsing and twitching in the same way, he smelt of shit and piss as he voided his bowels.

Aebbe wasn't going to wait to see the priest's skull when the knuckle was full and neither were the children she ran to them and wrapped her arms around their faces clutching her eyes shut as the priest fell to the floor.

"HE'S BACK!" gurgled Wiglac in that awful voice.

"How did it get out of the chest?" Aebbe wailed.

"It didn't, it's right here!" yelled Milian he shoved his dagger into the knuckles mouth before it could escape and looked around for the one that had killed the priest. Then what he feared was going to happen happened.

~

A second knuckle came flying and landed in the middle of a picnicking couple. Within seconds a quick-thinking man was trying to pull it off the young woman's neck but it was too late the fangs had dug in deep enough that it tore her throat open when he finally got it off. The knuckle then slashed at the man's wrist with its fangs nearly taking the hand off with one bite before succeeding with the second.

A third landed on the stage it scampered towards the prisoner being pushed towards the now lit fire and sank into the heel of one of the guards.

By now, screams were being heard from every direction it was complete chaos. Milian made sure his weapons were within reach and h Aebbe and the children were covered.

He grabbed his bow and quiver. There were about twenty arrows: he didn't need them for the knuckles, steel and iron killed them. He should conserve his arrows for The Nix. Bastard had at least one friend with him, maybe more.

But with the knuckles being flung and protecting the trio keeping him in one place, he saw little choice but to fire. He drew his bow halfway, aimed, and with full draw sent the arrow flying into the twilight sky, where it looped and tore through a knuckle that had been launched from somewhere.

"Are there cells under the seats?" he shouted but Aebbe's look meant she didn't know.

The struck knuckle meanwhile was making a sound like two rocks being scrapped together but so loud the whole amphitheater could hear as it burst into flames on its descent to the ground.

There must have been six no seven knuckles on the amphitheater grounds causing carnage and butchery everywhere they landed.

Some guards had gotten their act together. The one that landed on the stage was being hacked to death by two guards although not in time to save their comrade's leg which ended at the thigh.

The prisoner who was about to be burnt reached into the fire and retrieved some lit kindling. He waved it with a vacant smile and jumped off the stage to where King Cissa was sitting. The dead king had a knuckle shaped hole in his stomach. The knuckle filling the hole turned up to look at the grinning fool and instead of attacking it gave a ghastly squeal and leaped out of the hole to find other prey.

Far too late for the king but one guard noticed. "Fire! Everyone make a torch!"

~

Two more knuckles were shot down by the arrows. Milian decided The Nix had exhausted his supplies, so it was time to join in with those hacking and burning the ones still causing bloodshed. Then the remaining knuckles all at the same time began to wriggle their way in the same direction at a surprisingly high speed.

"They're going to feed the bastard," Milian realized and broke into a run following them as they reached the seats and vanished into a hole. Then out of the hole emerged a massive bear.

CHAPTER 23

Milian drew an arrow but too many people were in the way. The bear was fast, faster than any bear he'd ever seen. Finally, he got the bear firmly in his sights.

He then cursed and dropped the bow. It had just caught fire! He'd noticed a flame appear out of nowhere on the upper limb and dropped it before it reached the grip.

While he was stamping on the flames the bear was stopped by the warty old bear handler who in the confusion must have mistaken the speedy thing for one of his maimed beasts. The handler swatted at the bear's nose with a club. The bear seemed to smile as it stood 8 feet upright and took the handler's head off with one strike of its paws.

"Fuck!" screamed Milian as the knuckles began to rain down on the amphitheater again. The bear was a distraction for The Nix to feed and now they are being sent back for his second course.

~

Aebbe quickly snapped out of her shock and with one of Milian's daggers she moved among the chaos making sure the children were holding onto her dress. She made sure to stuff their hands with any sharp rocks she could find.

"You see any of those things or if a grown-up tries to make you go with them, you give them a whack and run!" she screamed in their ears.

They then headed to the gates. Someone must have made it

back to the city walls as more guards surged in, and these were armed with spears, much more effective against the knuckles.

The bear looked up from eating the face of one of the youths that had been watching the bear fight and roared his disapproval. He bounded towards the new guards and swatted two of them aside breaking their necks instantly. The remaining new guards warily made a circle around the bear which growled.

Then something happened that Aebbe had never seen before. The night air sparkled around the bear and when the sparkling stopped where the bear stood was a hawk. The hawk flew into the air and it swooped down to one of the guards ripping an eyeball out with its talons. It flew to safety about thirty feet from the spears. Then with more sparkles, it resumed its bear form roaring as it bounded towards a group of wounded unarmed wedding guests.

"Shifter! It's a shifter!" cried Milian, not sure anyone was listening. He looked at his ruined bow. How had that happened? He drew an arrow from his quiver.

"This is the only thing that will kill it, this and sunlight," he told no one in particular. The sun had only just gone down. It would be hours before they saw it again. Wounding such a beast to incapacitate it was unlikely with the men they have, the beast heals too quickly. It would have to be an arrow.

~

"Free me! Free me and I'll kill it you poxy streak of piss!" Lots of curses were being screamed around the amphitheater some were exhausting Milian's Saxon vocabulary but this one was screaming in Brittonic.

"Saig?" said Milian.

"Free me, give me one of those arrows and I'll stick it up his hairy bunghole!"

Milian nodded, he found one of the heavy iron swords and slashed at the rusty chains. Two hacks had them loose enough for Saig to tear himself free.

"Good luck, Saig," said Milian as he handed him an arrow.

Saig let out a blood-curdling scream and launched into a sprint towards the bear.

"Cut me too!" said the bald prisoner. "I can fight!" This one only had rope restraints after freeing him Milian offered him an axe; axes and daggers lay all over the place but the man ran straight for the wedding feast tables which some clever soul had arranged into a defensive kind of fort and was doing a good job of repealing the knuckles.

"Milksop rabbit," Milian muttered, stepping out into the melee and stabbing at any knuckles he could find.

~

Psyche sat on the stone seats trying to stay out of sight. She was annoyed she couldn't fully enjoy the carnage, but she had fulfilled her orders well kind of.

"Destroy the arrows!" had been screamed into her head all day from Londinium as she slept. She hadn't been able to; she had tried so hard to get them to alight but nothing had worked, even the chants that Alecto had told her were foolproof and could cause anything to alight into an inferno hadn't worked.

Almost anything, she thought. Even worse the arrows seemed to fire something back at her – impossible! But the harder she tried the crashing sensations of pain ripped through her skull and her nose and ears started bleeding.

She screamed when she saw the Briton had Vitium in his sights and managed to set the bow alight just in time. She could still hear the bear roaring so he was still alive for now but what went wrong? She lay on her back panting.

"Are you okay, love? Did you get injured out there? I think it's safe here in the seats, those creepy crawlies don't seem to like climbing."

Psyche looked up at a young woman with kind eyes, reeking of wine and swaying a little. Red dye dabbed around her lips and a couple of faded dyed patches on her tattered dress told Psyche this was one of the whores enticed in by the guards by the prospect of a full belly.

No need to trouble such a woman, indeed from her human memories Psyche remembered whores to be good company with decent humor and...

"Fancy a swig of this, love? Good stuff, the reeve splashed out on Frankish wine. First time I've ever had anything that isn't ale, gone right to my head. G'wan, you need a swig, you look well knackered, ha! Which one of the guards did for you, Mad Mort? I've heard tales about how demanding he is...or was, I don't think he'll be in the business of bothering us anymore, not since the bear crippled him, ha!"

Psyche laughed and took the flagon. "No, if Vit didn't kill him then his family will have to carry him around in a basket, probably better if he gets finished off. Tonight, when I recover and rejoin the fray, I'll look for...wait, what? You think? Me? I am the creation with the most potential in a century my sire said and you think I'm one of you? Argh!"

Still exhausted it strained Psyche to sit up and give a feeble slash to the woman's cheek.

"Bitch! I'll kill you!" the whore spat.

"You'll do no such thing," said Psyche. "You will walk down the stairs to the fighting and find a man with a birthmark on his eye and kill him by whatever means are available to you. Now go!"

The woman's jaw wobbled in fright as she found herself descending the stone stairs.

"Stupid bitch will probably get a knuckle to the throat five seconds in," Psyche muttered to herself. Still, she might get lucky.

Now, she thought, how long was it going to take to recover from these headaches? Usually, her wounds healed in minutes, at most a hacked off limb takes an hour to re-grow, or a knife to the gut takes 30 minutes to seal over. She took a gulp of the flagon and lay down on the seats groaning.

~

Alfwen made sure there were no gaps in the space she'd made with the tables that had collapsed onto the floor when the first knuckle hit face-first into the big wheel of cheese.

They had already seen the destruction from the first three which had the table screaming, a couple of the male guests ran. One towards the knuckle to fight it and one to the gates, but when the knuckle stood up almost looking comical wearing the wheel of cheese like a hat, it was Alfwen who told herself that she could be just as quick thinking in a crisis as her sister.

She pushed the table forwards sending the monster to the ground. Yelling the others to help she knocked over the others and together with Heiu, they pushed four tables around them to act as a barrier.

This wasn't foolproof: the knuckle could have chewed through the table with its fangs or simply leaped over it. But Alfwen's gamble that the creatures were unintelligent, guided only by instinct and sound, paid off.

The only danger in their enclosure appeared to be if a knuckle landed inside or if the bear noticed them. Alfwen clutched a dagger she'd gotten from somewhere as a defense against the former and prayed the latter would be struck down soon.

"Torold!" cried the reeve; his son lost in the mess outside.

"Keep quiet!" Alfwen hissed. As she slashed at a knuckle on the other side that had become curious at the noise, the reeve looked furious and even raised his hand to strike her but then they were interrupted by a bald, smelly man tumbling into the mini fort. It was one of the prisoners.

"You!" said the reeve. To Alfwen's surprise, his eyes were afraid.

~

The bear had plucked the jaw out from a lad of no older than ten when Saig was catching up to it. Saig had done some violent things in his time, but he'd never made people suffer in a prolonged death. Well, not Britons anyway, he couldn't be sure when it came to his scraps with Saxons and Jutes. A kind of red mist descended upon him then, it's because they're ungodly he reasoned.

The same sort of mist was upon him now and before he knew it he found himself on the bear's back, hanging on trying to stab the arrow into the beast's hide. The skin was as tough as leather and he could only get the arrow to make the tiniest of scratches before being thrown off.

He looked up at the stars and was ready to feel the bear's claws tear through his guts and die a martyr. Instead, he heard inhumane howling from the bear. He looked up, the bear was holding its head in its hands. Blood poured from its eyes, mouth, and nose all over the beast's body. Welts appeared to be forming on its skin but then they would disappear and reappear on different parts of the bear's torso and legs.

The bear began shedding fur at a rapid rate. It was almost bald by the time it sank into the form of a human. Saig tried to get up but the force of the throw had broken something, days chained up in his filth had also weakened him, it took him too long to rise.

He yelled, "Finish the bastard!" to any nearby guards, although many were by now having a degree of success in dealing with the knuckles and focusing on evacuating survivors and the wounded. Two gingerly ran up to where Saig was watching the man. "Finish him! He killed your mates didn't he?" Then Saig saw why the men were reluctant to approach.

Ever since the orphaned boy giant had found himself taken in by the monks he'd heard about hell on a daily basis. Stories that had terrified him, and when he'd grown to such a size that Arthur's men demanded he be given to their army that fear had grown as death was just a battle away. Now he was seeing hell first hand. He knew he would die soon but was calmed by the firm sudden epiphany that whatever awaited him, it would not be as bad as what was happening to the former bear.

Blood was still pouring from his mouth, ears, eyes, anything. The man screamed spluttering his teeth onto the floor, his beard and hair falling out in clumps.

The furious-looking bright red welts continued to appear and reappear after fading, almost as if traveling across his body. The air glittered and he tried his trick again and turned into a hawk but instantly the hawk crashed to the ground a featherless runt.

He tried again this time a hound but doubled over in agony whining as its torso shriveled and the welts reappeared. The dog began to smell of burning flesh even though it was nowhere near fire. The pathetic beast then turned into a grass snake, and it suddenly seemed to be detached from its distress it hissed with malice at its audience before disappearing into the grass.

Saig grunted, "Let's finish it off." The two guards didn't respond. "Don't you understand me?" he cried.

They surely didn't but what was distracting them was the six-foot tall scaled man with a frog's head standing at the top of the hole in the seats from where the bear had emerged.

The big, bulging eyes scanned the scene in front of him. The Nix saw the arrow in Saig's hand and Saig launched it exhausted and at a difficult angle, still managed to get it on target. The monster ducked at the last second the arrow missing him by an inch.

The creature looked at the arrow and screamed a cry of revulsion; a shrieking, piercing cry that the entire amphitheater could hear. It turned to look down on Saig and the last thing Saig saw in this life was its tongue hurtling towards him as it attached itself to his neck and ripped out his throat.

CHAPTER 24

The backlog of wagons around the city gates was making the road crowded. People were frustrated and yelling.

"Too early to close them," said Allyn. "What do they expect us to do sleep outside? Five to a cart?"

"Who said anything about you using my cart to sleep in?" said the cart owner who had picked them up in exchange for Allyn's hammer.

"It doesn't matter," said Iga. "Digoth needs herbs for his hands and feet or the burns could turn foul and force us to cut them off."

"No!" yelled Digoth from the cart, but he was getting feverish so she wasn't entirely sure if he were reacting to her or not.

"Cwenhild needs some bones setting as well I think. You're right though," she said pointing her thumb back. "This isn't just them wanting peasants out of the city at night, seen carts with merchants and even warriors, must've been out inspecting their farms for the day. They'd want them in through the gates! What's happened for the city to go into lockdown?"

"We can check the amphitheater," said Allyn. "Wedding should still be going on." They had to leave the cart which was stuck in gridlock with the two unwounded helping Digoth and Cwenhild navigate the path around the river and stagger across the fields to the amphitheater.

~

What they found in the field just outside the entrance was a scene bloodier than any battlefield story they had heard.

Propped up against the outer walls of the amphitheater were scores of dead, dying, and wounded some wore the light mail of the guards, others the dyed tunics and dresses of merchants and tradesfolk, others the rags of serving slaves.

Some people were still being dragged out. Screams and shouts came from every direction. One of the priests who, from the blood-stained apron, Iga took to be the city leech or medicine man was directing underlings in every direction he was clearly overwhelmed.

Iga again was quick thinking and ran towards the man. "My friends need help, the man has serious burns and the woman broken bones."

"Are you blind? You flea ridden sack of shit! We have half the city in need of help! I've never seen your friends before," the man screamed spraying spittle in Iga's face.

"I'm a medicine woman," lied Iga. "While of course I don't have your knowledge, sir, I was in charge of tending to the sick and infirm in my slave hut," she said truthfully. "Most of the people I treated made full recoveries," she lied. "Please give me access to your herbs and tools and I'll stay and help with the rest of the wounded."

The leech wasn't happy but she could tell when a man was desperate. "Go!" he shouted. "The herbs are in that cart over there. Spend ten minutes tending to whatever ails them, and I want you over at the wall with the wounded drain the blood of any still conscious, and apply horse dung to their wounds."

At the cart, Iga dug around the baskets each marked with runes in charcoal. "Can any of you read?" she asked to silence. "Never mind, got it, rose petals, thyme, lard…shit, bear's urine works best for burns, there's never a bear around when you need one. Well, I guess human urine will have to do, can anyone help me with that? What? Do I have to do everything around here?"

~

After mixing the potion and rubbing it on Digoth's feet and hands the air was filled with new screams as Iga tried her bone-setting skills on Cwenhild.

Iga propped them both against the cart to rest while she prepared to begin her bloodletting duties. "Keep an eye on them," she told Allyn.

"No!" Digoth gasped still suffering from the fever. "Allyn, my sisters…" Outstretching his hand, his voice wavered. "Help them please."

"Look," Iga whispered to Allyn. "We know what has caused this, the same evil that destroyed the village, the girls may well be in…" She jerked her thumb to the stack of bodies some breathing, some not pushed against the wall.

Allyn thought about it for a second before unfastening Digoth's weapon belt, putting it on and running towards the entrance, only pausing at the gates when an outraged shriek pierced his and the ears of all for miles.

~

The Nix chewed on Saig's gullet and shuddered as he looked back at the arrow and how close it had come to landing between his eyes. He saw what just a tiny scratch of it had done to Vitium and figured the shifter wouldn't be of any more use tonight. He needed those arrows burnt! All of them!

But how when he can't even touch them? Psyche had been given that job but the arrows still exist! What the hell was she doing?

The two guards who had been next to the giant man were now running up the stairs. The Nix expelled his tongue in two short bursts towards the guards. The first time, it came back with a piece of skull with a nice bit of mushy brain in it, the second time an eyeball with a spot of the brainy goo that went behind it. Both figures that had been approaching him slumped to the floor.

Tasty treats! he thought, but the tongue was for killing: it didn't deliver nearly as much bloody goodness as the knuckles with their full bellies, but the knuckles were all dead or dying. They'd created a bit of carnage and their bodies full of axes and daggers were also full of flesh and blood, but The Nix would have to wait to drink them dry.

For now, his job was to mop up any survivors and take his prize. He spotted what he wanted and with a giant leap began to hop towards his target.

~

"You planted those jewels on me!" yelled the bald former prisoner at the reeve. "I knew you were siphoning off King Cissa's Fiscburna collection and adding it to your own. Since the king's mind has gone it was my job to take care of him. You turned him against me you eel skin full of shit!"

"Ator! Please it's all a big misunderstanding."

"They were going to cut my arms and legs off and leave me for the rats!" The prisoner tried to wrestle the dagger away from Alfwen making his fingers all bloody in the process.

Alfwen struggled back as the reeve cowered in the corner Heiu tried to help by whacking the man over the head with the arrow she had.

"Stop it! Stop it!" cried Alfwen. "Don't you hear? The fighting is dying down I think we might be okay. I don't hear the bear anymore."

Then came the shriek that made everyone pause. The four members of the table-fort peered over the tables as they saw a monster unlike anything in the stories leap from the seats to the amphitheater grounds and begin to hop at a fearsome speed. "It's coming in our direction!" screamed Hieu.

~

"Now or never," said Milian, he had lost some of his arrows in the fighting but a fair few still rattled around his quiver.

He saw at a distance what had happened to the bear and knew that Saig had managed to hit a blow. "Good job man, good job. May your foot washing god reward you well."

The guards were finding their spear work and the shield wall was reaping rewards when dealing with knuckles.

"Took you dumb foreign bastards long enough to work it out," he grunted, while bending down to slide his pugio through a lone knuckle trying to make his way back.

"Time to die, Nixy," he said. Then he grunted. His stomach felt warm and damp as blood rushed to the exit of the hole that had just appeared.

He went to his knees and panted: breathing had become difficult, everything had become difficult.

He turned around and saw a young woman with a red mouth standing over him with her dagger. She went in for another jab and pierced the other side of his stomach. She looked distraught.

"I'm sorry the witch with the bog accent made me. I can't stop!" she clenched her eyes and raised the dagger as high as she could when a solid thud sounded.

Half the woman's face was covered with blood pouring from

her hairline. Winfred and Wiglac threw rocks at her head, forcing her to her knees. Aebbe gave a second whack with the iron sword to the back of the skull and the red-mouthed woman was down and out.

"We need to get you to the leech," she said. Helping him up and then screamed as she saw the monster hop in bounds towards her sister's location.

CHAPTER 25

"Aebbe! There you are!" Allyn shouted and ran over to her. "Your brother is outside, he's hurt but…" He saw Milian was hurt too.

"What happened?" He turned his gaze towards the monster who had stopped about twenty feet from the improvised fort and had his eyes on something.

"What in Hel's name is that…?" Allyn gasped.

"The arrows…only thing that kills it…did enough to the bear… no bow…no bow…burned," Milian got out.

Allyn took an arrow out of the quiver. He was about to charge the monster when a man, a slave probably, from the rags he was wearing and a former Briton warrior from the tattoos on his chest charged forwards with an axe screaming. Without even looking the beast's tongue hurtled out returned to its owner's mouth with the slave's guts on the end of it.

~

"Who was that?" Alfwen asked.

"Some Briton captured in battle last year or so, we had two of them. They were going to fight to the death with the winner gaining his freedom for the final part of the feast. I think the bear got the other one," said the reeve.

"Always playing gods with the lives of others," spat Ator.

"Shut up! Why has it stopped?" said Hieu.

The Nix had stopped because for the first time since the assault he was receiving instructions from Londinium.

"Quite the mess you've made there Nixy! Right now I think most of your work here is done. If you can get the Brit bastard on the way out that's a bonus mate, but from my viewpoint, he's done for. Psyche assures me everyone who was in the village is dead. What you want is in that little nest over there. I got a buzz from it and there's something I want as well. The big chest is full of treats and its new owner won't have need for it in the lochs with you. There's just one problem."

The Nix squatted, his long legs pushing his knees over his head.

"It's those fucking arrows. We heard the hunt had a new weapon they wiped out Eard's crew out near Salinae way but we never got the details, none of Eard's crew lived. But we know now. Do not let it pierce the skin – you saw what happened to Vit. I've got Alecto working on it, but I don't know how to reverse it yet. A direct hit, and its bye bye Nixy. Psyche claims they won't burn despite her efforts. For now, avoid them and get a sample in that chest if you can. Anyway, approach the chest and the girl with caution one of the humans has an arrow, not sure which one. I've told Psyche and she's sending in one of hers to clear the scene best wait until it's cleaned up before going in."

That's why The Nix didn't react when a young boy with scratch marks on his face walked towards the table fort. He did use his tongue to rip the leg off a woman who ran out trying to pull the boy away. The boy showed no reaction as he climbed into the table fort. The Nix munched on the leg and waited.

~

"Torold, thank Woden you are safe my boy come here and…"

Torold was faster than any child that age should be as he fished the dagger out of his leggings and slashed his father's throat the instant he was released from the hug. Just as quickly an axe came out of the other side of his belt and buried itself into Ator's forehead.

Torold's trademark sneer curled up more than ever when his brown eyes flashed yellow and he began to speak in a creepy woman's voice.

"Put that fucking arrow in the chest you pointy nosed bitch."

Hieu stopped screaming and whimpered as she surrendered the arrow although Alfwen noticed that Torold's eyes looked manic at the sight of the arrow and he backed away.

Too far away for her to use the dagger on, Alfwen was torn at stabbing a child no matter how deranged and dangerous but when the arrow was locked in the chest. His confidence grew, as did Alfwen's. She moved into position when he corned a sobbing Hieu.

"Torold, please…" his sister sobbed. As he raised the axe, Alfwen slid forward on her belly and slipped the dagger between Torold's ribs. He screamed and knocked Hieu out with the flat of the axe as he sank to one knee.

He turned his head. "You bitch!" the woman's voice from the boy's mouth hissed. "I'll have you for that someday." The voice then called out in a language Alfwen had never heard before.

"Nix! Sagitta tegitur! Abeamus!" Torold then buried the axe into his own skull.

Everyone in the amphitheater looked on in horror as the frog-man made one giant leap into the enclosed space and peered down at Alfwen.

Aebbe screamed as he opened his mouth showing curved fangs, more teeth than she'd ever seen in a beast. Green sludge and slime poured from the monster's face onto the face of a hyperventilating Alfwen, the monster croaked in a low voice that none of the onlookers could hear. A sobbing, shaking Alfwen tried to resist but her body wouldn't respond to her brain's instructions. She got up and climbed onto the beast's back.

The beast picked up the chest and with three leaps the giant frog was back in the stone seats with a final push, he leaped out of the amphitheater and disappeared into the night.

CHAPTER 26

Iga was exhausted. She could only spend a few minutes on each patient pushing horse dung onto the wounds and randomly mixing up combinations of herbs to mix with the dung.

There was a bucket of leeches to bloodlet feverish and conscious patients and a saw to remove mangled limbs. More often than not, Iga got called away for duties with the saw. She was less squeamish about it than the others who were assisting the leech.

She noticed the screaming had stopped. A small trickle of survivors were now leaving through the gates. A few were sobbing but on the whole, most were stunned silent, their hands clasped onto their chests, grabbing onto each other, their faces drained white, their eyes wide but also sunken. It seemed as if everyone had aged 20 years in one night.

A guard started yelling. "Open the city gates! The beast is gone!" She heard her name called.

Aebbe and Allyn ran towards her. They were supporting an unconscious Milian. "You must fix him!" Aebbe said with tears in her eyes. "Him or his people, maybe they can get her back."

Iga nodded not knowing what to say to that. "Your brother is safe but wounded; over there."

Aebbe thanked her and ran off.

~

Aebbe found Digoth. He had managed to climb onto the herb cart with Cwenhild and they lay looking at the stars together. The leech passed by occasionally yelling at them to get off but he was distracted by his duties and eventually gave up.

Aebbe could tell they were holding hands under the rug. She took her brother's other hand and said, "Digoth…I have some terrible news…"

He cut her off.

"Father is dead, Aebbe. I'm so sorry I couldn't save him. One of the guards became cursed and…where is Alfwen?"

~

"Can you help Milian?" Allyn was furrowing his brow.

"See that woman over there?" Iga pointed her thumb. "Spent just five minutes rubbing my potions into her belly. She's already woken up, even moving a bit."

"And her head wound?"

"Potions didn't work on that, head must be weak, so she's simple now still alive though, besides she's the fishmonger's wife how much brain does she need?"

"And you treated all the people between her and here," he said gesturing to a row of corpses.

"Weak in body and mind," she said. "Now go to the herb cart and get me some pigeon's blood, lard, ale, and dormouse droppings. The Briton is going to need the lot!"

~

Finally! The Nix thought, he had chosen to put a bit of space between him and the city so he had bypassed a few rivers and streams, but now he was sure he couldn't be caught. It was nothing but forest he croaked triumphantly as he found a knee-deep stream to dampen his skin in.

He threw Alfwen off. She landed on her arse and started to get up at once. "Stay there," said The Nix. As soon as Alfwen tried to run off, she found herself unable to, it was as if her feet were rooted to the ground.

"Someone please help me!" she cried.

"Shut up too!" The Nix commanded, and Alfwen's jaw was clamped shut. *Should have done that hours ago,* thought The Nix as he bathed. Her screaming was fun at first but it didn't half get boring quick.

Alfwen was trying her hardest to scream but only muffled sounds could come out. She abruptly stopped when the air behind her chilled and the smell of burned charcoal began to linger.

"Hello, bitch," Psyche said from behind her.

"Look here's the thing, I had left the child by the time he caved his skull in as ordered, so didn't feel a thing but I was in full control when you slid that knife into him and it stung! I'm not allowed to kill you but this journey isn't going to be fun for you, honey-haired bitch!"

Alfwen's tears started to flow as Psyche clamped her fangs onto her shoulder and sucked in the blood.

"Enough!" shouted The Nix, who was now damp enough and getting out of the stream. "You will not touch my wife! Don't forget who is senior here and you failed to alight the arrows you deserve no blood from mine!"

Alfwen's eyes were wide making her spill more tears: *wife?*

"This blood won't last forever! Once Spurius creates her she will be full of the same green goo that runs through your veins.

I'm just taking a little from her" Psyche said.

"I said enough!" In temper, The Nix crashed his fist onto a nearby rock turning a frog that was sitting there into a squishy mess.

"You always do that to frogs, I've noticed," said Psyche. "Why is that? I would have thought you would keep them as pets or something. A little collection of mini Nixes," she laughed.

"Shut up!" said The Nix. "We have an hour until sunrise we need to find caves big enough for the three of us to spend the day in."

"Okay, let's get moving. You too, Lady Nix." She gave Alfwen a slap on the arse and laughed.

Then Psyche noticed something. "Nix, look! The frog!" The squishy piece of goo was moving, more than that, it was regenerating. It shook a leg and the cracked bones healed, its flesh bubbled for a bit and then its torso was back to its original shape, its ruined skull appeared to expand until its head could move. Within five minutes it had completely recovered from being crushed to death. Psyche knelt to move her head next to the frog "Vitium? Is that you?"

~

As the sun came up over Chichester, the dead were still being counted as more succumbed to their wounds. The meeting the leech held in the great hall was very sparsely attended with those only of Churl rank and upwards who rented lands being allowed to attend. The king, the reeve, many merchants, and warriors all dead.

The slaves and peasants, aside from a handful that were unlucky enough to be selected for preparing and serving the feast had been largely banned from the affair. Iga wondered how the land was to be farmed or the stores run with owners dead or maimed. The food situation could become grim quickly.

Iga stood behind the leech her hands red up to the elbows her dress and apron drenched in blood. The medicine man had good leadership skills at least, two priests had died in the amphitheater, leaving him as the most senior man currently in the city. He stood tall and lean with only two tufts of grey hair sticking out from behind his ears.

"The current tally is seventy-two dead, eighteen missing, and fifteen crippled," he announced to murmurs of shock and disbelief from the crowd.

Having seen the monsters worm-dog pets at close quarters, Iga could well believe that ten or so thrown into a crowded enclosed space did such numbers.

"I will be running the city's affairs until the Atheling hears the news and comes for his coronation. I propose that we begin by dividing the land of the deceased fairly so we can pull in what is left of the harvest," the leech continued.

"And forget about Hel's monsters that did this to us?" cried a voice from the back.

"We shall send hunting packs into the forest to track down whatever feral beasts assailed us." The leech said, murmurs of disquiet grew.

"The bodies of the creatures that did most of the damage burned up in the sun we can't explain that to anyone that wasn't here, the bear can be explained but not the damage he did and we would all be executed for allowing it to happen; a frog monster controlling worms the size of a hound and talk of some strange woman spellbinding people with offering no proof," he explained in a drained tone.

"Hundreds of witnesses!" someone countered.

"Maybe the West Saxons have learnt to train wolves to attack and disguised them, their leader could have worn some frogskin armor," offered the leech, adding, "There are certain herbs that can play tricks with the eyes and mind." this was at least greeted with murmurs of approval.

They had an enemy now to blame. Digoth was still unable to stand but roared "STOP!"

Massaging his temples he said "A West Saxon army in disguise does not explain the bodies burning up, the way the monster was able to leap over the amphitheater walls, what he wants with my sister! It's clear we are dealing with something far beyond our comprehension, something the gods have kept from us until now!"

"Do not talk to me about gods boy!" yelled the leech. "Do not forget I am the head priest as well as healer!"

Iga was beginning to see that Digoth's urgings had already been forgotten. When the Atheling arrives the entire city will be singing the same song.

The leech continued. "Bowden!" he shouted to the town smith, a burly man who had killed a knuckle but lost a son in the fighting. "I nominate you as our new reeve." When a stern expression from the man turned into a thoughtful nod, Iga knew the argument was lost.

"They can't just pretend nothing happened!" a furious Aebbe clenched her fists tightly around the children's hands making Winfred yelp and Wiglac scowl.

"People see what they want to see," said Iga. "How long do you think the monster's been at it? He's surely left survivors before and within the week they're telling themselves that it was a trick of the light or a bandits costume designed to frighten."

"How about the Britons? You claimed they know of this

island's terrors?" asked Cwenhild.

"Our Briton does, can't speak for all of them, the slave at the feast and the giant prisoner seemed surprised enough. Clearly, they have their secrets and our Briton has access to them or some of them. Problem is, it's unlikely he'll ever wake up," Iga said.

CHAPTER 27

They walked into the reeve's house where they'd stored Milian and were planning on using it to sleep and rest in, after that they had little idea what the future would entail. None were in a hurry to return to the village, Bowden was probably taking possession of the house once selected.

A stench greeted them upon opening the door. "His wounds have gone bad," said Allyn who had stayed behind to watch. "No wine to pour on them so I used ale."

"Waste of ale," grumbled Iga, and the group sat around in sullen silence drifting off to sleep one by one.

They all dreamt that night.

~

Milian dreamed he was walking down a cobbled street. The shape of the houses was different from the Saxon city he was in and the people wore longer and more colorful tunics and looked healthier. A column of soldiers wearing hooped metal around their body, at their head a commander wearing a helmet with a crest of red hair. The scene changed. Milian was on the same street but it was now made of mud with the buildings now crudely made of stone and the people dirtier and more gaunt. Both men and women wore long black tunics with the women having some form of white coif on their heads. Then someone noticed him; it was a tonsured monk, he'd never seen one in a city before. The monk's dome was splashed with the same purple color that was around Milian's eye.

"We are building this city anew," the monk said, "make this happen." Then he melted away and Milian found himself on the same street, but the buildings looked more like the first scene.

Two stories and made of bricks but crumbling. It was light but also dark, and the floor felt cold. He heard the sound of a snake hissing and two yellow eyes appeared. The snake seemed to know he was here and hissed furiously as the coldness grew.

~

Iga dreamed of living in a wooden room, a room that she just knew was far away, it smelled of sweat and cooked meat and terror leaped into her heart when she saw the door begin to open. Next, she dreamed of being on a ship and she felt at peace despite the ship being in a storm. Soon the storm got stronger and she peered over the edge and frowned. Something dark was in the water. It moved under the ship and the ship began to shake.

~

Aebbe dreamed of a stone building full of men wearing mail praying, but not to the gods: to someone different.

~

Allyn dreamed of a hag with a snake around her neck when the hag pulled back her hood half her face was a melted ruin.

~

Cwenhild dreamed of bearded men in row boats sailing through a marsh, and she could sense someone watching from a hidden island.

~

Winfred dreamed of a stone building, taller than she'd ever seen, with enough space for forty people to live in.

~

Wiglac dreamed of The Nix, Alfwen, and Psyche.

~

In the back of the cave, The Nix had had his two hours of rest that was all he needed, he shook his head at Psyche who was standing upright as she slept. Could she do that when she was a human? The Nix wondered, if it were a skill Spurius had bestowed on her then seemed pretty pointless. He shrugged, made his way to Alfwen who had passed out from exhaustion. His tongue slithered out slowly and licked her cheek softly.

The Nix thought about the cold man's promise to him. There were other Nixes but they were all pretty useless, no intelligence and nothing between their legs. Whether they had been male or female in their human lives, it didn't matter. Useless mouths fortunately they only had to pull down one fisherman or drunken straggler on the shores of the loch every few months to fill their bellies but their stunted vocabulary and lack of sexual organs meant they were poor company for a lonely Nix.

"After what happened at Housesteads..." Spurius had explained back in Londinium. *"Lilith took me north into the Pict forests for a time. Taught me how to hunt, how to talk to the wolves, and soon I was ready to make my first creation...well it were a mess, the first wolf-man hybrid I made walked straight into the sun on his second day! Can you believe it? Eternal life and he lasts two fucking days! Eventually, I grew stronger and made the red caps..."*

"Good lads," The Nix had said.

"...and The Nuckelavee."

"Fucking poser!"

"Before Lilith told me my powers had increased and it was time to leave the Picts land and cross the wall, but I remember when I was making the first failed hybrids. I counted the Nixes as a partial success as they would rather dive to the bottom of the loch when confused rather than walk into the sunlight. Always had a soft spot for the village of Picts I turned into Nixes so when I returned north of the wall all those years later and you came sailing into my cave the thought of making an intelligent Nix was too much to resist."

The Nix was quiet for a time after that.

"I understand these thoughts of yours have been growing and growing," Spurius had said. *"Do this task for me, and I will turn the human of your choosing into a Nix to keep you company in the lochs for centuries to come."*

~

Iga was woken sometime that evening by a young bloody girl with a pointy nose and bandaged head.

"Who are you?" she murmured.

"This is my house! Who are you?" was the reply.

Eventually, Iga got up listened to Hieu's sad story, made her some porridge, and gave her some ale which put her to sleep. Iga still exhausted returned to her dream of crashing waves and darkness in the water. It was preferable to being in that wooden room.

It would be in the early hours of the next morning that most of the group were awake again.

"We should leave soon," said Iga.

"And go where?" Aebbe asked, she had no answer for that.

"When the Atheling becomes king he will let me stay right?"

said Hieu.

"Might be up to Bowden," said Digoth.

"Then I'd like to come with you," said the girl. "You are going to find Alfwen and that evil woman who made my brother kill my father, aren't you?"

There was silence to that and then from the stinking pile of straw that Milian was laying on they heard him croak. "Londinium."

~

"It's long been rumored to be their base," Milian explained, panting between each word.

"A Roman city on the Tamesas, a big river, it starts in the Frisian sea. Spurius that's kind of their king used to move around the island setting up little groups of them, Nixes in Caledonia to the far north, Sirens in Dumnonia in the far west. The city dwindled in size after the Romans left. It was easy pickings for Spurius to make it his throne when he rested between travels. They'll be in Londinium, Alfwen too if she's still alive."

"How far is it from here?" asked Digoth.

"Two to three days on foot."

"Would they keep her alive long enough for us to get there?"

"Perhaps, must be a reason The Nix didn't kill her on the spot, like he had the brainwormed lad do to the others."

Milian looked up, Aebbe and Digoth had exchanged eye contact and he knew the decision was made, Allyn would go along with whatever Digoth wanted and Cwenhild too. The two village children would go with Aebbe and the girl who claimed to live here seemed to be eager too.

He turned to Iga. "It would be suicide, just three of them slaughtered nearly a hundred people; how many more are behind Londinium's walls?" But even Iga felt determined.

Milian was surprised Iga had always seemed the smartest of the group plus he could tell that she and Alfwen didn't care much for each other, but she said, "We go and fight, this time I'm going to fight back."

"What do you mean this time?"Aebbe asked to silence as Iga shrugged.

Milian felt himself recovering at speeds that shouldn't be possible, and he wondered about the cause of this. Could Avalon be sending some sort of spell from afar? He'd never heard of such a thing, but now he saw to himself as he got up clutching the blankets around him to stop him from shivering, that his next task was keeping this amateurish group of Saxons alive.

"The boy is not to come. Until The Nix is dead he can use his eyes to spy on us. I propose Cwenhild, Allyn, and the children go to the West Saxons and try to treat with this King Cynric. Ask around the market stalls and ale shacks there will be some who aren't happy with the priest's cover up but be discrete. Cynric will be interested once you tell him the South Saxons are trying to blame him for the slaughter. If this Atheling blames Cynric for the death of his father it could mean war. Tell him to treat with the Dorset Britons; he'll have fought them in the past and mention to them that Milian of Avalon, one of the representatives of Merlin's seat on The Lost Hunt requests that this Saxon delegation be given passage and escort onto Avalon."

He took a deep breath. "Those of us that survive the journey to Londinium will join you once we are done."

"As for us…" He reached for his quiver. "Shit, not nearly enough left, we should cover the amphitheater before we leave. I fear we will need every one and I think...what's that chest?" He pointed to a small wooden box in the corner.

"The handgeld, don't you remember? The reeves gift to father," Aebbe said, comforting Hieu who bit her lip and held back tears at the first mention of her father.

"If I finally find luck in here then I might start giving Saig's foot washing god a prayer or two."

He put his hands together in a mock prayer when upon opening it he found three pugios, from the sharpness of the blade he reckoned they had never been used and the carvings in the golden hilts showed these blades had been designed for decorative purposes.

He gave one with a bow and arrow carved onto the hilt to Aebbe, one with a blacksmith's hammer carved onto the hilt to Digoth, and one with a three-pronged spear carved onto the hilt to Iga. For himself, it was the heavy looking two-edged iron sword with a cross on the hilt.

"What weapon do I get?" said Hieu, surprising everyone who was engrossed and fascinated with the craftsmanship of the swordwork, the quality far superior to anything any of them Saxon or Briton had ever seen before.

"You're going west with the other children," Aebbe told her.

"They killed my family!"

"They killed many people's families, mine and the other two's." Aebbe stuck her thumb at Winfred and Wiglac. "And we're going to rescue Alfwen not get revenge besides the reeve's daughter is an important witness to show King Cynric."

Hieu opened her mouth in a shocked gesture, not used to being told 'No'.

Milian spent the day in the reeve's house resting and taking various parts of the reeve's furniture apart until he decided he had sufficient parts to begin carving a new bow. Cwenhild and Allyn started asking questions around town in a bid to find any sympathizers, and the remaining five headed to the amphitheater to go arrow hunting.

~

The amphitheater had some slaves pouring water on the gritty floor to try to wash away the bloodstains. Some others under the supervision of a carpenter were dismantling the execution stage.

The fire that was meant to burn one of the prisoners had gotten out of hand in the chaos and bits of charred wood stuck out of the ground like rotten teeth.

The table and chairs from the feast were arranged in a circle and slaves were digging a large pit, "cremation," one said when asked, "King Cissa and a few others might get a burial somewhere outside the city but it was such a mess when we started the clean up it was too difficult to tell where someone begins and another one ends. Can't tell if this foot or arm comes from the head merchant or the latrine digger slave."

They found seven arrows after a whole day of searching. Hieu found an eighth but frowning decided to bury it between two loose stones. It would be easy to find later.

The stones were next to the pool of bear blood, or human blood, or hawks blood, or dogs blood it had come out of the monster in all of his forms and it wouldn't wash away. Even when the sand and stone were replaced it, it reappeared within a few minutes.

~

"I think I've got what you asked for." Now back in Londinium,

Psyche had spent most of her time with Alecto in the old Roman temple; a place she was seldom bothered. Most of the city's inhabitants claimed the place made them feel restless and unwelcome.

Psyche could kind of see where they were coming from, the place chilled her but it was where Alecto was often found. Vitium now in an adder form slithered on the stone floor.

"He can return to human form anytime he wants! Whatever the weapon he got stung with was it didn't take away or reduce his powers. I've tried but the examination spells show both the body of a healthy snake or frog or whatever he's deciding to be at any given moment and the mind of Vitium contained inside." Alecto said.

"Can't some of the others speak in snake?"

"Yes, but I don't trust them, best to get it straight from the snake's mouth." She took the chalice off Psyche. "How many did you get?"

"Six snake brains, best I could get, mixed them in with some pieces of shell from a snake egg I found."

"They're pretty tiny. Well six should give me ten minutes or so of being able to talk to him."

She then picked up a dagger and stuck out her tongue; it was as green as her skin. She made a deft motion with the blade and a gash appeared on the tip of her tongue, splitting it in two, giving it the impression of being forked. Blood dripped from it into the chalice. As soon as the chalice was half full she downed it in one.

Alecto then began to hiss and Vitium hissed back. Psyche was surprised to detect different tones to the hissing sounds when the two conversed some were short spurts of high pitched hissing others more like an angry long groan.

Alecto gave a long hiss and the fork in her tongue healed up.

"Well?" said Psyche, "When is he turning back into a human?"

Alecto said, "The arrow poisoned his blood, set it on fire. Basically, when he's human or any other animal with warm blood the blood boils like a cauldron on a fire. It causes unbearable pain and would destroy the body, so he had the quick thinking to turn himself into a snake but he's stuck as cold blooded animals, turning into a man or mouse would be like us walking into the sunlight only a million times more painful."

"How do we cure him?"

"I don't know, I think it's permanent."

"He's stuck as a snake forever!"

The temple grew cold and the sun was blotted out as they heard hoof steps clop, clop up the temple stairs.

"Not necessarily a snake forever are you, Vitium?" Spurius said with a sad smile. The snake was cringing in a corner.

"Any creature with cold blood is doable and there are thousands of them, sadly if your only reference is this island then just weak venom snakes and useless lizards. Not far from the land I was born in there is a great river which runs for miles, longer than anything in Europe it has living in it these wonderful beasts! Lizards the size of wolves only with much more teeth and longer jaws and a bite so strong it can cut through steel! One of those would be very useful to me, do you think you could become one without having seen one."

Psyche had never seen a snake concentrate before but that's certainly what Vitium was doing his snake's head shaking with intensity.

"Doesn't look like it's going to happen," said Spurius, grabbing the snake by its tail and shaking it. "Don't worry. A cure will probably pop up in a few centuries. In the meantime, my bath can always do with another leech to help me balance my humors."

He turned and left, Vitium in his hand hissing furiously.

"Don't let me down, ladies," he called as he clopped down the temple steps. "There are worse things than ending up as a leech. Can't think of any off the top of my head but I have a big imagination."

CHAPTER 28

The two groups ended up leaving through the city gates at different times.

One group just before they closed that night comprised of Milian, Aebbe, Iga, and Digoth, and the next morning the second group of Cwenhild, Allyn, Winfred, Wiglac, and five other witnesses to the amphitheater butchery departed.

The latter group used the bustle of the morning city gate traffic to leave in pairs to avoid suspicion. They would gather in a large group for protection a few hours outside the city. The first group, all adults largely unknown to the city watch, were dismissed as farmers or peasants getting back to their huts a little late.

~

Alfwen's wedding dress was now tattered rags that barely covered her modesty. The man in the cage to her left didn't notice, at least his eyes stared vacantly at a wall, his hair had been burned off and his scalp was a melted, charred mess. His brain had quite clearly been irreparably damaged.

The man in the cage to her right was in slightly better shape; a mess of hair tangling over his head making it impossible to know where his beard ended and his hair began. Now and then he mumbled something in Saxon so Alfwen strained to hear.

She even asked him, "How long have you been here? Have you tried to escape? How many of them are there? What did they do to you? What language are they speaking?"

She didn't get much useful information. The hairy man just moaned about a shade, an army of shades, horses that could fly, and other stuff that made no sense. Alfwen realized with a shudder that in a few weeks or even days, her own mind would snap and she'd end up some hairy hag of a woman muttering to herself about talking frogs and yellow eyed bitches. She cringed as if feeling something crawl down her back: someone was coming down the stairs, one of them.

~

The Nix was at the bottom of The Tamesas trapping fish with his mouth and spitting them onto the banks. He reckoned he'd need the guts from around 50 to make a decent-sized knuckle this time and was hoping that a chat with Alecto would speed up the process.

He wanted an extra big one to give to Alfwen as a present as soon as she was turned into a Nix. Then the two of them would swim down The Tamesas for a nice old feast. This time he thought he'd take Vit's old advice and swim east, see what these Angles bogmen tasted like.

Poor old Vit! he thought with a chuckle. The Nix was cold blooded too and had no doubt that the arrow would make his blood boil, he'd got enough from touching it to know that was the case. Vit must just have gotten lucky that he got stung as the hot blooded bear so he could cool himself down by changing.

Lucky or not! Thought The Nix in gurgled chuckles then he got the command rattling around his head as soon as he hit the shore. Sometimes Spurius' words couldn't get through when he was underwater so bouncing around rapidly once he resurfaced, as if to childe him for missing them the first time round. Well, the message was clear; an important meeting in the bath house.

~

After covering some good ground on the first night and with the weather good, they decided to sleep in a clearing during the day with each taking shifts for the watch.

As Milian settled down to sleep he warned Aebbe who was keeping first watch. "We're being followed. A young lad, he won't bother us I reckon as he's keeping far enough back might have to tackle him. If he's still tracking us when we think it's safe to leave the forest and join the Roman road then I'll tackle the little bastard. When I last scouted ahead I tracked back and got a look, kind of familiar but certainly not Wiglac which I feared, the beast still has control over his eyes."

~

The Nix had reminded himself to take a look through those eyes before the meeting in case. He was surprised to pick up the boy so soon, it meant he survived the amphitheater battle unscathed. Injuries would make it harder to see through his eyes, and of course nothing would happen if he had perished.

The boy was walking through a forest staring at his sister's back like usual but there was a long row of them. More company than an orphan boy should have thought The Nix. He was pondering whether to tell this to Spurius. Amphitheater survivors travelling in large numbers; seemed like something he should know.

Then he took a deep sniff and through the boy's nose he smelt the sea -- not the sharp tang of the water that flows into The Tamesas, but a clearer, saltier smell that told him they were to the west walking away from Londinium.

~

"A road? Made of stone?" Iga looked reluctant to step on it.

"Sounds a lot of work when you can just cut down the trees between where you are and where you want to go."

"Extraordinary!" said Digoth "We can travel in rain without having to stop!"

"That's why I let the other group take the ox," said Milian.

"Are you sure it's not dangerous? I mean we have to climb on it?" said Iga.

"It's been elevated with ditches they have these roads all over the island. There's a good foot of gravel on there to prevent collapse it's safer than the mud roads and it goes all the way to Londinium," an exasperated Milian explained.

"Besides, one other advantage is your lot never use these roads, you love your mud tracks too much. Most of you aren't even aware of their existence, so our lot find them a convenient way to navigate the island, and as there aren't many of our lot left in the south we should have a clear run."

"How can people forget about roads?" asked Aebbe.

"We are going to a city that has been forgotten and ignored for about a century, you Saxons are not famed for your curiosity... oh and before we start, come out boy! There's nowhere on the road to hide yourself," Milian yelled in the direction of the forest.

Only Aebbe looked surprised when Hieu, dressed in a boy's tunic and leggings with her hair hacked off in places, stumbled out of the forest.

"You horrible little turd!" screamed Aebbe. "Now we've got to head back and hand you over to the others, we don't have time to…"

"She can come with us," said Milian. "The road should be incident free and it was a wise idea to disguise yourself as a boy, but we leave you when we reach The Tamesas, you do not enter the city."

~

The bath house was crowded with creations. All of Spurius' inner circle were ready to witness the opening of the chest, except for Vitium now living in his new home at the bottom of the bath.

Psyche had been to the dungeon and returned with a Saxon prisoner; the man with the horrific head burns from the melted helmet. Psyche's claw marks on his neck indicated he should be compliant but she sometimes had trouble with her commands.

"Is it a language issue?" Spurius asked. "I can get Alecto to whip up something that will allow him to understand Latin for a few hours."

"No," she said. "He speaks the same tongue as me. It's that parts of his skull are sticking into his brain, it's difficult for my commands to get through but the other one we need for Herla's amusement, and the bitch is Nixy's thrall so I can't touch her."

"Well make do," Spurius telepathically replied.

The Nix entered in time to see Psyche on the verge of a meltdown finally get the dull-witted Saxon on his knees in front of the chest and the whole congregation of creations took a step back. They had felt it. A feeling of repugnance when getting too close to the chest.

For much of the journey, The Nix had made Alfwen carry it, even having in his hands made his skin suddenly dry up which caused him great discomfort. Now the kneeling man was going to touch what none of them could touch.

"Open the chest," said Psyche, the man gave a vacant stare. "Open the chest," she repeated. "Arms out, arms touch wood, arms up." After about three attempts each one accompanied by a Psyche tantrum when the man failed the chest was opened. "Arm out, arr... I mean stick get."

As the kneeling Saxon held the arrow aloft, discontent and moaning began among the crowd, whilst the Saxon if he could still think wouldn't have noticed a thing the creations began to smell charred dust and burnt bones. Usually, these smells brought happiness to them but they all knew it was their flesh that was the dust, their bones that were burnt and blackened.

From one of them, a shade The Nix guessed from the histrionics, a wobbling high pitched howl started to echo around the room.

Spurius laughed. "If you are reduced to mewling mice just by the sight of it think of the touch! How was it Nix?"

"Not too nice," the frog-man croaked. "Worst burns I've ever had, had to sit out most of the fun in Noviomagus Reginorum, still sore today."

"And how long did you touch it?"

"A few seconds at most."

"Can you imagine the torture if one of these pierced your skin! Infected your blood! Alecto! Burn it!"

"Yes, sire." She shuffled towards the arrow, her hands quivering. Psyche, who The Nix remembered had failed to do this at the amphitheater, looked on intently.

Alecto chanted Latin that was far above The Nix's grasp on the language, some other stuff was mixed in too. Alecto would be crying if she had eyes, she was bleeding heavily from the nose and mouth when the tiniest spark set the arrow alight.

The man holding it was startled and dropped it on the stone floor and the flame died out.

Alecto gave a cry of sheer rage and stormed over to the man and kicked his head clean off, it was a strong kick as the head went straight through a hole in the roof and disappeared.

Alecto shrieked when she realized how close to the arrow she was and fainted.

A ghoulish sound came from the back of the room. "I will take my host to Avalon myself and murder all of these cruel, filthy robed men who have made my people forget the gods of their ancestors!" The clopping of horses' hooves came from the entrance and the king or former king made a rare appearance.

"King Herla!" said Spurius. "It's been a while!" The king entered on horseback a foot and a half taller than most of the creations only an ogre reminding at eye level. He was wearing a suit of armor that only exposed his legs and head, his legs despite being skinless showed thick layers of tendon wrapped around unbreakable looking bone, draped over each side of a skeletal war horse, and under his crowned helmet a skull looked at the crowd defiantly.

"Making these abominations was an act of war and if it's war they want, we can oblige turning their island and castle to rubble!"

Much like Spurius, the lack of tongue was making the bulking skeleton communicate telepathically and when two of them were doing it at the same time it didn't half make The Nix's head rattle.

"War?" said Spurius, almost as if it was an amusing sounding foreign word he was hearing for the first time.

"You do remember the arrangement we have with Merlin? They stay far from Londinium as long as we leave their precious castle and island untouched."

The Nix noticed Spurius had a short reddish beard, he'd never noticed it before it was as if it appeared when he began talking to the moaning old bag of bones with a crown.

"Now they have the means to kill us do you expect the Christ loving bastards to keep to their word, we must strike before they do!" And with that, the king turned his horse around and trotted out of the building.

"I will think about what you have said," Spurius communicated for them all to hear.

Then, "Get some kindling around that arrow for Alecto to have another try when she awakes."

It took another couple of hours but finally, the arrow was burning nicely and the atmosphere improved.

It had taken Alecto two more attempts and the creations had taken to making wagers as to how many it would take. The Nix was upset at losing to Heslop he had to bring him an arm back from the next hunt now.

Spurius stepped over a now again unconscious Alecto and looked into the chest.

His eyes lit up, a flicker of flame appeared in them when he realized what he was looking at.

"Roman treasure," he almost purred. "This is good for us...very good for us, if this had fallen into Merlin's hands or even worse, those dirty old monks giving him counsel. Old hands made these, old hands who worshipped forgotten gods, but they would have prayed and made offerings while making them. Men back then had real faith, not like these Saxons who need some trickster or angry brother and sister in the sky to blame whenever their crops fail or their wife is barren!"

He pawed the goat statue looking at it with lust. "Alecto will have a treat turning these into weapons we can take out on the hunt, or use them to defend our home. I daresay Herla may get his wish sooner rather than later!"

He was then rendered speechless by a discovery at the bottom of the chest; a golden cross, one side was decorated with jewels and the other had engravings, a beautifully drawn craving of a long-haired man, naked apart from a loincloth nailed to a wooden cross.

"Crux gemmata...on this island!" he gasped. "Nix, you done all of us an honor, had the monks got their hands on this it could destroy us all." He stood up and clapped his hands. "We needn't wait for the full moon, that's just pomp and decoration, a couple of days to prepare the amphitheater and capture some subjects for the games might be needed, we are running low on Saxons." He gave the headless man a look. "But let's bring the ceremony for your brides siring up to this Saturday."

CHAPTER 29

The quintet sat on the Roman road eating some bread and roasting frogs legs that Milian had caught from the river they were about to cross. He said, "You'll all be pleased to know that we leave the road from now and return to your beloved mud."

Iga gave a visible sigh of relief.

"This road may not be used much anymore but Spurius knows my people use it so will have eyes on it close to Londinium, some dwarf or shifter waiting in the shade. They can use their magic to inform Spurius instantly, and he'll know we are coming. No, we follow this river, Aeman I've heard it called, although I've never followed it, but from the direction it's going it should lead us to an advantageous point in The Tamesas to enter the city unnoticed."

"This isn't the first time you've mentioned Spurius," said Aebbe. "Was he one of the ones at the amphitheater?"

"No, I'd have known if he was. Men feel dread in his presence, a feeling of hopelessness and emptiness overcomes you as soon as you are sharing the same air as him. It means that even against the greatest warrior the battle is half won but it gives others fair warning of his approach. Probably why he holds court in Londinium and sends his pets to soak the land red whenever he's bored."

"But who is he?" asked Digoth.

"Their king for want of a better word. No, their father. He

makes them you see; The Nix, the shifter, the one we didn't see but who turned the whore and Hieu's brother into thralls were all as human as us once. We don't think anyone other than Spurius can create them, other than whoever created him of course."

"Where does he come from? Why is he doing this? What does he want?" Digoth pressed on.

"There are more details back in Avalon. I'll tell you what I can. The Romans didn't get along with the Picts from the far north, and from my brief visits there I can't say I blame them, so they built a wall. It still stands today but back then it was manned we are talking hundreds of years ago when it was just us and The Romans here, happier days I'm told."

"Will you just get on with it! You can be a right windbag sometimes."

"Alright sorry, Iga. I will get to the point there was a slaughter there. Hundreds dead, no explanation, imagine what happened at the amphitheater but on a bigger scale with no survivors, or none they thought. Rome was furious they remanned the fort and even sent a cohort that's like about 500 odd Romans into the Pict forests but none were ever seen again. It was seen as unlikely that the Picts had the numbers, weapons, or leadership but what else? Well, how about an influx of Picts trying to get over the wall several years after making stories that did not sound unlike to what you lot sounded like straight after the amphitheater…then they started popping up in our lands; giants in Bernacca, real ones this time, trolls in Pengwern, warlocks with the heads of pigs in Gwynedd, sirens in Dumnonia and more it was then one of our kings decided to form The Lost Hunt."

"The lost what? That sounds silly!"

"Thank you, Iga, I do wish you had been around to advise my

ancestors in naming their demon hunting organization, I'm sure you'd have come up with something more fearsome."

"Too right I'd have gone with fearless stags," Iga said

"Could we get back to the discussion?" asked Digoth.

Finally, Milian was allowed to continue. "The hunt has a representative from each of the Briton kingdoms. Seven seats for the Britons, two for the Picts, one for the Hibernians, one for the Bretons, one for the church, one for Merlin, and one for the chief king. Constantine since his father fell in battle…"

Milian looked distraught at mentioning this. "Remember five years ago when the sky turned black for a whole year? Happened straight after Arthur fell. I wouldn't be surprised if the filth inside Londinium had something to do with it so Constantine is the chief king now. He's a good lad, he just listens to the monks a bit too much for my liking."

"The monks are the ones who made the arrows?" Iga asked. When Milian nodded, she said, "Well, I'm not bloody surprised he listens to them, if not for them the whole city of Chichester would be dead."

Milian sighed, "Anyway the hunt meets, discusses strategy and sightings of the creations as Spurius' monsters are called. If the situation calls for it then each seat holder has to pledge at least a hundred warriors who are aware of the dark forces of this island and trained to fight them. It's a system not unlike your Fyrd. I am a member of Merlin's warriors."

There was a period of silence after that. Milian finished with, "It has been decided that as you hairy foreign bastards aren't going anywhere there should be Saxon representation on the hunt. It will not be a popular move out west, it's why I sent Allyn and Cwenhild they are for Saxons at least a bit more affable than…y'know." He gestured his hands towards the other four.

~

Allyn and Cwenhild slept contently next to each other in their linen tent. They even pulled their bodies against each other for warmth before pulling apart in an awkwardly friendly arrangement. They both murmured the same annoyed sounds and Cwenhild gave him a soft punch in the head for farting just when a head popped into the tent.

"Winfred?" said Allyn.

"It's the king, he's agreed to meet us!" the girl said.

~

The West Saxon king shunned the old Roman city of Wintanceaster due to its proximity to South Saxon lands and the other main settlements were too close to the Briton borders. Knowledge that a king resided in either would lead to constant attacks, so he stayed on the coast in a well-armed fort.

Going on from what Milian had told them the stone walls were probably constructed by the Romans to have a force on the shore to tackle pirates straight away. Certainly, Cynric's guards were far more disciplined, trained, and equipped than the frankly half-arsed city guard of Chichester. They had intercepted the group a few miles from the fort and had them camp under guard while they sent word of their arrival to the king.

Cynric was a forty-something-year-old man whose long ginger beard was just beginning to turn the same grey color as his hair. He made quite an impressive figure, still strong looking and at least half his teeth remaining.

He wore furs and hides rather than the linen that most Saxons preferred, and was eating beef from a trencher when they approached. He noticed their eyes linger from the hides to the beef that his guards were also sharing sitting at the king's table as if the king was just another man, and to their surprise at least two of the guards were women.

He laughed. "Can always tell when a man comes west for the first time. Yes, we've taken a few Briton traditions like making the women folk do their share of the war duty. Animal skin fares better against the pig fucking weather out here but don't worry, we haven't adopted their more backward ways like… well pig fucking." He burst into laughter at his own joke which the guards had heard several times already and were long past humoring him.

Once he had recovered he told the group, "Tell me what you told my men about beasts in the east, especially Subseaxe's plan to blame me." His face turned sour at that part.

When the group finished their story his face betrayed no emotion. "Relations with the Dorset Britons are not as bad as they once were, we haven't had any raids for a while and even discreetly trade with them." He held up a sleeve of his seal skin shirt as evidence. "But Britons are Britons and I'm expected to risk my men on the say-so of this Minny man."

"Milian," Allyn perhaps unwisely corrected earning himself a scowl.

"Milian who sounds little more than a bandit!" the king finished.

~

Once the newcomers had departed for their tents Cynric commanded the guards. "Bring me Brennus!"

It took another few hours for them to locate the old man, a mash of twisted and ruined flesh poked out the hood. Cynric had never asked but assumed it was a fire that had ruined his face although a captured Briton warrior had once claimed

Brennus had done it to himself.

One eye still worked and half of it peered out of the melted folds of flesh. A blue smudge which Brennus told him had once been a tattoo of a star was half-visible on his forehead. Half Briton, half Saxon and despised by both Brennus had become very important to King Cynric. Important enough so that the king didn't ask too many questions about who he was and how he acquired his information.

"So what you told me was true," Cynric began. The burned man made a sound that could have been laughter or could have been pain. "Tell me what your spies in Chichester have reported."

In accented rasping Saxon that most wouldn't be able to understand but Cynric had grown used to it Brennus recounted the story he had heard in pieces. After the group had arrived from the east he had dispatched messengers and now had the most of it.

His three men inside Chichester were now one man. The other two were city guards who weren't responding to his men's message drops, and he had a feeling that was now a permanent state of affairs. His other man in the city a slave trader who had not attended the wedding due to a grudge against the reeve, had however given a full account of what he had witnessed from the city walls, as he saw body after body being dragged out of the amphitheater. He had been at the meeting when the leech suggested covering the affair up and even blaming Cynric.

The next Briton outlaw to catch himself in one of Brennus' traps would be a suitable reward for that information, Brennus thought, even if the old fool always complained spraying spittle in the air at the poor value of lame slaves.

But the story he told Brennus which Brennus wheezed to the king matched what Allyn had told him earlier that day. Allyn's previously outlandish story was now scarily believable, and Cynric had retained several Britons who like Brennus were unwelcome among their own people. Over the years, he had become aware of the belief in monsters and overtime, his obsession had grown with stories of a dead Roman and his grotesque army.

"What I want to know is true or not is that this hunt is willing to welcome a Saxon king to treat with them? This Milian, can he be trusted?"

"I know of him," was the raspy response. "He is fierce but he is Merlin's creature."

"What does that mean?" Demanded Cynric.

"Merlin hates Saxons but has come to terms with the need for you on the hunt, but since the king fell the new king listens more to the monks who hate your gods. They had had great success converting the west and were about to have the whole island to themselves when you bastards arrived in the east."

"I'm not interested in the mewling of monks!" said Cynric menacingly. "I want to be the first Saxon king in that cabal, the legitimacy will set me high above Subseaxe and bring men to my cause when I have to crush them!"

"You are thinking of making the hunt's existence public? I really would not…"

"Inform the Dorset Britons we will be entering their land soon!" The king stamped his foot on the floor in temper.

CHAPTER 30

"It's a swamp! Surely you can't mean the city is just half a day away?" Iga said, sneezing violently in the stout stone building they were spending the night in.

"It's just a bit boggy and from this mansion standing, trade was once done around here. I imagine the Romans used this area as a herb garden for medicine and there's still a few of the plant's descendants growing as weeds which is the reason your humors are distressed up making you sneeze," Milian said.

"It's good that I'm sneezing, it's a sign of good luck from the gods!"

"Never mind that!" said Milian irritably. He disliked traveling with groups of Britons, and a group of Saxons was trying his patience. Digoth at least looked rapt as he scratched the floor stones that were illuminated by the fire with a stick scratching soot onto the stones deftly.

"Is that a map?" Digoth asked.

"Memorizing the Roman towns is part of the test to get into your lord's army of warriors. From the south, the way we are heading from only one bridge is still intact. Well, it was intact fifty odd years ago the last time a Briton laid eyes on it. Regardless eyes will be on it whatever the case, so that's out. Now if we swim across we can follow the city wall to the east of the city and look for gaps. The area near the gate where the road leads out to Camulodunum might be our best bet, now who here is a strong swimmer?"

Hieu's hand was the only one to go up. "Well, who here can swim at all?"

Still only Hieu's tiny arm remained raised. "For fucks sake!" Milian was on the verge of losing his temper now.

"At least the wood around this bog will be well water worn as it looks like we are spending tonight making a raft!"

~

Alfwen kept herself sane by talking to her hairy cell mate, the mostly crazed Saxon who muttered about shades and flying horses.

She told him about her family, her sister and brother, and a boy she was once betrothed to.

"Holt, you see his father's village is twice the size as ours, but his father had trouble finding him a match because he was kicked in the head by a mule as a child, so his wits were gone, but he was handsome and his lands were rich. I think I would get his mother's Frankish brooches some of them were even sparkling red you know, but Holt died when the plague came around the year the sun went out. It took most of his father's villagers too so they couldn't get the harvest in time before the clouds blocked everything out, still, they didn't starve. A group of Jutes came along and killed them. Holt had a younger brother, I wonder if they took him as a slave? Strong looking boy anyway, now onto Pleoh one of Digoth's boyhood friends, one time me and him went off to the woods together and…"

Her heart leapt back into her mouth as the chill and burning smell hit her and she heard the tap tap of footsteps descending.

"Lady Nix," said Psyche with a smile that could make milk go sour. "Don't worry, I'm not here for you, your turn is tomorrow. I've come for your hairy friend, two new creations in as many days not common." She turned to the insane man.

"Herla said you shit yourself when you first faced him, not at first he says you were a good fighter for a pirate, but your mind snapped when the horse began to fly and breathe fire. Would have thought a seafaring man would be used to unworldly sights anyway, before Lady Nix's metamorphosis as the main event tomorrow, Herla fancies a rematch, and to make it fairish the boss man is going to make you the same as me. Not a half human-animal freak like she's going to become but a strigoi one who can move among men…"

"The pale mare, its eyes red, it floats it wants me to float too…" moaned the captive.

"Yes, very interesting, ghosts are scary blah blah blah…eternal insanity sounds like a laugh. Maybe should old Herla allow you to live tomorrow I'll take you on my travels now Vitium is otherwise indisposed." She tore the chains off the cage door and grabbed the whimpering former pirate by the ear, before turning to Alfwen's cage and cackling.

"I've heard your skin will turn green first before your jowls and eyeballs start to expand, the webbing of the hands comes next. I do hope you keep that pretty head of yellow hair, the only one of your kind I've met is The Nix, and the boss once mentioned he was bald when he sailed into that cave and…"

"What the fuck are you talking about you piss eyed freak!" Alfwen had had enough of this creature's rambling threats.

Psyche made a deep roar-like hiss in anger and held her hand back at the last minute.

"Once you can't die I'm going to kick the shit out of your ugly green hide." She composed herself a little.

"They say that when frogs mate the man mounts the woman and she has to carry him around like that all day, you must tell me what that's like." And with that, she dragged the man out of the dungeon to his fate.

Despite Psyche being incoherent with her rantings and the frogman being vague with his threats, Alfwen knew by now what their plan was, somehow in someway she was going to become like the frog-man. She had been restrained in such a way that smashing her brains out against the bars or stone floor was impossible. The monster himself came down to feed her, he cowled himself in a brown hooded cloak, was that to spare her the discomfort of looking upon her face, she wondered?

~

"Open," he always croaked on his visits, and unable to resist he spooned gruel into her wide mouth, even when she gagged on the rotten fish he'd mixed into the gruel.

"Need to get used to that heh!"he muttered in accented Saxon. It was like he was trying to be kind but he'd long since lost any notion of what human kindness was. Alfwen thought back to how she'd treated her sister and Iga and the other slaves even her brother at times, the way she'd dismissed the trauma of the two orphaned children. I can't blame them for having already forgotten about me she thought sadly.

~

Cynric led the procession of men out of the fort. Allyn, Cwenhild, and the children as well as the five Chichester citizens made up the rear.

"Who are those wretched creatures?" Anfeald, the town's fishmonger, asked, referring to a bunch of chained, filthy staving men in the middle of the procession. Having lost his brother and his wife struck on the head and rendered simple in the slaughter he was in no mood to appease the leech and Atheling so had hitched his fortunes to the group. Cwenhild, who predictably enough had found herself entrusted with the responsibility of tending to his poor wife, thought that Ar was still noticeably more intelligent than her husband despite the injury.

"Britons caught in battle or raids and waiting to be sold. The Franks don't like enslaving their own so send ships along the coast regularly to buy. King Cynric thinks the Dorset Britons will be less likely to rain arrows on us if their kinsmen are in our ranks. They will be released if we treat them and are allowed safe passage through their lands some of them are kin to high ranking Britons," Cwenhild explained.

"What happened to Gildas' cousin?" Cynric on horseback asked Brennus.

"Ah! Such a fierce warrior woman, sold her to the Franks last month."

"Right, how about his chief archer?"

"Well, we cut Jikel's hands off so I've left him in the pen with the mad and lame I think Gildas might consider it an insult to return him in such a condition."

"Do we have anyone of value?" Cynric said, wondering if leaving the captured Britons wellbeing up to Brennus was a mistake. Truth be told he didn't trust him enough and only had him on the trip as someone had to interpret.

"Hmm, a bastard brother, third from the left in the front row."

"So a rival for his chiefdom, yes I'm sure he'll be delighted to see him. Open the gates!" bellowed Cynric and the procession of King and advisor, forty warriors, ten Briton captives, and nine confused Saxon messengers started their journey.

~

By the time they got within sight of the city Milian had them crouch down and crawl on their bellies through the marshy grounds on the southern side of The Tamesas. On the northern side, they could see stone walls and above it, buildings shaped differently to anything found in Chichester.

Milian was more familiar with the designs. The Britons had preserved the Roman buildings in their cities better Corinium Dobunnorum a place he was a regular visitor to had buildings like this, but even he had never seen anything on this scale or size.

The smell of burning of charcoal and sulfur faintly lingered in the air from the direction of the wind it was coming from the city. They crawled and crawled in an eastern direction until the city was well behind them.

"Even without demon lookouts that bridge couldn't have supported four of us," Aebbe said.

"Five," replied Milian. "The girl is the only one of you that can swim she has to cross the river with us in case one of you falls in and needs saving." Hieu turned to Aebbe and gave her a broad smirk.

The city was now just a distant speck in the distance. Digoth and Milian stood and unloaded the bundle of branches from the Crohdenu bog. Aebbe and Iga provided the limited pieces of rope they had found at the mansion and made up the rest with stout-looking plant vines.

None of the crew appeared to have much idea of what they were doing, even Milian had to look away as he gritted out the confession that he had never built a raft before, but they worked quickly and quietly nevertheless.

Two rafts were made with each one having a swimmer Milian and Hieu on it. Aebbe and Hieu would travel together. Milian figured that if one of them fell in, the child would stand a better chance of recovering Aebbe rather than the heavier Digoth or Iga.

It took a few hours but at around midday the rafts were ready.

The Milian piloted one took off first sailing in zig zags with its two passengers clinging on for dear life. Aebbe piloted her raft not having any idea what to do but copy Milian, who unfortunately didn't have much more expertise.

The first capsize happened from Milian's raft about twenty meters into the journey: he grabbed Iga and flopped her over a log he found before diving underwater to look for Digoth who had disappeared in a current.

Aebbe's raft drifted by Iga choking and sputtering on her lo. Aebbe and Hieu flailed at the log and somehow managed to push it along. About halfway over the river, they looked back to see Milian and Digoth but there was nothing. As they shouted and screamed the men's names a cold chill tore through the air.

CHAPTER 31

Silence: Digoth felt calm as he sank he had no desire to fight the current anymore soon it would be all over, he'd be with the source of the song that was coming from somewhere, a most beautiful song.

Why had he never learnt to swim? Digoth wondered, his father had in his cups spoken about his grandfather braving the journey across a hostile sea and of the old country; beautiful Germania filled with thick rivers. There were only steams near the village he never felt the need to learn but it was okay. She was coming, she'd come to him at the point of panic when he realized the current was too strong. She'd told him to relax to calmly sink. She would be waiting for him.

~

Echolle sat in a squat position on the bed of The Tamesas. Long black hair, bright green eyes, and porcelain colored skin without a blemish, they looked beautiful.

They hated this form it was too different from how they were in the Gaulish village they had brief memories of when their name was different and then marching up a road in armor, a man with a plume on his helmet screaming at them in Latin. A journey by ship, the overcrowded boat swaying, a wave taller than any they'd seen before engulfing them, nothing but water, the taste of salt and brine, coughing, endless coughing, waking up on a beach with a man standing over them. A horned man with a snake drooping out of his mouth somehow managed to say, "Welcome to Dumnonia."

Something else had happened at the bottom of the sea. Something so bad they couldn't remember it. As long as they remained underwater they couldn't remember it.

That was a very different form, one which didn't seduce men to the depths. Never mind soon this man would sink to the bottom, and their true form could be revealed. Lamisa had a different challenge with the other raft with the female food on it. They'd probably have to pretend to be a drowning girl and hope to get close enough to the raft to pull it down.

Women trusted strangers less than men, and would be less impressed with Lamisa's curly blonde hair and wide blue eyes than men would. Still, all they needed was to get within an arm's length and if needs be they could show their true form above the water. The boss man's spells provided some protection against the sun as long as they didn't stray too far from the city walls.

The Sirens of Dumnonia were pledged for two of their kind to patrol the bed of The Tamesas in case the hunt attacked from the west, or Saxon raiders came in large numbers from the east.

Spurius took the security of Londinium seriously but these were just stragglers no real threat to the city. A tasty treat, a bonus for the hardship that kept Echolle and Lamisa away from the beautiful coast of Dumnonia, with its rocks and its cliffs that they could lure juicy and tasty fishermen, pirates, smugglers, Briton envoys, Frankish trading ships, and more to them.

Digoth fell into their arms they sang a bit more of the Saxon lullaby that had just come to them when they saw Digoth for the first time on the river banks. They rested his head between their two breasts and then they revealed their true form.

This resembled the human they had been even less, but when they made this form it was time to eat so they didn't mind as much.

Their canine teeth grew into giant tusks, their jet black hair fell out as their skin shriveled and their muscles bulged. Their skin turned grey the texture of oysters, long whiskers spouted from under their nose, and their bright green eyes now piggy blots of red.

They rested a tusk against Digoth's heart – still beating! They loved it when the food was still alive. The food's eyes flashed open in terror when the first tusk ripped the belly open! Echolle noticed a second figure coming towards them.

~

"Help! Help! I can't swim!" The young woman had appeared out of nowhere.

"We don't have room," Iga warned.

"We can't just leave her there to drown," Aebbe said and began flapping her hand to steer the raft towards the woman.

The raft went nowhere but the woman was getting closer it appeared to Iga that she was not as useless in the water as she was trying to appear.

"Something's wrong with this one! Steer clear!" Iga screamed.

"What are you talking about? Here!" Aebbe grabbed a stick and held it out to the woman. As she leant forward effortlessly for the drowning woman to grab it, Iga felt another surge of fear.

"It's a waif but it has tits the size of a baby's head! That isn't a woman! It's some man's dream of what a woman should look like! Throw the stick back!"

"How rude!" said the Siren, its arm morphing into a tentacle and throwing itself around Hieu's throat.

~

Echolle had turned back into their beautiful enchantress form as the second figure made himself clear.

A tatty-looking man without much meat on the bones but his lungs must be large they thought he was still conscious despite being underwater for an age. They liked the lungs; chewy with a bloody tang.

The man's face was now just a few feet away. They extended their forked tail and swished it to increase the currents that had brought the men here. What to sing to the man to render him limp and harmless? They wondered, reading the man's eyes often told them. A Briton battle chant was the surprising answer that came into their head.

They opened their arms wide and giggled. *"Sons of the west born to defend our father's land! Where ever we are the valley and hills beloved in our heart."* They purred the lyrics they plucked from the man's mind in a voice that oozed warmth and comfort despite the lack of air they knew he'd be hearing every word.

When the man was just inches away Echolle smiled at his birthmark. Branded food? Is that good luck or bad? they thought giving another giggle between verses. That was their final thought before Milian pulled an arrow out of the sack he was carrying and rammed it right through Echolle's left eye.

~

Aebbe fought to get the tentacle off Hieu's neck while Iga still clinging on to the log spat and cursed at the siren until their other arm also turned into a tentacle and slapped against her head stunning her.

Hieu was turning blue and the tentacle was gripped tightly around her neck spittle was drooling from her mouth and her eyes were thick with tears.

The blonde woman was now a terrible sight. Aebbe was reminded of the picture on the floor of the giants...no the Romans building near the village. The woman's hair was a bunch of eels, and her face had begun to protrude outwards it was almost as if she were growing a beak, but when this beak opened it was full of sharp triangled teeth.

Aebbe screamed in fear, frustration, and most of all anger. This wasn't fair! She had never hurt anyone! She had always wanted everyone to be happy. She had tried her best to keep everyone safe. She had never wanted too much for herself, no gold or power she just wanted enough land to ensure she never went hungry, a kind man, and healthy and happy children, was that too much to ask?

Instead her mother butchered, her father slain by some magic, her brother drowned, her sister enduring unspeakable torments behind the city walls, and her and her last two remaining companions; friends even now were soon to be slain and eaten by this twisted monster disguised as a drowning woman.

Another of her screams echoed across the river from bank to bank maybe even audible beyond the city walls. Aebbe didn't care. It was just so unfair!

Then something happened. The monster's face had turned back into that of a beautiful blonde woman but something was wrong with its face. It looked distraught with tears welling up in its eyes and its mouth opening and closing in shock. It looked so pitiful Aebbe thought without giving it an inch of pity. A new experience for her; a complete lack of empathy was something she'd never felt for anyone or anything.

The woman moaned and whimpered in their native Greek but the meaning was obvious even to Aebbe, Hieu, and a groggy Iga who didn't share a single word of Greek between them.

"Oh, oh my, this...this...I don't think...this is not good...this is not supposed to happen."

And with that, the tentacles shrank. They unraveled from Hieu's neck and with a final tearful look, the siren disappeared under the water.

A panting, puking Hieu somehow managed to look up at Aebbe and with awe in her eyes gasped, "You are the greatest warrior I've ever seen."

Smoke seemed to float out of the water and the whole river began to smell of rotten eggs. The three of them gagged. Iga now recovered screamed, "To the banks quickly! We need to get out of the water now!"

~

Milian sat on the south bank of the river an unconscious but alive Digoth beside him. He was panting and his hands were shaking, swimming while carrying his weapons including the sword had taken every bit of energy out of him.

He'd never felt like this before. It was those arrows. When it had gone through the siren's eye something had been released. It felt like the shades of hundreds of fishermen and sailors that the sea bitch had taken had received a boon.

They weren't here, they were far away in new bodies some in distant lands, some in other worlds, but the trauma and terror that the siren had imprinted on their souls were still there, even in their new bodies the sight of a sea cliff or the sound of song would trouble them and keep them awake for reasons they couldn't explain until now.

He'd avenged them and their souls had been cleaned. The violence they were born anew into and the violence that they found themselves inflicting on others in a cycle was broken;

they could start afresh.

It must be the arrows, he thought, he'd killed before, even killed a creation; a dwarf's head he'd smashed in so hard that it couldn't crawl back to its cave before sunrise but had never felt like this.

The knuckles were pretty brainless so the siren was the first intelligent creature he'd killed with the arrows. And he didn't even use a bow! He barked a nervous laugh, he'd have to compare notes with the lads who took down the shits in Salinae.

"This island can be saved. We can break the cycle," he said to himself. He then noticed the smoke and the smell and laughed. "Burn well, you bitches."

Out of all the creations, he had a particular loathing for sirens. The memory of the chill in his gut when he noticed the damp hand reach up to the raft seconds before Digoth had tumbled overboard joined a few other foul memories he had of them.

He put his hand over the water and gave a yell of pain at the heat. He scanned the horizon. The woman's raft must have gotten to the north bank by now, it was too far out to return to the south bank…if not, then all on board were doomed.

~

Iga was yelling in pain as the raft pulled the log she was clinging to onto the shore of the north bank. Aebbe had felt it too, the water going from icy cold to lukewarm, to uncomfortably hot, to scalding hot in about a minute.

They had panicked and flailed and somehow gotten to shore without getting too burnt. Aebbe collapsed. She couldn't take anymore, she laid on the small beach, soon a whimpering Iga was laid next to her. Hieu completed the trio by squatting next to them.

"Do you think they made it?" Hieu said, her voice raspy after the tentacle had throttled her neck.

Digoth! He still had burns from the fight at the village, Aebbe remembered. Being in the water would inflame them.

Then the steam from the river drifted over them and they all screamed in pain. They looked out at the river in horror. It was boiling and bubbling like the contents of a pot left on a fire. Digoth's burns were the least of his problems if he was still in the water Aebbe realized. A new smell greeted them with the arrival of hundreds of dead fish now floating on top of the river.

CHAPTER 32

Alfwen had awoken early that morning. Some ogre-like creature had unchained her and carried her up to the bath house where she met a grinning Spurius laid out in his favorite bath.

It was her first time seeing the creature but she wasn't surprised at his outlandish appearance. It was partly due to her being desensitized to the horrors of Londinium by her trauma but Spurius gave off a sense of familiarity to all.

He's always been here in some way, she thought, a sudden gloom overtook her, and tears sprung from her eyes. These were the tears of despair, not fear.

Reading her thoughts he replied, "Not always but certainly for as long as those limited by a human mind can imagine, at least for now."

Talking to a human he had to retract the snake to his lips and then the snake's skull expanded grotesquely allowing the snake's mouth to merge with his.

The sound out of his mouth was different to what the creations heard in their head and it even made the ogre grimace it was brittle like two stones being struck together harshly to make a sound.

Alfwen covered herself as best she could with her arms and hands; her dress long since reduced to rags that barely covered a thing.

Clink, clink, clink, went his voice in what she imagined to be a laugh.

"You have nothing to hide from me. Soon you will join my children, besides, I don't have any human desires anymore, I haven't for quite some time. Well not of the nature you're thinking of I still enjoy watching battles in the amphitheater of course and I would kill to see a panmtomimus again, of course you know I'm talking literally, but finding anyone on this island that can play the instruments is as likely as finding a Briton who doesn't prefer his goats to his woman…"

He rambled more in this manner before saying, "Some of your Saxon riddles appeal, but they are too easy and… how is my Saxon? Surprisingly easy tongue to master with its stunted vocabulary…where was I? Of course, today's your wedding day and you look and smell like shit my dear get in the bath with me."

Alfwen gave a horrified whimper but barely had any time to think before the monster made some sort of communication with the ogre who lifted her up and unceremoniously dumped her in the warm water.

Practically naked under the water her rags drifting away, Alfwen squirmed to turn her body away but Spurius stood up and got out of the water.

"Perhaps your husband should be the first to see you in all your glory. Don't worry about the rags, I have prepared a gown for what will be both your wedding and your ascension to one of us this evening. Morchan here will be your guide and chaperone for the rest of the day."

Spurius gestured to the ogre. "A Hibernian monk before I met him I doubt he'll be interested in…"

A young man with yellow eyes and hollowed cheeks somehow

slid into the bathroom without anyone noticing. When Spurius felt his presence he turned and yelled at the man in the same watery language that the monsters spoke on the journey from Chichester. At first, Spurius sounded furious. The interruption was unwelcome but then he began to sound bewildered.

"I must go," he told her in Saxon. His voice rang with confusion.

Alfwen groaned with relief when he left the bath house it was as if a stone weight on her heart had been lifted.

~

Spurius was greeted with bows and ashen faces as he strode down the streets of the city. He could feel the heat coming from the river well before he reached the gates of the city wall. The doors had long since rotted away but Alecto was there to greet him as he stepped outside of the city walls.

The sight was unlike anything he'd seen and he had seen pretty much everything.

The river was bubbling furiously and they had to shield their faces from the heat. He even thought he saw a glow from the river bed. Could it be burning down there?

"What the fuck?" he asked. "Do you see what I'm seeing?"

Alecto turned to him so he could see the skin stretched across her eye sockets. "Ah, sorry, I mean can you sense it?"

"The gifts you gave me mean I can feel it far greater than anyone sighted."

"Are Echolle and Lamisa still alive?" Spurius usually could sense it when a creation left this world. He thought maybe the sirens had left the water, although they shouldn't do that for too long. It would make them begin to remember.

"They are still alive unluckily for them," Alecto said. "Boiling alive perpetually until the river calms then they have Hades to look forward to."

"When will the river calm?"

"I'm sensing a few months maybe, a year at most."

"A whole fucking year! What caused this?"

"Those fucking arrows, "she spat with rage and fear. Spurius had never heard her swear before or her voice quiver.

"Preparations for tonight's ceremony remain unaffected, we will talk about what to do about this afterward. Whoever is responsible for this is dead or stranded on the south bank," he said and turned on his hooves, and clopped back into the city.

"Best keep an eye on the bridge just in case," he called back.

~

Digoth had woken up and was being assessed of the situation by Milian. "So we are back on the south side of the river?" he asked.

"Yes."

"And the others are on the north side?"

"They should have made it yes if they didn't well…"

Both their heads turned towards the smoldering bubbling river.

"They made it," Digoth said with a bit of steel in his voice surprising Milian somewhat.

"There's still a problem if they did," Milian said and pulled out the quiver of arrows from his sack. "As I'm the only one who can fire these, I kept them all for myself so all three of them are on the monster's side of the river with only the pugios for protection."

"We must hurry and join them!" Digoth said excitedly.

"How are we supposed to cross that?" Milian gestured to the river. "We can't swim or cross by boat a drop of that water touching your skin would wound you, imagine what falling in would be like?"

~

On the other side of the river, the two women and one girl had moved inland, and recovered from the scalding they'd got on the beach by sitting in the shade of a small forest a couple of miles east of the large city. Still visible the city gave them a cold feeling when they glanced at it. Londinium appeared to have black clouds always lingering over it no matter what the weather was like elsewhere.

Iga was mixing up some moss and mud into a paste. She rubbed it on parts of her and the other's bodies that had been scalded.

"Well that's it!" she said. "No chance of saving her ladyship with those magic arrows at the bottom of a boiling river."

"I'm sure Milian saved my brother." snapped Aebbe still exhausted from the screams and the crazed race to get to the shore.

"Where are they then?" Iga said.
"What would you have us do? We are three women travelling alone, we can't go south until the river calms, go east, and Angles will enslave us, go west or north and it's a toss-up between wolves, the winter cold or Briton bandits that will be our doom," Aebbe said.

That shut Iga up for a while.

Hieu felt the arrow under her leggings, she'd found it at the amphitheater and so wanted to show it to Aebbe to give her the same courage she'd given Hieu on the river crossing, but at the last minute, she remembered why she'd brought it along. "We should continue on and enter the city," she said.

"We rest and wait for dusk," Aebbe replied.

Iga gave the city a worrying look. "It doesn't seem to be the sort of place you want to visit at night," she said. "A few hours gives us time to heal and maybe the men will find us?"

An uncomfortable silence fell as Iga returned to making her paste, Hieu touched the arrow for luck, and Aebbe stepped out of the forest to look at the bubbling, steaming river.

~

Gildas listened to his scout's report on the incursion into the forest.

"The idiots are armed with sword and spear they will never have the space to wield them when we fall on them! We should attack with haste."

He raised his hand to quiet the man.

"Such weapons are to quickly dispatch of the prisoners when the first arrows begin to fall and my brother is among them," he explained.

"Bastard brother, and he only travelled south to find passage to Armorica once we discovered his plot against you."

"We don't know that for certain," the small man said calmly. "He was apprehended in the wrong part of the land if that was his intention. I smell Brennus' foul work in this I take it he is with them?"

The scout nodded. "No missing that freakish looking bastard."

"We talk…I don't suppose Jikel or Nonn are among the

prisoners?" The scout shook his head.

"That is unfortunate," he said slowly. "and King Cynric will answer for it at some point but I feel he hasn't come into the forest for a fight."

~

Cynric sat on a log as the smaller man approached him. An arrow had hit the head of one of the south Saxons making up the rear of the party that morning, the dull-witted one who stank of fish. He was stunned but otherwise unhurt; the head of the arrow had been removed and the spin filed down; a sign that this was an invitation to talk.

Soon Brennus was shouting at the trees in the Britons' tongue and this meeting was arranged. Of course, the Britons were shorter than the Saxons. Their style of fighting made height and brute force less necessary although being chased out of the best farmland several generations ago had hardly helped Cynric reasoned, but even for a Briton Gildas was short he barely came up to Cynric's chest when they both stood. Red hair in pigtails and a freckled face made him look like a…

"Dwarf, yes I know what you're thinking." Brennus stared at the floor as he translated the chiefdom's words.

"I always make it my business to meet new friends under the blazing sun despite it being no good for my skin. I want word out around the forest that I'm as mortal as the next man, it isn't good for your health to be mistaken for a dwarf when the hunt is about!" He smiled as he saw Cynric's face light up at that.

"Now what of my cousin Nonn and my best bowman Jiken?"

Cynric sighed. "I imagine your cousin is on her back in a Frankish brothel by now and as for your bowman he killed five of mine on his attack on our fort, five who had kin and friends living in my walls…sometimes we forget to feed him."

Brennus decided to offer a tactful translation of this. "Sadly, both of them passed away of the flux soon after capture despite excellent care I ensured they were buried with their weapons and ornaments as well as food for their souls journey to its new host."

Both Cynric and Gildas understood more of each other's language than they let on and were testing each other for trust.

Gildas was satisfied that Cynric was telling the truth even if the interpreter feared his reaction. Cynric was relieved that he wouldn't have to smear the trees with Briton blood should Gildas attack him. Sure the forest gave the hairy little bastards an advantage but too often Britons were overconfident of their chances. Saxons drove them out of their lands for a reason, stronger, better disciplined, and better trained. Well the West Saxons were anyway and becoming their king had not been easy. Cynric had never been raised as some pampered Atheling he'd become king by being the strongest of the strong.

Gildas signaled for a barrel of ale to be brought to the clearing to toast their temporary truce. Truth be told Cynric left them alone most of the time seeming content to consolidate his own lands which were plagued by infighting among the Saxons, not to mention the Jutes, now well established on the island of Wihtwara who kept Cynric busy with their raiding.

Cynric had no heir and the instant he was gone alliances could be made that would lead to trouble for the Dorset Britons. No, if this king wants to meet then they meet and if the meeting goes sour then Jiken and Nonn might be avenged sooner than expected; every nook of every tree had archers trained on Cynric and his guards. They would be away with the prisoners before the rest of the lackwitted Saxons realized their king and best warriors were on their way to the next life, and the Dorset forest could be unforgiving to those stranded with no way back.

He was surprised when Cynric waved his hand and beckoned over a stocky looking Saxon and a slightly smaller woman whose nose had been broken several times over her lifetime.

"Never go hungry in the forest with them two! Just have to roll them about a bit and bound to crush a squirrel or snake or two," he chortled. Brennus, the only one who could understand him, stared at the floor. *Miserable burned bastard still got to have a word with that one about how my kin fell into Cynric's hands and...*he quickly stopped his internal monologue when he heard Allyn begin to describe the events of Chichester. Cwenhild spoke after about the creature that had somehow controlled Aart's movements and actions during that terrible day back at the village.

Finally, King Cynric passed on the message from Milian.

"Aye best you tell this tale to them at Avalon. You won't find it without us so I feel we're going to get better acquainted. It's still a good way away. Further west than any Saxon has been I'd wager. Just got to hope they don't hang me for treachery when they see us approach together." The small man finally replied.

~

Getting dressed in front of Morchan wasn't the trial Alfwen had feared. Although his grey skin, hulking frame, and brown slabs for teeth unnerved her and the smell of dirty water coming from him made her gag, it was quite clear from Morchan's eyes and expression that he was deeply unintelligent. It was like getting dressed in front of a cow.

The dress that had been left for her was more beautiful than the gown she had worn to her first wedding. A robe of pure white tied with a woolen belt. She had eventually taken over and tied it herself after Morchan's thumbs proved too misshapen for the task.

An egg yolk yellow hairnet and a red veil made up the multi-colored ensemble, Morchan then lifted her up and carried her through the city.

Dusk was beginning to fall and the streets while not busy were not as deserted as they were during the day. Alfwen clenched her eyes shut among the chatter beneath her. It was all in a language she didn't know but it sounded so sinister so old.

Smoke stung her eyes after a while and she made the mistake of looking. A group of men standing around a brazier, boys really from the height, then she saw a bushy tail flick out from under one of their tunics, and one must have heard her gasp as they turned their head and their hood fell off revealing a foxes snout protruding from an otherwise human face. It stepped aside and led the other foxmen in a high-pitched snigger as she saw a human foot on the brazier.

She swung her head away to see in the half boarded window of a crumbling villa on her right a young woman dressed in a similar tunic, her eyes were closed as she smelt the head of the infant babe she held in her arms, the tired but contented look of a new mother on her face. The scene was so out of place, so normal in this horrifying bizarre city that it calmed her for a few seconds before the woman opened her eyes revealing the yellow color. She smiled showing fanged teeth and then looked at the baby's head with desire licking her lips.

Alfwen started screaming at this much to the amusement of the foxmen. Morchan reached up and one of his foul-smelling, watery hands clamped over her face silencing her and thankfully blocking her view from the sights as he walked moving through the crowds.

She heard screams and laughter, blood-curdling cries and tears both in the far distance and sometimes close enough to hurt her ears. The laughter was mostly mocking, but sometimes she detected fear in there too. Morchan took his hand away and allowed her to see again; despite no other creatures being in view the fact they were inside an amphitheater brought back unpleasant memories, and sent her screaming again.

She squirmed and wriggled as the enormity of what was about to happen sank in. *This is it! They're going to turn me into one of them! Make me like him! Force me to be with him!* She only saw Morchan's fist from the corner of her eye before her head exploded in pain and everything went black.

CHAPTER 33

The two men approached the one remaining wooden Roman bridge to reinspect it. At the first sight of it on the journey, they had dismissed it as being unable to support their weight as well as giving the inhabitants notice of their arrival. Now it appeared they had little choice and both groaned with dismay when they saw how rotted away the bridge was.

Most of the deck had been lost to storms and time with gaps of as much as three or four feet, with nothing but bubbling, steaming water underneath.

"I don't think I can make those jumps," said Digoth.

Milian surprised him with a bit of humility. "Nor me, maybe under normal circumstances but with the heat…"

A hairless pink thing with welts and blood all over it lay motionless at the foot of the bridge. "Beaver must have been in the water when it started getting warm. Poor bastard didn't get out in time," said Milian.

Digoth said, "The beams and girders are still intact we could hold onto them and crawl across. It's dangerous but…"

"There's no other way," Milian finished for him. "We need to do it in the next hour the water is going to make the wooden base soften and bend, and then the whole bridge is going into the water."

~

On the northern side of the bridge, Jrim watched with growing annoyance.

No Latin, Saxon, or Brittonic for him. He could only communicate in a language that to non-trolls was just a series of screams. Alecto had taken a spell to learn it so she screamed at him he was on bridge duty during the ceremony.

"A troll guarding a bridge! It's a stereotype! I want to be at the feast!"

"He has asked for you personally! Are you going to defy him?" At that, he had cowered a bit.

"It's an easy job, not even a troll can fuck it up. Watch the bridge if you see anyone trying to cross rip out the support beams and send the whole blasted thing into the boiling river complete with intruders!"

The feast was going to be a marvelous thing. The boss had sent some of his yellow eyed freaks out in every which direction over the past week to round up captives; Saxons, Britons, Jutes, Angles, Picts, Franks, old, young, men, women. The dungeons under the city were going to be full to the brim from what he'd heard. Only scraps for old Jrim once he returned from his watch.

That's why he hadn't kicked the bridge into the steam and bubbles once he'd spied two men climbing upside down on the remaining horizontal girders that once supported a deck. He'd found a nice little ditch to rest his enormous frame in, and his grey head was well camouflaged by the overgrown terrain just outside the city walls. Wait! One had slipped! Jrim whined, *half my meal* he thought. Even if he washed up on this side, all the flavor would be gone.

~

Digoth's hands had tried to grip a piece of wood that had too much rot in it and snapped away falling into the river.

This had left Digoth hanging on to the girder by his legs, and his head was so close to the water he felt his scalp scalding. He began to scream in terror and pain.

Milian reached down with one arm to try to get all Digoth's four limbs back on the bridge before he fell. He heaved reaching but the sack on his other shoulder had the arrows, the bow, and his sword and that was weighing heavily on him as well.

He briefly considered letting the sack fall but to take on Londinium's horrors unarmed would be suicide.

He let his legs fall so he was in the same position as Digoth just the other way up. He then swayed and booted Digoth in the chest where he was able to grasp onto the girder with his hands and continue his crawl along the bridge.

Milian tried getting back to his original position, but it was proving difficult and Digoth was powerless to help him. One hand slipped and the sack slid down his arm, he clasped it with his free fist at the last moment, but now was completely stranded.

He lost his composure and started to panic with each fleet of fear surging as he could feel the girder begin to snap.

He had never felt like this before but what a terrible way to go. Make it quick and have me awaken far from any rivers in the next body were his final thoughts as he let go, and with lightning fast reflexes, grabbed the rope that had suddenly appeared dangled in front of him.

Milian was light and Digoth strong but Milian was still an adult man carrying a sack full of weapons and Digoth still only had one limb free with which to heave and pull up. If he could get Milian back to a position clutching to the bridge they might just make it before the bridge falls.

Muscles were tearing as he heaved as much as he could. Inch by inch he was doing it, the rope shouldn't be this strong it was just hanging in front of him to find as he crawled forward attached to the girder.

He pulled again screaming in agony as muscles stretched and it felt like his bones would pop. Two, three, four…he stopped counting how many giant heaves he made but it worked!

Milian was back with all four limbs clinging onto the girder and the sack stuffed down his front. Neither of them said a word as they shuffled their bodies along and along grunting and panting, both in agony from the day's exploits.

They dropped themselves onto the small stone beach on the northern side of the river and looked up at the city walls, crumbling and overgrown with weeds and plants, and with terrors behind them, the two men still couldn't wait to walk through them and leave this river behind.

While they were still panting and puffing and groaning they heard a creaking sound and sat up to see the remaining parts of the bridge, the girders, the support beams, the pillars, and posts crash into the boiling river.

~

Aebbe, Iga, and Hieu watched from a grove of trees around the north eastern side of the wall.

Milian had said the gate that the road to Camulodunum started from was a good entry point, but none of the three could read the curvy characters carved into stone posts that they found on the paths that probably told them what the gates and road were called.

Saxon runes were just squiggles to them let alone this strange alien alphabet. They couldn't get too close not knowing if they were being watched.

Aebbe thought that one of the gaps in the wall might be best to gain entry through while Iga harshly asked what she intended to do once inside.

"Your sister won't be waiting behind the gap, we are going to have to search for her in that place," Iga said, spitting on the floor at the mention of the city. She asked herself constantly why she'd thrown her life away on this foolish mission her odd comment in Chichester about how this time she was going to fight back now made no sense to her and she had no idea why she had said it.

With dusk hiding their movements more they had edged closer to a promising-looking gap in the city wall when they heard sounds behind them.

Looking up the Camulodunum road they saw a group approaching in the distance so they raced back to the trees to hide. The noises grew louder, not voices but the clomp of a large group marching at the same speed and rhythm. Could it be soldiers? Iga had heard of some armies that marched in such a way although none of the Saxon fyrds she'd seen march through fields and mud tracks on their way to battle ever had such discipline.

The first few marchers became visible, they were, they were… normal.

"Townspeople?" whispered Iga.

"Right some peasants too," Aebbe confirmed.

"That one's rich," said Hieu pointing at a blonde woman. "Her beads are crystal, not amber."

Aebbe, for whom amber beads would be an unimaginably luxurious item, and Iga, who had never worn a bead in her life, just nodded.

Most of the men were in dirty tunics and smocks, the women in the same ankle-length gowns that Aebbe and Iga were wearing.

They all looked so ordinary until you caught sight of their eyes. Either dead inside, like they had retreated to a warm place in the deepest part of their mind. Switching off while their bodies shambled and stumbled to where they were supposed to be, or widely awake but sensing something was gravely wrong. Eyes either raw red from crying or brimming with tears.

A rumbling came from the back and an ox dragging a wagon came through forcing the marchers off the path. Two men came forward and slowly dragged some sheets off whatever was in the wagon.

~

Ordo felt the fading daylight on him as the sheets were pulled away and held up his hand – not even an itch. The sun was mostly set which was usually safe to walk in, but until it was pitch black there would be unbearable itching and irritation of the skin so most creations didn't bother.

However, there was nothing to fear near within sight of Londinium. He sat up, threw his long brown hair back, flashed open his yellow eyes, and climbed out of the wagon.

"Alright," he shouted, "all of you in single file. Some of the alleyways we need to get through aren't that wide!"

He turned his head even from the distance he could tell something was wrong with the river.

"Is that smoke?" he said to no response he'd ordered complete silence from the collection of East Saxons he'd rounded up during his travels through that new kingdom.

The scratch and bite marks on their faces and necks had

rendered them robbed of free will and he had about fifty-odd to offer to the bossman as his contribution to the feast.

Like Psyche, he'd learnt from Alecto how to make the goo that went under the nails or on the teeth that would keep the thralls conscious and aware as their self-determination was stripped from them but controlling fifty at once was something he'd never done before and half were already in a mindless haze.

Still aware or not what Ordo said they did and the cattle were lining up to dutifully march into their slaughterhouse.

After going inside the city to check that there were no other parades of captives blocking their way, he returned to outside the city walls, and started to count as they filed through the city gates, but got bored and stopped at around twenty. It was hardly possible that any wandered off.

He gave an odd look to the woman at the rear with a twitching eye: there were a few he didn't remember making his own. So many and they all look the same he reasoned but he decided to give the few at the back a closer look.

~

The trio had worked out what was going on quickly.

"My brother had the same mark on him when he did what he did," said Hieu quietly.

"I remember! I think the whore that nearly killed Milian had similar," said Aebbe.

"What can it…ow!"

"Shut up," said Iga, her fingernails now bloody. "Come here girl," she then said to an unhappy-looking Hieu.

"Promise you won't cry out. I bet that yellow eyed bastard has good hearing, after I do you I want you to mark me. Your nails are sharper, never been filed down by hard work I bet."Iga finished the job.

The group's leader walked through the city gates and disappeared for several minutes allowing them to sprint towards the group of East Saxons, drawing some confused looks from them, although many others just dully gaped at them.

~

Now Iga felt cold sweat pour down her back as the smelt of rot and burning coming from the man lingered as he stared at her.

"Stop twitching your eye!" he snapped at her.

Iga felt rage no matter how many times the older slaves or Aluhburg had beaten her for it, she couldn't control it. She forced it shut and waited: if the monster asked her to open it again it would close and shut as rapidly as Milian's mouth when the conversation topic turned to him.

The man stared at her for half a minute before moving to Aebbe. His face half an inch from hers he said loudly, "I'm hungry, as there's more of you than I thought. I'm of a mind to have a warm-up before the ceremony."

He glanced at Hieu before staring at Aebbe a bit longer.

Please don't piss yourself thought Iga who was confident and grateful that just one week as a freed woman hadn't yet given her a frame of someone who ate more than once a day.

He was still staring at Aebbe when he shouted, "You -step forward."

Iga wondered what would happen if she refused. The man would know her for an imposter but would he suspect more of them?

Aebbe was pushed aside by a young man with a long nose and a mop of blonde hair. He looked stunned. "Yes, you. Come closer." Aebbe could smell the man's fear it was like his sweat was tanged with some sort of grassy smell.

"You can speak," said the cruel-looking man with a smile on his lips.

"Please, please let me go…I have children…my wife, she is with child again," the man stuttered and wept.

Then a look appeared on his face as his eyes caught Aebbe's.

"Look, let me go, and I can tell you that when you were inside the city something…"

"Silence!" screamed Ordo, shutting the man's jaws.

Why did they never come up with anything original? Whining about their family! Did he really think that's the first time I've heard that? Ordo thought, and does he think all the other times it worked?

He put both his hands on the man's head and pulled him far enough from the line so that they could see. With a display of strength that looked impossible as the blonde man was both taller and heavier, he gave his neck an almighty twist, wrenching the head clean off.

He threw the head behind him and lifted the body up by the torso tipping it to an angle so the blood poured from the open throat into his mouth. He drank until the contents of the body were dry and threw it to the floor his head drenched red.

"Well, I'm feeling better now into the city we go!" He then whispered to Aebbe, "You, to the front with me."

CHAPTER 34

Alfwen woke to find herself tied to a post in the middle of the amphitheater with the unpleasant sight of the frog-man and a green skinned woman with no eyes staring at her…well, the frog-man was staring at her at least.

The woman finished muttering to herself and blew some dust in Alfwen's face: suddenly everything became extra vivid for her and she felt a little light-headed.

"Just a little thing to make sure you stay wide awake for the ceremony, no fainting or taking a nap, you will never sleep again as a human," she said in flawless Saxon.

Alfwen began to swing her head from side to side. The amphitheater was a third full and beginning to fill with monstrosities.

"Time for me and your husband to retire to the seats, his greatness has a private area where we will watch the festivities. I will return to you at the end of the night with your new father to ascend you to our higher form."

The Nix burped making her scowl. She snapped something at him before departing behind her to a part of the amphitheater Alfwen couldn't see. The Nix gave her a lingering look before following the green woman.

Alfwen clenched her eyes shut but they tore themselves open seconds later: she tried to shut them again, but a chill ripped through her heart when she found she couldn't.

She couldn't even blink! The crowd began to stir like they were sensing something she couldn't and in the distance below the first row of seats, a wooden door slid open. She tried to turn her head away but found whatever the blind, green woman had done to her, it had robbed her of that as well.

~

"Greetings to all my creations! No, my children, on this night we welcome our newest member, lady Alfwen, soon to be our newest Nix and the first intelligent female of the species I've created. But the creation comes at the end of the evening. First up, each of my strigois have been sent across the island to gather a feast and games for all of us. Our first benefactor is old Hain, he's spent a week in his old stomping ground of Bernicia and let's see what he's brought us!" Spurius relaxed in his private box, acknowledging the arrival of Alecto and The Nix with a wave of his hand as he boomed this message into the minds of all the creations.

"Some of these northerners will be descendants of Romans on the wall. I may have broken bread with their ancestors I'm curious to see how they fight," he told the new arrivals.

~

A cheer went up among the monstrosities with the first sight of whatever lay beyond the doors. A barrel bodied man strode out waving a heavy sword and screaming. His face was a forest of browny orange hair but two eyes the same yellow color as the bitch who delighted in tormenting her stared right through Alfwen. Following him, some looking in a daze were a group of bearded young men. The fearsome-looking man bellowed for the crowd to hear him in that watery language again.

~

"I give my friends my contribution to the feast! King Eoppa's fyrd, blood-thirsty warriors the lot of them, and since I've borrowed them leaving the king defenseless a bloody civil war is probably going on up there now. Might pop up there to pick off the refugees. Will you and your lady wife join me, Nix? It's on your way home."

Despite The Nix's dislike of the strigoi creations, he didn't mind Hain. More than once they'd been stuck together on some errand or another, and the Northman had never been greedy when they divided up whoever had wandered across their path, and ended up as their meal.

"Maybe so," croaked The Nix from Spurius' private suite, from here one's voice carried far. In truth, The Nix was hoping to spend some more time in the southern Saxon kingdoms once he'd matched with Alfwen. He thought he had the makings of becoming a legend there; one whose foul deeds would be talked about until the end of time.

~

Alfwen wasn't catching any of the dialogue's meaning but orders were barked to the young men and two of them squared off opposing each other. The monster waved his arm and the two moved to within sight of Alfwen so she could see the bite and scratch marks on their necks.

Both men were well built, they stood facing each other shirtless with only rags of the lower part of their tunics and leggings covering them.

The monster who was dressed in fine furs and a cloak bellowed more stuff that was gibberish to Alfwen and she got the sense neither of the two young men who were shaking and shuddering with both terror and rage understood it either. The monsters in the seats did from their cheers.

Then the monster strode towards the two men and started speaking to them in a dialect of Saxon that was difficult to follow as it was so fast and slurred but the gist of it she got.

He said to the two men, "Just promised the crowd an unarmed fight to the death between two brothers. A bit of a tame opener but the only way to win is to rip your opponent's bits out with your teeth in this order; right eyeball, tongue, balls, left fingers, and liver, if he's still alive after all the blood loss."

He backed away. "Well, off you go then! It's not often I get two fighters with good teeth! I'm going to have to get most of the others to stone each other to death."

Alfwen yelled at them. "What are you doing? You don't have to…" And then screamed as the brother on the right leapt at the other only to have his ear ripped off in mid flight. Soon the brother on the left had him pinned on the floor, and was biting and snapping at his brother's right eyeball, eventually forcing it into his mouth before ripping it out.

~

Digoth and Milian didn't know how long it took them to recover and find the strength to sit up and continue their journey, but the sky had grown noticeably darker.

"Can you go?" panted Milian.

Digoth nodded before asking, "Should we go around the wall and find the others?"

"If they survived the crossing, wisest thing to do would be to head for the woods, we would never find them and if Alfwen is still alive we don't have the time."

They got up and looked at the gap in the city walls where once a large thick gate had stood.

It was Digoth who noticed the statue; the huge grey arm

sticking out of a ditch by the city wall. He was startled as he'd glanced at that same place while they were recuperating on the beach briefly and he couldn't remember seeing a grey arm statue then, but before he could cry out to Milian the arm moved, and with a sweep that looked ominously effortless threw the pair of men back towards the edge of the beach.

Both of them screamed in agony as the boiling hot waves lapped onto parts of their body and howling, they pulled themselves away as fast as they could. Digoth had scalded his right leg, making him limp.

To his horror as well as his agony, Milian had landed with his head facing the water. His scalp was scalded and his eyes opened in shock and rage at the clump of his hair that he now held in his hands. He reached for his sack and attached the bow and quiver to his back and the sword to his belt. He saw Digoth hobbling but still had his pugio.

"Let's meet the owner of that arm and pay him our regards," he shouted. Digoth nodded.

~

Jrim yelped to himself which was the best way he could really express laughter or convey any humor at all. He had started to dig when it looked as if the pair were going to make it. Especially after the ginger one found the ropes that Alecto had ordered hung up after several of the flightless and non swimming creations such as Jrim himself had complained about the poor condition of the bridge. She had refused to build a new bridge or repair the Roman one.

"We don't want Saxon hoards becoming aware of us, they may team up in difficult numbers. Seclusion is best!" Alecto had scream-talked at him.

But she had agreed to arm the bridge with ropes only the creations would know to look for and had used some of her dark arts to make them able to support the gargantuan weight of things like Jrim's arms which were twice the size of his body. Digging with these huge tools meant he had hollowed out a section of the ground beneath the beach, and he dug down a bit not wanting to risk going outwards and letting the water in.

~

The two men went back to where Digoth had first seen the giant arm but it was gone. They cautiously walked around the beach. "Maybe it sneaked into the city?" Digoth said.

"It's a troll, not a stray cat!" growled Milian still seething and spitting with rage at the clump of hair. He threw it on the ground.

"Bastard! My hair! My fucking hair!" He was about to say something else when the giant grey hand reached up from under the stone beach and just missed him by inches allowing him to roll away but again in the direction of the deadly water just missing it this time.

A second hand bursting out sent Digoth tumbling in the same direction. They were both now at the edge of the shore their backs facing the water.

The beach was short, barely twenty feet in width, and above it was a stone ledge wide enough for men and even wagons to pass by on and on that ledge rested the city wall and open space where the gates once stood.

"We should run to the space in the wall," said Digoth

"It got too close, it can sense our movements. It'll either drag us down or throw us back towards the water," Milian said.

"So what do we do? The arrows don't go through stone!"

Milian counted his arrows. Only ten, a few had been lost in the water he couldn't really afford to waste any. He could run out and then try to stick the troll in the palm before his head was popped like a berry but a clear shot with the bow is more doable he thought.

"How do you feel about being bait?" he asked Digoth.

~

Jrim had dug deeper he was planning on eating the little bug men piece by piece so he needed a bit of space to store them.

He may miss out on the feast but with a full belly, the bridge in the river, and having fulfilled his obligation as the troll's representative for the ceremony once he finished eating and got there for the end part the event would have been a splendid affair. Then back to Hiberian and the open plains and green valleys, so convenient to chase bug men in, so fun to hide from them and snatch them before they knew they were gone.

No wonder the larger creations; trolls, giants, ogres and the rest were recently preferring that beautiful island to this smelly one which was just full of nothing but forest, and populated by stunted angry Britons or Saxons who didn't even have the manners to wash before you ate them.

He heard the pitter-patter of feet from above him. Only one? He expected them to make the run together in different directions, forcing him to smash up the entire beach to trap them. One after the other? He'd have to be fast.

~

Digoth treble checked that Milian had notched his bow and then began to sprint towards the ledge as planned, but he froze when he saw the section of the beach he was running towards had disappeared. There was a large hole which had suddenly appeared and he was heading for.

He stopped running but skidded too close to the edge and out of nowhere a grey hand appeared for a micro second to flick his ankle and Digoth crashed to the bottom of the five-foot trench.

He lay there for a second wondering what had just happened before fingers looking like ten small grey tree trunks pulled him into a second smaller hole at the base of the trench and he disappeared under the beach.

Milian had seen the flicker of a grey hand before Digoth fell, but had no chance to fire off a shot.

Probably miss and get Digoth instead he thought glumly; his was confidence not what it was after the swim and bridge crossing had wrecked him physically and mentally.

He remembered what Merlin told him the day he was told he had been chosen as one of his warriors. *"You will never know what you are capable of until you tell yourself that it can do done."*

He staggered towards the trench and saw no sign of Digoth or the troll. He wriggled through the hole that the troll had dragged Digoth through and found to his horror he had wriggled over a cliff edge and crashed deep down into the underground cave the troll had built.

~

Jrim heard the crash onto the floor. The second bugman or his second course had landed right into Jrim's trap.

Bugmen always saw the sloping brow and wide nose smeared across his cheeks, and assumed trolls were unintelligent but the cold man didn't go to all the trouble of making creations just to be mindless beasts of burden, well except for the ogres he reasoned.

Jrim's arms were strong and agile enough to hollow out an underground cave big enough for the three of them in a shockingly short time. He picked up the first man he'd trapped by his head who had fainted; he only needed to use his forefinger and thumb and was just going to twist the neck a little to…he felt something.

Shit! The man was playacting being out of it and had stuck him with something in the neck. A little pain and a shudder of fear went through him as he remembered the rumors about arrows that could cause creations to perish in all manner of horrible ways, can't be that the pain would be too much. This was really just a nasty sting, time to…the time he'd spent thinking and brooding over the wound had given the man time for a second stab this one to the eye.

This fucking stung and Jrim sank to his knees releasing the man. Fuck! It'd take a couple of minutes for the wounds to heal and his body to regenerate. After that he'd kill both bugs slowly. Like bugger the ceremony he planned to find Alecto and ask for something that'll keep them alive for weeks while he toys with them.

Digoth rolled over stones and pebbles grunting but finally some luck his body hit Milian's.

"We need to go now!" he shouted.

Milian looked up at the wall of stones next to him and then the gap of sky he fell from.

"Impossible," he moaned.

"What is wrong with you? I thought Britons could climb better than squirrels was that all horse shit just like about you being brave fighters?"

Digoth's temper angered Milian but then did what it was intended to do and shamed him into action.

"Come on then, you ginger foreign twat," he said, and grabbed hold of one of the rocks and hoisted himself upwards, and then upwards onto another. He'd been rock climbing on Crib Goch since he was old enough to walk.

Digoth carefully studied the moves Milian was making as he followed him up.

Before starting to climb Digoth sheathed the pugio with which he'd stuck the monster and did a double take when he saw the blacksmiths hammer engraved on the hilt was glowing bright red. "What the…"

"Come on you arsehole! The troll will be on us soon," Milian hissed. Digoth began to quickly climb.

~

Jrim's eye had healed itself, although not without a bit of pain. It was difficult to push out the damaged jelly and replace it with new jelly, and it stung a bit. The neck wound sealed up without any sensation he barely noticed it. He looked around and saw the two men clambering up the walls of the cave to the surface.

This should be easy, he thought as he picked up a large rock. Jrim had amazingly good aim probably from nights of doing little but playing a sport where the trolls tried their best to knock each other out and sometimes they would allow the human captives to escape from the cave giving them a twenty-second head start before turning their heads to goo with a well-thrown boulder.

Not this time with them moving up the wall slowly, he reckoned he could pop their kneecaps and send them crashing to the ground still conscious and aware of what was about to happen to them.

So he aimed, stretched back his arm, clenched his fist around the warm rock, and let out a yelp of pain, the rock shouldn't be warm, and was now so hot it burned his palm. He threw it to the ground in shock and his beady eyes widened as he saw it on the ground; it was glowing orange from the inside and smoldering. He looked at it in amazement but another rock emitted an orange glow from its base and then another, and another, and another.

~

Digoth and Milian had noticed the warm feeling from the foot of the cave and how it had quickly turned from an uncomfortable humid feeling into the air becoming painful to breathe. They scrambled faster and faster up the walls.

Digoth followed Milian's every move and crucially cried a warning when Milian's eyes clenched shut from the growing steam nearly put his hand on a rock that had just started to glow orange.

It was as they were wriggling out of the hole Digoth had been pulled into and Milian had fallen in that they began to hear screams from the bottom of the cave. Inhuman shrieks and howls of agony.

Back in the open air, they stood and the howls had faded a little but were still ongoing. Looking down and seeing the whole cave glow orange, they wouldn't be stopping anytime soon. Climbing out was impossible for the beast, with two-thirds of the wall the two men had just climbed smoldering and more and more rocks were beginning to glow.

"The whole cave has become a giant kiln!" said Digoth. "He must be roasting alive in there."

"Rather him than us," said Milian. "We should seal up this hole in case its screams attract passers-by not that there's likely to be any this side of the Tamesas, but still wouldn't want anyone falling in. The women are still wandering around somewhere remember."

Finding a slab of stone on the ledge and some parts of the city wall that had crumbled enough that they were easy to break free was simple enough, but carrying them back to the beach took its toll on their already exhausted bodies.

Finally, the hole was sealed and the screams reduced to a faint if horrifying sound.

"How long will those stones burn? Will it kill the beast?" Digoth asked and Milian shrugged.

Digoth showed Milian the pugio with the glowing hammer and his eyes went wide. "You keep that thing near, I daresay we will need it again."

CHAPTER 35

Ordo sat on the stone bench inside the villa while Aebbe was staring at the floor. A circular mosaic pattern was her view with at the center of the circle made of tiny tiles, the figure of a man naked apart from a cape and loincloth, with a crown of leaves in his hair reclining on a giant orange and black cat.

"We call it a tigris," said Ordo his face stained from chin to hairline red with dried blood. "There's no word for it in your language." he took a swig from the clay jug spilling wine down his chin. "I had the pleasure of seeing one in the Colosseum once."

Aebbe had no idea what the monster was talking about, but nodded as long as he was talking he wasn't eating her.

Iga and Hieu were hopefully free from the enslaved East Saxons. Ordo had marched them to an amphitheater in much better condition than the one in Chichester.

Staring straight ahead as she walked through the city, Aebbe had tried to ignore the ash floating through the air, the stink of rotting flesh from every building, and the screams coming from a distance with the occasional one shrieking from a nearby point.

At an amphitheater gate, he told her to step aside, and yelled directions to the next brainwashed Saxon in line before snapping, "What's your name, lice carrier?"

"Wann," answered the large jawed man dully.

"Everyone follow Wann into the building I'll be back in a while." To Aebbe, he said, "Follow me!"

So now she was all alone, no sister, no brother, no Briton bandit/warrior or whatever he thought he was at this moment in time, no former slave turned ally, no cross-dressing brat with an inflated sense of her intelligence who she was somehow becoming fond of.

It was now just her and the monster. She hadn't seen a chance to sneak away and didn't know where she would go if she did. She just kept hoping something would turn up. Now it hadn't and she was defenseless she regretted not making a run for it.

Before joining the procession of thralls into the city they had taken their weapons off their belts and hidden them. Her pugio was tied to her forearm by string, a few tugs and it would be free. She doubted it would be any use against these monsters it was just a pretty-looking dagger and not magic like Milian's arrows, but if needs be she could use it to open her own throat and deny the monster the pleasure of what he had planned.

Ordo stood up and handed her the jug. "Drink," he said, and she lifted the weirdly shaped clay jug by the base.

"Use the handles of an amphora to drink with, it's not like the wooden crap you pig fuckers use it keeps the wine fresh for longer." She took a sip and her tongue lit up. The fruit-tasting liquid, both sweet and sour, as it passed through her lips, the flavor of the fruit so intense.

She'd only ever drunk stagnant water and ale before, sometimes mead at a special occasion such as the harvest feasts. She took another, longer sip. "Frankish swill," said Ordo, "they don't use the right combination of herbs to sweeten as was done in Rome's day of course they had access to more ports…" he trailed off.

"Maybe we should conserve it, swill or not. The sirens swim out to the east and south to feed and always bring back something of the wrecks they make but I wonder where they are? I hope they weren't in the Tamesas when it turned that way. No, conserve we must, the villa's sleeping quarters are just the other side of the courtyard so stand up, and…"

Her hand was about to untie the pugio when the door opened and another figure entered the villa.

Ordo looked annoyed but still greeted the intruder. *"Salve Psyche."* She shot him a bemused look and snorted. "Why are you speaking Latin, you goose! You know the boss man doesn't care as long as it isn't business and…"

She then noticed Aebbe sitting on the floor and suddenly finding the mosaic design the most interesting thing in the world.

"Oh, I get it! You found a pretty one among the East Saxons and fancy a private piece of the feast, you old goat, you never change! Hey love has he told you about his days in Rome and Alexandria yet? Drunken fool was born in Cynwidion, this city is the furthest south he's been, still, it's likely his father was a legionary, although which one is impossible to say given what the boss man told me about his mother so half-Roman at least. Mind, for you East Saxons that must be remarkably common so…"

"Shut up, woman!" screamed Ordo. Psyche gave him a menacing look with such a hideous smile and expression on such a beautiful face it startled both Aebbe and Ordo with its uncanniness before she burst into cackling laughter.

"I will never understand you men! Hain takes them and rips out their throat halfway through the act, while Heslop always says he eats the pretty ones slowly, and now there's you always trying to impress them. I mean they're just food! When you were human did you sing a song to your porridge to get it to like you better?" She cackled again.

Aebbe had heard enough. She knew the voice she was hearing taunting the man, it was the same bog land accented Saxon of the Angles. She remembered where she had heard it first.

Coming from the mouth of Hieu's brother, the whole amphitheater heard, *"Put that fucking arrow in the chest, you pointy nosed bitch,"* from Torold's mouth towards the newly orphaned Hieu.

Aebbe felt loathing towards the creatures, hate she had never felt before, not even when confronted with the water whore on the river but a voice told her in a rattling sound that bounced around her skull. *'She's not the worst, you ain't met me yet.'*

This snapped her out of her terror-induced daze she moved her arm against her stomach and was ready to thrust the pugio through her gown sleeves into her belly when Psyche started another rant.

"I've just come back to get changed, the ceremony is already underway. Oh, you should have seen Hain's northmen fight so fierce! I had to take one down to a private part of the dungeons myself and well look!" She gestured to her black gown which was caked with dried blood.

"You aren't the only one to have a wandering eye, you boar. I'm just more discreet. Anyway I'm due in the boss's private seats for the rest of the ceremony so need to look the part. Erm, even if you are seated with the plebs you might want to wash your face you are going to have to face him when you make your offering."

"I won't be with the plebs for much longer once he sees how much Saxon flesh I've brought him maybe I'll take your seat! The frog has been talking around town about how little use you were down south."

"The frog is full of shit! I captured one of those arrows so he could get his hands on the chest with the shiny cross, and win the boss's favor not to mention saving Vit from the arrows, fat lot of good it did him."

By now, they were bickering at each other on the fringes of the courtyard. Aebbe hoped for a brief second that she had been forgotten about until Ordo snapped his head back, growled, "Don't move" to her, as he and Psyche walked into the courtyard.

"Why don't we get messy eating her together and then we can wash the blood off each other's bodies?" said Psyche. "I'm sure that'll be more to your liking than some mousy little Saxon." She pulled down her gown, displaying her breasts.

"What's gotten into you?" Ordo asked a bit confused.

"Maybe it's the blood lust from tasting one of Hain's or maybe the look in the blonde Saxon girl's face when she had to witness it from the middle of the amphitheater, but I am on fire right now. Might as well make the most of it before we see blondie turn into a grisly, slimy, croaking thing that The Nix will mount straight after, because trust me, nothing will dampen those fires than that."

"I thought you were with…"

"We enjoyed each other for a time but then he got the arrow in his blood, and I don't fancy having a leech as a boyfriend for the rest of eternity!"

"I hear you, Psyche," said Ordo grinning. He stopped to wash his face in a stone basin.

"Wait!" Psyche told him. "We wash after we eat the Saxon, you idiot! It's not going to be a clean feed and we may need to conserve our water until we work out what's wrong with the river!"

"I'm pretty sure that if the eyeless snot-skinned mare can burn one of those arrows, which you couldn't then magicking up a bucket of water should be easy for her."

"Did you talk yourself out of sex as often when you were a human? You're lucky I've already tasted blood tonight it'll take more than your flapping fangs to put me off. Now let's head back, I think I'll start with the rat-girl's face and you start with her feet. We can meet in the middle like a pair of hounds with a sausage, hah!"

They walked back into the room they had just left only to find it empty.

The room appeared to be silent for a long time before Psyche said, "No...no...you didn't forget I remember you asking her to stay, and I saw the scratch mark you left on her face this is..."

"Impossible," Ordo finished for her as he was racking his mind desperately trying to recall the faces of the female villagers he'd marked at Mucking. Failing to do so he wondered about the merchants at Camulodunum, a wife or sister of one perhaps? No, he'd had a fun time there so all the faces were still fresh. He was panicking.

~

Aebbe still had the pugio resting against her belly as she hurried down the streets trying to remember the way back to the amphitheater. She still needed some assurance that if captured, and the odds impossible, she had a way out, but this meant her sister was surely alive! In fact, the disdain the evil bog woman had used in her voice when talking about her assured Aebbe that she was talking about Alfwen and not some other unfortunate blonde Saxon girl they had come across.

She had to get back to the amphitheater, find Iga and Hieu and work out where the middle of the amphitheater was, free her sister and head somewhere far, far away from this terrible city.

She slipped through an alley, and was sure that it was just a left turn here, through this gate, she froze in fright as she'd somehow found herself in an open air square fenced off by crumbling stone buildings.

In the square were market stalls, shacks, and shops manned by yellow eyed creatures. The stalls had racks of meat hung behind them. The smell was overpowering and flies buzzed everywhere. Through the haze of insects, Aebbe could make out the torsos hanging on hooks behind the stalls certainly weren't swine. She knew exactly what animal they were from, and had to cover her face with her sleeve from the smell.

Most of the customers, some ordering bowls of the foul-smelling meat from the stalls were cowled in black hooded cloaks which made their whole face retreat into a pool of darkness with only eyes glowing red, yellow, green, purple, and some colors Aebbe couldn't name.

Towering above the hooded customers was a blue skinned woman as tall as two men, naked from the waist up, she wore a necklace of three human skulls.

Aebbe could see the amphitheater from here it was just on the other side of the square but how could she get across without being noticed by the monsters? Even if they were blind she gave herself away by vomiting the second she got close to the stalls. Her best choice was to retreat the way she had come and try to find a way around the square.

She turned to see the space in the walls she had come through was clear and slowly began to edge towards it. Her insides turned to jelly as she heard from behind her shout in almost a yelp, "Where do you think you're going, dearie?"

She broke into a run but made barely made it a few yards before she felt something tug on the hem of her dress pulling her to the ground.

Next thing she knew, she was laying flat on her back and standing over her were four young men, youths really but they had the snout of a fox where their noses and mouth should have been and triangle shaped shirt ears on the top of their heads. One had a piece of cloth from her dress in its mouth.

"A live one! No need for piss-eyed stew! Their best meat is fighting inside. Old piss eyes only sell old women and cripple's meat in the forum. Oh, to get a young one to eat alive what a happy day lads?"

That strange yelping sound asked the question and was greeted by excited yelps of approval.

Tears streamed down Aebbe's face as the frustration ached and wracked her body more than the fear did. She had the pugio pressed in the right place and was ready for the final push.

Perhaps she'd see her parents again in a new world, perhaps she would open her eyes as a baby somewhere older and far away, perhaps she would see and feel nothing for the rest of time. The priests were very vague on the question of where we go after this life with each one having a different story.

She would find out soon enough as she clutched the hilt of the pugio under her sleeve and closed her eyes it felt warm, it felt nice.

Could she already be dead and at peace?

No, she could smell the smell of raw meat coming from the snout of the creature nuzzling her neck. Her thoughts began to race, every last memory she had appeared in random order and a sense of elation went through her from head to toe as she withdrew the knife from her sleeve and slashed at the snout. The blade was so sharp even a tired hack from her sliced a chunk of flesh off it.

"Bitch is going to get it now!" screamed the stuck fox man in rage as the hoots of his friends rang around him. He shook his head in fury, blood splattered the face of his companions.

"What are you going to do, Gizo? Make her more dead?" More hooting.

Well, I guess it's time, thought Aebbe unable to understand why she was feeling so good. Her eyes grew when she saw the pugios hilt for the first time since it started feeling warm. It was glowing green.

Then a fog descended, it was an invisible barrier but one she could see or sense. She knew she was in here with the fox men and no one outside had any idea that this space existed. It was outside of the world but connected to it, some of its rules applied and others didn't. It was inside the forum, but bigger than the whole city.

The wounded fox man Gizo knew something was wrong.

"What is happening! Black Annis! Can you see us?" He appeared to be shouting towards the blue she-giant who absently looked in their direction, but that seemed to be all as if she had heard an unusual bird squawk or something, enough to only attract her attention for a second, before she moved onto a stall to yell at a yellow eye over something or another.

Aebbe couldn't stop smiling. She had no idea where she was but had a massive sense of confidence that she was safe.

She looked around all she could see was the bustling and ghastly market place and that's all she would see even if she walked for miles, which she was sure she could.

"I didn't know the Saxons had their own magic," yelped one fox man sounding worried.

"It's nothing, Alecto will have us out in a jiffy," said Gizo. "I don't know what you're grinning about bitch! You're trapped in here with the Vulpine lads!"

"Am I?" Aebbe said calmly. "Because it appears to me that we aren't alone here, and someone wants to talk with you more than they do with me."

Aebbe had sensed the growling before it had started. She could smell the blood on their breath it was fresh not like the rotten stink the fox men had on theirs. Two red eyes appeared behind Gizo.

"What the fuck is…" were the last words they ever heard from him before a growl and a snap, and he disappeared into a misty fog.

The remaining fox men started to jostle and edge away from each other, each wanting to find a way out of here alone and then the screams started.

The screams of someone being eaten alive, someone having their face torn off, their bones crunched, their belly torn open, and the sounds of this happening to someone who couldn't die. Aebbe grew up more or less in the woods that surrounded the village she knew the smell of fox piss and was smelling it now.

A growl and a set of red eyes appeared behind each of the fox men.

Aebbe turned away and sheathed the pugio into the pocket hanging off her belt. Suddenly the fog lifted and she was back in the reality of the square. The cold air hit her face like a slap. She had returned alone. Where ever she had left the fox men, they had remained. With self-belief charging through her for the first time in her life she strode out the way she came and navigated herself towards the amphitheater.

CHAPTER 36

Iga and Hieu had stayed in the line as they walked through damp stone corridors following Wann along with all the other thralls. Unlike most of them, Iga was aware of her surroundings. She could still pause and look at the blood on the walls, and listen to screams and cheers from above.

She also noted they were descending; the paths sloped never so slightly, but she was aware they were going further and further beneath the city. Soon she found herself with fifty other souls in a cell.

There wasn't much space to move. Iga wasn't too worried about her confinement as the locks, and indeed half of the caged cell door, had long since rusted away, and unlike the fifty unlucky thralls, she and Hieu could walk out at any time. She was just concerned about what awaited them.

More screams from above, a bellowing voice in a language she had never heard before. With Aebbe surely dead and the two useless men at the bottom of The Tamesas, her obligation to this mission was over. She was not without pity for Alfwen, but there was no need to throw away her life and the child's life on what was surely a doomed mission.

She should get out of Londinium somehow and go where? Back to Chichester? The new reeve would not welcome the sight of Hieu, which could lead to inheritance questions about the old reeve's house and possessions, and making the pair of them disappear wouldn't be too difficult for Bowden.

West maybe, to catch up with Allyn and Cwenhild? How would they survive such a journey? The prospect of being enslaved again made her shudder.

She pulled Hieu who was transfixed by the graffiti on the walls by the arm. "Don't look at that!" she snapped. Some long-dead prisoner had drawn a picture of himself with grotesquely oversized genitals with some of that curvy writing underneath. "We are leaving!"

She squeezed her way past the statue-like but sometimes swaying East Saxons and soon they were both in the corridor. "Do you remember the way out?" she asked Hieu.

"Right," she said, and the two started to sprint then in the distance they heard voices coming faintly from the way they were heading.

One was too faint to hear although a burst of female laughter sent a chill up Hieu's spine. The other voice had the annoying habit of speaking upwards, making every sentence sound like a question it was unmistakably Ordo's voice.

"Quick! Other way!" Iga hissed, and she and Hieu ran past the cell in the opposite direction.

Ordo leaned into the cell and shouted, "Left arm up." They all did so at the same time he couldn't spot any hesitation.

He said, "bash your brains out on the floor." A sudden flurry as they pushed each other in order to clear space with which to get on their knees and begin. Eventually, thuds started and cries of pain and grunts intermixed with sobbing and heavy breathing rang out as all the East Saxons were trying to crack their skulls open.

Ordo looked; not one of them was faking it or being half-hearted: in fact the opposite, he was going to lose them at this rate. "Stop right now! Stand up!" he screamed.

Groggily the captives complied. Trickles of blood rolled down most of their faces.

"I swear sometimes Morchan has more going on between his ears than you do, boss turned the wrong one into an ogre. Just ask one of them!" Psyche said.

"Ask them what? Are you a spy? The thralls will deny, as will the rat girl's companions, so how do I find out who is a liar?"

Psyche walked to the front of the cell and took the hand of a young woman, her gown while filthy from the journey was made of better material than most of the others, and her beads were crystal which was rare among Saxons.

Psyche lifted her hand to her mouth and bit and drank. Hmm, she thought the taste of pork was in her blood this once got to eat meat regularly; lucky girl... until now.

The sight of the woman's blonde hair reminded her of lady Nix she paused to see if she could recognize that cow's screams amongst the others up above; futile!

She drank slowly the corners of her mouth curving upwards as the Saxon woman's tears launched into a flood. She took the hand out of her mouth and gently put it back by the woman's side.

"There, there my love, no need to cry just got to make sure you and I have a nice little chat now. Are any of you different from the others?"

"Different how?" stuttered the woman.

"Oh you know, less lice, better fed, different dialect of Saxon, the fucking ability to make decisions of their own free will."

She slapped the woman across the face.

"If you give me another stupid answer I will take your arms

and legs from you and leave you for the rats to eat slowly. Again, are any of you different from the others?"

Between gasps and tears and pleading, she got her answer.

"Before we entered the city, three joined us; they had our mark but we hadn't seen them on the journey down, he—" she pointed at Ordo "--went into the city before us, so we didn't see."

Ordo muttered. "Fuck!" Then, after a pause, "You better keep your Saxon whore mouth shut!"

"Of course she will," said Psyche. "She has about an hour to live and is hardly going to spend that marching up to the bossman's private suite not when we can both control her, but you are going to owe me big time!"

She turned back to the woman. "We know who one of these three is but point out the other two."

"I can't," said the woman, now convulsing with sobs before Psyche could jab one of her long nails into the woman's eyes, she saved her sight by gurgling, "Two just left, walked out as if not a care in the world, they went right then left."

"Thank you, dearie," said Psyche. "Well Ordo my love, let's go have a bit of fun!"

~

The Nix poured some water over himself. The heat from the river was making his skin dry faster and he didn't like that.

"I need damp skin to breath!" he snapped at Alecto's tutting. She had previously complained to Spurius that magicking water for the whole city would be time-consuming. "Given the other tasks you have given me."

"I'll send the ogres north from tomorrow," Spurius had said. "Surely, not all of the tributaries can be boiling."

Now, The Nix joined him on the edge of the suite as he looked at the carnage below. He shuffled a bit usually he just wore a loincloth. There was little point in dressing up when he didn't need to feel the warmth. He spent most of his time in water and mud but today at the cold man's insistence he was wearing a bulky and long toga. He shuffled some more slowly so he didn't trip over and stood next to him.

"You…uh messaged me sire?" he said.

Spurius clad in a toga only his had a blood-red border, unlike The Nix's plain white one turned to him.

"You have had the same word rattling around in your head whenever you think about me or the girl or the ceremony, 'when'. It's driving me to distraction, just enjoy the festivities. I have enough on my mind! Your time will come before the sun rises I swear! Do not question me again you have pleased me and will be rewarded but my patience has limits."

It was always risky to ask the man questions but it could stop him from wondering when he got to unwrap his gift. "What do you have on your mind sire?" He was rewarded with a grin: he had made the right choice. Spurius was dying to brag about what was on his mind.

"Alecto has been making great progress with the Crux gemmata: it appears to enhance her mind and powers whenever she is working. She has finally come up with a spell that can defeat our oldest enemy."

"You mean those hunt boys giving us trouble out west?"

"No, picking them off will be like squashing worms once we defeat the sun. She thinks she can make it powerless against us then imagine it Nix! With no restriction to our movements, I will add to our ranks. We will have a creation in every village farming them, how fat we will grow!"

"When will this happen?" The Nix asked.

"Within days," Spurius said so excitedly the snake's skull rattled in its head. "Maybe even tonight!"

A cry went up from below as neither had been paying attention, they didn't move in time to avoid the blood that splatted over their togas and faces. After a moment's silence, they both burst out laughing.

They walked back inside the suite. Heslop was sat on his usual stone bench gnawing away at an arm. He'd nearly got the upper arm down to the bone, but the forearm tendons were proving tough for him and he was getting frustrated.

"Where are Psyche and Alecto?" asked Spurius.

Heslop threw down the arm in a tantrum and yelled, "Fucking Britons swinging on branches all day makes it too tough to chew! Tell me the next lot are Saxons, meat slides right off them, salty too."

An irritated Spurius repeated his question in a tone that made Heslop remember that being in Spurius' inner circle had not saved a few others from his wrath in the past.

"Erm, sorry sire Alecto popped out saying you'd know where she was going and I ain't seen the loud one for a while. She was in good form at the start but went home to get changed and is late returning. Say, she has been looking a bit off if you ask me. Maybe she misses Vit, if she's lonely do you think…"

The Nix's tongue whipped out and stripped the forearm bare to the bone. "Don't think she'll be into a man whose hair smells like his feet," he said with his mouth full of flesh. "You can have the hand if your teeth are strong enough," Heslop sputtered his outrage.

Alecto entered, behind her Morchan was clutching the jeweled cross protectively. She opened the sack. "Happy wedding day, Nix." A dozen knuckles began to crawl out.

Two shot straight for the hand and fought each other while feeding, only leaving a skeletal claw.

"How? With the river boiling there's been no chance to fish?" the Nix said.

"A little trick that just came to me thanks to your discovery in Noviomagus Reginorum. I swear everytime I get stuck it… it's like it speaks to me. The message comes in a dream, I ask and it provides a guide that leads me to the answers to all my questions. I only needed a slither of fish scales to make these."

She turned her eyeless face to Spurius. "I have asked it how to render these arrows worthless," she said with glee in her voice. "I hope that the answer comes to me in my sleep after the sun comes up."

"Well, if you remember, Alecto, I asked about no longer being the sun's captive any progress on that?" Spurius asked.

She gave a surprisingly beautiful smile for such a peculiar face.

"I've found a way but it will require treating each creation individually."

"Then tonight we have two ascensions, young Alfwen to a Nixess, and you yourself, Alecto, can be the first of us to walk in the sunlight."

The Nix gave an excited croak. "Seems everything goes to plan when you put a Nix in charge eh, Heslop?"

The dwarf screwed up his face in disgust as The Nix picked up the knuckle, drained it of whatever blood it had retrieved from the hand, and launched it over the balcony and onto the amphitheater grounds.

~

Alfwen was watching bloodbath number ten or eleven. It couldn't be more than the twelfth one surely, but she had lost count by now.

This one had two yellow eyed monsters each present a tribute.

She recognized one as Jutes from their thin shields. The others must be some type of Briton tribe by their reluctance to use shields at all but strong armor.

They had been forced to fight each other to the death. Truth was, the losers were the real winners as their body parts were thrown to the now capacity crowd after they died. The survivors of each fight had to turn on each other with the final one returning to the dungeons for god knows what, but Alfwen suspected they would soon envy their fallen comrades.

None of the Jute or Britons would have this issue she knew as with a thud a second knuckle fell on the ground. The first had already sent the Britons fleeing after it landed on one of them. The yellow eye that had brought them to the area had screamed at them to stand and fight.

They had been left with their arms and armor for the fight but were exhausted by the time they made it to their comrade to reign blows down on the foul thing. It had already detected movement and jumped away leaving its first target bleeding out, his left leg from the thigh down a mess of ruined bone.

The second knuckle was around a Jute's throat and his comrades were running in the opposite direction with their yellow eyes disinterested as to their attempted escape.

He shouted something up at the elevated area with a balcony some kind of special suite for important people, and the same strange language came from there in an all too familiar croaking noise as a back and forth dialogue went between them.

Eventually, three more knuckles fell from the air, and then the yellow eye screamed at his Jutes to stand and fight.

Her face was drenched in blood, the gown a ruin with the insides of Woden knows how many men, women, and children dripping off it.

Only the area around her eye sockets remained clear. Something that eyeless bitch had done to her to prevent being blinded by blood she guessed.

How her mind hadn't snapped and gone the same way as her pirate cellmates was beyond her, but reasoned the witch had a hand in that too. Was she becoming indifferent to it?

The Jutes had begun fighting each other in their panic with the knuckle looking on curiously before deciding to dive into the melee.

Was that part of their process when they turned you into a monster? Make it so normal that when it was your turn to start hurting people, it seemed like the most natural thing in the world?

Soon it was over and just like the end of all the previous rounds the yellow eye who had made the tribute threw the maimed and mangled bodies into a rabid crowd who pushed and fought for the body parts.

The yellow eye would for him or herself keep an eye out for any dying people who seemed to have a particular thirst for live blood.

Orders were shouted down from the high balcony on occasion and body parts that had been requested by the occupants were thrown up.

Soon the crowd started cheering; they were reacting to another announcement that Alfwen was unable to hear. At least unable to hear yet.

CHAPTER 37

Digoth and Milian were more than a little unnerved by how quiet the entrance to the city was. Milian remembered his training where it was said about Londinium that for every set of creature's eyes, you saw fifty more hiding in the darkness watching everything you do.

Up until around fifty years ago or so, Britons, both hunt members and bandits seeking gold or revenge, would fall on the city during daylight hours hunting for monsters to slay and Roman treasure to plunder.

A very small handful survived and had recounted their stories to the people back west, well to Merlin's people back west. Merlin, for whatever reason, didn't want the priests who wrote in that curvy script the Romans had left them to know. He wanted their accounts to be preserved only orally or in the runes.

Retreating raiders some now blind or half-mad, others aged by decades by spending just a few hours in the city; they were all picked up by his men scouting the roads and brought back for an audience with Merlin in Avalon.

From there had come the blood-chilling accounts that made up Milian's training. These were all out of date as fifty years ago some said less, some said more, Merlin had shocked very Briton kingdom and tribe by one day striding into Londinium in the dead of night and then walking out just before sunrise.

There are probably less than five men on this entire island who know what was said and done that night but afterward, no Briton had entered the city and if any Saxon had there was no record of them making it out. Until now.

They had taken a right and Milian's attention was caught by a building that had been hollowed out and gutted by fire. He peered inside a charred open window space his bow and arrow notched.

"This place looks familiar," he saw nothing but soot and rubble but a cross had survived nailed high enough to escape the flames. It was stained black from smoke and would probably crumble to pieces at the slightest touch, but it told him this was once a church. Similar structures albeit wooden stood in the towns and villages to the west he travelled through. This was the first stone one he'd seen and it gave him the strangest feeling, almost serendipity.

Then the skull started chattering.

Digoth gave a shocked gasp when he heard it.

"What after all you've seen a talking skull is what sets you off? It's pretty harmless all things considered" Milian said.

They both peered into the window and looked closer at the chattering thing on top of a pile of burnt rubble. Time and smoke had charred it to an oak stained color.

"It didn't set me off," said Digoth. "It's just the other things we've seen aren't quite so ordinary. I mean, skulls? We dig up several dozen whenever it's time to till a field. Probably a bunch of your ancestors who fell out with another bunch of your ancestors, anyway is it trying to talk to us or something?"

"Can't talk without a tongue. I think we should carry on doing a perimeter of the inside of the walls until we work out where the movement is and where it's heading."

~

The Nix had watched Spurius turn from furious to concerned in a second. He had proudly announced to the crowd the entrance of Ordo and his East Saxons, only for nothing to happen when the gates opened. His face had turned from its usual olive red mix to a violent shade of purple.

"Where the fuck is he? How dare he be late?" he snapped at the occupants of his suite who suddenly wanted to be elsewhere.

They had all heard tales of creations who had been in the wrong place during one of his rages and had woken up in several pieces in some far-flung area with little time to literally pull themselves together before the sun came up and most never made it.

There was even talk of a strigoi who had talked over Spurius while he was ranting about someone who had displeased him, and that soul had been chained to the bottom of a boat and spells had been cast to push it far, far out from Dumnonia into the Sea of Atlas, forever sailing west.

"Always said Ordo thinks himself special, even the other yellow eyes say he's too proud, and that's like pigs calling one of the others a glutton!" Heslop was going with the idea that keeping the boss enraged with Ordo would distract him from themselves.

Eventually, some spare bodies were sent down to the cells to shuffle the East Saxons into the area grounds the crowd started booing and jeering when the stumbling and distraught Saxons looked around for an escape rather than fighting.

Some were able to move independently, Ordo's power fading after so long since the scratches and bites but it still pained them to walk far. One did get close to the barrier separating the seats from the grounds and was yanked into the crowd where a mass of green, grey, black and white bodies fell onto it and blood was soon spraying onto the damp red sand.

Most were still in Ordo's thrall and couldn't move without his instructions, some were in pain at having to be dragged out of the cell unable to leave without his say so.

All in all, it made for a poor show. But Spurius had lost interest his face had gone from purple to pallid white and he beckoned Alecto over for a private talk.

"Remember Luicus?" he asked her.

"The skull? He's still around? I thought he'd have asked to be put out of his misery by now." she said.

"It's easy to please Christians, especially priests. He cut the throats of the boys after he was done with them, and weighted them to the bottom of the river. Raving bastard was terrified of their hell when it was his time I could have offered him a slug's body and he'd have taken it."

"Their hell…does it exist?"

Spurius didn't answer but went on. "He keeps a look out for me in the old church, hoping one day I'll give him a body I suppose. He's just spoken to me. We are being invaded."

CHAPTER 38

Iga and Hieu were completely lost in the bowels of the amphitheater. Even though they could hear footsteps they knew the yellow eyes were close; it was the smell.

A quick right turn gave them hope. It was too dark to locate the entrances from a distance but a burst of cold air told them that an exit to the outside was in this direction.

They couldn't run due to it being close to pitch black. Whoever usually roamed these halls had no need of light other than a torch every dozen yards. They headed towards the source of the cold and heard doors slam both behind and in front of them. The pale face of a pretty yellow eyed woman appeared under a flame from a torch that appeared to alight instantly.

"Found them, Ordo," she said, making Hieu break into hysterical sobs at the sound of hearing that voice again. Iga cursed in anger: it was all over now, the pugio strapped to her leg was too far: she knew that in the seconds it would take to grab it Ordo, by now surely behind her, would twist her neck around or simply snap her arms like twigs.

~

Both Psyche and Ordo felt it at the same time: Spurius screaming in rage.

"Where the fuck are you! Get to me at once!" Psyche bit her lip, and Ordo gave a terrible shake. This only made Hieu cry and scream louder.

"What are we going to do?" Ordo hissed.

Psyche snapped her fingers. "Got it! Take the big one out to the arena floor with the other Saxons and I've got an idea that'll cheer up the boss. I'll head to his suite and make good with him maybe offer this little bitch as a gift."

~

Aebbe had found the entrance she and Ordo had left the remaining Saxons to march through unguarded. The roar of the crowd had changed and she heard boos and jeers ringing out from above her.

There were no signs of Iga, Hieu, or the marked Saxons. She clutched the pugio as she examined the scene soon finding an empty row of cells and footprints indicating some recent movement.

She heard footsteps approaching and with no one else to use it on drew blood by cutting her palm. The clear fog descended again and the air shimmered and grew thicker and she was back, back in the land where she had taken the fox men to and left.

They were here as were their tormenters but they were far away she was in a different part of this land now. She could still see the dark, dank stone corridor she was in now. It was more visible as if the darkness had a glow and was certain she couldn't be seen.

She watched as Ordo dragged Iga by the throat and Psyche pulled Hieu by the hair. They talked, but from her blurry vision point Aebbe couldn't make out what they were saying. It was Saxon but through the haze, it sounded so slowed down it was like they were moaning and groaning, and coupled with the different dialect Aebbe struggled to make out more than a few words, "mark", "fight", "Spurius".

Then the two creatures separated with Ordo, taking a different direction to Psyche and going down a different corridor. Psyche waited for a while before loosening a few stones to reveal a stone staircase in the rubble. She floated over some awkward lumps of rock and brick that had congealed together over the years, not seeming to care that Hieu's head smacked against the lumps a few times and disappeared, ascending.

~

"What do you mean, invaded? You said the hunt and you had an arrangement when it came to Londinium?" Alecto said.

"This isn't the hunt, it can't be. They know what I would do if they tried. I was attempting it when that old fool came to treat with me." Spurius was breathing heavily. "This is something else."

"Two men Lucius said? Probably just bandits who are lost… very lost," Alecto said.

"Normally I'd agree! I'd make a sport of it to see who can chase them down the fastest but The Tamesas…" He trailed off. "Lucius said that one of them had arrows, and when one was pointed in his direction he could feel himself being dragged towards a lake of fire…his words, not mine."

"Then it must be the hunt!" she said. "What the fuck are they thinking? Do they know about The Nix's haul from Noviomagus Reginorum? They must, that's made them break the deal! They're scared of what new magic I can create with these tools."

"Perhaps," replied Spurius. "We need to send a message. I've called Herla to my quarters I will tell him his fight with the newcomer is off."

Then the crowd started mock cheering turning their attention to what was happening on the area floor.

"Ordos, back," said Heslop.

"He had better have a good explanation for fucking around!" growled Spurius.

He turned back to Alecto. "The two bastards were last seen using the wall's perimeter to find their way here. Should be easy to find just send someone reliable after them! Now let's see what that whoreson has to say for himself."

~

Iga was thrown choking onto the damp sand and gazed in horror at the contents of the seats.

Hundreds of cheering monstrosities. Some human looking, some as black as coal, others green or gray, men and women with the heads and features of animals, human looking figures who you could see through as if they were made of smoke, human shaped bodies of unnatural sizes and proportions. Worst of all the normal looking ones. Their grins revealed more teeth than a person should have. The yellow from their eyes seemed to have the power to invoke nausea when she locked eyes with them.

She tried to focus her eyes on some people, real people were on the sand with her. Their attempts to shuffle away or crawl up into a ball ended when Ordo screamed, "Stand up, look in my direction, and pay attention!"

Instantly although with pain etched across their faces they complied. Iga recognized some faces from the trip to the amphitheater, they were her former cellmates.

Also there, in the middle of the sand in a mess of blood, guts, vomit, and who knows what else around a wooden pole stuck out the head of Alfwen. Her eyes blinked in surprise as she recognized Iga. Iga found it admirable that she still had any sanity left. She looked away as she couldn't take it if Alfwen's next gaze asked for hope. She had none of that to give.

Ordo started a loud and booming speech that after a bit of booing and jeering at the start was heard by every person in the seats although Iga couldn't understand it. It was in a language that she didn't understand but something about it gave her the strangest sense of familiarity.

Ordo bellowed, he could locate the best surfaces that would give his voice an echo effect and had been a loudmouth as a human, it hadn't taken him too long to give the vocal upgrade he'd received when he ascended to strigoi plenty of practice.

"My sire, my friends on this wonderful night please a million pardons. I beg you for my tardiness but I have a treat. I give you the offerings of the new kingdom of East Saxon, a fertile land for sure they aren't as boney as most Saxons and…"

"Shut the fuck up!" came the scream from Spurius. "You kept me waiting! Give us all a satisfactory explanation now or risk being given a new form. We can always have two transformations tonight! And trust me you don't want to see where my imagination will lead me! Maybe I'll turn the Saxon girl into a strigoi and you into a female Nix to keep my good friend here company for the rest of days as his reward!"

"Now hang on, I'm not sure about…" came The Nix's croaked response, before The Nix thought better of talking over Spurius.

The threat had Ordo bursting out, "I had to capture some intruders. I have one here!"He pointed to Iga. The crowd began to stir. No human had set foot in the city for half a century, at least voluntarily: they assumed Ordo had made it up and some mocking laughter came from the seats when it sunk in that Ordo had probably gotten himself deeper into trouble.

That soon turned to silence when Spurius turned his back and disappeared into his suite. It started to rain. Iga felt bile at the back of her throat and the blood started to smell of rotting meat and shit. Suddenly in front of her stood on hooves with faded scales just visible against the skin of his torso, a neck of raw, red the texture of leather, and a snake lolled out of his mouth. The horns on his head seemed to twist in ways that no matter in what direction he moved his head that blocked out the moonlight. The snake retracted into his mouth, his jaw clicked and fanged, and able to speak he said in Saxon, "Are you with the hunt?"

Iga's eye twitched harder than she'd ever imagined, and then the monster peered a bit closer and said something strange. "Could it be you? No, surely not. After what Kai saw he wouldn't want to return. At least not so close. Still, maybe you don't get a choice. I've not been to that side, and never will."

"Are you okay, Sire?" asked a petrified-looking Ordo.

"Just a feeling that this isn't the first time I've seen this one. Tell me all you know of this intruder."

Ordo recounted the story of him and Psyche tracking the two down. He wanted to leave out Aebbe's involvement but was terrified that Spurius would look into his mind. To what extent he could see and what he couldn't when he peered into his creations' memories was unknown to them all maybe even unknown to Spurius himself. But he was sure Aebbe's existence would jump out.

He instead stuttered an explanation that had him catching the trio at the city gates allowing the child and the blinking one to escape while he dealt with Aebbe, and teamed up with Psyche to capture the two remaining invaders in the amphitheater.

He left out any mention of his intentions towards Aebbe, leaving her unattended and letting her escape, and practically inviting the three into the city. Despite being almost certain the wrench didn't have a word of Latin he still gave her nervous looks every few seconds.

Spurius nodded, it sounded amateurish, and Ordo would not enjoy the fate he had planned for him for allowing such a desecration, no matter the circumstances, but he guessed most of it was true, and Ordo could enjoy one final night in his current form before he was summoned and made to account for this.

He dismissed the strigoi for the moment and focused on Iga. "Why did you come? Do you remember anything about last time? You couldn't stop yourself?"

Iga answered the first question by jerking her hand in the direction of Alfwen. She didn't have any idea what the following two questions meant.

Spurius grabbed her chin. One minute his hands felt like dry wood, the next the texture of worms. Looking into her eyes, his brown ones flashed blue, yellow, green, some colors she didn't have words for.

She was drooling before long and the panic that she had likely minutes left to live had been relegated to a vague, troubling feeling she couldn't find words for. All that mattered was looking into those eyes and doing whatever their owner asked.

"Tell me everything," he commanded.

CHAPTER 39

So Ordo had led them into the building before he discovered he was duped thought Spurius with fury. There was no time to mull on his punishment.

Despite this wretched body Kai was now inhabiting insisted that they were dead, and she must have believed it as there was no lying to him not know he'd put his hex on her, her brain would be mush within the hour, he knew the two men were still alive and inside the city walls.

He also had confirmation that the blasted arrows were in one of the men's possession. She offered no information about the river boiling nor about the whereabouts of this mystery woman who Ordo claimed to have disposed of.

He spoke slowly to her. "Thank you for speaking frankly, I know you didn't have much choice but you have paid a great price. Human minds weren't meant to look at me for long. But I give you back your free will for the short time you have. Thanks for the lamb, shame I never got to eat it."

He looked at Ordo with a charming smile. "Thank you for everything. Please come to my quarters as soon as the festivities are over for your reward." He walked away and Ordo, who had noticed a queasy unfamiliar feeling in his stomach since the smile, noticed the cold man walking away more briskly than usual.

He called back to Ordo, "Have your East Saxons tear her to pieces, it's a kinder fate than rapid brain rot, and it'll get us the crowd back onside."

~

Back in the suite, Spurius was greeted by Psyche. "Great minds, Sire! Forcing the intruder to fight Ordo's Saxons was what I suggested to him to put to you, and…"

"She's not going to fight, she is unarmed and will lose the ability to walk in minutes, but it should be a death to please the crowd, each limb being ripped off one by one. I understand you've been running around with that soon-to-be cursed wretched Ordo. Be careful, Psyche, I'm in a bad mood in regards to that."

Psyche, now on the verge of tears at his tone, held out her arms with a now passed out Hieu in them. "Take it, please, a gift for my lapse in not informing you when we were tracking down the invaders. This is the woman's companion. I recognize her from Chic…I mean Noviomagus Reginorum. The invaders must have come for Nix's bride." A furious snort from the frog-man came out, and he started spluttering about the need for haste.

Spurius ignored them both and walked to Alecto. "It's done?" he asked her.

"The Faerie are engaging them as we speak," she replied. "They weren't with the hunt, after all, so Herla?"

"Bring him to me anyway, we have matters to discuss."

~

The two men were spotted crouching against the wall edging their way towards the amphitheater still keen to avoid being spotted and so far successfully so. The city was largely deserted, the handful not in the amphitheater were goblins who preferred the deep underground even at night.

~

"Two mortal men, one not even a warrior! Spurius forgets himself with this summons! He has a legion of beasts to command. Does he consider us to be the same level as his amateurish creations?" said the red-haired, green skinned beautiful woman the size of a chicken.

"It is tiresome mother," said the beautiful brown haired man who towered over the woman. He was the size of an upright dog, both were clad in silk light pink colored robes that were so flesh-colored it gave the appearance of nakedness, for the man anyway.

The man continued."While we do not answer to him nor anyone it does not hurt to have him in our debt given his powers show no sign of waning. The strigoi in particular is troubling me, I'm not sure he knows the potential for that to get out of control."

"But why us?"

"These arrows are mortal to Spurius' creations. His witch suspects that because they were all once human, the gibberish the priests or druids, or whatever they are calling the old fools these days, cast over the arrows makes the creatures vulnerable due to part of them deep down still believing in it. With us being from a higher realm the arrows will be as harmless to us as everything else in this shitty realm is."

"What if his witch is wrong?" asked the green woman.

"These spells are weak, mother," said the man through gritted teeth. "It's two men, we will be back in Fae within minutes!"

~

Digoth heard the flapping of wings behind him and knew this was unlikely to be a bird or bat. He jerked his head to Milian who as quick as a flash spun and fired off a shot that tore through the torso of a tiny woman who had been approaching them in mid-air from behind. She lay prone on the ground.

"What is it?" Said Digoth.

"A dwarf?" offered Milian. "I've never seen one so well…pretty. Dwarfs are usually hairy, stinky things regardless of their sex. It's too tiny to be an elf. It is unlike anything I've ever seen before."

He walked closer. "And the arrow appears to have just killed it. It hasn't caused any of the distress we saw happen to the bear or what it did to the river."

Just then, a bright white light engulfed everything the men could see, and when their sight returned the creature's body was gone.

~

Everything was gone. They were standing in a field somewhere and it was freezing.

"Where are we?" said Digoth.

"Not Londinium," answered Milian. They took a step forward and he tripped on a root. Before he could even curse he tripped on another, then heard a grunt from Digoth who was having the same happen to him. The roots got bigger and he realized with horror they were growing out of the ground and engulfing his legs.

Both men were screaming seconds later from thorns digging into their legs and chest, and before long only their heads stuck out from the bushes that now trapped them. In the distance, two figures approached.

~

Their screams had slowed to moans by the time the beautiful

and diminutive mother and son were standing in front of the two bushes.

"Welcome to Fae," the man said with a grin that made his eyes dance.

Milian's eyes flashed with confusion when he saw the man's companion was the same tiny creature he had downed with his arrow. He tried to speak but cried out in agony instead as a thorn punctured his stomach.

"All wounds will heal and regenerate ready for you to be struck again. This is your new home!"

He turned to the woman. "Did the arrow hurt mother?"

She turned her nose upwards. "More so than most mortal weapons. It didn't leave a scratch as I knew it wouldn't but it did make me feel a trifle peculiar, still feel a bit grotty. Wretched thing!" she kicked the sack of arrows that now lay at Milian's feet before leaping away.

The man continued, "We are not of Spurius' blood, these weapons don't have the same effect we are not of your realm so they have no real effect really but intent is key, due to some trouble we had a time ago." He rolled his eyes. "We cannot just abduct humans into Fae as we once did. They have to wrong us and shooting a poisoned arrow through the body of the Faerie King's mother certainly has earned you both a place here for eternity. Now meet your jailer, Puck." A third figure wandered into view.

CHAPTER 40

Iga blinked blankly as drool covered her chin. It was so loud. She tried to think. She couldn't remember her name or why she was standing on sand with everyone screaming at her.

She clenched her eyes and thought hard. She wasn't blinking and twitching, she knew enough to mark that as unusual. Memories from long ago flashed through her mind but she couldn't remember who she was, where she was, or what she was supposed to be doing.

She remembered a face with a birthmark for just a flash, then a cruel blonde girl who was one minute mocking her and the next her face was a sea of blood. She remembered walking a long distance with a companion, a lamb in her hands she felt stronger, then she remembered being in a wooden room placing the lamb down, and hearing the door creak open to the sight of something her mind would not allow her to visualize.

Then she remembered something from a lost childhood. She was sitting outside a wood and thatch hut hearing screaming in the distance that blended into the screams she was hearing now from the crowd. A man leapt out of the hut, bare-chested, with blue marks on his body and face.

He looked at her as smoke started to come out from one of the huts behind them. "The battle's been lost, they will be coming over the hill soon! Get to the woods and hide girl!"

"Yes, father," she had said and ran. She'd looked back and seen a swarm of Saxons waving their axes pour down the hill.

There were just too many of them. She watched frozen as two fell onto her father, he swung his sword at the side of one's head making his skull shatter and half his face explode into a red spray, but the other had taken his knees out with the axe and was soon hacking away at his chest and wrists. Iga remembered to turn and run but collapsed sobbing. She tried crawling to the bushes that marked the beginning of the forest before everything went black.

That memory from twenty years ago was now vivid in her mind despite her previously having no memory of anything before the beatings in the slave pens, until she ended up being bought by Ribald.

Now the vivid focus shifted to the two Saxons charging at her. She squinted: somehow they had gotten axes from somewhere. The two men were wearing hoods but she saw the faces of the two men who had come to her village.

No point just taking one of them out, she told herself. Dad made that mistake no, they both go at the same time. The East Saxons with claw marks on their faces bellowed as they approached, and Iga lifted her dress and reached for the pugio that she somehow just knew was strapped to her thigh.

At the last possible second, she yanked it from her leg and swung it against the air, slashing the throats of both men.

The men looked surprised and even a little relieved as they slumped to their knees clutching their throats. The crowd jeered and the long-haired man with yellow eyes was screaming and this time sent three men and one woman charging at her. She gutted the woman in the stomach and kicked the first man in the balls. It was while the final man appeared to hesitate not knowing the best mode of attack that the swaying started.

A feeling that despite all the outlandish things she had seen and experienced over the past week or so was beyond unreal. The amphitheater area was moving. It was like standing on a giant wave. The earth was swaying back and forth.

She took advantage of the last man's shock to cut his Achilles heel and stab the one moaning on the floor clutching his balls in the side. Something told her to head to the post where the girl was tied up. She seemed important somehow. She made a few paces further towards her, and she fell to her knees from another violent shift under the sand.

The pugio spilled out on the sand in front of her. In the night the fork-like symbol on the hilt glowed bright blue. She looked up and saw the whole building was shaking not just the sand. The jeers of the crowd were turning into screams of panic and pain when a pillar holding a section of the seats up collapsed sending the seat's occupants tumbling on top of each other. Some spilt on to the sand and others fell to the deep chambers beneath the amphitheater.

~

"What magic is this?" asked Psyche. She and Alecto began to hover while Heslop looked like he was about to throw up.

From their high viewpoint they could see a building outside the amphitheater, a forgotten brick and timber building, a quarter-house for amphitheater guards, or a storehouse for grain before it was sent east to the garrisons in Camulodunum. Few of the creations remembered, but now it was dust and rubble as it fell to the ground, the smoke and the ash floating into one half of the shaking and crumbling seats full of terrorized creations.

"The whole bastard city is shaking!" screamed Heslop, before vomiting all over a carpet Spurius was fond of.

"It's called an earthquake. This island doesn't have them. It's one of the few things about its natural conditions that isn't shit," Spurius told them coolly although he made sure to keep his back to them so they couldn't see his face contorting with rage.

She had lied to him and he hadn't detected it, this hadn't happened for hundreds of years.

"I was deceived!" he bellowed. "She must be with the hunt! Such spells can only come from one mortal on this wretched island!"

A stone block fell smashing into the floor, making them all cough furiously. Then the clop of hooves came from the entrance and cold air breezed into the room.

"Herla," coughed Spurius. The armored skeleton rode into the suite seemingly unfazed by the chaos as Heslop clutched to a trembling pillar and The Nix began to choke on the dust.

Herla did not get off his horse as he couldn't. The two stared at each other in silence their thoughts bouncing back and forth but Herla was hearing what he wanted to hear.

"To dust! I tell you I want the dust of their stones and their bones mixed into one pile I want no trace of the shithole left standing, let the future generations of this island, who Lilith willing will be our beasts of burden and food have no memory or knowledge that a fort ever stood there! In fact, fuck it! Get rid of the island if you can think of a way!"

He turned to the others. "The sun will be up soon. Nix, Alecto, our plans will have to be delayed while we find somewhere safe to stay. The temple is my favored place. Romans won't have spared any expense on materials lest they anger their gods."

"Nooooo!" howled The Nix. "Tonight I get my bride, you promised me! Always promising old Nixy and now so close!"

"We leave in five minutes. Alecto, cook us up something to help us on the way to the temple, doesn't have to be 100%. I know it's short notice, I just need any loose bricks or boulders to stay the fuck away from our heads, if they bounce where they aren't supposed to go. Nothing worse than being knocked out and unable to move when the sun comes up. Well, Nix what are you waiting for!? Go and get her, I'll perform the ceremony in the temple!"

Quick as a flash, The Nix leaped over the balcony and down to the chaos below.

~

Iga was crawling closer and closer to the tied-up girl. By now she had forgotten how to stand and walk as well as talk, and even the chaos around her wasn't troubling her that much as she had no idea what the trouble was. She was happy to ignore the screams and stamps that rang around her and just keep crawling in the direction that the voice in her head just kept dully repeating. *"To the girl, to the girl."*

The other people on the sandy area were rooted to the ground, not even trying to escape, and now and then a panicked monster would run onto the arena grounds in search of escape. If they saw any of the unfortunate humans who were just blankly staggering around they would stop and feed their blood lust overtaking self-preservation. One thing with moss green skin and pointy ears had been so preoccupied with chewing a woman's armpit off that it hadn't noticed several large slabs of stone come down on the both of them.

The woman was out of her misery now but from the twitching of some green limbs under the stone, the beast was somehow still alive. Thankfully they ignored the demented, exhausted woman crawling slowly towards her target. The shaking of the ground had stopped happening so frequently, and for so long, but now and then it was like the earth groaned, and there was another thud against her body as the earth shifted beneath it.

After what seemed like a lifetime she had made it.

The girl gasped. "Iga, oh my! Thank you! Please, quickly." None of the seven words had any meaning but she used the pugio to cut the binds around the girl's feet and waist, and numbly gurgled as she hacked against the rope bonds getting one arm free.

She then felt a jolt of smashing intense pain in the back of her head. It was only for a second after it was over she felt a fierce wind all around her, and the amphitheater turned bright white. She had her language back now and could speak, if not for the voices around her. Every word she had ever spoken, every word she had ever heard was chattering in her ears. She mouthed the words, "Not scared anymore," and fell flat on the floor as everything went dark and calm. *So peaceful* was her last thought.

~

Alfwen watched in horror and despair. Her vision was blocked by the sand cloud that seemed to cover the whole arena. The tongue had shot straight out of that sand cloud and taken the back of Iga's skull away with it when it shot back into the cloud.

She knew what figure would stride out of the cloud next. She was powerless to do nothing but obey him. She moved her free hand, and her body shook something felt different.

~

The Nix arrived in front of her as promised. His tongue with bits of brain on it licked against his lips.

"Come on wife! To the temple. I ride you tonight this…" he searched for the Latin word neither his nor Alfwen's native languages having a word "*terrace motes* is not to stop us quick to the temple with us." That was strange, he presented his back to her but she hadn't climbed on.

"On quick! The boss will leave without us and it's not safe to… why are you smiling?"

~

She was smiling because she knew the venom that made her obey The Nix instantly, no matter what wasn't working. She didn't know if it was because of the blood, or if the glowing fork on the pugios hilt was doing this, but she was full of a feeling she had never had, a sense of purpose.

The voice of her mother, of Iga, of all of the Nix's victims over the years was whispering and giving her the same message.

"Come and get me, husband," she said, not even needing the pugio to wrench her remaining tied hand free.

The Nix leaped forward so he was a few inches from her face and opened his mouth in a primal scream of frustration. His revolting tongue twitched and twisted. Alfwen clenched her eyes in shock she had blown her chance, any moment now that bastard tongue was going to shoot out and rip off her face.

A vision of her mother standing in front of her with her face missing was all she could see behind her shut eyes.

"Stupid girl, always with your head in the clouds. No revenge for my soul, or the others now!" The eyeless skull somehow said blood pouring out of the teeth and eye sockets. Alfwen forced herself to open her eyes and accept her fate but The Nix had closed his mouth.

"If you won't come, I will take you!" he said in accented Saxon. "You won't like that, so come! I will not give you up! Not after waiting for so long!"

Alfwen took a deep breath. "I will come," she stepped closer to The Nix. "You want my company for the rest of time? I will grant you your wish, husband."

The Nix looked close to tears, as his lips curved up in a smile and he said, "That's all I ever…"

His sentence was finished with a shocked grunt as Alfwen lifted the pugio with both hands and plunged it into the crown of The Nix's skull. She was still grinning when the ground beneath them opened up seconds later, sending them plummeting into the depths below.

CHAPTER 41

"Fuck," said Spurius, and Heslop crawled to the balcony to see what had happened, and quietly said "Yeah, fuck."

The entire arena ground, the pitch of sand, had vanished. Just a giant hole remained and it appeared everything underneath it had disappeared too. The newly formed pit looked bottomless and anyone who had been standing on the ground when it collapsed Saxon prisoner or hungry creation was now lost.

The shaking now got fiercer and fiercer, and it was clear that this suite, designed for the old governors of Londinium and visiting VIPs was not long for the world.

"Come on!" commanded Spurius and he walked out trailed by Heslop, Alecto, Psyche and still clutching the jewel-encrusted cross Morchan. Psyche almost forgot about Hieu but at the last minute remembered to grab her by the ankle and drag her unconscious body along with her.

~

Aebbe followed the procession down the winding staircase she hadn't had an opportunity to grab Hieu while in the large room. No sooner had she followed the yellow eyed woman up the staircase, then the whole group had exploded into fierce arguments in a strange language. Then the shaking had happened. It looked surreal to see everyone in the room swaying and screaming when inside her own space she couldn't feel a thing.

All other thoughts had deserted her as she had run to the balcony where she saw the chaos and the deaths of Iga and her sister. She was now the only one left. All the others were dead, but then the sight of Hieu's ankle being crudely grabbed as an afterthought, as the beasts made their retreat suddenly dissolved the feelings of despair. She still had someone to save.

Outside more buildings were shifting and swaying it appeared anyone of them could come crashing down at any moment. Some of these buildings were hundreds of years old and in no state to withstand a fearsome earthquake.

~

Around the amphitheater were the ruins of brick houses and villas that had already fallen during the waves of shaking. Among the ruins were moans and cries from trapped creatures.

"We can't help them all," Spurius said. "If they are lucky, the rubble will protect them from the sunlight and we can help later. Any we lose, I will make more. I'm out of patience with these freezing shit holes inhabitants. Saxon or Briton they pay. For everyone of us we lose today we take a thousand of them!"

He staggered cursing with rage as he tripped on stones and rocks that blocked their path. The sky was now a dark shade of blue. "Hurry!" he shouted.

~

Aebbe followed, the stones bounced off the invisible cloak that had her in a place that was different but somehow the same.

When a giant brick was about to crush the head of the ugly grey-skinned giant, the green eyeless woman pointed her finger at it and screamed in a foreign tongue. The brick had somehow changed direction and the eyeless woman was bleeding from the nose.

Aebbe was exhausted she soon fell behind and struggled to keep the retreating group in sight. Other monsters fleeing the collapsing amphitheater were bouncing against her shield, too panicked to realize that there was a space in the street they couldn't enter.

Another terrible shudder of the earth and another series of buildings heaved and seemed to moan as they collapsed onto the street's occupants. Aebbe found a second wind and saw them climbing into a large marble building with huge pillars that so far looked undamaged.

~

Puck was getting bored. The bush torture had been fun for the first few years but now he was trying out new stuff.

Burning was old hat! Too many realms that had found themselves with human captives couldn't resist the effect fire had on them, but Puck wondered what extreme coldness would do to them for a decade or two.

Digoth and Milian shivered in the same field they had been in for as long as they could remember; now it was covered in snow and shrieking cold winds. The bushes they had been imprisoned in were gone but moving was impossible their veins were full of icy water instead of blood.

Puck had allowed them movement for a while. Once allowing them to make it to the edge of the field before doubling its size leaving them stuck in the middle once more, or by having them climb over the fence into an identical looking field which they would run across only to find Puck and the two bushes waiting for them in the middle of this new field. But, after six months or so, Puck had abandoned this. What's the point in cracking their minds? It would be like torturing animals and he wouldn't sink to those levels so he'd upped the physical torment but hoped to keep them sane by offering hope.

Two Pucks stood in front of the shivering men. Somehow he had managed to make a complete replica of himself. They were identical in every way from the hair which resembled a white transparent dandelion, to their stubby little noses, to their hairy cloven legs, to the leaf on their crotch that was the only piece of clothing they wore.

"We both know the way out of here, one of us is compelled to answer you truthfully while the other will lie. You may only ask us one question before you select one of the two paths we will present to you. If you choose wrong, we…"

"You will what, torture us some more? That became an idle threat some time ago," Milian muttered. Milian felt his jaw snap; Pucks preferred method to get one of them to shut up. The body horror of removing the tongue now bored him as he couldn't really see it disappearing and it always grew back quickly. It would take his jaw a bit longer to pop into place.

"As we were saying before we were so rudely interrupted you may ask one of us a single question before selecting the path but the wrong path will not only lead you back to your torment. You will return with a new companion the lady Aebbe, your good sister, sir, I believe?"

"Aebbe?" Digoth said in a haze. "She would be an old maid by now if she was still alive. Unlikely she made it into Londinium, and if so, certainly not out again."

He turned to Milian who was jerking on the floor in agony. "Remember the boat ride over The Tamesas? That was when we last saw them and then the water started boiling. Maybe we should have stayed in the water. It would have been quicker."

"You silly sausage!" The left Puck said lazily. "We choose how much time goes by here. How much time passes in the real world is irrelevant. How long do you think you've been here?"

"I don't know the sun never sets here and there's no moon… thirty years?"

"Good Digoth! Twenty-eight in fact, but barely an hour has passed where you come from. It's the opposite kind of mind trick that Spurius pulled with old King Herla when he borrowed our land for a trick. To think one morning passing in your world brings you over a lifetime of pain in this one. Think of how much you've got to look forward to?"

"We…we…were told that your people couldn't abduct humans here. That's why the queen tricked us into thinking she was a threat…" said Digoth.

"By standing behind you? Yes, she must have seemed fearsome. Still, you've had plenty of time to reflect on that mistake, as will Aebbe reflect on her venturing into other lands that humans are best well out of, should you choose wrong. Where is she? It is and isn't Londinium at the same time, but it's a place that makes it fair game for us to arrange a permanent family reunion that is if you choose wrong."

The two Pucks looked at each other, beaming. They could expect a few good years of fierce fighting and arguments between the two men debating, and driving each other mad over what question to ask and which Puck to ask it to.

The risk of stranding Digoth's sister would be an added piece of drama, making the debate fiercer and when they returned, having chosen the wrong path, they'd have a new companion. Even if they chose the right one, Puck could think up a plan to stall them and get them right back to where they started. They waved their arms and two paths leading out of the field appeared. One made of stone, the other made of sand.

~

"Which one would your double choose?" said Digoth to the

Puck on the right.

"What? You've decided already!" shrieked the other Puck in outrage.

"Answer my question," Digoth said in a cold dreary voice.

"What do you think you are doing?" panted Milian, his jaw healing quickly but more painfully. "We should talk this over for quite some time. If what he said is true we don't even have to rush!"

"Which one would your double choose?" said Digoth, louder this time.

"Are you sure you want this to be your only question?" said left Puck.

Milian saw how uncomfortable he looked he was almost squirming. "Answer him," he demanded to right Puck.

"He would choose that path," right Puck spat out, on the verge of tears pointing to the sand path.

"We choose the stone path," Digoth told them.

Right Puck disappeared in a fizzle of sparks, leaving left Puck scowling. "Never liked that chicken hearted fuss bucket! Ugly little fellow too!"

Puck looked up at the two men. "You ain't out of the woods yet. I make the rules and I can make them up as I go along too! Follow me, lads." He turned on his heel and made his way towards the edge of the field in bow-legged hops.

CHAPTER 42

Allyn opened his eyes and smelled the smell of sweat and shit that was all around him. Had been since he'd been thrown in this dungeon filled with other men. Despite flights of fancy as a younger man, he had never considered how smelly it would be to share cramped quarters with several other men.

Not to mention how dangerous it was to be shoved into a cell full of hardened Briton criminals, who had been taught from the cradle to despise the yellow haired invaders from the east, who had enslaved and murdered so many of them while stealing their lands.

He was thankful for Colby, one of King Cynric's surviving guards, who had been shoved into the same cell as him. They had barely been in the cell for more than a few minutes when Colby smashed the face of the nearest Briton prisoner into the damp stone wall as a message to the others about his strength. It became an unspoken message that his fellow Saxon was under his protection.

Allyn thanked the gods for Cynric having women guards among his entourage. A few had avoided execution after their capture and he prayed that they were giving Cwenhild similar protection where ever the women and children were being held.

~

It had started with a bright light shining through the bushes as they approached the end of the forest. It shined so bright they had to shield their eyes when they hacked through the final cluster of bushes on the forest's edge. What they saw would have taken their breath away under any circumstances.

Staring down into a beautiful valley at the foot of the mountains, which began where the forest ended, and in the middle of the hammer-shaped lake in the valley laid a small island, upon it a Roman fort.

Well, it had started as a fort the foundation, and base of the structure was similar in design to King Cynric's base, but this structure was built up with stone floors stacked one after the other, making it soar into the sky higher than any building Allyn had ever seen before.

"It must be five floors high!" he gasped to Cwenhild who yanked his ear and pointed to the shores of the lake. There, a group of armored men smashed their shields on the floor and let out a battle cry. They then locked their rectangular shields together, making a packed formation.

The first row of men had their shields covering the front of the formation, while the rows behind hoisted their shields towards the sky, and placed them horizontally over their heads creating a roof for the formation which began to march up the mountain.

Cwenhild hissed and pointed, a boat of armored men was disembarking on the shore and making the same formation. A further boat had just departed from the island. Murmurs of worry went through Saxon and Briton alike from Cynric he heard bellowed, "Is this betrayal, Gildas?" Followed by Brennus' reedy translation of the question in Brittonic, which caused the Britons to start screaming and chanting, although telling when the screams ended and the chants began was not easy.

Every Saxon in the party expected betrayal and arrows to rain down at any moment and were shocked when the arrows flew upward instead. Falling on the hedgehog-like formation, now halfway up the hill, when the arrows bounced off the shield roof harmlessly. The Saxons knew it would be their sword to shield fighting skills that would determine the outcome of the battle. Soon chants in a language the advancing troops had never heard before rang out from the forest.

~

Allyn hadn't fought in the battle at first. He wasn't a bad fighter with an axe, but Cynric's guards formed a shield wall and he fell behind it ensuring Cwenhild, Ar, Wiglac, and Winfred were as far as he could get them from the fighting to the back of the shield wall.

More arrows rained down from the treetops thudding onto the invaders' shield roof with a random cry of pain that signaled the arrows had found a gap in the shield roof. By the time he felt he had the women and children far enough back that they would be safe for the while, he charged back towards the fighting with his axe in his hand, and was unsurprised to see Cwenhild right behind him charging axe in hand herself.

~

The numbers had overwhelmed them and only Brennus' insistence that his witness testimony from Chichester was of use that prevented his head from being taken off with one swoop. The children and Cwenhild were allowed to live for the same reason.

Although he couldn't understand the soldiers' discussions he figured they were discussing taking Ar as a slave, as they only stuck their pugio through her eye when it was evident her damaged wits were beyond following even the simplest gestures.

Cynric himself was hacked down from his horse but they took care to maim rather than kill; hacking his heels bloody as he was dragged away. Colby and a few other warriors managed to communicate in broken shouts of Brittonic that persuaded the Briton troops that they may have value in the slave pens. The rest of the surviving warriors were cut down where they knelt. The victorious Britons left the cruelest fate however for their kin.

~

By the time the small boats taking the prisoners to the towering fortress in the middle of the lake departed the shore was lined with thick wooden beams. One posted upright, the other horizontal with screams coming from the surviving Britons who were being tied, or nailed to these cross shaped posts. Allyn had no idea why they were doing this to their people he scanned the other boats for signs of Britons or Gildas but most were pinned down to the boat's floor and soon so was he.

The next thing he remembered was screams as the children and Cwenhild were dragged off in a different direction. Before long, he was kicked down a ladder into a cellar that doubled as a dungeon with Colby, the only companion from the boats kicked down with him.

~

Now he was in trouble as Colby was ill. He laid in a curled-up ball, no space to stretch out, coughing and hacking up blood.

The criminals used any spare pieces of straw to cover their mouths and noses. He noticed a few make a peculiar gesture where they touched their forehead and then their stomach, before touching both shoulders left to right.

They all chattered to each other in their strange language of long sounds, that sometimes resembled whistles and bursts of songs. It sounded a lot nicer in its original form, unlike when Milian spoke Saxon with its accent, but he still suspected they were planning to kill him the instant they were sure Colby would never recover. A conclusion they would probably reach in minutes rather than hours.

A long wheeze out of Colby, and a prisoner stepped up to Allyn and pointed at his belly before gesturing to his mouth and laughing, his breath almost smelling as bad as his arse, both holes having a lot of unpleasant wind come out of them.

"You want me to eat?" said a confused Allyn. "You want to eat… ah me." He headbutted the stinking prisoner scattering his remaining teeth around the cell. Another prisoner picked up the wooden pail that they had been using for a toilet and threw it over a third prisoner who was sneaking up behind Allyn.

It had been intended for Allyn, but he was holding onto the rope which had been dropped down in front of him and was being lifted towards the open trapdoor on the cell roof. He looked down to see the remaining prisoners tear each other to pieces and clung on as he was pulled through the trap door. Upon seeing who had been pulling the rope, he said, "Cwenhild?" before passing out.

~

Aebbe felt pressure on her chest making each breath more difficult than the last. She figured she'd been under this barrier or whatever it was for too long without taking a rest and it was beginning to suffocate her. Just sheathing the pugio would let her breathe but she'd then be revealed in the middle of this large building.

Carved into the wall was a statue depicting a man slaying a bull. A clay bust of a curly bearded man was at the head of the room and the mosaic was of a beautiful woman playing the flute. The five figures with their unconscious hostage/meal stood in the center of the room were talking in their watery language. Aebbe looked around for a hiding space so she could come back into the real world if only for a while.

~

Morchan started a ghastly whine.

"What the fuck is wrong with that greasy grey golem?" shouted Heslop, who was pacing around the room with worried stamps every time the building shook.

Sunlight gradually peeked through the windows, making his pace smaller and smaller and forcing him closer to the others which pleased no one.

"He says there's a human here," said Alecto, looking up from the cross now laid on the floor and beginning to glow and make a humming sound. She had been in the middle of feverish whispered chants that had made her face glisten with sweat. She had already cast two spells. One to drown out the screams and cries of fear and pain from the chaos outside. One to make the temple invisible to other creations to prevent a crush from those wanting refuge.

"Do not interrupt her again!" yelled Spurius staring at her as if she was the only thing in the world.

"Of course there's a human in here." Heslop leaped up to Morchan's shoulder and started snapping his sharp teeth. "The human is the one Psyche brought for us, as we are going to be stuck in this temple all day." The final two words were spat out while the dwarf's teeth tore at the ogre's earlobe.

"You're so horrible to him," said Psyche with a cackle.

"I'm a monster! I'm not supposed to be nice!" he replied.

"Don't worry too much about Morchan, he's a rare one whose taste for human flesh predates me meeting him, and we won't be stuck in this temple all day if you just allow her to focus! It's all clear now, the gift of conquering the sun coming on the same day the hunt take their last swing at us and miss leading to their ruin! It's all connected!" said Spurius his voice sounding like chipped ice.

"These earthquakes have cost us many of our kin and…" He stopped as the temple shook and the bearded man's bust crashed to the floor shattering into pieces.

"Serapis," said Heslop, "a foul omen he knows the world under our feet well." A crack appeared in the mosaic floor.

"It means nothing he was the easiest to carve, so the priests ordered his likeness in bulk. There are probably half a dozen Serapis busts in storage somewhere in here!" Spurius said.

Then came another shake. Alecto groaned. "The city is sinking. Whatever that bitch used to start the earthquakes, she didn't undo it before she died. We need to defeat the sun before we end up buried under tons of Londinium."

~

Aebbe crouched behind one of the pillars, sheathed the pugio, and returned to the world. If she wasn't visible, she was certainly audible panting like someone forced underwater for a while, but the monsters were huddled together as thick as thieves.

Also being in the presence of their leader; the snake tongued one, without the protection the mist from the pugio gave her, was giving her a wretched feeling. Like being thumped in the stomach, again and again, while a fog took over her brain bringing tears to her eyes.

Only the wretched woman from Chichester was away from the group, hovering a few feet off the ground and looking around nervously.

~

It was then that Psyche locked eyes with Aebbe and her mouth opened in a shocked O shape. She snapped her head towards the huddled group and then had second thoughts. She left the still sleeping Hieu slumped against another pillar and began to glide towards an exhausted Aebbe. Aebbe looked at the pugio in her hand and struggled to lift it her strength had been so depleted.

CHAPTER 43

Digoth, Milian, and Puck stood standing at the top of a mist-covered mountain looking down into a deep valley.

"As I've explained, all you have to do is go down there beat whatever you find, and return here with proof. Then I will send you back to your realm for a couple of hours for you to find replacements."

"Replacements?" said Digoth.

"For you both, you mutton heads! Queen Mab went to a lot of trouble to create the field of torture if it went empty and unused she would get the notion to use it on poor old Puck! What a thing to happen!"

Digoth and Milian now reunited with their pugio and arrows and iron sword respectively looked at each other and sighed. Thunder came from the bottom of the valley.

"What is down there?" asked Digoth.

"It doesn't matter," said Milian, who started trudging downwards forcing Digoth to stumble after him.

"There's not a word for it in Saxon or Briton!" yelled Puck. His shouts followed the two men on their descent. "Maybe the Franks have made a word for it yet. They call it Luhng in the place where Oberon acquired it all that time ago, a realm far from here called Youdu, if my memory is correct."

The thunder sounds got louder and the fog got thicker the

further down they went. Soon both men were having to scream nonstop just to make sure they stuck together.

Then came the heat. Something close to them was burning. Flames appeared after a while in the distance, and it was then they came across it.

They couldn't tell what it was, its shape or appearance, but flames would shoot out from the same two points.

Eventually, Milian, with an archer's sharp eyesight felt confident enough to judge. "It's sleeping and those flames are coming out of its nostrils."

"What is it?"

"I can't see much, it's like a massive snake but…it's beautiful."

"How can a snake be beautiful? Never mind, just shoot it!"

When whatever it was breathed in, the orange glow deep in its nose illuminated the valley, just enough to make out a silhouette of the beast.

Milian used this chance to fire an arrow. It bounced off the side of the beast's skull harmlessly. The valley was then illuminated by the glow of the beast's orange eye that had opened.

"I don't think your pugio is going to be much good," said Milian.

"Why?" said Digoth.

"Well, when you nicked the troll with it, it appeared to warm up everything around us, and…"

He leapt and threw himself and Digoth as far as he could in any which direction to get away from the steam of fire that was coming from the creature's mouth towards them.

"I think that bastard thing is well accustomed to fire and we don't need more of it now! Run!"

He looked back to see a sight he would never forget. The beast roared and its teeth were as clear and unblemished as marble, and a shade of green he had never seen before in his life. Sharper than the finest sword he'd ever seen, too.

~

Puck watched from the mountain top. His vision was obscured by the mist but he didn't want to clear it even though he could. He'd taken too much of a risk by bringing them here but he hadn't thought that one of them, especially not Digoth, would be able to solve his riddle so quickly.

The idea of the Luhng had just come to him but they couldn't be allowed to beat it. Not the rarest prize in all of Fae. He covered his ears at another thunderous roar from the valley.

The spells Queen Mab had to use to contain it in the valley! He remembered the day that Oberon returned from Youdu!

Ordinarily, the different realms had no link due to the little people sticking to their little villages and huts, but the Romans with their roads changed that!

It had started with a couple of Dobunni savages who the conquering Romans had liked for their size. One of these Britons had ended up in their army out east fighting off the Huns. A gambling problem not to mention the Huns not being fun opponents had our man bodyguarding a caravan across Persia after deserting.

The Dobunni had died of a flux in India, but his son would one day bring a caravan of his own into the city of Chengu, and mentioned his father's old tales from his boyhood about the magical land of Fae to a courtesan he was hoping to impress with his tales.

She didn't care for the stories, and he was soon stabbed to

death over a dispute about the ownership of some camels, but that didn't matter. Fae was alive in the minds of the little people of the Middle Kingdom, well, one of them. That meant Oberon could visit their realms; at least for a while. The courtesan buried the story to the back of her mind, and it would likely die with her.

Cheating Yama for one of his beasts had proved simple. In most cultures, death deities loved to gamble too much. A weird song-like sound was now coming from the depths of the valley. Puck thought it sounded beautiful. It had been a long time since he had thought anything was beautiful. It stopped. Oh well, time to trudge down there once the beast is asleep, gather up the charred bones, and carry them back to the field and wait for them to regenerate.

He waited for a long time. He wasn't sure how long, but he finally felt the beast sleeping and left the top of the mountain. He was only ten yards down when he saw a flash of gold and Milian's marked face popped out of the shadow.

"Hello, Puck, me old mate, reckon you're up to a trip to Londinium? Or if I call for Queen Mab will she hear? Be nice to have you contorted in the bush in between me and Digoth, eh?"

"You sniveling cowards! I gave you the chance to win your freedom and you just ran away from the Luhng!"

"His name is Fucanglong," panted Digoth, struggling from behind carrying something heavy, something green, something beautiful. "And we came to an arrangement of sorts. He yields and offers this as proof." He looked as if he was about to faint but managed to drop the tooth onto Puck's feet, making him scream and weep like some giant baby.

~

"It's working, it's working!" screamed Alecto in her native Greek as she felt her blood run hot so hot, hotter than it had been for a very long time. Her heart thudded at a speed that would kill a mortal on the spot. Finally, the cross she'd been clutching let off a small bang and flames danced across Alecto's face. She smiled enjoying the sensation.

It seemed to take an age for the flames to die out. Wordlessly, she walked to a corner of the room where the light was shining in and let the sun's rays pour onto her face.

Deep down the others had a dreaded feeling this was going to all be for naught and their fate might lie in trying to escape from the depths of the city, hoping the collapse doesn't bury them too deep.

When the sunlight illuminated Alecto's eyeless face without a single hint of discomfort on her part she had never looked so beautiful to them and then she smiled.

Two long white fangs which had been carved and chiseled into an array of jagged spikes over the years, each one skillfully self-applied to ensure maximum suffering in her victim's final moments appeared in the sun for the first time.

At first, they looked eerily unnatural in daylight that even Heslop shivered a little before he reflected that soon, all of their fangs would have the same access to the day and the flesh that walked the land then. He was trying to think of something clever to say when he looked around and asked, "Where's Psyche?"

~

Aebbe wept as she walked downstairs, with the slash on her cheeks she was powerless to stop. Psyche walked behind her looking curiously at the pugio she had ordered Aebbe to hand over after she had given her her mark.

"Faster you stupid sow! Ordo told my sire that we had disposed of you. I can't let him see you!"

Finally, they reached a large cellar. Psyche flicked her fingers to light a torch she found on the wall. "Don't really need it with my eyesight, but I want to look into your eyes when I...what the fuck is that smell?"

She walked away from Aebbe and opened one of the many barrels piled up by the cellar walls.

"Phew! 200-year-old wine! Not even the goblins have supped here. Oh well, can't help myself..." She took a sip and immediately spat it out.

"Tastes like hag's blood! Oh well, I have a pretty young one here to devour, two, actually. Where did I leave the other one?"

She was answered by a shrill scream coming from the stairs, and her mouth opened wide in amused shock as Hieu charged into the room. "Why, it's the little..."

She was cut off by Hieu tearing the arrow out from the back of her leggings and shoving it into Psyche's mouth.

Psyche went to pull it out and screamed at the touch as the skin on her fingers crackled. She spat it out and screamed with rage. "Pointy-nosed bitch!"

She grabbed Hieu by the cheeks and spun her head around with a fierce display of strength and power that Aebbe heard a fearsome crack, and she gave a terrible moan when Hieu slumped to the floor still as a stone her neck flopping in a grotesque angle.

Psyche turned back to Aebbe and opened her mouth. "You are going to..." Her teeth fell out and rattled as they bounced off the stone floor.

With a look of terror on her face, Psyche clasped both her hands over her lips, but the amount of blood filling the inside of her mouth was too much, it seeped out between her fingers, and she bent to the ground to vomit it all out.

Aebbe was able to edge away and move towards the staircase the rooms only exist. Closer and closer she got, but she couldn't resist taking one final look.

She met Psyche in the eyes, well eye; the eye socket flesh around her right eye had melted and fused, trapping the eye underneath. Her long black hair was now a few sticks of frayed white. The fingers on her left hand had also fused making a crab-like claw. Her cheeks had melted so much they drooped down to her shoulders.

The earth shook again and the cellar was full of dust. Bits of clay from the roof and even some seashells that had been used to decorate the ceiling clattered down. The shaking made Psyche bend over but her bones were now as fragile as bird bones, again grim cracking sounds rang around the room only to be drowned out by Psyche's screams.

Aebbe watched in terror as the now hunchbacked Psyche tried to get up only to crash further to the floor.

The last sight Aebbe had of her was a final wretched view of her trying to say something. "Wun app muh?" she moaned. The bog accented Saxon and the missing teeth and now lips made it impossible to be sure but Aebbe was sure she was saying, "What's happening to me?" and that slurred whine would stay in her head until her dying day, which she decided wasn't going to be today, and found the will to run up the stairs.

She first clutched her nose to prevent smelling the contents of Psyche's bowels, which had long since been emptied, and ran forward to retrieve the pugio that Psyche had dropped before running out of the cursed room as fast as her legs could move.

CHAPTER 44

The last thing Digoth and Milian remembered about Fae was the ludicrous sight of Puck lying on his chest, pounding his tiny fists into the ground. Screaming and crying about how they had cheated somehow.

"Just wait," Milian said calmly, his sword now glowing gold.

"We made a promise we can't keep!" hissed Digoth

"We will keep it even if it takes us a hundred lifetimes."

Then their view was filled with brilliant white light, and they both screamed as it burned their eyeballs with red hot heat. They then opened their eyes and with only a slight soreness in the eyes found themselves blinking in the dawn light of Londinium.

~

Or what was left of Londinium: the wall they remembered using to find their way around the city in the dark was now just a few chunks of jagged bricks with massive gaps between each chunk.

They turned to look into the city. Only a few buildings remained upright with most reduced to uneven piles of bricks and cracked shards of clay and tile where the buildings once stood.

"The little shit lied to us," said Digoth. "He told us we've been gone for hours. It's clearly been years since we were last here.

Maybe decades, maybe Spurius won and we're the last humans on the island."

"From what I've heard of him he wouldn't leave his city looking like this. Look." Milian pointed at a heap of bricks and rubble that had been a long if low single-story structure, a stable perhaps or slave quarters. "Dust is coming from that one and, look at that one too! These buildings collapsed recently!"

Noises started to come out of the pile to their left. A sort of guzzling groaning and moaning. Digoth started to attack the pile with his hands throwing debris to one side with gusto.

"Digoth! Not a good idea!" said Milian.

"What are you talking about?" snapped Digoth as he pulled out the moaning survivor.

To his shock he saw it was a monster; an ugly thing with an egg shaped head as big as its tiny body, its skin was a greenish yellow color and its eyes like two little berries looked on blankly, but it was clearly unhappy about being rescued. Its mouth opened hissing showing fangs, a sharp row of teeth, and a long triangular tongue shot out, but it was weak and Digoth threw it to the ground with ease.

It scrambled on the floor like it was trying to swim. It was panicked and the reason became apparent quickly when the sunlight shone on its back: its skin began to bubble and crack. Soon the beast was screaming an ear-bleeding, guttural scream as smoke began to engulf its body and just a few minutes after being thrown to the ground, only a charred skeleton remained.

Digoth gave the misshaped skeleton a tiny tap with his foot and the whole thing dissolved to dust.

"What was it?" asked Digoth.

"Imp maybe, could be a goblin, but it would be very unusual. They usually are deep underground by the time the sun comes up. Unless it had found somewhere cozy to sleep and awoke to find the house on top of it."

"What the hell happened here?"

"The destruction of the city must have been instant," replied Milian. He found another skeleton; this was human sized at least, a further one was at least seven feet tall with antlers. Both skeletons turned to dust at the faintest touch.

"These two were on the street when the sun came up. The houses must have all fallen by then, or a few remaining ones were too full for them to get in. Spurius' creations are craven and selfish creatures at heart. Once the houses started to fall they would have realized shelter was in jeopardy and barred the doors as soon as they secured their own. We will probably find more of these some will have wounded themselves or others in the rush to get into a remaining house leaving them helpless, I reckon, and the others…"

"Are buried," Digoth finished for him looking around the wreckage.

"Hopefully buried deep, with shattered bones. They are no threat to us in the sun," Milian said.

The ground gave a furious shake forcing both men to their knees and the wrecked houses groaned and shifted. "What the fuck was that?" Milian spat.

"I've never felt anything like that before," said a white-faced Digoth.

Milian spat, "Now buried deeper, we can't get to them and they can't get to us. Nothing stopping us from flushing out the buildings still standing. Should be simple enough."

Digoth nodded at that and said, "Remember what Puck…"

"I remember what he said well enough. We will give him two."

He blinked and shielded his face. For him, this was the first sunlight that his face had felt for decades and it burnt. "Let's move into the city."

~

Allyn took a swig of wine as he sat on the edge of the mountain looking down into the lake and Avalon rising from the center of it. The evacuation had finished an hour ago. Only the ancient old man remained. Allyn had caught a glimpse of late King Cissa before the carnage at Chichester, and never thought he'd see an older man than that, but then minutes after being dragged out of the dungeon, he was dragged through corridors and doors, up stairs, and was propped up for dear life by Cwenhild across a wooden rope bridge which led to a windowless tower, the only door connected by the bridge.

Soon Allyn was looking at a long boney finger being jabbed at his face. The owner of the finger was toothless and misty-eyed with long white hair reaching the floor his beard coming to his knees.

Random tattoos, etches of green that made no sense to Allyn, were all over his forehead and cheeks. The man was dressed in a white toga and smelled of...

"It's called sapo," said the man in perfect Saxon. "You boil ashes from the fire and mix it with tallow, it produces a substance that is most pleasing to the skin and clothes." His voice sounded gentle until he snapped, "You know Milian?" Allyn and Cwenhild nodded. "His foolishness has brought ruin to us all!" He bowed his head and the gentle tone resumed, "This is why all of us must make sacrifices to rebuild the hunt."

~

Now that old man was the only soul left on the island, most of the women, children, and cripples had been sent on a march further through the forest but further west this time being accompanied by half the Briton army.

The other half about fifty men and twenty women with fighting experience remained and three exceptions, Allyn, Cwenhild, and a cripple; Father Maeleg who was sharing his wine with Allyn.

"The old bastard will sink with the island if that's what it comes to the sentimental old goat." He took the wine sack back as they watched a hatch open in the tower's roof and the old man climbed out looking stronger than his years, whatever they were, but still hanging on for dear life as an icy wind blasted through the valley.

Father Maeleg had been given the responsibility of being Allyn's handler or bodyguard, due to his ability to speak Saxon with a degree of fluency, when Allyn asked how this was the burly old man told him.

"Battle of Natanleaga, back when I was no more than a boy. My shield shattered at the first Saxon axe that swung at it and I froze. Was furious with myself for years, while I toiled as a slave for you bastards." He brushed off Allyn's awkward apology while Cwenhild rolled her eyes.

"So, I resolved to run away but they caught me, and everytime they did they took something away that would make it harder for me to blend in on the road." He was missing one eye, both ears, his nose, and one foot.

"When they took the foot I thought that was it, and I would die a slave, but then one day something amazing happened. I thought it was mischief-makers from Fae, but once back with my own kind I was taught there's no such place and it was god's will that returned me!" He held up the wooden cross around his neck and cried, "Praise the Lord!"

Cwenhild rolled her eyes again, while Allyn asked what had happened. "Five years ago or so the sky went black. It was endless night and cold. I was able to walk into the woods unnoticed and anyone I came across couldn't see I was marked as a runaway slave. When I found my kind again the monks said God must have sent the fog for me although a lot of them at another settlement later told me the devil sent it as it had unseated Arthur and brought him down."

Allyn said, "That's amazing."

"Wait," Cwenhild said. "How did you walk for so long with one foot? And how did you know what direction to walk in? How did you feed yourself? And even if they couldn't see your face your accent would have marked you as a Briton."

Father Maeleg shrugged and said, "God?" This only made Allyn's face light up more and Cwenhild roll her eyes harder. Then the temperature dropped and Father Maeleg shuddered and said, "They're here."

~

Darkness had fallen quickly but Allyn could see at the foot of the mountain from the way the moon
seemed to make the horse's bones glow. The armored figures on the horses were covered from head to foot with hooded cloaks. Only at their head did a single figure throw the cloak off and reveal a skeleton clad in finer armor than Allyn had ever seen before.

Its horse hovered off the air and roared. The light from the flames that came from its mouth lit up the lakeshore and Allyn thought he counted twenty skeletal horses in the light. Surely more were out of sight from silhouettes and shadows that loomed into the space. They had appeared out of nowhere seemingly, getting a mounted host through the forests would be impossible.

Then the figure at the head screamed in rage. "Praise the Lord!" whispered Father Maeleg. "The sacrifices! They cannot pass!"

It was then that Allyn saw the skeleton was screaming at the dead men and women on the crosses who had been nailed there earlier. Gildas and his tribe, along with some criminals from the dungeons, Merlin had decided wouldn't be necessary to take along after the evacuation.

Then from the trees that towered over the trio, arrows began to fall.

CHAPTER 45

Milian and Digoth found a stout looking brick building that was still upright. Its one window had been boarded up, and it was small. Anymore than three people inside would be uncomfortable.

"I reckon it's part of a larger building that collapsed. They built this bit with a few extra layers. Maybe it's where they kept their gold," Milian said.

"And you think some are inside?"Digoth asked. Milian nodded and said, "Let's find out."

He unsheathed his sword, which glowed gold, and had ever since Fucanglong had coated it with fire, and smashed it against the wooden door which splintered into thousands of pieces.

A horned thing charged out and out of habit Milian got into a swordsman's stance by standing with his feet at shoulder width before he realized it was a waste of time. The demon or imp or goblin or whatever it was screamed as he began to burn up, it was soon a skeleton, and soon after that a pile of dust.

Inside the building were a yellow eyed woman and a figure with the head of a badger and the body of a man with two-inch sharp-looking claws where his nails should be.

"These good enough for you, Puck?" yelled Digoth. The badger slashed at Digoth's face ripping off half his cheek. Digoth had enough sense and speed to jab the monster through the bottom of his jaw with his pugio and roll back into the sunlight before the monster could retaliate.

The woman let out a scream and cowered in a corner of the room as sun rays poured in from the vacant door space, while the badgerman fell back clutching his throat and face. She then started laughing.

"That won't kill Mani here you rotting freaks! Come in here to finish us off if you dare! If not, once the sun goes down, we hunt."

"I dunno," said Milian. "Going by the sun's position, I reckon you've got another ten hours before you can be sure you're safe to step outside and that's going to be a long ten hours for you."

"Why?" spat the woman, and then she felt something. She turned around to see the bricks glowing orange as heat rose off them.

~

Digoth and Milian walked further into the city as they heard screams of agony behind them.

"So Puck has forgotten about needing replacements for the field?" said Digoth who turned his head behind him to check on the building.

"Yes! He was the first one out!" he said watching the badgerman make a run for it in the distance before burning up.

"Really?" said Milian. "I guess the old boot is tougher than she looks." A female scream was heard next as she ran out and frantically looked for a hiding spot before crumbling onto the floor as a pile of fragile bones.

"Lucky Saxon prick! Beat me by seconds!"

"Bets a bet, you owe me an ale."

"Sure, as soon as we stumble across a shack or better yet, a tavern, and as for Puck, who knows what he's thinking? He's had his chance."

~

They both came to the amphitheater. The large stone blocks that made up the seating areas were still intact. At first, they thought to try to flush out any creatures that maybe in the bowels of the building.

However, the underground passageways that people used to climb staircases to the seats and the passageways a level below that once held the captives and fighters didn't exist anymore. In fact, the whole ground underneath the amphitheater didn't exist anymore. It was just a giant cavernous hole with seemingly no bottom.

The stone blocks were clinging to whatever land that they were built on that remained, but they were crumbling and creaking, having lost so much land support.

"Bastard thing is sinking," said Milian.

"So we should move?" Digoth suggested.

They heard creaking beneath them and jumped to safety seconds before the block of stone amphitheater seats they had been standing on crashed into the abyss where the arena had once been.

"Maybe we should leave the city?" said Digoth.

"It's looking that way," replied Milian. "Could check out the woods around the city for escapees, we'd lose a bit of our advantage under the tree's shade, but with the arrows and what we know the sword and pugio can do, we can do a spot of good I wager."

"What about my sisters and the others?"

"If they survived they can't still be in the city. Maybe they'd have headed north as the northern wall is nearest but nah… Aebbe and Iga are too smart for that, it would be full of monsters running for their lives. I reckon south to see if the river has calmed, and if not to follow it west." He looked south holding his hand to his forehead. "There's a building just to our south that looks remarkably untouched want to take a look?"

Digoth groaned. "Must we? Our advantage over the beasts is here in the light!"

"When we leave this city it's the bandit's life for us. The hunt will have orders to kill me on sight and I don't imagine a return to the farmer's life is in store for you. Your village has probably already been taken over and burnt down and rebuilt a few times over by rival Saxon bastard tribes by now. Before we leave, a spot of savaging might not be a too terrible idea? That building has barely a scratch on it if the Romans left treasure it would be somewhere like there. Might still be there, what use do monsters have for gold?"

~

Allyn ran through the forest clutching Cwenhild's hand for dear life. Somehow she was strong enough to hoist Father Maeleg up on her shoulder, and somehow had enough strength to carry one man and pull the other one forward making him keep pace with her strides as the forest fire chased after them.

Thank god that Wiglac and Winfred had been sent west with the rest of the women and children. 'Thank god' as in just the one god? What a strange thought for a Saxon to entertain. Been listening to Father Maeleg too much? Allyn wondered.

~

The arrows had spooked the skeletal horses massively when they landed, throwing the host into disarray, and when one lodged in the rib cage of one of the cloaked figures it let out a rattling scream that could surely be heard for miles around. The scream continued as a sharp hissing sound almost as loud came from the cloaked skeleton.

Allyn couldn't see what was happening to it but the noise of confusions and the sense of dread and fear that was coming from the gathered host was clear to all who watched.

"The lord's arrows blessed to send the demons to hell slowly," whispered Father Maeleg. Then it happened all at once. The skeleton in the fine armor that had been screaming and chanting in a language that sounded to Allyn like a drowning man at the dead and dying men and women on crosses then turned his skull around 180 degrees. He looked up at the source of the arrows and then his horse rose and rose until it was level with the archers in the trees at the top of the mountain.

The skeleton turned the horse around and with its skull now facing the right way made the horse gallop on nothing but air. A hail of arrows sailed harmlessly over his head the thickness of the archers hiding places making shooting at point-blank range difficult.

The horse opened its skull wide and fire torched the trees and the archers in them.

~

The fire just wouldn't stop. The remaining seventy or so Briton soldiers and archers had lost half their numbers in the initial blast, and a further twenty or so were out of sight.

Allyn hoped they were the fast runners way ahead of him because if not there was nothing but fire behind them.

The back of Allyn's tunic was in smoldering tatters, his back was red raw and in agony due to the heat. He had no idea how he was going to outrun the fire and grabbed Cwenhild's hand tightly.

He needed to tell her he loved her, not in the way she needed, but she had been a rock ever since they stepped off that ship and he needed her to know that he felt something.

"Cwenhild!" he shouted. "I..." his words turned to a scream as the floor turned to air underneath them. Soon all three were screaming as they plunged off the cliff they had inadvertently leapt off.

CHAPTER 46

Aebbe panted and heaved deep breaths, as she made her way up the stairs back to where the other beasts were.

Thankfully the screams of the melting woman had stopped but another shake of the ground. Dust and gravel and soil filled her vision, making her cough and gasp and finally vomit.

She gave one final look back and saw rubble and dirt now blocked the staircase. She staggered to the top of the stairs and looked for the door she'd walked through.

She struggled to get her bearings, as when she entered she was in her place and her view of the outside world was a little hazy. She crept and crept.

The monsters were still excitedly chatting about something. She didn't want to cut herself with the pugio and hide in the fog again. She was too weak for that. These monsters had very good senses and the smell of vomit from her dress or the sound of her hands crawling on the floor would surely be picked up, so she kept the pugio pricked against the palm of her hand. Her panting and crawling seemed to go unnoticed by the creatures who were engrossed in whatever they were discussing.

She was inches from the thick bronze doors and got on her knees to push them open and escape to the freedom of the sunlight when the doors burst open smashing her on the forehead, sending her sprawling.

Two figures excitedly talking to each other strode past. One was clutching a rag to a ruined and bloody cheek and looked familiar. Their eyes met and her last thought was, *"Digoth?"* before she passed out.

~

Digoth stared in shock and horror at his sister lay prone on the ground covered in vomit with blood pouring from her head. He then turned his head to the other end of the hall where he saw a group of monstrosities at the far end of the room.

Milian had turned white upon seeing them at a distance. "It can't be…in the flesh."

He put his hand out to calm Digoth but it was too late. "What the fuck have you freaks done to my sister?" he bellowed.

Four figures who had only had eyes for each other or rather three had only had eyes for the green skinned, eyeless creature, and the strange noises she was chanting suddenly swung their heads towards the entrance of the building.

~

"We get out of here and get far away from that thing. That's Spurius!" Milian pulled Aebbe's body up and put his ear against her chest. "She's alive, to the sunlight we can regroup there safely."

A drained Digoth took a step forward but then Milian's words seemed to seep through and he staggered backward, helping Milian prop Aebbe up with one of them each taking one of her arms. They panted as they departed through the thick doors and out into the sunlight.

~

Spurius and the others didn't speak for a minute after the interruption. It was as if something significant had happened. The interruption had taken place the very second that Alecto had finished her final incantation, this one giving Morchan who was still clutching the cross the same boon that the rest of them had received.

"I think it's a sign of their timing, don't you?" said Spurius with a grin.

"What were they saying?" spat Heslop, who hadn't bothered to learn Saxon convinced their time on this island would be short. "Soft as shit," was his assessment of the newcomers.

"Nothing important," said Alecto. "Although they seemed to know who you were sire and the one with the mark; his Saxon was strange."

Spurius laughed. It was a terrible, terrible sound. It sounded like the screams of a mother that has lost her children, the wailing of a soldier bleeding out on the battlefield, and the lamenting of an old man with a lifetime of regrets, knowing he would soon enter the other side having achieved so little.

"The hunt sent an assassin in case their magic didn't do the trick, and the craven has taken the safe ground outside. Well, let's give him a surprise. Let's give them all fair warning that they can destroy Londinium but we don't need Londinium anymore for we have conquered the sun!"

~

Digoth and Milian sat in the sunshine panting, exhausted. Aebbe was still unconscious and Digoth cradled her head in his arms. "I never expected to see you again, please wake up, please."

Milian watched the buildings doors like a hawk. He unsheathed his sword which had returned to its original silver. Scowling he put the sword down and started to notch his bow. "Once she's awake I'm going to need you both to get those doors open and keep them open. I've got seven no six arrows left if I can make half count then we stand a chance of…"

There was then a deafening sound like a thousand trees falling at once. A giant plume of dust appeared from the building's entrance. More crashing sounds and as the plume cleared the doors had been kicked or thrown clear, and standing in the doorway was a seven-foot tall horned man with a long snake dangling from his mouth. He took one stride on his hooved feet and stood in the sunlight for the first time in 365 years.

"No, no, no…this can't be." Milian's mouth hung open in gaped shock and horror. "This is it! It's over. Everything is over." The sense of ennui overtook him from both shock and the effect Spurius naturally had on people.

He sank to his knees, put his head to the ground, and started banging it back and forth.

"What the fuck is wrong with you?" yelled Digoth. "Those arrows work in the daylight, don't they? After everything we've been through you're just going to lie there and cry?"

Milian cried out, "Can't you feel it too? The hopelessness?"

"I feel it. I just don't care anymore. Whatever we do something always comes along to fuck it up, so what if this twat can walk in the sunlight, and makes you feel suicidal with just a glance? At the end of the day, compared to some we've met, that's normal. If he bests me, fine, but I will not leave this world whimpering!" He pulled out his pugio.

"I fancy making those hooves dance on a hot surface!" he said, and he charged.

CHAPTER 47

Digoth felt something strike his stomach. It happened so fast it took a while for his body to register that anything was wrong about five seconds after he felt the blow, he stopped.

He was halfway between Milian and Aebbe, and the monstrous group that was beginning to edge outside and follow their leader.

There had been a movement from the group but it was over so fast. A flick of dust from the ground it could have been caused by a nearby ruined building collapsing further under the ground but it moved in a strange way turning this way and that.

Digoth didn't notice it until it was too late.

~

Milian was too far away by this point. It had moved faster than anything he'd ever seen, even if he'd been standing next to Digoth he was unsure if he could have prevented it.

~

Digoth put his hands to his stomach after stopping. "It feels so soft." were his final words. He sank to his knees and vomited blood.

Some more dust whirled around him and when it settled, an ugly little thing was standing under him, its mouth open, eagerly swallowing the blood Digoth was chundering from his mouth.

~

Milian had never seen such an ugly thing. Its skin reminded him of a boyhood friend who had once drunkenly claimed to be able to leap the bonfire one Beltane eve, and had fallen face down while halfway over the fire.

This thing's face was even more twisted and warped than his friend's new face after his fall it was something more than fire that had turned it into such a spine-chilling sight.

It then disappeared leaving only a flicker of dust in the air. It reappeared, beckoning at one of the figures just emerged from the building. It took Milian a moment to realize that the monster was simply capable of running at speeds that were unimaginable, faster than any man or beast. It had run to the building and back in seconds.

~

Heslop giggled in between gulps of blood and bile that was gushing from his victim's mouth. He kind of wished he could speak Saxon as the man's eyes were open. This was a strong one, no lights out for him yet.

He shrugged, maybe the rotting thing could understand Latin.

"How'd it feel, matey? Head butted you right in the gut at that speed ha! All that goo inside you, all the pink, and brown, and orange, and purple, and even blue squishy bits in you, they're all leaking out now! And they're going to leak and leak until there's nothing left! You ain't a barrel, matey, no way to plug that leak! Lots and lots of juicy red stuff for me still to come out of your mouth! By the way, have you started bleeding from the arse yet? It's just that...well it's a shame to waste any of it and..."

"If I had eyes they would be rolled to the back of my skull you disgusting little imp! You actually would eat from…"

"Alecto! I only asked for Morchan to pop the head! Back with you, hag!"

"While he holds the Crux gemmata, I go where he goes," she told him.

~

Milian had his bow drawn but anything that could move at such speed was an impossible target. The lumbering beast was far simpler, but something told him the green skinned woman was more important, take her out and the rules of the game change. He told himself sadly there was nothing more he could do for Digoth not with the blood he'd lost.

Nothing other than vengeance.

"Remember you take our promise to the next life, friend," he said and aimed.

~

Alecto and Jessop were still bickering, when they sensed something that made their stomachs heave, and their throats touch the roof of their mouths, making them retch and drool out a pool of bile on the floor.

Alecto felt as if the sky was about to fall on her head and for just a split second the helplessness and terror that her victims had felt in their final moments was repaid to her tenfold. She couldn't see it ever ending she was going to feel like this until the end of time in the next world nothing but sheer torture ahead. Then it stopped.

Heslop was on the floor rolling around clutching his belly. Alecto sensed the arrow that was aimed for her, the arrow that she somehow knew would make her a wretched, runty thing in constant trauma in another realm for all time was half an inch from her forehead.

Morchan had blocked it with the cross; despite this, it had torn through the metal at first like a knife through butter, before something had made it slow as two objects of immense power cancelled each other out.

The arrow had passed straight through the cross stopping a second before it would have sealed Alecto's eternal fate.

Alecto took all of this in. She knew things the other creations didn't, she could analyze objects from a glance especially those with mystical qualities, but she had never comprehended that these arrows could do far more than maim and kill them until one was so close to ending her.

She looked up at Morchan but before she could say thank you she fainted.

~

Milian squinted. He was sure he hadn't taken the woman out but she was down. Something shiny the big ugly thing was holding got in the way. He decided to get closer. He didn't want to notch again, he had to save his few remaining arrows for Spurius himself. He couldn't be sure that just one would do the trick especially now that somehow the fiend was able to walk in the sun.

He took careful steps forward. Hand-to-hand combat might be needed unless that sword started glowing again. He unsheathed it anyway, a fine blade even if it couldn't kill them it could put them on their back long enough to jab them with the arrows.

He had to make pace very carefully. Whatever brought Digoth down could be coming for him.

He felt something brush past him, just the faintest of faint sensations, he walked forward, and there he felt it again!

Someone had pushed him, but it wasn't a real push, it wasn't like he was being physically touched but something was blocking him making it difficult to walk.

In fact, he was finding it difficult to see the air was getting blurry. It was like the dust from the ruined buildings was clouding the air in front of him. It was just strange that this was happening when there wasn't a gust of wind in the air.

Nevertheless, he went onwards until the dusty mist appeared to block his eyes, and then all of a sudden it disappeared, and when his eyes were clear again Aebbe was standing in front of him with a pugio at his neck.

~

"What the fuck is wrong with you? You saw what happened to my brother and you are doing the same thing! No change to your strategy or anything!" Aebbe shouted.

"I thought you were out cold?"

"I clearly didn't intend on that being a permanent condition and woke up!"

"Your brother…"

"I saw," she choked back a sob and biting her lip, continued.

"This blade we found in Chichester can do things, wonderful things it made me believe in us! In people, we don't have to be afraid of these shits. A long time ago some people knew what was coming and they made these things with help from people like those shits, but good ones people with the right power. I know it's difficult to explain but just let me pass and I will find a way to get rid of those three, I promise you. Charge in there and that dwarf will destroy your insides with his head like he did to Digoth."

"It was a dwarf?"

"I was doing some scouting before I had to come back and stop you from throwing your life away. I woke up too late for Digoth but not for you."

"That's the thing Aebbe me and Digoth we went through a lot to get here…"

"We all did!"

"I do not doubt that, but I cannot allow his sister to put herself at risk for this. We agreed more than once that vengeance was a job we entrusted to each other and we would ensure it or die trying and…ahhhhhhhohhhhhhh!!!"

His scream bounced around the hollow ruined buildings that surrounded them, as he sank to his knees clutching his balls.

"I didn't mean for it to hurt that much. I was recently in an underground collapse. I think some pieces of bricks got stuck to my boots, some lead too. I will be as fast as I can. I think you still have work to do." And with that, she slashed the back of her hand and vanished.

CHAPTER 48

Heslop climbed to his knees and let out an ear bleeding whine at the sound of the scream in the distance.

Another one! Yes in the temple there were two of them babbling in their grunty sounding language, and one the boss man said was from the hunt. Heslop had always stuck to the far north east on his hunting trips away from Londinium and avoided those fuckers who these days seldom left the western half of the island, but he remembered a chase after him way back in the day.

Scum had disguised themselves as defenseless villagers and then bolted. Heslop and his crew were expecting a feast as they flew their bodies forward at a furious speed as if propelled by trebuchets only it was a trap.

The bastards had lured them out to Beast Cliff, and so many of his tribe lay with shattered bodies on the beach helpless and unable to rejuvenate in time before the sun rose and turned them to dust.

Heslop only saved himself at the last second hearing the screams of those that plummeted ahead of him. Well, Heslop's head going straight to that bastard's guts would-be vengeance for his old friends at least.

He turned to Morchan and saw that Alecto was passed out, but beginning to stir. "I don't have the strength to run at him put me on your back and I can launch myself at him from ten feet or so away."

Then in a flash, some dust swirled and blotted out his vision. He thought he saw something strange it was a silhouette of a figure around five foot tall with long curly, messy hair. It was standing right under Morchans hulking frame and as quick as a flash its hand shot up in the air and stuck Morchan in the lower jaw. Blood drenched the silhouette and sprayed all over Heslop's face.

Exhausted and disgusted he sank to his knees as everything faded to black for him.

~

Heslop woke up in the same space but it felt different. He could see the temple in the distance and there was another shake of the earth, but not where he was standing he saw the dust rise from the ruined buildings he saw the temple still standing but shaking. He looked back and saw the hunt bastard get up and then sink to one knee from the force of the shake. Heslop felt nothing the ground beneath his feet was as still as the *"the grave"*, a woman's voice rang out finishing his thought for him.

He got up, he felt dizzy seeing the city rumble around him. He saw Spurius looking stern in the temple entrance, he saw a now conscious Alecto crawl on her hands and knees dragging the pierced cross with her. Wailing and retching at the arrow's proximity but he wasn't part of that.

He looked up and saw who had made the silhouette. He sniffed. "You're just a human! A rotting thing and a woman one at that!"

"Out there I am," said Aebbe. "In here the rules are a little different. I don't think you're going to like it in here." They both turned their heads at the sound of the clopping of hooves.

~

"Well met, Aebbe," said the shrill little man. "Awfully sorry about your brother but he did ensure me that replacements would be arriving in Fae soon for him, and Milian and it looks like he's a man of his word even after moving into the next life. I'm sure he's having a wonderful time nearly as much fun as me and this little lad are going to have in the field…"

"I'm 280 years old!" an indignant Heslop bellowed.

The shrill little man gave him a sad smile. "You won't be alone little lad. Aebbe was kind enough to ensure your friend would be able to keep him company. Morchan, where are you?"

Silence. "For fuck's sake if I have to come and find you I will not be happy, and when I'm not happy you almost certainly are not happy!" The shrill little man was cross.

Out of the mist came a gaunt middle-aged man with patches of orange fluff randomly appearing in patches on his bald dome.

"Morchan! Turned back into a rotter!" said Jessop in shock.

"Just easier for me to navigate him as a human instead of an ogre, so I gave him the form he enjoyed before he met Spurius. Doesn't seem to have improved his smell," the shrill little man explained.

"Why didn't you change his teeth?" Heslop pointed to the jagged triangle shapes in Morchan's mouth.

"He was like that when he met Spurius. Must have done it to himself. I daresay we will find a use for them!"

He turned to Aebbe. "Shame you couldn't have struck the witch she would have had her uses but Milian and Digoth's debt to Fae is paid. You tell them to never come back in any form I don't give a shit what they promised that overgrown lizard!" His face was now nearly as twisted as Heslops as he screamed these commands his tiny fists beating against Aebbe's legs.

Then just like that he was speaking to her calmly, friendly even as he wiped his tears away and with a smile told her, "Best if you bury that pugio or chuck it in the sea, my lovely. Rott…I mean humans, would you believe it he's got me doing it now." He jabbed a thumb at a now nervous-looking Heslop. "Anyway, humans don't do well in these worlds between worlds. Hiding in the temple would have popped your lungs like a berry if you'd done it for much longer. So go on love give yourself a prick and return to your realm I think the Briton twat is in a spot of bother."

"Goodbye, Puck," said Aebbe, wondering how it was that she knew the strange, shrill little man's name.

~

Milian staggered forward, his body swaying as if it had become used to the random shaking of the ground. He reached over and spat, and then on one knee vomited the wine, crushed oats, and dried grass they had eaten as their final meal before attempting to cross The Tames is. That was the last time they were all together now it was only him left.

Digoth had thankfully stopped breathing and looked at peace. He had managed to close his eyes one last time. Aebbe was responsible for that. She had vanished and taken two of the monsters with her. Where she was and how and if she could find her way home was as mysterious to Milian as the nature of the twinkling stars in the sky, smaller than the moon but still visible.

Milian who knew a thing or two about being whisked away to a strange land and the troubles involved in getting home felt his insides knot up in an extra painful way whenever he thought of her. Alfwen, Iga and Hieu, he had no idea about their fates but their absence told him the cold fear he'd had in his heart about them for some time now was accurate.

He clenched his fists and went on. There was one left; the

green woman who was still moaning and howling. She was desperately trying to grasp at a cross shaped thing. The same shape the mewling monks back home wore around their necks but this one was shiny. Its base was the color of the sun and star like things twinkled from it.

The woman was rasping in some foreign language not the soppy-sounding stuff the priests chanted and not the Frankish tongue, Milian had spent enough time on Dumnonia beaches and inlets where smuggling went on to be able to at least understand the numbers and drunken threats of that language. No this was a weird one.

"Far from home love?" Milian said as he pulled an arrow out of his quiver. He recoiled when she gave him an eyeless glare. No amount of meeting these monsters ever prepares you for a one-on-one chat he thought as he notched his bow.

"Please," the woman then said in Saxon "you don't understand, the cross it can do so much. I need to get that arrow out of it! But if it burns it could damage the precious… " she then realized she was talking to the man with the arrows. In a last gasp effort to save her skin, she uttered a scream that penetrated away beyond the eardrums.

Milian knew this was another language she was trying to communicate something but this was a different one to the one she was speaking before. Indeed he wasn't sure if it was of this world. He startled as the arrow caught fire and he dropped it to the ground. The arrow inside the cross was burning too.

The witch turned and ran stopping to pick up the cross she screamed as the flames licked her hands but still she ran. Milian smelled smoke coming from his quiver and threw it to the ground. He stamped the flames out and fished through the few remaining arrows, managing to salvage one that was only lightly burnt and notched again.

He had a clear sight of the fleeing woman's black cloak as she ran in a straight line back towards the building the group of monsters had emerged from. The second he was about to fire the bow and arrow crashed to the group and he screamed louder than he ever had in his life.

The snake! The snake that had come out of nowhere. The huge black headed thing that was sinking its fangs into his arms. The bite burnt and Milian fell to his knees as the blackness filled his blood, his veins now looking like the grayish-black lines on a fruit that has begun to rot.

CHAPTER 49

Spurius withdrew the snake back into his mouth and made the torturous looking movement to contort his face around the snake's skull allowing him to speak.

"A dose of my special sauce in your bloodstream for you. I don't want to kill you too quickly. It's been a while since I felt human pain, but one lad I stuck with my venom described it as the blood boiling under his skin, and as each inch of flesh rots it feels like it's being eaten away by thousands of tiny little snakes. Of course, that was after he'd passed on and I bought him back as a goblin. No one has ever got bit and stayed human it's either a long death or a long second life as a creation. I had a mind to turn you into similar and send you back broken and deformed to hunt your Volcae mates for a bit of payback and I still might but for now, I'm content to sit and watch. How are you feeling friend? Looking a bit poorly eh? Should have stayed in those beautiful valleys you lads have. There's nothing for you in Londinium. Never will be. Briton and Saxon alike. Franks, and Jutes, Angles, Basques, and Ostrogoths. Gepids, and Byzantines. Lands beyond my reach that only Lilith knows of, it doesn't matter if you are a human and set foot in this city you are nothing more than a menu item, and soon that condition extends to this entire cursed to Hades island!"

~

Milian gasped and hyperventilated as his arm burned and rotted. His hyperventilation was at least partly due to the mental trauma of watching his fingers turn grey and into small chunks, his skin shriveled and twisted until it looked like the skin of an old man. It then twisted further still ripping and tearing the flesh apart in open sores exposing the bone. Ash poured out from the veins as they rotted to nothingness.

The monster was looking at him with excitement and Milian tried to push himself backward on his remaining arm, clenching his eyes and crying at the sight of his other arm now handless and withered to dusty flakes of skin and bones the texture of chalk, wearing away rapidly.

"It will spread all over the body now," Spurius said. "All are of the dust, and all turn to dust again. Read that a long time ago."

He smiled. "It was a lie not all of us will return to the dust but I like how with you it's going to happen while you are still alive. Wait till my special sauce gets to your belly that's always a laugh to watch. Alecto? Morchan? Heslop? Psyche? Where are you? Come out and watch this I want you to see this in the daylight! That's strange I can only sense two of…"

~

He was cut off by the appearance of Aebbe. Out of nowhere she came from, it was as if the sky had a sudden slash in it she stepped out of. She looked from Milian to Spurius and unleashed a fearsome scream as she picked up the large sword she found on the ground and sliced Milian's arm off at the shoulder.

~

Milian sucked in and prepared for the pain. He knew it would be intense and the shock from losing a limb could slow his breathing and his heart. A warrior of many battles, he had seen countless amputations and prayed he would never be on the receiving end of the blade. He knew the look of terror in a man's eyes as his chest tightened and breathing became an agony. He knew the whitening of the face as a never-ending flow of blood gushed from the stump until eyes closed never to reopen.

Even worse was when a wound or stump turned greenish black and the rot spread to the rest of the body making your flesh smell like shit. Even if that awaited him Milian was eternally grateful to Aebbe. The alternative was such an unearthly fate.

He sucked in hard and clenched his eyes shut before opening them and he felt, fine. Better than fine, the exhaustion, the pain, the fear it was all gone. He sat up and saw the final seconds of his detached arm as it dissolved into ash and blew away in the breeze. He looked at his stump. It had healed in seconds.

He turned to an open-eyed, and open-mouthed Aebbe who was gripping the sword with both hands tightly, and said, "Thank you deeply and truly I am in your debt for all of the time to come. Until the very end." She looked down at the sword which was glowing gold.

"The last time the sword did that I made a similar promise which is yet to be repaid but it will be one day to both of you. The sword awed the most impressive creature I've ever met. Someone who makes dick-tongue over that look like a woodlouse in comparison. I wonder if dick-tongue knows how much trouble he's in." Spurius snorted but there was doubt in those dark eyes.

"Aebbe, give me the sword." he shouted standing up and then slipping the experience of standing with one arm for the first time disorientating him.

"Not so much the great archer anymore are we, Briton!" Spurius screamed he turned his head towards the newcomer. "I'll add that to my collection, bitch!"

"Don't let him bite you Aebbe!"Aebbe was frozen in terror along with the familiar pit of gloom again, and the snake hurtled towards her at breakneck speed before it stopped just an inch shy of the golden blade.

The snake's head turned sidewards looking at a glint of light that was on the blade. Aebbe sweated and panted expecting to be bitten any minute but the snake seemed transfixed on this glint.

Spurius looked impatient and doubt clouded around the crow's feet running from his eyes. He gave his neck a jerk to provoke the snake into moving and the snake finally opened its mouth. Bright green goo dripped from its fangs and it bent its jaws at a 90-degree angle and snapped its mouth shut on the blade.

The sound of the snake's head exploding was louder than any thunderclap or battle cry either of them had ever heard. Aebbe was covered with blood and guts and slithers of snakeskin and flesh were caught in her hair. Exhausted she managed a final smile somehow the feeling of dread that Spurius' presence brought was lifting from her belly. A piece of snake dropped from her eyebrow. She looked at it and said, "Smells like chicken," before collapsing in a heap.

~

Milian ran at her and secured the sword. He looked down at her, and whispered something he had said to many women but had never meant before until now.

He turned and looked at Spurius. The beast was furious and distraught it was trying to speak but was in enormous pain the headless snake has retreated to his mouth. He closed his mouth encasing the snake/tongue and bent over.

Milian raced towards him and a few feet away Spurius raised his head and glared at Milian in the eyes.

Milian nearly doubled over as the sight made his stomach lurch and his eyes water as he felt the most immense sadness at everything he had lost in life, he had never had it brought into such focus before, but Spurius' eyes told him and emphasized how they were all gone. His mother, his sisters, Arthur, all of his comrades in Merlin's army were all gone.

Digoth, Iga, Alfwen and Hieu all in the ground. Allyn and Cwenhild he couldn't tell if they were living but sensed they were in great pain.

He saw all of that in the cold man's gaze only Aebbe was left he knew that for sure and that thought made him smile. Spurius was enraged by this he grimaced as blood dripped and dribbled from his closed lips. He opened his mouth to reveal the snake had rejuvenated.

Milian not only smiled as knowing Aebbe was still a reason to continue lifted from his gut but he laughed out loud. The fearsome thing that had cost him an arm had rejuvenated as a tiny little thing. No bigger than a large worm. He didn't doubt that it would get bigger quickly so he taunted Spurius with, "And it's not even that cold!" before slashing it with the sword.

The now detached worm gave a shrill screech this time before exploding showering both Milian and Spurius with its guts. "Can you talk now? Or do you need the snake to do that creepy thing with the jaw? How long till it grows back anyway?"

Spurius took a step back making sure to be at least a meter away from the end of the sword. He looked around for a weapon to use the only bastard thing he could see was the quiver of arrows on the ground and just looking at them made his skin crawl running to get them would expose him to the sword.

His main weapon was regrowing inside his mouth and it couldn't defeat whatever was protecting that sword. His minions had all died or fled. This Briton was strong and he could tell how much he hated him how much he wanted to win. He silently said to Alecto, "Where are you?" then turned to run.

~

Back in the temple, Alecto was panicking. The arrow had burnt away a hole in the middle of the cross and it wasn't responding to any of her fevered chants or incantations.

In fact, the cross seemed…angry. Her fingers felt sore. She couldn't bend them anymore without her joints creaking and bones cracking. The cross had turned on her she lamented. It showed her unlimited potential but since it had that cursed arrow in it now made her ill to look at it. She had to get away from it.

She heard Spurius' command and for the first time ever since that day she was about to walk into The Tamesas her hands still warm and sticky with her husband's blood only to see him rise from the water his figure against the moonlight seeming to tower over the whole city. The smile on his face silently whispered one word to her, "Algea."One of the many entrances to the underworld. That's what his smile looked like; Algea.

For the first time since that day so many years ago she felt torn and hesitated as to run to him. His voice, it was shaky? She turned her head towards the cross and recoiled. She started to run.

~

Spurius got to the entrance of the temple and didn't look back. He knew that he was being pursued. Where was she? When he made her he gave her an extra sensitivity to the secrets of the other side so he wouldn't have to learn all that. He would always have her to use as a tool and he needed his tool now!

Make the Briton bastard start bleeding from the eyeballs or talk to the rats in their language, and get them to swarm him and slow him down. Why hadn't she answered his call?

He kicked the temple doors open so hard they crashed into the inside of the building. He had a strength advantage, he could pop the Britons head like a grape but one scratch from that sword he wasn't going to risk. He feared it was as strong as the arrows if not stronger.

The temple was empty. He called for her and instantly knew she had fled. Bitch! And where had Morchan and Jessop gone? All the others would be buried and no use until the sunset including Psyche he had had high hopes for that one. What a let down!

He turned and strode around the temple for a minute. He looked at the relief structure of Mithras slaying the bull and decided this is where it ends. With a god slaying a dumb beast.

CHAPTER 50

Milian stood in the doorway. He surprised Spurius by saying, "History has been made here today. There will always be a darkness in this city but the narrative will be set on our terms," in Latin.

He then charged. Spurius unleashed the rejuvenated snake and pulled a giant stone slab from the floor and hurled it at the charging man.

~

Milian slid to one side. Stopping the snake was vital he couldn't recover from a second bite but the slab was impossible to avoid. Praying that he would be able to move quickly even with a smashed-up face he held the sword in front of his face in instinct only to be blinded by a flash of light as the slab shattered into thousands of pieces.

There was ringing in his ears by the time his sight returned. His face was covered with scratches and his head stung like it had received a heavy punch. He sat prostate and saw to his horror he had dropped his sword and it was just out of reach.

Spurius stood over him. The snake lolled out bleeding from scores of cuts. Blood trickled down from Spurius' right eye. He retracted the snake and made the cracking sound with his jaw. A sign that he was going to speak. Milian knew he had lost already, but he willed himself to stay conscious and listen to whatever tedious guff the monster was about to gloat over him.

Aebbe probably wouldn't be able to get far enough away, but it was a big city and she could be forgotten about and hidden for long enough to escape if the beast forgot about her due to his triumph over Milian and the sword he wielded.

If, if, if…if she had a strong head full of wits which he knew she did. If she was kissed by her gods with luck, which he was less sure of, given the events that had led to well everything that had happened since they met.

He made one last grasp for the sword, which ended in a frustrated groan. He suspected he would pass before he had a chance to repay the deal he made in Fae but more years to hone his…he couldn't think anymore. It was time to rest.

~

Spurius spoke, "You're the third human I've met that has troubled me. The wizard was the first and the second he was fiercer than you both. Still three in a century! Are the people of this island finally getting their act together? I do hope so. The newcomers are fucking useless though! Did you see the red-haired one? He just charged forward and walked straight into Heslop's gut and head butt. Reason why they're so soft I reckon is their gods. No imagination! It's from your minds that the other realms come you know? That makes these visions flesh, like my creator she saw something in my mind something that told her, I could listen and absorb the feelings and fears of others, and create things from the unspeakable parts of their minds. What do the hairy savages from the east bring us in terms of gods and traditions? Just idealized forms of themselves. There is nothing to inspire me! I'll always keep a few of your tribe around to terrify and pick their brains for new ideas but the Saxons? Pah! Good for flesh only. Well, Briton, time to go home. Back to the…"

Milian heard a thud and the Spurius started to smirk.

"Someone has sneaked in and..." He put his hands to his temples and the smirk turned into a twisted, horrific mess.

~

Aebbe screamed this time as she launched a second blow to the back of the monster's head using the cross she had found on the floor. It felt not unlike the empowering sense she got when she wielded her pugio.

She had heeded the words of the strange, shrill little man and put her pugio away when she spied the cross. She wasn't sure this monster could be contained in whatever that other place was and the cross glowed in a way she wasn't sure others could see or sense.

Now the monster was emitting a howl as the back of his head started to smolder.

It turned to face Aebbe, and its face was the most terrible thing she had ever seen. Far worse than the horrors of the amphitheater's in either Chichester or Londinium.

The forehead was the color of blood, not fresh blood, but the type of blood long since expelled from the body, the type you saw in puddles outside a butcher's stall or on a battlefield. Thick lines creased across every part of his face and she could tell he was in an enormous amount of pain.

His mouth made a distressed 'O' shape and she could tell it was a struggle for him to open it. Before he could release the snake and doom her, she hacked at his cheek with the cross sending him sprawling.

~

Spurius staggered and struggled to remain upright. His mouth tasted of dirt but the dirt burned. His eyesight was bloody, the only color he could make out was red and one shiny light coming from somewhere.

He tried to speak but only dust and broiling dirt came out of his mouth. Never mind, that didn't stop the snake from making an appearance.

He decided the first one he struck he would turn. Nothing special, but stronger than a goblin or imp maybe a savage dwarf or a strigoi. The creations retain a sense of clarity of their former selves for a while after turning some for much longer than others, but they can't overcome their new instincts watching one struggle with feeding for the first time was a splendid way to spend the time he had always thought.

Well this time watching one of them eat the other alive... slowly would cool his anger for a fraction of a second. His stomach ripped apart from the inside, making him grimace in agony, and he could feel his skin burning.

He sent the snake straight for the throat of the red blob that was standing the one the shining light was coming from but suddenly he felt cold. Not in body temperature in from sheer terror.

The last time he'd felt like this was in Housesteads when still human. The sight of the slaughter had made him shake violently as the sight of one tortured body after the other made him fear that what had caused it was near and waiting.

When Lilith had given her gift to him he knew he would never have that feeling again but now. He couldn't move. Not one inch. As long as that light was shining at him he was trapped. His movement had been slowed to such an extent that moving his head a millimeter to one side took a gargantuan amount of time and excursion.

It's that fucking light! It's doing something to his body and mind he realized. There was nothing he could do until he felt a thud somewhere on his torso. It gave him a dull pain that faded quickly. He then realized he felt nothing at all.

Not even the breeze of the air on his skin or the touch of the ground on his hooves. Every part of him was numb and unfeeling apart from the cold. Not the invigorating coldness that flowed through him when he strode through the streets of Londinium feeling the adoration of all who passed or the exhilarating coldness that struck him when he looked into someone's eyes and saw the gloom fill them. It was a cold of nothingness like the bones of the dead. He brushed these troubling thoughts aside and made to end these worthless rotting things.

He still couldn't move. The stiffness was complete paralysis now. Still as a rock. In this world but not a part of it. Aware of everything but powerless to do anything. He tried to step forward but couldn't. He tried to launch the snake but couldn't. He tried to scream in rage and finally in a plea for help but couldn't.

~

Aebbe and Milian stood in front of the stone statue that had been Spurius.

In shock Aebbe dropped the cross when the metamorphosis was complete, and clasped her hands to her throat in shock and horror at the clanking sound as the cross hit the floor, as if it would make the statue come back to life.

After sending him sprawling Aebbe had thrust the cross at him hoping to stall him in time for Milian to recover and the two of them to flee. She found the creature staring directly at her. It was trying to move see could tell but was grimacing and panting as stiffness and some force rendered his body slug-like in movement. Aebbe didn't know what was happening but kept doing it.

The light that shined through the hole in the cross that the arrow had made a dot like shape of light on the beast's torso.

She moved it up and down his body, across his face and arms, but never took it off him. He sweated, he shivered, he was in the most discomfort he'd ever been, but he couldn't do a thing about it.

"He can't move? Can he?" Aebbe had called to Milian. "I'm not sure I can hold him like this for much longer. Maybe we should flee?"

Milian slightly stood up and gave Aebbe a nod. He picked up the sword and said to it, "I thank you and whoever made you." He strode over to the prone Spurius and pierced the sword through the point on the torso just below the chest where the dot of light was shining.

As soon as he pulled the sword out the wound and the flesh around it turned grey. A cracking sound came from the source of the grey and Milian fell onto Aebbe and they both crashed to the floor and held each other clutching their ears and screaming as the most terrible sound came from the creature's body.

Aebbe later likened it to millions of giant spiders stomping on the ground as they charged, for Milian it was like a man trying to scream while his tongue melted and ice grew on the inside of his throat.

When the sound had faded, they found themselves alone in the building. Alone in what Milian suspected to be a temple from the strange sights on the walls. Alone in this city. Perhaps the last two people who would ever be in this place, he thought. They backed away from the statue, still holding each other. Milian picked up the cross and gave it to Aebbe. Then they turned and ran.

~

Spurius saw the two red blobs get smaller and smaller until he sensed he was alone. The building shook again. He felt some chips of lead from the roof hit the top of his head. His sense of touch was back. Not only could he still see he could now feel. He was merely unable to move, to speak, to shout, to threaten, to plead, to cry. He stood there and seethed.

~

The two tumbled down the temple stairs. They gave the temple one final look back and noticed most of the shaking seemed to concentrate in the area around it. Londinium was a ruin, even the strongest buildings The Romans had built were half-standing at best.

The route to the wall was the southernmost gate that bordered The Tamesas and that was going to be easy to find. They just had to walk in the direction of smoldering smoke and the smell of dead fish.

"Home?" said Milian.

"Where is home?" asked Aebbe taking his hand.

"I'm going to rule out Londinium for now," he said, "but it's a big island. We will find room for us somewhere."

EPILOGUE

Vale. Ken arwech all. Wis thuhel.

Allyn was waiting for Cwenhild to come back from foraging. He clutched Father Maeleg's wooden cross and murmured what he thought were Christian words that the old man had screamed on his death bed.

He didn't know he was saying, "I am in so much fucking pain, kill me now!" in Brittonic.

After the fall he knew his legs would never work again. He could feel his bones move under his skin in places they shouldn't but counted himself lucky, as Father Maeleg lay next to him screaming as a shinbone and forearm bone stuck out of his flesh.

Cwenhild would fall at some point during the few hours and with all her limbs being in order was tasked with dragging them both to a nearby cave where Father Maeleg had died and was buried, and Allyn had not left since and probably never would.

Cwenhild had had her fall from the cliff broken by a tree, so had not been crippled but had remained high enough for the fire to burn off her hair and melt half her face.

It had been two or was it three months since they made their home in the cave just waiting to die and for the pain to end. She had been gone for longer than usual. Maybe Cwenhild's pain had eased enough for her to attempt a route out of the never-ending woods, and he was left here to starve.

It would be for the best, he told himself. Then he caused himself a lot of pain by snapping his upper body upright on instinct in response to hearing two, no three sets of footsteps approach from the cave entrance.

His senses were still sharp, but it was useless with every bone below the waist ruined. Bandits come to slit his throat for his rotting leather boots and the handful of nuts he had left.

He yelled one of the chants Father Maeleg had manically repeated to himself in his final hours. He had memorized the Brittonic sounds word by word, surely this was a chant to open the door to the place Father Maeleg had called heaven.

"So you're sorry for buggering a chicken when you were a lad and wish for forgiveness?" said the twisted face of Brennus that peered out from under the cowled hood, illuminated by the torch being carried by one of the hooded figures that stood to each side of him.

"Your Brittonic is good. I've never heard a Saxon get the intonation so right. But as to your particular plea for forgiveness, I fear you must talk to your priests. It's time to go."

"Go where?"

"Cripple or not, the deal you made with Merlin still stands. You are to be Cynric's Atheling. He's a cripple too now! Ha! What a pair you will be for the West Saxons! Better hope he's been using his time finding loyal replacements for those cut down in the forest. Going to need a long of help holding onto his throne. Luckily, Merlin has an idea or two up his sleeve that will ensure you become king after him. The first Saxons to be tied to The Hunt! We have the future queen outside waiting for you too. It was stories from local hermits about her appearance that led us to finally locate you. I swear on Arthur's grave me and her could be taken for twins although when I said that to her she wasn't happy!"

He slipped off his hood to reveal scratch marks from his left temple to his neck.

~

Cwenhild was waiting outside as Allyn was helped into a large wicker container. Brennus' two companions had initially expected Cwenhild to carry it cursing at her and pushing her towards it. The sight of her claws and the deranged smile causing cracked and crisp skin to twist made them think twice.

Soon both men were grumbling as they hoisted the container with Allyn inside on their shoulders.

"They are saying that with these woods being full of bandits they need to be daggers drawn at all times in case of a surprise attack," Brennus translated for them.

"Personally, I think Cwenhild makes a fierce deterrent, besides lately bandits have been sparse in these parts. It's to do with the new chief of the Dorset Britons. I will have to treat him one of these days he's said to be a savage leader. The one armed warrior, they call him."

"What happened with the monsters and the old man and

where are the children?" Cwenhild demanded to know.

"The children are far west. The boy is speaking normally now, just started one day I heard. He'll be trained for a spot in the hunt's fighting ranks when he's old enough. The girl too if she decides being a wife and mother isn't for her. To have that experience of the island's darkness at such a young age and Saxon speakers to boot they will both prove invaluable to the cause and will be treated well."

He stopped talking for a long time as they struggled through the thick wood. Darkness fell but Brennus seemed to know each bush, tree, clearing, stream, and hill like an old friend and guided them through.

"Merlin lives but is far away. Herla is also far but not defeated. Avalon is gone."

~

The Nix heard nothing for the first time in what seemed like forever. He had finally managed to wriggle enough arm space to pull the dagger out of his skull and at once the never-ending rumbling and shaking seemed to stop.

The Nix was in a bad way. There was no water down here. None that he could get to anyway, he was wedged between mountains of rocks, and his skin was dry and coarse which left him in agony. He needed dampness to breathe and suffocated every few minutes only to wake up soon after passing out to resume his torture.

Maybe this can help me get out of here? He thought eyeing the pugio but then the rocks trapping him shifted, and the floor opened up under him and he fell and slid down a gap in the rocks.

He remembered falling when the bitch betrayed him. It felt like he was falling forever. He wished it was as the pain had started once he landed.

He bumped on the surface of his new home and had a brief pang of hope as he thought he could sense water somewhere, but cursed when he realized it was on the other side of the giant pile of rocks that was entombing him. He had also dropped the dagger somewhere!

One advantage he had down here was being able to see in the pitch darkness so he adjusted his eyes and attempted to make out his new surroundings. He had more space than before, the underground pocket between tons of rock and rubble above, below and to all sides of him was about six foot long, two foot wide, and two foot high.

He couldn't stand up or even sit up but he could wriggle his legs a little and move his head forward to have a view of what lay at the end of his confined space.

It was her.

"You betrayed me!" The Nix whined at the skeleton in the white wedding dress that sat across from him when he next came to from suffocating to death.

The skeleton didn't answer.

But eventually, someone did. "I was never yours." The voice drifted down to him. It was neither Latin or Saxon or Pict, regardless The Nix could understand every word. "You can spend forever with my bones. I've escaped you and am older and far away."

The Nix screamed, "Where?" He would be screaming at the skull with its wisp of dry yellow hair for quite some time. He never got an answer.

592 AD - Wessex

The old woman hobbled her way to the gate of the coastal fort she was escorted by a group of stout young warriors. The warriors hoisted a black on yellow flag that depicted a sword piercing a snake's head.

A grey haired woman with an eyepatch greeted her as the gate swung open.

"Good day to you, Mother Aebbe!"

The old woman gave a toothless smile. "Winfred! How are you still in armor? You should be resting in your old age!"

"Like you are?" smiled Winfred who still had ten or so teeth left.

"Someone has to take care of the forest villages while my offspring are either west on hunt business or up north fighting Angles. What of your brother?" Aebbe asked.

"Accompanying King Cuthwine in Wintanceaster," she said naming both Allyn's and Cwenhild's grandson and the stone-walled Roman settlement that King Cuthwine had grown fond of holding court at.

"Trusted me to hold the fort against any bastard Frankish scum who fancied playing pirate!"

Aebbe chuckled at Winfred's infamously foul tongue but she meant what she said. The pirates had long since given up on attacking the West Saxon coast. Winfred had an army of skiffs and hard bastards with axes and daggers to board them secured in every creek and cave on the coast.

Any approaching ship was swarmed and boarded before the pirates knew what was happening. Winfred herself would lead these charges, and the skiffs would return full of a handful of Frankish slaves and many more Frankish heads.

It would always be Winfred at the head of the returning fleet hoisting the captain's head to a cheering fishing village. Now the pirate ships, mostly Frankish but some Britons from Dumnonia, sailed far from the coast in a straight line to the South Saxon lands for easier pickings.

And easy they were. Each of King Cissa's successors had been more useless than the last, and the current one Cynefrid, his great-grandson was losing land so much to Jutes and Angles that Cuthwine's younger brother Ceolwulf was hotheadedly urging an invasion so they could absorb the kingdom into theirs.

The much more cautious Cuthwine was urging restraint with poor old Wiglac stuck in the middle as the two brothers' weary advisor. A role he'd had since returning from his tour as a travelling ambassador to various Briton kingdoms.

~

Aebbe gave a bittersweet smile at the thought of the two brothers. It had been rumored that Allyn was incapable of getting Cwenhild with child, something Allyn never seemed troubled by as with child she got many a time.

That old goat Cynric was responsible for most she was sure but Milian had visited Cwenhild at Allyn's request and Aebbe reluctantly gave her blessing.

Two of the princesses had the telltale raven hair and faint birthmarks around the eyes complimenting the chubby cheeks and flat noses they'd gotten from Cwenhild, but the eldest son and future king Ceawlin was a male Cwenhild huge shoulders and a ruddy face with a tuft of orange hair he surely had nothing to do with Milian she assumed. But as for Ceawlin's two surviving sons, the youngest Ceolwulf had the angry, dancing purple splashes around his eyes, and the eldest Cuthwine was planned to be called Cutha but when they saw that the mark stretching from his cheek all down his neck just like a wine stain they changed their minds.

Milian by then was concentrating on his own family and giving Aebbe few complaints there. Leading a band of Britons and controlling the woods of Hwicce, a vast territory that covered the valleys and rolling hills of the area between the land they were now calling Wessex and the powerful grouping of Briton kingdoms that people were starting to call Cymru. Aebbe and the eight of her eleven children who lived past infancy never wanted for much.

Five daughters, three sons, she'd stopped counting at thirty grandchildren but every village and forest settlement soon had a charismatic set of residents with Aebbe's messy brown hair and Milian's purple marks scattered among their features.

Milian acted as the conduit between Wessex and the Cymru kingdoms where The Hunt's leadership had retreated.

~

This position allowed them safe passage to Gywnedd, where

King Constantine now held his seat. In a stone hall with colored glass that dazzled both Milian and Aebbe. Arthur's son the unspoken king of the Britons spoke down to them.

"The castle in Caerleon is to be taken apart piece by piece its too much of a target for surviving creations Merlin assured me that this part of the island is particularly strong for spells so… I say what is your woman doing? Is she choking?"

It was because Constantine spoke to them in the same language Spurius and his inner circle had used when Aebbe was unseen watching them. Two men in black cloaks on either side of Constantine rapidly interpreted every word in Brittonic and Saxon to the pair of them. They were both wearing the wooden cross that Allyn had taken to wearing since he had returned from his time in the forest.

The king continued, "We sent some of our best forces into Londinium at night who reported the city is again completely deserted save for a few pathetic creatures who were easily disposed of. We took zero casualties. The city is in ruins as you said. Perhaps we owe you thanks…"

He then went on to describe what Merlin and Allyn had agreed on or rather what Merlin had dictated to him.

Wessex was to receive a seat on the council of the hunt and Briton spears and arrows to defend it from aggression so it could grow and establish itself. Some of those who today wait on beaches and inlets axe in hand for Winfred's commands came from this agreement. There are other groupings too that watch Wessex's borders as a result of this.

In return, King Cynric (unable to attend due to foot amputations) would send a squad of warriors to Gywnedd for training each year, and these warriors once returned to Wessex would be on alert for any dark stirrings in the Saxon kingdoms. With knowledge of Briton language and customs as well as being the best-trained warriors in their land would greatly deter and weaken further Saxon aggression or so Constantine hoped.

Neither Aebbe nor Milian appreciated the looks Constantine or his priests gave them, but it gave them the idea to break into the stone hall later that night.

"Such a gloomy place," said Aebbe.

"They call it a church," said Milian. "Priests want one built in every village, doubt they'll be as grand as these. See that long wooden bench the king had a nap on while the priests were droning on. Looks comfy with those silks and furs all over it. Let's have a go."

Their first child, a girl, Aela was made that night.

~

Now with her body so old that every step was a struggle she wondered what had made Aela and that night pop into her head. Maybe it was the flags fluttering over the fort, they certainly contrasted with the ones her warrior guards had brought with them.

Each of the fort's flags displayed a creature that no person on this island had ever seen, but Aela had created this wonderful golden image that went on the black flags she carried into battle.

~

When Aebbe asked where on earth she'd gotten the idea for

what appeared to be a giant winged snake, Aela had answered.

"When father got delirious after the fever last summer, he spent one afternoon just repeating, 'back to Fae, back to Fae,'. It meant nothing to me, then he screamed the strangest sound word. 'Fukan' or something. I asked him what he was talking about to keep him awake. He scratched an image into a piece of wood, it took him ages. I thought it looked beautiful and recreated it as best as I could, well from memory, when father recovered he disposed of the wood and said he had no memory of speaking during the fever."

Aela was gone now. She'd survived two tours of Caledonia with the hunt, where a few surviving creations had fled and won praise for her bravery. Soon, many Wessex fyrds were using her creature on their banners. A Jute axe on a failed invasion of Wihtwara to claim it for King Ceawlin had cut her down in her prime.

Milian too died the following year. Allyn, Cwenhild, and Cynric all long in the barrows too. Only her and the "children," both grey and nearly toothless, remained.

~

Back to the present, now she warmed herself by the fire in the same hut Allyn and Cwenhild had met with King Cynric all those years ago.

Two of the men who escorted her, Dorset Britons came in carrying a large wooden chest. She thanked the men, and Winfred nodded to some crates of Cray jugs full of wine confiscated from some former pirates.

The Britons used to weak ale would leave the two women alone to talk with such treats.

Winfred opened the chest and counted "thirty that should be enough, they've all been blessed?"

Aebbe smiled. "The hunt has taken some creations alive, the howling when just a few of these are thrown into the dungeons is unlike anything you've ever heard. These will work, believe me. Why did you ask for them?"

"Hobgoblin or dwarf, shitty little thing, is bright red and we think it's from the Frank's land. It appeared just after we caught the last ship. That was a fucked up case. They were all dead when we boarded them. It was like a wild hound had been let loose on the ship, nearly broke my neck slipping on the bloody deck. After that, the sightings began on land and the disappearances. It must have killed the crew at night and swam to shore."

"I do not recommend hitting it with the arrows when it's in water!"

"I've heard that story enough times, mother Aebbe. Seven months it boiled! I like my fish pie too much to lose the sea." Winfred laughed. "We have a rough idea where it sleeps during the day and…" She trailed off.

Winfred then said, "Do you ever think it's going to stop? Spurius made enough to still keep us busy decades later and now from across the sea."

Aebbe sighed. "Soon it won't be our problem. Best we can do is kill as many as we can so those in the future don't have to."

She closed her eyes. "Our enemies can no longer control our fate as if we were cattle. If that is how I've helped leave us, I'm happy." She exhaled a deep breath and spoke no longer.

AFTERWORD

Author's note.

If you are reading this then I finally got around to the steps required to publish this and you in all likely hood either bought or rented this and read it to the end. For that I'm sincerely grateful, this is my first effort at a novel so I understand it's not perfect, but I enjoyed every minute of writing it.

If you did enjoy the story then I would be very grateful if you could leave a review on the page where you bought/rented it. Here is a link: https://www.amazon.com/dp/B09WLBQKRX

The idea that early Saxons believed The Roman ruins they inherited were the works of giants comes from folk stories that historians of the Middle Ages took literally I believe. There's no evidence that this was a real belief but it fits the story and with no literacy, technology or education then a gap of a century may as well have been a millennium. Certainly, the tiny number of educated Saxons were well aware of who The Romans were and what they had left.

Londinium was abandoned during this time. The Roman wall still remains in places. The amphitheater remains were dug up in 1988. The Temple of Mithras was discovered in 1954. Parts of the amphitheater can be seen at Guildhall Art Gallery which was built on top of it and artifacts from the temple can be seen at the Museum of London.

The site of the amphitheater in Chichester is displayed in the park it now is in.

Strigoi is a Romanian word with Latin roots, I have taken the liberty of guessing 6th century Latin speakers may have used it or something similar to refer to vampires.

Some of the creations are based on myths and legends, some are the product of my imagination.

Thank you for your patience in finishing the book. I hope some people enjoy it. I am working on a follow up novel set a few centuries later, where some descendants or reincarnations of familiar characters should appear. As well as a few baddies who escaped the great earthquake of Londinium.

NK, Tokyo, Japan, January 31st, 2022.

ABOUT THE AUTHOR

Neil Kay

Neil Kay was born in 1979 in Croydon (it's in Surrey or London, depending on who you ask). He currently lives in Yokohama, Japan. His interests include; history, books, TV, Crystal Palace FC, Indian food, and beer. He can be found at the following links.

Twitter: @neilkay1979

Facebook: https://www.facebook.com/neilkaywrites

Website: www.neilkay.com

Email: neilsbooks@neilkay.com

Printed in Great Britain
by Amazon